it

Raymond Hawkey

NEW ENGLISH LIBRARY

Quotations from 'The Second Coming' by W.B. Yeats,
from *The Collected Poems of W.B. Yeats* (1977) are
reproduced by kind permission of Michael B. Yeats,
Anne Yeats and Macmillan London Ltd.

Extracts from THE LAST DAYS OF HITLER by
Hugh Trevor-Roper (1947) are reproduced by kind
permission of Macmillan London Ltd.

First published in Great Britain in 1983 by New English
Library, Mill Road, Dunton Green, Sevenoaks, Kent.
Editorial office: 47 Bedford Square, London WC1B 3DP

Printed and bound in Great Britain by
Biddles Ltd, Guildford and King's Lynn

Typeset by Fleet Graphics, Enfield, Middlesex

ISBN: 0 450 04892 6

Books by Raymond Hawkey

WILD CARD (with Roger Bingham)
SIDE-EFFECT (published by New English Library)
IT (published by New English Library)

This book contains descriptions of
procedures for contacting so-called
discarnate entities. Since such procedures
are potentially hazardous, the reader is
warned that they should only be carried out
under the supervision of an experienced
parapsychologist.

And Saul disguised himself, and put on other raiment,
and he went, and two other men with him,
and they came to the woman by night:
and he said, I pray thee, divine unto me by the familiar
    spirit,
and bring me *him* up, whom I shall name unto thee.

The First Book of Samuel

PREFACE

The Dictionary of the Occult (compiled by B.W. Martin; Rider and Company, 1979) defines paranormal as 'a term that may be used to describe all those powers and areas of experience which lie outside the "normal" but which nevertheless exist alongside them; it thus includes extrasensory perception [the ability to perceive things which cannot be perceived with the normal senses], out-of-the-body experiences [any state during which there is awareness of the existence of an exteriorised counterpart of the physical body], psychokinesis [the imparting of physical motion to an object by the power of the mind], spirit communication, and occult practices such as magic and divination'.

Although during my years as a journalist I participated in the investigation of many aspects of the paranormal, at no time did I witness anything which could not – or so I believed – be satisfactorily explained in terms of either heightened suggestibility, misinterpretation, conscious or unconscious fraud.

However, as the 1960s drew to a close I began to have second thoughts. If all alleged paranormal phenomena could be explained in such mundane terms, why, I wondered, had the ultra-conservative American Association for the Advancement of Science voted six to one in favour of admitting the Parapsychological Association (parapsychology being a term coined by J.B. Rhine to designate the academic study of the paranormal)? Why had the number of American colleges offering courses in parapsychology increased a hundredfold during the past decade? Why had the US Defense Department's Advanced Projects Agency commissioned a translation of all available Soviet literature on paranormal phenomena? Indeed, why had such a seemingly worldly people as the Russians become interested in such an apparently unworldly subject as the paranormal?

The answer to these and many other such questions was inescapable: for many of the world's most distinguished scientists paranormal phenomena had become an accepted reality, and as such seemed a promising theme for this, my third novel.

However, one important element continued to elude me. Although I was to spend the best part of three years researching the subject, try as I might I again failed to experience anything which could be described as paranormal. Or at least such was the case until I began writing the book in the autumn of 1980, when, with somewhat mixed feelings, I experienced the first of what became a long-drawn-out series of poltergeist-like phenomena. (NB. Although by no means the full list, all of the events set out below were witnessed by at least one other person apart from myself.) Extraneous, unexplained voices appeared on both audio and video tapes; objects inside closed cupboards were set in violent motion; pictures were removed from walls (I use the word 'removed' rather than 'fell' because not only were both the cord and the hook always found to be intact, but on no occasion was any damage done to either the frame or the object on which it came to rest); sounds reminiscent of footsteps were heard in unoccupied rooms; electrical equipment malfunctioned in ways which defied rational explanation; and objects which had mysteriously disappeared reappeared in what was often an even more mysterious manner.

Although various 'occult' explanations have been offered to account for the above (the most common of which was that as a result of my 'delvings' I had attracted the attention of earth-bound spirits), it is my belief that in some as yet inexplicable way the phenomena resulted from the abnormally high level of tension induced by writing what proved to be by far the most difficult and demanding of my books, and as such conforms in part at least to the archetypal conditions under which poltergeist activities manifest themselves.

However, although I would venture to suggest that my hypothesis is given some credence by the fact that since completing the book I have ceased to be troubled by such disturbances, one further mystery remains. It is this: why did two of the people who kindly offered to check the manuscript (people who, like myself, had never before experienced any form of paranormal phenomena), report similar outbreaks of poltergeist-like activity while it was in their possession?

Finally – and for any reader who might find the proposition central to IT highly improbable, i.e. that a modern head of state would seek guidance from a discarnate entity – I would like to draw attention to the case of W.L. Mackenzie King, Prime Minister of Canada from 1921-30, 1935-48.

Through the mediumship of Miss Geraldine Cummins, Mr Mackenzie King not only received guidance from alleged discarnate entities on personal matters, but also on matters of public policy.

Raymond Hawkey
London, January 1983

ACKNOWLEDGMENTS

I would like to thank the following people for the advice they so generously gave me during the writing of IT.
Albert Allen, Roger Bingham, Charles B. Bovill, Eric Clark, Jonathan Cunningham, Jim Dowdall, Peter and Pamela Evans, Eileen Finn, Richard B. Fisher, Paul Lethbridge, Austin John Marshall, Nico Preston, Patrick Tilley, Pierre-André Tilley and Merrick Winn.

Finally, I would like to thank Barbara Leigh-Mason not only for her help, but for having so stoically endured the phenomena which accompanied much of the writing of the book.

PROLOGUE

THE MAN they had code-named Big Boy sat staring out of the window of the Mercedes that was speeding through the dark, rain-washed suburbs of Frankfurt, his mind suppurating with hatred. Hatred not only of those from whom he was defecting, but of those *to* whom he was defecting.

Characteristically, he had given no thought to the moral implications of what he was doing. After all, he had long ago reconciled himself to the fact that he was an amoral opportunist. Had he not been, how would he – the son of a Georgian peasant – have risen to become one of only fifteen men who ruled a nation of 254 million?

Neither had he given much thought to the expediency of what he was doing. He hadn't needed to: caught between the hammer and the anvil, there had been no alternative but to defect. Or at least, no acceptable alternative.

Of course, had he gone to his comrades on the Politburo things would have been different. They would either have bought the evidence with which he was being blackmailed by the imperialist lackeys from the CIA, or, failing that, have taken steps to make it appear as if it had been forged in order to embarrass the Party and undermine the cause of international communism.

Not that it would have saved *him*. In such a situation, the best he could have hoped for was to have spent the remainder of his life in the Serbsky Institute of Forensic Psychiatry.

This way, however, he would be able to avenge himself on both the hammer and the anvil, and although he didn't yet know how he would achieve his dream, he clung to it like a drowning man to a lifebelt.

A lifebelt afloat in a sea of . . .

Blood.

The Russian closed his eyes, not to dispel the image the word had conjured up, but rather to bring it into sharper focus.

Blood, fresh and warm and smooth as liquid silk. Blood oozing from savaged breasts to form a scarlet pool on the pale, still quivering belly . . .

Aware that he was developing a tension headache, the Russian pushed his tinted spectacles to the top of his bald head and began massaging the bridge of his bulbous, pock-marked nose.

He had black, bushy brows, close-set, heavily lidded blue eyes that were as piercingly cold as a Siberian winter, a petulant mouth and bad teeth. Folds of flesh like a blood-hound's dewlaps all but hid the knot of his black tie, and his sagging cheeks were threaded with congested capillaries. Although the first and second fingers of his right hand were stained with nicotine, his inordinately long, horny finger-nails were as carefully tended as those of the most fastidious woman.

'How much longer are we going to be?' he asked, in his heavily accented English.

'About twenty minutes – twenty-five at the most,' replied the man sitting next to him.

'And when we get there, what?'

The man began fumbling for a handkerchief with which to shield himself against the Russian's fetid breath. 'A medical, mug shots, voice and fingerprints, and then a plane— ' He stopped, his attention diverted by a cluster of fuzzy, flashing blue lights which had suddenly appeared through the drifting curtains of rain.

The Russian turned to peer through the windshield, but could see nothing which would explain the almost palpable increase of tension within the car.

However, when the lights reappeared a moment later it was possible to see that they were mounted on top of two green-and-white Porsches which had been parked at right angles to the kerb to form a roadblock. Standing alongside

2

the cars were half a dozen men wearing the white-topped peaked caps and long green raincoats of the *Kommunale Polizei.*

'Why the fuck weren't we advised of this?' demanded the driver, peering anxiously around for a means of escape.

As one of the policemen stepped forward and signalled to the driver to pull over, the man in the front passenger seat snatched a microphone from the two-way radio and pressed the transmission button. 'Babysitter to Watchtower,' he began, in a hoarse, frantic voice. 'Babysitter to Watchtower. For chrissakes, Watchtower, do you read me?'

The Russian felt himself break into a cold sweat. Were the men ahead of them really police officers, or a squad from Department V posing as police officers? '*Mokrie dela!*' he muttered, but instead of reassurance all he got was a reprimand from the man trying to coax a response from the radio. 'If you have to speak, speak English!' he growled, as the driver began to reduce speed. 'Jesus H. Christ, we're in enough trouble as it is . . . '

Shaking his head disbelievingly, the Russian took a deep breath, folded his arms and waited. When he had first learned that he was to be taken to the defector centre by car – even one which had been bomb-and-bulletproofed and equipped with a mass of auxiliary safeguards – he had protested. What if the plan for concealing his defection were to misfire? he'd demanded. Was the CIA not aware that in such a situation his former colleague in the second-floor office of the Lubianka would move heaven and hell to have him liquidated before he could be debriefed? But his case officer had been adamant: Escape and Evasion wouldn't *allow* the plan to misfire, and even if by some unforeseeable mischance it were to do so the last thing the KGB would be expecting was for him to be delivered in an ordinary-looking family saloon. 'If you wish to hide something,' he'd told him, quoting an ancient Arabic proverb, 'hide it in the sun's eye.'

The driver drew up alongside the policeman and rolled down the window, acknowledging his salute with an amiable '*Guten Tag!*'

The policeman held out a gloved hand. '*Darf ich bitte Ihren Personal Ausweis sehen?*' he asked, his breath smoking in the cold night air.

As the driver passed his papers through the window, the Russian turned his attention to the submachine-gun being carried by another of the policemen. In the poor light and at a distance it looked disturbingly like a Soviet weapon, but as the policeman moved closer he at last recognised it for what it was: one manufactured by the Oberndorf company of Heckler and Koch.

The Russian stopped worrying, and instead, occupied himself with trying to decide whether it was the MP-5 or the more powerful HK-53. Probably the latter, he concluded.

'*Darf ich bitte Ihren Personal Ausweis sehen?*'

A nudge in the ribs from the man sitting next to him brought the Russian out of his reverie. Turning, he saw that the policeman at the window was holding his hand out to him. '*Ihren Ausweis bitte!*' he ordered, snapping his fingers impatiently. '*Schnell!*'

Although the Russian hadn't understood what had been said, there was no misunderstanding the manner in which it had been said. And he resented it, particularly coming from a petty official of a nation which had killed twenty-five million of his countrymen during World War II.

'Your identity card!' hissed the man next to him. 'For Christ's sake show him your identity card!'

Still the Russian did not react.

The policeman moved from the front to the rear door, tried the handle and found it locked and began rapping on the glass with his flashlight. '*Auf!*' he cried, his voice now almost half an octave higher. '*Auf!*'

Tut-tutting, the Russian unfolded his arms, turned towards the policeman and wound down the window. What he wanted to do was grab him by the throat and squeeze it until his eyes popped from their sockets. What he did was to spit in his face.

The policeman turned purple with rage. Stepping back from the window, he began fumbling for the catch on his revolver holster.

4

The last vestiges of the Russian's self-control snapped. For a man weighing seventeen stone he could, when he wished, move surprisingly fast; sweeping aside the hands of the other man in the car, he hurled himself at the door, his teeth bared and a murderous glint in his eyes.

'Let's get the hell out of here!' someone yelled.

Snapping on the main beams, the driver gunned the highly-tuned, six cylinder engine into life and surged forward, his horn blaring.

Scattering policemen in all directions, he tore past the first Porsche, swung the steering wheel violently to the left and stood on the brakes. The rear wheels lost their traction on the wet road, and, throwing up a great curtain of spray, the Mercedes spun counter-clockwise around its centre of gravity, hitting the offside of the second Porsche with a deafening crash.

As the Russian cannoned into the man next to him, the door by which he had been about to leave burst open and he saw the policeman with the submachine-gun raise it to his shoulder and take aim. An orange flame flickered briefly from the muzzle, and was followed a millisecond later by the whine of high velocity bullets ricocheting off armour plate.

With its Hostile Fire Indicator flashing and bleeping, the driver wrested the groaning Mercedes around the front of the damaged Porsche, straightened up and accelerated, then activated an armoury of anti-pursuit devices.

Unaware that he had sustained anything more serious than a few bruises, the Russian reached out to slam the still half-open door. As he did so, his eyes glazed over with pain and disbelief and he crashed unconscious to the floor.

Experiments using blocks of gelatine to simulate human tissue have shown that a bullet, as well as producing a permanent wound track, radiates shock waves which blow apart the tissue surrounding the track. Known as cavitation, the severity of this effect is directly related to the amount of kinetic energy which is transmitted by the bullet to the tissue. Thus, a bullet fired from a high velocity weapon will do more damage than one of the same weight fired from a low velocity weapon.

The bullet which had struck the Russian – the only one of five to have found its target – weighed fifty-three grains and had been fired from a weapon with a muzzle velocity of 2,460 feet per second. Leaving a temporary cavity twelve inches in diameter in its wake, the bullet had passed through his large and small intestine, his stomach and his spleen, and had exited amid a fusillade of bone fragments from between what remained of his ninth and tenth ribs. As well as virtually pulverising the organs through which it had passed, the shock wave from the bullet had also damaged his lungs, liver, pancreas and kidneys. Furthermore, because the pressure inside the temporary cavity had been subatmospheric, the entire missile track had been contaminated not only by his own excreta, but also by a variety of pathogens which had been sucked in from outside.

Immediately, each of the arteries and veins severed by the bullet began both to contract and retract within their fibrous sheaths, reducing the rate at which his blood was being lost, and, more importantly, exposing it to a surface which triggered the blood's clotting mechanism.

This reflex, however, succeeded only in sealing the smaller of the severed vessels; in the major arteries the pressure of blood, though falling, was such that it swept away the clots as quickly as they were formed.

Responding to the now steeply falling pressure, his body's autonomic system began a desperate attempt to compensate for the loss of blood by diluting what remained with fluid withdrawn from the tissues, at the same time diverting the flow away from his skin to his brain and kidneys, organs which, had they been starved of oxygen and glucose for more than a few minutes, would have begun to die.

Consciousness has been defined as the totality of sensations, memories, thoughts and emotions which make up the self, and in that sense the Russian never fully regained consciousness. Nonetheless, he did manage to put together

6

some sort of picture of where he was and what had happened to him.

At first he was determined to die, for by dying he would not only escape from his pain and helplessness, but would also deprive those ultimately responsible for it of their prize. However, the thought of death brought him little comfort. Dying, he decided during one of his rare moments of lucidity, was too negative a response, when what he wanted – and wanted with a savage, aching intensity – was to destroy everyone who had played any part in his own destruction.

'*Live*!' From somewhere deep within his skull, a voice seemed to be calling to him. A voice he knew of old. '*If you're to destroy the bastards who've destroyed you, you've got to live*!'

Suddenly he became aware of light shining through his lids. Summoning all his strength, he opened his eyes to discover that he was no longer lying on the back seat of a car, but on a trolley which was being rushed along a green-tiled corridor lit by fluorescent tubes.

'*Live*!' The pitch of the voice seemed to have risen, and become more hectoring in tone. '*If you're to destroy the bastards who've destroyed you, you've got to live*!'

The men pulling the trolley shouldered open a pair of swing doors, and he found himself in a room milling with people wearing green surgical gowns and caps. The trolley was manoeuvred alongside a table overhung by a huge reflector studded with lamps, and, even as he was being lifted from one to the other, the people began frantically hooking him up to the array of machines and monitors with which the table was surrounded.

'*Live*!' The voice was now coming through painfully loud, drowning out the babble of voices in the room. '*If you're to destroy the bastards who've destroyed you, you've got to live*!'

Turning his head, he saw that a tube had been plugged into his left forearm. Standing alongside it was a man filling a syringe from a rubber-stoppered bottle. After clearing the syringe of bubbles, he took the tube between his fingers and thumb, pierced it with the needle and depressed the plunger.

Almost immediately, the effort of keeping his eyes open proved too much. As the light shining through his lids faded into darkness, he once again heard the insistent but by now rapidly receding voice. '*Live*!' it shrieked, as if from the very depths of hell. '*If you're to destroy the bastards who've destroyed you, you've got to live!*'

CHAPTER 1

DR SARAH STUART read through the last of that morning's batch of letters. It was from a television station in Cleveland, Ohio, inviting her to appear on a late night chat-show to talk about her work as director of the Institute of Biotechnology and Human Research. Although flattered that the writer of the letter had described her as 'one of the world's foremost parapsychologists', when she switched on her Pearlcorder it was to dictate a polite but firm refusal.

Ever since her paper *Paranormal Factors in Healing* had been published in *Nature* a month earlier she seemed to have done little other than be interviewed. Of course, she realised that publicising Biotec was an important part of her job; not only did it bring to its doors the psi-gifted subjects who were the life blood of an institution such as hers, it also helped generate funds at a time when neither federal nor foundation money was as easy to come by as it had been during the seventies.

Even so, enough was enough: quite apart from the fact that too much exposure in the mass media put her at risk of being branded a populariser by a scientific community inclined to regard science as a fit subject only for other scientists, it hugely increased the already large number of crank letters she received every day. Letters from people claiming to have had encounters with everything from Bigfoot to little green men from Mars; people who believed themselves to be haunted, possessed by devils or bewitched by neighbours; people who insisted that the world was flat or hollow or about to end.

'You haven't forgotten you're having lunch with Cyrus

Shaw in half an hour?' asked her secretary, as she entered the office.

Without looking up, Sarah rose from behind her desk. She was tall and slim and moved with an unselfconscious, fluid grace. Her pale, Garboesque face was framed by shoulder-length auburn hair and a deep fringe, and she was wearing the bottom half of an impeccably-tailored cream linen trouser suit and a bronze silk shirt tied at the neck in a huge bow. Like her lipstick and nail-varnish, her high-heeled Italian leather shoes, belt and handbag matched the colour of her shirt perfectly.

'No, I haven't,' she replied unhappily, handing the secretary the letters and the tape. In fact, ever since the president of the university to which Biotec was affiliated had called Sarah the previous evening, she had found it difficult to think of anything else. She had only met Shaw three or four times during the whole of her tenure at Biotec, and then always on campus. So, why was he taking her to one of Boston's most expensive restaurants, and at such short notice? Had she somehow managed to put the scientific establishment's nose out of joint as Targ and Puthoff had done a few years earlier? If she had she would have to keep a tight rein on her emotions, for, with only forty-eight hours or so to go before the start of her period, she was feeling decidedly pre-menstrual. Her breasts were sore, and she had begun to feel tense and irritable even before his call.

Taking a powder compact from her handbag, she checked her make-up in the mirror. 'Och, no!' she cried, peering at the shadows under her widely-spaced, blue-grey eyes. 'I look like a panda, and that's a fact!' Although she had lived in America for five years, she still spoke with the softened consonants and the rolled 'r's' of her native Edinburgh.

The secretary laughed. 'Were you late getting away from the dream lab last night?'

'Late enough.' Sarah opened a bottle of foundation. After patting a little of the cream under her eyes with the tip of her ring-finger, she freshened-up her grey eyeshadow and began applying mascara to her long, upswept lashes. 'Still, I now know why we've been scoring zero for the past week: the percipient had only been popping Seconal before getting into bed, if you please! Anyway,' she added, as she blotted her lipstick on a tissue and began brushing her thick, glossy hair, 'it seems that Hayakawa has finally managed to talk Art Trumbull into staying overnight, so maybe we'll start making some progress at last . . . '

The secretary took Sarah's jacket off its hanger and helped her into it. 'Is there anything you want me to do while you're out?'

'I don't think so,' she replied, glancing at her leather-bound desk diary to make sure she'd remembered the address of the restaurant correctly. 'Winter Street? That's just south of Boston Common, isn't it?'

The secretary seemed taken aback. 'Sure, but didn't you know? He's sent a car for you. The chauffeur's waiting in the lobby . . . '

'A car!' she exclaimed, as if she had just learned that she was to be taken in a gold coach drawn by a team of white horses. 'Shaw's sent a car for *me*?' She snapped shut her handbag. 'Now I know he's up to something, and whatever it is I don't like it!'

Sarah arrived at the Locke-Ober to find Shaw sitting at what was obviously one of the best tables in the crowded, handsomely appointed Men's Grill.

'Sarah, my dear!' he cried, rising to give her a perfunctory peck on the cheek. His voice was plummy, and he affected an accent that was more British than her own. 'How *very* nice to see you. As always, you're looking quite delightful.'

'You're not looking so bad yourself,' she lied, as a waiter wearing a winged collar, tails and a white apron broke open a linen napkin and draped it over her lap. Although still something of a dandy, Shaw seemed to have aged ten years during the intervening ten months. His face had become more pinched and fox-like, and he had lowered his parting in an attempt to conceal the fact that he was losing his now almost white hair.

11

After ordering Campari and soda for them both, he engaged her in ten minutes of rather forced small talk, then abruptly changed tack.

'I read your recent paper in *Nature*,' he began, perusing the menu through a pair of gold half-frames. 'And if I may say so, I found it most impressive.'

'Really?' Sarah felt as if a great weight had been lifted from her shoulders.

'You sound surprised . . . '

She laughed. 'A little, perhaps . . . '

'Surprised that I should have read it, or that I approve?'

'The latter, I suppose. After all, it is a pretty contentious area.'

'Contentious, certainly. But then, as I had occasion to tell the regents only last week, if quantum physics is permitted to violate the laws of nature as they were understood by classical physics, I don't see why psi shouldn't claim the same right.'

The suggestion that he'd had to defend Biotec from an attack by the board of governors had not escaped her notice, nor had she failed to recognise that the line he'd claimed to have used was one stolen from Koestler's *The Roots of Coincidence.* Pompous old fool, she thought.

'Now,' he continued, as the waiter returned to take their order. 'What's it to be? The lobster, perhaps? Or the Trout Meunière? I must confess I've always found the trout here to be quite irresistible!'

'Fine,' said Sarah, not caring much what she ate. 'The trout sounds fine.'

After making a great show of choosing an appropriate wine, Shaw helped himself to a wholemeal roll from the wicker breadbasket, pocketed his spectacles and at last settled down to what was obviously the real purpose of their meeting.

'Just before I called you yesterday, I had a call from the Chairman of the Joint Chiefs of Staff,' he began, breaking apart the roll with his carefully manicured fingers. 'Asking us for our help.'

'*Our* help?'

12

'More specifically, for your help,' he replied, after waiting for a peal of laughter from the next table to subside.

'In what way can I possibly be of help to the Chairman of the Joint Chiefs of Staff?'

'Uhm . . . ' Shaw caressed his pursed lips for a moment, apparently deep in thought. 'I must confess, I'm not entirely sure. As a matter of fact, all I really know is that he'd like you to get together with their people at the ONR . . . '

Somewhere at the back of Sarah's mind, alarm bells began to ring. 'The ONR?' she echoed, as she tried to recall what little she knew about the Office of Naval Research.

For a start, it had been the ONR which had funded much of neurophysiologist José Delgado's early work on electronical stimulation of the brain. Although she had never much liked the idea of such experiments, it wasn't that which had made her uneasy. Nor was it the fact that —

Suddenly it came to her: the Philadelphia Experiment! Of course; it was the ONR - or so the story went - which had been responsible for carrying out an experiment in which a destroyer escort vessel had been made invisible and teleported from the Philadelphia Navy Yard to Norfolk harbour and back, with disastrous consequences for its crew.

'You don't seem very happy about the prospect,' said Shaw, popping a piece of buttered roll into his mouth.

'No I'm not!' Sarah replied, rather more forcefully than she had intended. 'In fact I'm not at all happy about Biotec taking on any kind of defence-related experiment, and specially not one involving the Office of Naval Research. With the Philadelphia Experiment now part of the folklore of this country, if it were ever to get out that we'd been working with the ONR, the lunatic fringe will immediately jump to the conclusion that we've got together to - I don't know, develop psi as a weapon, or some such nonsense. And frankly - well, frankly I can do without that kind of hassle right at this moment.

'My God, Cyrus,' she added, suddenly picturing herself being buried beneath an avalanche of crank mail, 'do you realise that the Navy still gets letters asking about the

13

Philadelphia Experiment – something which was supposed to have taken place in 1943?'

Shaw shrugged non-committally. 'I think you can rest assured that any help you were able to give the Navy would be treated with the utmost confidence. Indeed, they would insist on it . . . '

By now the sommelier had returned with the bottle of Graacher Munzlay Riesling which Shaw had ordered. After sniffing the cork he savoured the bouquet, then rolled a little of the wine round his mouth. 'Admirable!' he pronounced. 'Quite admirable!'

As soon as their glasses had been filled, Sarah returned to the attack. 'In other words, what I'm being asked to do is take on a classified project.' She shook her head. 'I'm sorry, but the answer's no. Absolutely no! Everything we do at Biotec *has* to be publishable . . . '

Shaw sighed the sigh of a man who, because of another's intransigence, was being driven to do something against his better nature. 'I'm sorry that that should be your attitude, because to use a useful if somewhat out-moded expression, we have been made an offer we can't refuse.'

'*We*!' By now Sarah was so angry that she could have strangled him. 'Cyrus, would you please stop using the word "we"! It isn't *we* who are being asked to compromise ourselves, it's me, for God's sake!'

Unperturbed, Shaw turned his attention to the food which had just arrived. 'Let me tell you something,' he said, lifting a forkful of trout to his mouth. 'Approximately eighty per cent of our funding comes from the Federal Government, the largest proportion of which is defence-related.

'Now, if even a part of this funding were to be diverted elsewhere – and believe me, with the possible exception of Harvard, there isn't a university in this country which wouldn't accept it with open arms, defence-related or not – our activities would be severely curtailed. It would then become a matter of priorities, and I'm very much afraid that the consensus opinion would be that maintaining a facility for the study of paranormal functioning was of a very low order of priority.

14

'And, of course, there is another consideration,' he added patting his lips with his table napkin. 'If I'm not mistaken, you are at present being evaluated for permanent residency in the United States, are you not? Now, if it could be shown that you were willing to be of material help to the United States — '

'Okay, *okay*!' said Sarah, groping in her bag for a handkerchief. 'I get the point . . . '

Shaw beamed. 'I was sure you would!' he said, seemingly unaware of the fact that she was on the verge of tears. 'Now, let me see,' he continued, consulting the gold half-hunter he carried in his waistcoat pocket. 'As I understand it, there should be a helicopter waiting to take you to Maine — '

'What, *now*?' she exclaimed, loudly enough to attract the attention of the people at the next table.

'After you've finished your lunch,' he replied, as if making a great concession. 'I'll have my secretary let yours know where you've gone, and to expect you back by the end of the afternoon. The car which brought you here will take you to Logan, and, of course, will be waiting for you when you return.'

'But why *Maine*?' she demanded, as her anger re-emerged to sweep away the final remants of self-pity. 'Good God, man, ONR have an office only a few blocks from here!'

Taking a gold MasterCard from his snakeskin wallet, Shaw twisted around in his chair and signalled to their waiter. 'That'll be explained when you get there.'

After miming the action of writing a bill he turned, took one of her hands in his and patted it. 'Just think,' he told her, with a sardonic smile, 'if you do a good job they might even name a battleship after you!'

CHAPTER 2

'THIS IS it, ma'am,' yelled the pilot of the JetRanger that had brought Sarah to a point somewhere well to the north of what she guessed must be Rockport. In spite of her blatantly flirtatious attempts to draw him out, it was the first time he had said anything of significance since they had lifted off twenty minutes earlier.

Ahead of her was a sandy bay embraced by low, rocky promontories. On the northernmost promontory was a handful of gabled houses; on the southernmost, a rambling, three-storeyed mansion standing in grounds aglow with the scarlet and gold of maple, aspen and birch. The landward side of the mansion overlooked a three-tiered fountain and a driveway flanked by a colonnade of purple beeches, lawns and planted beds; the seaward side, an informal terraced garden that fell away in great sweeping semicircles to the edge of the cliff.

As they swept over a cluster of outbuildings, a flock of gulls rose from the grounds and wheeled away to the east. By now, she could see that the mansion was of the type which had become fashionable as the summer residences of the rich during the early 1870s: picturesque and unashamedly eclectic, it had steep, gabled roofs pierced by a great many ornate chimneys and dormers; a tower capped by an arcade and a conical roof with a dolphin-shaped copper weather-vane; balconies, terraces and verandas, even a *porte-cochère* to protect those getting into or out of horse-drawn carriages from the vagaries of the weather.

She could also see that a checkpoint had been set up behind the wrought-iron gates which opened on to the driveway, and that the wall surrounding the estate was topped with gleaming coils of barbed-wire.

Amid a cloud of dust and swirling leaves, the helicopter dropped gently on to the north lawn and one of the men who had been awaiting its arrival alongside a naval fire tender ran forward and yanked open the door.

'Dr Stuart?' he yelled, reaching up to shake her hand. 'Welcome to Seacrest.' The top half of his lean, deeply-tanned face was hidden behind a pair of mirrored sun-glasses and he was wearing a short-sleeved khaki uniform bearing the insignia of a major in the Marine Corps. 'My name's Piroschka,' he added, as he helped her to the ground. 'Hank Piroschka, Naval Intelligence.'

'Naval *Intelligence*?' she yelled back at him. 'But I was told I'd be met by someone from the Office of Naval Research.''

'You were – Rear Admiral Calder.' Holding his cap to his head with one hand and Sarah's elbow with the other, Piroschka hurried her from beneath the spinning rotor blades. 'The admiral sends his apologies, and hopes to be joining us shortly.'

As the helicopter's engines were shut down and the dust began to settle, she was suddenly able to see that the estate was badly dilapidated. The lawns were parched and balding and the planting beds overrun with ragweed, goldenrod and black-eyed Susan; icicle-like pendants of dripping green algae were hanging from the fountain's stone basins; and most worrying of all, the salt-encrusted, stick-and-shingle mansion looked as if the first northeaster of autumn would reduce it to matchwood.

After following Piroschka through an ankle-deep drift of curling leaves as crisp and brown as cornflakes, she found herself on a gravelled forecourt choked with crab grass and moss. 'I don't know quite what I was expecting but it certainly wasn't anything like this,' she complained. 'Who does it belong to, Hammer Films?'

But Piroschka either did not understand the joke or was not amused by it. 'It belongs to the Navy. They bought it back in the early seventies with the idea of re-developing the site as part of their Seafarer programme. However, when over-the-horizon radar started getting a bad press, the local environmentalist lobby raised such a stink that the project had to be re-located.'

'So, what's it used for now?'

'Projects such as this,' he replied, unhelpfully. 'Projects which are too sensitive to be contracted out, and yet don't fit into the Navy's own scheme of things.'

'Huh-huh.' Sarah gave him a sideways glance. 'And just what sort of project comes within that category?' she asked, as they passed beneath the ivy-clad *porte-cochère*. 'More to the point, what is it you're expecting from me?'

After leading her up a short flight of steps and across a creaking, worm-eaten veranda, Piroschka pocketed his sunglasses and threw open an elaborately-panelled front door guarded by two Marines armed with automatic rifles. 'In just a couple of minutes all will be revealed,' he promised, ushering her into a cavernous, two-storey living hall.

Although after the brutal heat of the garden the air felt pleasantly cool, it was tainted with the musty, mushroom-like smell of dry rot and there were dust motes dancing in the shaft of sunlight that was pouring through an enormous stained-glass window set high in the west-facing wall.

The hall was clad throughout with ornate oak panelling, and it had a ribbed ceiling from which hung a wrought-iron wagon wheel chandelier draped with cobwebs. Sliding doors had been set in the walls on either side of the hall, and at the far end a massive staircase with carved newel-posts rose to an arcaded landing beneath which was a deep inglenook with built-in seats and a Tudor-arched fireplace. Apart from the huge grandfather clock with an exposed bob pendulum and a moondial that was standing near one of the doors leading to the rear of the house, such other furniture as there was had been shrouded with white dust-sheets.

Could buildings retain a record of highly charged emotional events? Sarah found herself wondering as she waited while Piroschka logged her arrival. If it were possible, something indescribably awful must have

18

happened to produce an atmosphere as malign and threatening as that which permeated Seacrest. When talking of projects too sensitive to be contracted out, to what had he been alluding? The Navy's notorious series of experiments into the nature of aggression, perhaps? Or the programme in which men being trained for commando-type operations were said to have been subjected to a particularly obnoxious form of audio-visual desensitisation in order to convert them into ruthlessly efficient killers?

'Okay, let's go,' said Piroschka, bringing her out of her reverie with a suddenness that made her jump.

Sarah slipped her jacket over her shoulders, and, with their footsteps echoing between the walls, they crossed the vast expanse of uncarpeted parquet floor and began climbing the stairs.

'So, how did you come to get into your particular line of work?' he asked.

Although tempted to reply in the same deliberately arcane manner he'd employed when answering her questions, she decided it would be childish to do so. And anyway, if she were to be open with him perhaps he'd feel under an obligation to be open with her. 'I suppose I just sort of drifted into it,' she began, thinking she could smell surgical spirit. 'When I came down from Oxford — '

'*Came* down?'

'Graduated,' she explained, making a mental note to add 'come down' to her list of English words and phrases which when used in America were either meaningless or misleading.

'In what subjects?'

They were now on the first floor landing, and, as they turned a corner into a long, brightly lit corridor, she became absolutely certain she could smell surgical spirit.

'Psychology and philosophy. My first job was evaluating the psychological profiles of paranormal metal-benders.'

'You mean guys like Uri Geller?'

'Yes, except I didn't get to meet him until much later.'

'Tell me, what did you make of Geller?'

'As a man or a magician?'

19

A flicker of a smile disturbed the almost perfect symmetry of Piroschka's face. 'I guess that answers my question!'

'Anyway, what I saw there – at Birkbeck College, London, that is – got me interested, so, after I'd taken my PhD, I began looking for a full-time job in the same field.

'However, with very little serious work being done on paranormal functioning in England and nothing really to keep me there, I thought what the hell, why don't I throw a few things into a suitcase and try my luck in the States.'

By now they had come to a standstill outside a panelled mahogany door at the end of the corridor. With his hand on the brass doorknob, Piroschka waited with ill-disguised impatience for her to finish her story.

'After a while spent working as a secretary cum reception-ist for a fashionable New York shrink I was offered a job at Duke; from Duke I went to Stanford, and from Stanford to Biotec where — '

'Interesting,' he said, throwing open the door without further delay.

Like the rooms she had glimpsed during their walk along the corridor, the one in front of her was enormous. It had a bay window hung with white Venetian blinds, panelled walls and a carved chimney-piece. What made it startlingly unlike the others was that it had been equipped as a fully-operational intensive-care unit.

Lying on a wheeled ripple bed in the middle of the ICU was an enormous bald-headed man with bushy eyebrows and a bulbous, pock-marked nose. Like his pubis, his shoulders, chest and the backs of his forearms were covered with grizzled hair, and his skin was the colour of yellowing putty. Cotton-wool pads had been placed over his eyes and his jaws were clamped around the mouthpiece of an endo-tracheal tube connected to a respirator. As well as having been hooked up to an array of sophisticated monitoring equipment, he had drainage tubes in his nose, chest, abdomen and bladder, and an intravenous line in his right arm. His swollen belly was traversed by an ugly-looking surgical scar held together with metal clips, and above it yellow faecal fluid was oozing into a disposable plastic bag attached to a livid ileostomy stoma. Apart from the rhythmic hiss of the respirator and the steady, sonar-like bleeping of the cardiogram, the room was still and silent as a tomb.

'Who — ' Sarah began, but shock had left her speechless.

'Who is he?' said Piroschka, asking the question for her. 'He's Marshal Andrei Illich Itzhevnikov; defence minister, chief of the Soviet armed forces and member of the Politburo.

'Or at least he *was*,' he added, in an exasperated voice. 'Unfortunately the poor bastard died on an operating table in West Germany a couple of days ago . . . '

CHAPTER 3

'WELL, HI there!' boomed a voice from the end of the
corridor. 'You must be Dr Stuart . . . '

Sarah turned to see a tall, powerfully-built naval officer
striding towards her. He was wearing a white short-sleeve
shirt with blue epaulets and blue trousers. Like the epaulets,
his cap was emblazoned with gold rank insignia and there
were five rows of ribbons above his left breast pocket.

Hurrying to keep up with him was a nurse and a short,
wiry and somewhat agitated-looking doctor wearing a white
coat and tortoise-shell half-frames.

'This is Admiral Calder,' she was told by Piroschka. 'The
admiral's in charge of the project . . . '

'For my sins,' he chuckled, shaking her warmly by the
hand. Although even his own mother could never have
thought of him as handsome -- his eyes were too small and
too closely set, and his hooked nose jutted over a mouth that
was too wide -- he nevertheless came across as being more
attractive than the conventionally good-looking and much
younger Piroschka. Much more attractive. To her surprise,
she even found herself waiting for an opportunity to see if he
was wearing a wedding ring, and, moreover, feeling just a
little disappointed when she discovered that he did.

'So, has the major put you in the picture?' he asked, as
soon as he had apologised for his late arrival.

Stepping aside to allow the doctor and the nurse into the
ICU, Piroschka replied: 'I thought I'd leave that to you,
sir.'

'You did, did you?' Calder took off his cap to reveal a grey
crew-cut. 'Well thanks a million!' With a sour smile, he

shepherded Piroschka and Sarah into a path lab adjoining the ICU and closed the door. 'I hope you've at least been told who he is,' he said, nodding in the direction of the man-machine symbiote on the other side of the between-glass Venetian blind.

'I know *who* he is, but not what's he's doing here or why you think he's dead,' she replied. 'According to the cardiac monitor he's certainly not dead . . . '

'Ah!' Putting down his cap, Calder leaned across the bench that was standing in front of the observation window and pressed a switch on an intercom. 'Commander Kessler . . . '

Looking faintly irritated, the doctor turned from studying one of the items in the array of patient monitoring equipment to peer at the admiral over the top of his half-frames.

'Commander, would you mind talking us through what you'll be doing? For the benefit of Dr Stuart . . . '

'What, the whole work-up?' he demanded, speaking into a microphone that was suspended over the bed. The voice from the intercom was crisp and clear, and behind it Sarah could hear the clink of instruments as the nurse bustled about preparing a trolley.

'No, just the brainstem reflexes.'

'All right, but first I'll have to check out a couple of problems with ALF.'

As Calder began questioning the doctor about what had gone wrong, Sarah turned to Piroschka. 'Who or what is ALF?' she asked in a hushed voice.

'It's an acronym for Automated Library Facility. The one we're accessing is at Bethesda Naval Hospital, and what you do is key symptoms into it from the VDU over there – ' He pointed to a computer terminal that was standing alongside an electroencephalogram ' – and within seconds it comes back with both a diagnosis and a recommended course of action.'

'Sounds like a hypochondriac's dream of Christmas morning.'

Piroschka frowned. 'Ma'am?'

23

'Forget it,' she said, determined that this would be the last time she would attempt a joke for the major's benefit.

Calder released the switch on the intercom and turned back to her. 'Now, where were we?'

'You were about to tell me what all of this has to do with me . . . '

'Okay.' Calder took a Meerschaum pipe from his breast pocket, blew down the stem and began filling the bowl from a pigskin tobacco pouch. 'So far you've been told who he is but nothing else, right?'

'Right.'

'Well, I won't burden you with the story of how the CIA came to recruit him, except to say that it was probably one of the biggest intelligence coups of all time, certainly as far as the West was concerned.

'However, running a so-called "defector-in-place" in as closed a society as the Soviet Union isn't easy – particularly one as highly placed as Itzhevnikov – so we weren't exactly surprised when we heard that the CIA were going to have to bring him out, and fast. It was a pity, but at least we'd now have a chance to do what we'd been itching to do for a long time: debrief him in depth.

'Except it wasn't to be. There's an inquiry still going on into just what did happen on the night he was lifted, but as a foul-up it looks like being a contender for the *Guinness Book of Records*!'

As Calder paused to light his pipe, Piroschka took up the story. 'To appreciate what happened next, you have to understand one thing,' he told Sarah. 'In order to gain the greatest advantage from Itzhevnikov's defection, the Russians hadn't to know he'd defected. And in order to achieve this the Directorate of Operations set it up to look as if he'd drowned while swimming near his dacha on the Black Sea, at the same time issuing a directive saying that only personnel with an absolute need-to-know should know what was happening.

'Which,' he added, before conceding the floor to Calder, 'ruled out just about everyone except Escape and Evasion.'

'Let's face it, they screwed up for exactly the same reason

24

as they screwed up when they tried to rescue the Iranian hostages,' he told Piroschka. 'They became so goddamned obsessed with secrecy that the right hand not only didn't know what the left hand was doing, it didn't even know there *was* a left hand!

'Anyway,' he continued, turning back to Sarah, 'we now know that it was agreed that he should be taken to our defector centre just outside of Frankfurt, and from Frankfurt to Camp Peary.'

'The CIA's Williamsburg base,' Piroschka explained.

Calder blew a smoke ring at the ceiling. 'Which was all fine and dandy except for one thing: because Operation Big Boy had been set up as an eyes only, sealed orders exercise, the guys at the defector centre only found out what was happening when it was too late to advise the guys who were bringing him in that the Germans had mounted a big anti-terrorist operation for that night.

'To cut a long story short, they got stopped at a roadblock, and, during some chickenshit hassle about IDs, Itzhevnikov takes a round in the gut. As if that wasn't bad enough, when they finally got him into the base hospital he gets given stale blood – that or the level of anaesthesia was allowed to become too light. Either way, the upshot was that the poor sonuvabitch suffered a cardiac arrest, and by the time they got his heart beating again his brain had been without oxygen for over four minutes and was irreversibly damaged.'

Piroschka tut-tutted.

'When the Director of the CIA finally plucked up the courage to tell the President he'd been declared brain-dead – Itzhevnikov, that is, not the President, although when I tell you what he's come up with you may well think he's been brain-damaged too! – he went ape. After kicking the Director's ass all the way back to Langley, he had Itzhevnikov moved to the National Security Agency's hospital at Fort Meade, where some of the best neuro-physiologists in Britain and America were drafted in to see what could be done for him. When they came up empty he even had the Advanced Projects Agency try to figure out a

25

way of -- I dunno, using computers to tap into his memory banks. But it was when they, too, came up empty that the President fielded the *real* zinger — '

Suddenly the intercom crackled into life. 'We're ready to check the brainstem reflexes,' Kessler announced. 'But first, may I ask Dr Stuart how much she knows about the function of the brainstem?'

Sarah leaned forward and spoke into the microphone. 'I know it's essential to the maintenance of consciousness, respiration and blood pressure,' she replied, watching the nurse as she finished sticking the last of a dozen or so silver EEG electrodes to Itzhevnikov's skull. 'Also, it's — '

'Fine. That's fine.' Kessler moved to the head of the bed, took a pentorch from the breast pocket of his white coat and lifted the cotton wool pads from Itzhevnikov's eyes. 'So, what we'll do first is test the upper part of the patient's brainstem -- the part which controls eye reflexes,' he announced.

Using the first and fourth finger of his left hand, he raised Itzhevnikov's eyelids, switched on the torch and shone it into each eye. 'Although you probably couldn't see it from in there, in spite of the light the pupils remained fully dilated.'

After returning the torch to his pocket, he touched each of the exposed eyeballs with a twist of cotton wool, closed the lids and then pressed them gently but firmly with his thumbs.

'Well, that takes care of the upper part of the brainstem,' he told Sarah, as the nurse began filling an aural syringe. 'The absence of corneal reflexes together with the lack of facial movement in response to supra-orbital pressure indicates that the upper part of the brainstem is no longer functioning.'

Moving to a position alongside Itzhevnikov's right shoulder, Kessler looked inside the Russian's ear with an auriscope, then took the syringe from the nurse. 'What we're doing now is irrigating the external auditory meatus with ice-water,' he explained, as he inserted the syringe and depressed the plunger.

26

He straighened up. 'Again, no reaction. If the middle part of the brainstem had been alive his eyes would have moved.'

Laying aside the kidney bowl she'd used to catch the water which had drained from Itzhevnikov's ear, the nurse pulled on a pair of disposable gloves, opened a sterile pack containing a long plastic tube and handed it to Kessler.

'What I'll do now is check to see if there's a gagging reflex. If there isn't, it means that the lower part of the brainstem is also dead.'

After unplugging the air-supply hose from the mouthpiece, he passed the tube into Itzhevnikov's throat for a moment.

'Again, nothing,' the doctor announced, handing the tube back to the nurse. 'Later we'll go through the formality of pre-oxygenating the patient and disconnecting him from the respirator to see if by some miracle he starts breathing on his own again, but I'm afraid it's now only a formality.

'Just as checking his EEG is only a formality,' he added, as he crossed to switch on the electroencephalogram.

After watching the roll of calibrated paper pass slowly beneath the line of almost static pen-recorders for a minute or so, he said: 'As you can probably see, there is a little EEG activity, but I'm afraid it's not significant. According to all currently recognised criteria the patient is dead, and has been dead since he was first brought here.'

Calder thanked the doctor, switched off the intercom and turned back to Sarah. 'Satisfied?'

'Okay, so he's dead and I'm sorry. But what has all this to do with me? I'm not a neurophysiologist. I'm not even a doctor of medicine . . . '

'No, but you're a parapsychologist,' said Calder, fingering the metallic-thread gold oak leaves on his cap visor. 'And the President seems to think that parapsychology is – ' He shrugged apologetically. 'Well, I guess some sort of updated, computerised version of spiritualism . . . '

'Oh, no!' she cried, suddenly and painfully aware of what was coming next. 'I don't believe it.'

Calder nodded grimly. 'You'd better believe it, because what the President wants you to do is — ' He hesitated, searching for the words with which to express what was clearly an impossible concept.

Piroschka finished the sentence for him. 'What he wants you to do is raise Itzhevnikov's ghost,' he explained, looking her straight in the eye. 'The President wants you to raise Itzhevnikov's ghost so that we can debrief it!'

CHAPTER 4

WITH HIS buttocks resting against the edge of the bench and his arms folded, Calder waited for Sarah to come to the end of her angry outburst. 'I quite agree,' he said, taking the pipe from his mouth. 'The whole thing's crazy. However, what I don't understand is why you – a parapsychologist – should think it crazy?

'Surely,' he added, with a quizzical frown, 'attempting to contact the dead is what parapsychology's all about, isn't it? Or at least *part* of what it's about . . . '

Sarah laughed. 'No, no, no!' Suddenly the whole thing seemed clear to her: she had become caught up in this ludicrous project because of a simple and all too common misunderstanding of the aims and objectives of modern parapsychology. All she would have to do to extricate herself, therefore, was to put the record straight.

Reaching for a stool, she sat down. 'Listen, since the Society for Psychical Research first began investigating seance room phenomena at the end of the last century, most of it has been shown to be either deliberately fraudulent or the product of abnormal psychological states, right? And the tiny percentage of it which doesn't fall into one or the other of these categories can now be explained quite satisfactorily in terms of extra-sensory perception, clairvoyance or psycho-kinesis.

'These days, we no longer have to concern ourselves with whether port-mortem survival might or might not be a factor in such phenomena; it's as irrelevant to parapsychology as – well, as phrenology is to psychology!'

'That's as maybe,' said Calder, crossing to open one of a

pair of casement windows that were set into the wall either side of a boarded-over fireplace. 'However, the irony is that while the President would probably dismiss extra-sensory perception, clairvoyance and psychokinesis as bunk, he does happen to believe in an afterlife.'

Sarah eyed the two men suspiciously. 'But he's a Catholic, isn't he? So why hasn't someone told him that the Catholic Church expressly forbids attempts to communicate with the dead?'

'Someone did, and were told to check their facts,' Calder retorted. 'The situation seems to be this,' he continued, relenting a little. 'Although the rule applies to the general body of the faithful, the Church is prepared to grant dispensation to certain people under certain circumstances.

'Anyway, that's a problem for him and his confessor,' he added, a trace of impatience in his voice. 'As far as we're concerned, we've no option but to go along with what he wants.'

Sarah jumped down from her stool. 'You may feel obliged to go along with what he wants, but I *certainly* don't!' Scooping up her handbag, she set out towards the door. 'As far as I'm concerned, you can tell everyone up to and including the President to get stuffed!'

As unruffled as Calder, Piroschka looked up from absent-mindedly nibbling his fingernails. 'And discover in a couple of week's time that your application for an immigrant visa has been thrown out?' he said, as she opened the door.

Turning on her heel, Sarah glared at him. 'For refusing to raise the ghost of a Russian defector?' Out of the corner of her eye she saw the nurse look up from aspirating Itzhevnikov's lungs to exchange a questioning glance with Kessler. 'You're out of your mind!'

After making an unsuccessful grab at a moth which had flown in through the open window, Piroschka hoisted himself up on to the bench and reached for a black leather document case. 'Listen,' he said, as he snapped open the lid and took out a bulging file marked TOP SECRET, 'the guys over at Immigration and Nationality won't have checked you out as thoroughly as we have.' Pausing to lick

30

his index finger, he began leafing rapidly through the papers in the file. 'And unlike us, you'd find they wouldn't be at all happy to learn that at – yes, here we are – that at Oxford you were an active member of what was then the Communist-dominated National Union of Students; that you took part in a march in support of the occupation of Essex University; a sit-in in support of — '

Sarah burst out laughing. 'Oh, come *on!*' she said, trying unsuccessfully to catch Calder's eye. 'In those days we were all into student power. It was the in thing, like ethnic clothes and macrobiotic food!'

'Sure, but the INS isn't going to see it that way,' Piroschka explained. 'Especially if they were to be told that on the Police National Computer at Hendon you're — ' he paused to turn a sheet ' – yes, you're described as – and I quote – "an urban terrorist not connected with the IRA" . . . '

'A *what?*' she exclaimed, closing the door behind her.

Piroschka looked up. 'You were a member of the Hunt Saboteurs Association, were you not?'

Turning away from his remorselessly penetrating stare, Sarah saw that the moth had flown into a spider's web which had been spun between the chimney-breast, ceiling and wall. 'For a while, yes,' she conceded, as the moth began a frantic struggle to escape. 'But how does that — '

' — make you an urban terrorist?' Piroschka shrugged. 'In Britain the police classify members of the Hunt Saboteurs Association as urban terrorists,' he replied, as if it were as much a mystery to him as to her. 'And what about the ex-boyfriend who was charged with being a member of the Red Army Faction?' he continued, turning back to the file. 'Let me see, what was his name again? Hans something-or-other?'

'Hans-Dieter Scheele. But if you know about Hans, you'll also know that that all happened long after we split up,' she protested.

Piroschka tossed the file aside. 'Sure, but put all the facts together and to the guys over at INS it'll sound as if you belong to what the Immigration and Nationality Act calls a "subversive class", which means you might just as well start packing now.

'And there's one other thing you should know,' he added, almost as an afterthought. 'An unsuccessful application for immigration makes it damn near impossible for anyone to ever again get a non-immigrant visa. Once you've been turned down for immigration, you won't be allowed back into this country even as a tourist, let alone to work here.'

'Nonsense!' exclaimed Sarah, as Piroschka once again began nibbling his fingernails. 'If you so much as suspected me of being a subversive, you wouldn't be trying to pressure me into working on this God-forsaken project of yours.

'And let me tell you something else,' she added, with as much force as she could muster. 'If the INS turns me down I'll have my immigration lawyer go straight to the Attorney General. And if we can't get a waiver out of him, so help me I'll take the story of why I was turned down to the *Washington Post*!'

For a moment, the only sound to disturb the poisonous silence which had settled on the room was the fluttering of the moth. Glancing up, Sarah saw that it had almost succeeded in freeing itself. However, as Piroschka started speaking the spider suddenly darted across the web, paralyzed the moth with its fangs, and, spinning it like a bobbin, began enveloping it in a silken shroud.

'I'm sorry, what was that?' she asked, turning back to Piroschka in time to see him remove a sliver of nail from his tongue.

'I said you could always *try*,' he replied, amiably. 'Not that anyone would believe you. I mean, just think about it for a moment: the people at Biotec don't know where you are, only that you went off for what looked like a romantic lunch with Cyrus Shaw. If it comes to that, *you* don't know where you are. Okay, so maybe you could find the house again, but how do you prove you were ever here? None of *us* have ever seen you before, and if it comes to it Shaw'll say that the two of you spent the afternoon in the sack.

'And if you don't think he could make it stick, let me tell you something else,' he added, with rather more of an edge

32

to his voice. 'Three hours ago Shaw and a CIA operative who happens to look a lot like you checked into an hotel in Salem for the afternoon. So, it wouldn't just be your word against his, it would be your word against the desk clerk, the bellhop and the waiter who brought up the champagne . . . '

Now very frightened, Sarah returned to the stool and sat down. 'Supposing – just supposing – I were to agree to do what you want,' she said, as a prelude to what she knew would be her final attempt at extricating herself from the trap they'd so carefully and cunningly prepared. 'What's to stop me or one of my colleagues from telling the whole story once we're through?'

'The Espionage Act apart, as you yourself said a couple of minutes ago, if it were ever to get out that you'd been involved in something like this – and I think your actual words were "as unsavoury, unethical and unscientific as this" – you'd be all washed up. Kaputt.'

'Not if it were known that we'd been blackmailed into it.'

Piroschka began leafing through his file again. 'I don't much care for the word blackmail,' he said, indifferently. 'But if you insist on using it, you're the only one who's being blackmailed. The others will play ball because you ask them to play ball.'

'How can you be sure of that?'

'Because we've checked them out, and we know how highly you're regarded by all of them.' After pausing to reassure himself that the sheet he had found really was the one for which he'd been looking, he passed it to Sarah. 'Those are the names of the people who've been cleared to work on the project.'

Sarah ran her eye quickly down the list. 'There are several here who're going to take a *lot* of persuading . . . '

'You'll manage.' Piroschka put the file back into the case and closed the lid. 'Jesus, lady, you're a psychologist, and if a psychologist can't handle a little problem like this, who can?'

Sarah folded the sheet of paper and slipped it into her handbag. 'Tell me something,' she said, looking from one man to the other. 'There must have been plenty of people who'd have jumped at the chance of getting in on an act like this, so why pick on me? Someone you obviously knew was going to give you a hard time . . . '

'Because the President happened to see you on TV a couple of weeks ago,' replied Calder, tapping the ash from his pipe against the heel of one of his highly-polished, black leather shoes. 'He thought you were pretty impressive, and when he had you checked out with the American Association for the Advancement of Science he was told that yours was the best shop in the business.'

'After that, well, it was simply a question of us making sure you wouldn't say no,' added Piroschka, with a sardonic smile.

Calder finished re-filling his pipe and put a match to the tobacco. 'Listen,' he said, squinting at her through a cloud of smoke, 'it's not going to be *so* bad. In a week – ten days at the most – it'll all be over and forgotten.' He paused to blow out the match. 'And anyway, if you haven't seen Maine in the fall it's high time you did. I promise you, it'll really blow your mind!'

Sarah looked up from picking aimlessly at the hem of her jacket. 'You're not expecting us to work *here*, are you?'

'Where else?' asked Piroschka.

'Biotec!' she snapped. 'For God's sake, if Itzhevnikov's contactable at all, we stand just as much of a chance of contacting him in Boston as here!'

Piroschka shook his head. 'If you start fooling around with something like this at Biotec, in no time at all everybody'll know about it,' he told her, glancing at his wristwatch.

'But they're going to know about it if I and half my senior staff suddenly up and move to Maine!'

'They're not, because you're going to tell 'em you're here to talk over the idea of telepathy as a means of communicating with our strategic submarine fleet.'

'Telepathy?' Sarah exclaimed, as he turned, picked up a phone and asked the operator for a number. 'Och, away with you! Everyone knows the Navy dropped that idea years ago!'

'So, tell 'em we've gotten interested in it again,' he said, while waiting to be connected. 'Hell, it's no secret that we still haven't cracked the problem of shore-to-ship communication with subs operating below fifty fathoms.'

As Sarah began to protest, Piroschka held up a hand for silence. 'Dr Stuart will be leaving in five minutes,' he announced. 'As soon as she's airborne, call her secretary and have her set up a meeting of the personnel who've been cleared to work on Endor for say — ' he looked questioningly at Sarah ' — nineteen hundred hours?'

'Today?'

'Why, is that a problem?' he asked, covering the mouthpiece with his hand.

'I guess not . . . '

'Then nineteen hundred it is.'

'Endor? What did he mean by *Endor*?' she asked Calder, as Piroschka turned back to the phone.

'It's the code name for this phase of the operation,' he explained, looking faintly embarrassed. 'I'm sorry about that, but it was chosen before we knew it would be run by a woman.'

'I still don't understand . . . '

Through the open window came the high-pitched whine of the helicopter starting up.

'When Saul wanted someone to raise the ghost of Samuel, he went to — '

' — the Witch of Endor!' Sarah gave him a black look. 'Christ, that's *all* I needed!' she added, before picking up her handbag and storming out of the room.

CHAPTER 5

SARAH ARRIVED back at Biotec at 6.40, her mind a turmoil. Anxious to avoid her colleagues until she'd had a chance to get her thoughts into some kind of order, she had the driver drop her off at the rear of the imposing concrete-and-glass building, where she took the service elevator to the third floor, hurried down a length of carpeted corridor hung with framed Kirlian photographs and entered her elegant but somewhat untidy office.

After pouring herself some wine from one of the six bottles she'd bought on her way back from the airport, she stacked them in the refrigerator, crossed to the window and opened the Venetian blind.

Beyond the exquisitely landscaped grounds lay the great sweep of the Charles River, and beyond it the towers of downtown Boston, their windows ablaze with the reflection of the setting sun.

Was this the thirty pieces of silver for which she had sold her integrity? This and the sense of being in the very heartland of scientific innovation? Because in agreeing to work on Endor, surely that was what she had done?

Of one thing she was certain: if she were to change her mind and tell them she would have nothing to do with it, she'd have to make the whole thing public, and fast. It would be no good her saying no and hoping they wouldn't carry out their threats; by then so much water would have passed under the bridge that only the left-wing, lunatic fringe of the press would believe her story to be anything more than the product of paranoia.

However, no sooner had she found the telephone number of the *Washington Post* when another thought occurred to her:

if she were to do what she was about to do, not only would every waking moment be taken up with the wretched business for God knows how long, but she would be hounded morning, noon and night by the international news media.

Appalled by the prospect, she drained her paper cup and flung it into the bin. But then, just as she was beginning to think that she had no option other than to return to England, something Calder had said flashed into her mind – something triggered by the action of dispensing with a worthless object. Although she couldn't recall his exact words, the meaning had been quite clear: she should, he'd suggested, treat Endor for what it was – a worthless but essentially harmless, short-term exercise.

Maybe he was right, she told herself as she returned to the desk. After all, if she was to continue with her work she would have to remain in America. Apart from Russia, America was still the only country in the world which considered psi to be an area of scientific research on which it was worth spending substantial sums of money.

Feeling suddenly much less unhappy, she opened her handbag and took out the sheet of paper bearing the names of the people who'd been cleared to work on Endor. Although she hadn't noticed it at the time, she now saw that along with lab assistants, graduate students, administrative and maintenance personnel, two members of her senior staff – Weisz and McPhee – were missing from the list. Weisz she could understand: although happily married with two children, two cars and a Colonial-style house in Concord, as a student he'd burned his draft card and gone to Montreal, where he had studied physics at McGill until the amnesty. But why McPhee? Unless, of course, they thought his fondness for under-aged boys made him a security risk.

Although her instinctive reaction was to challenge the veto, she immediately dismissed the thought. Neither man would have thanked her for doing so, and anyway, with her deputy attending a conference in West Germany, someone would have to stay behind and mind the store while she and the others were fooling around in Maine.

37

But would they agree to go to Maine? To a large extent, that would depend on whether or not she told them about the blackmail angle. If she did, they, too, would be angry as hell. Indeed, in a group the likelihood was that one person's anger would fuel the anger of another to a point where they would no longer be receptive to even the most carefully reasoned argument.

So, perhaps the thing to do was simply not mention it, and instead, appeal to their sense of patriotism. Although the term had a curiously old-fashioned ring to it, it might just work. After all, there could be no denying that if there was a way of getting through to Itzhevnikov it would be of immense value to the United States, particularly at a time when the President was pursuing what many considered to be overly trusting peace initiatives with the Soviets.

So, she would begin by describing what had happened that afternoon, omitting only the blackmail aspect of the story. She would then go on to say that although the odds were against them achieving anything, it was still worth a try. After all, she'd point out, there is a vast body of anecdotal evidence which suggests that in certain circumstances the mind can survive the death of the body – evidence going back to the very beginning of recorded history. In rejecting such evidence, are we not guilty of the same kind of prejudiced thinking that had led the scientific establishment of an earlier generation to reject as great a body of anecdotal evidence that the mind is capable of both extra-sensory perception and psychokinesis, feats which are now accepted, if not fully understood – by all but the most die-hard reactionary?

If only as an exercise, she would conclude, it might be no bad thing for us to think about the unthinkable for a few days, in pleasant surroundings and at the government's expense.

Although she knew they wouldn't buy it straight off, the chances were that they'd do so eventually. All of them, that is, except the person whose help she would have welcomed most, the Caltech-trained mathematician and theoretical physicist, Jack Adams. In fact the likelihood was that Jack would tell her to shove Endor where it belonged the moment she revealed it to be a Defense Department project. And who could blame him. As a veteran of Vietnam, he had *plenty* about which to feel aggrieved.

Except . . . Leaning back in her leather-covered swivel chair, Sarah began tapping out the rhythm of a protest song she remembered from the early seventies. *And it's one, two, three what are we fighting for?* she sang softly to herself. *Don't ask me I don't give a damn, the next stop is Vietnam . . .*

And then suddenly it came to her. Of course! Although Jack had every reason to feel bitter, unlike so many who had fought in that most misguided and nightmarish of all wars, he had never shown any signs of bitterness. Okay, so there'd been just a trace when the Iranian hostages had been released. 'We got spat on and called baby-killers,' he'd said, shaking his head incredulously. 'They get yellow ribbons coast-to-coast and lifetime passes to baseball games!' But that had been it. He hadn't joined Vietnam Veterans Against the War; he hadn't thrown away his medals – the Legion of Merit, Bronze Star and Purple Heart – nor had he demonstrated against the previous Administration's proposals to reduce veterans' counselling, employment and education programmes. So, maybe she'd been wrong to write him off quite so quickly. Maybe those of his colleagues who suspected him of still being on a heavy heart-of-darkness trip were right. After all, despite legs which had been shattered by a Chicom mine at Da Nang he did spend several hours a day pumping iron and he was a championship-class clay-target shooter and archer. Except what did that prove? she asked herself. That he was *High on War* like the freaked-out grunt who'd first scrawled the slogan across the front of a helmet? No, the only thing it actually proved was that he had the grit and determination to overcome disabilities which would have left a lesser man permanently incarcerated in a Veterans' Hospital.

Anyway, all she could do now was wait and hope. And if he did turn her down, well there was always Andrew Svenson. Although as extroverted as Jack was introverted, like Jack, Andy was already well practised in thinking about the unthinkable, whether at a sub-atomic or a super-galactic level. The son of a cosmologist father and a molecular biologist mother, he had been raised in a house where talk of anti-matter, imaginary masses and electrons which move backwards in time was an almost daily occurrence, and on graduating as a physicist from MIT, had taken to psi as effortlessly as a duck to water.

Okay, so providing Andy was willing to go along with Endor she could forget about the other people from the hard sciences, and instead, turn her attention to picking someone from the life sciences. McPhee was out, so the choice was between Peter Brownrigg, Paul Quinsey, Minoru Haya-kawa, and Margaret Mintz.

Pete would have been ideal, but with his wife in hospital recovering from a miscarriage, it would clearly be unfair to ask him to leave Boston.

Paul, on the other hand, was still something of an unknown quantity, having only recently joined Biotec.

So, who was it to be – Minoru or Maggie? Of the two, she would have preferred the gentle if somewhat inscrutable Japanese-American to the bright but brash, spring-loaded New Yorker, except she was reluctant to interrupt what promised to be an important series of telepathically-induced dream experiments.

However, temperament apart, did Maggie have the right background for such a project?

Crossing to the cabinet containing the personnel files, she ran her eye quickly down Maggie's *curriculum vitae*. As she'd feared, although Maggie had done a lot of varied and distinguished work since graduating as a biologist from New York University, most of it had been as far removed from survival research as was possible to imagine.

Even so, it might be no bad thing to have her on the team, if only to help keep Andy's feet firmly on the ground.

Sarah slipped the sheet back into its file, closed the drawer and returned to her desk.

Right, well that was that. It would be Andy, Maggie and maybe Jack, if they could be persuaded to participate, that is.

CHAPTER 6

'AND WE thought you'd been getting your rocks off with Cyrus Shaw!' exclaimed Maggie, as soon as Sarah had come to the end of her carefully edited account of what had happened that afternoon. 'For the greater good of Biotec, you understand,' she added hastily.

Only just in time, Sarah stopped herself from pointing out that that was what they were supposed to have thought, and instead said: 'Cyrus Shaw? Not even for Biotec!

'So, what do you think?' she asked, looking from one stunned face to another.

Again, it was Maggie who was the first to speak. 'I think the whole thing stinks!' she snapped, tucking her long, glossy black hair behind her ears. She had an attractive, mobile face that was devoid of make-up, closely-set eyes and a Barbra Streisand nose, and she was wearing blue-and-white striped dungarees over a man's collar-less shirt, ankle socks and sneakers.

'Really?' Sarah tried to sound surprised. 'But why?'

'Why?' Maggie put down her can of diet soda and dug into a canvas shoulder bag for a packet of Kooltip and a Zippo lighter. 'Because if it were ever to get out that we'd been mixed up in anything as crazy as this we'd be finished!'

'But there's no reason to suppose it would ever get out,' said Sarah, wondering why someone who had recently taken up health food and aerobics was still smoking. 'The government doesn't want it known they have Itzhevnikov, so they're hardly likely to issue a press release. And we *certainly* won't!'

Maggie lit her cigarette and blew a plume of smoke at the ceiling. 'The government didn't want it known that they'd bombed Cambodia, but that didn't stop the Pentagon

41

Papers being published!' she replied, her words coming out like a burst from a machine-gun.

Sarah managed a laugh. 'Oh, come now!' she said, searching her crowded desk-top for an ashtray. 'It's not the same thing at all! In bombing Cambodia they were behaving illegally. But trying to debrief a dead Russian defector isn't an offence — '

'Except against common sense!' Maggie interjected, stabbing out her cigarette in the ashtray Sarah had uncovered from behind a pile of score sheets.

'I think she's right,' said Svenson, a heavily-built man with a blond beard and an open, friendly face. In his checked shirt, Levi's and tractor boots, he looked more like a lumberjack than a scientist, an effect heightened still further by his having chosen to sit on his chair backwards, with his legs straddling the seat. 'In spite of what Jack might think, I'm as patriotic as the next guy, and if I thought there was any way of raising Itz — ' He paused, not quite able to remember the name.

'Itzhevnikov,' said Sarah.

Svenson tried again, but still he got it wrong.

'Itz-*hev*-ni-kov,' said Sarah, syllabising the name. 'But if it helps, just call him It.'

'If I thought there was any way we could raise It I'd be the first to say fine, let's give it a whirl. But all that'll happen is that we'll end up with egg on our faces . . . '

Brownrigg nodded gloomily. 'I'm afraid Andy's right,' he said, amid a general murmur of agreement.

'Jack, you haven't said anything yet,' prompted Sarah.

Adams looked up from absentmindedly tracing a pattern on the carpet with the tip of one of his steel elbow crutches. He had a lean, disturbingly deadpan face, a mop of curly, carrot-coloured hair and a carefully-tended Zapata moustache. 'I think we should go along with what they want,' he announced, digging into one of the cargo pockets of his surplus store combat jacket for what Sarah recognised as his equivalent of Captain Queeg's ball bearings – a plastic-and-steel wrist exerciser.

Maggie pushed up her shirtsleeves as if preparing for a

42

fight. 'You've gotta be kidding!' she exclaimed. 'But why, for chrissakes?'

Adams sighed. 'Because, honey,' he replied, as he began pumping the wrist exerciser, 'this is no time to be putting anyone's back up, particularly not the backs of the people we rely on for our funding.'

'And you think that if we don't go along with them we'll lose our funding?' she asked, in a disbelieving voice.

'That, or have it cut back to a point where we're barely ticking over,' he told her. 'If it wasn't for Cyrus Shaw, the board of regents would've had our asses long ago. There just isn't enough Nobel prize potential in psi research for their liking . . . '

Maggie pooh-poohed the suggestion. 'I don't believe that would happen – not for turning down something as crazy as Endor. And if it did we could set up our own shop! With our reputation, surely to God there would be plenty of foundations willing to fund us?'

Sarah winced. 'Not at the level we're being funded at present, and even that's not enough.

'Take Minoru's project, for example,' she continued, with a nod in the direction of the bespectacled Japanese-American in the white lab coat. 'If we're to get that off the ground we're going to need the help of the National Institute of Mental Health, and you can imagine the reception we'd get if the White House has been putting it around that the President isn't happy about the taxpayers' money being spent on such a highly speculative area of research as psi . . . '

'Okay, but have you thought about the bad-mouthing we'll get if we take on the assignment and come up empty?' asked Maggie. 'And let's not kid ourselves, we will come up empty because what we're being asked to do is impossible.'

Sarah tut-tutted. 'I'm not sure we're ever justified in using the word "impossible",' she pointed out, trying not to sound too pompous. 'After all, the history of science is largely one of heresies which have become orthodoxies . . . '

'That, and a growing realisation that the more we

43

discover the more there is to be discovered,' added Hayakawa, pleased with the paradox.

'Okay, all right!' Maggie held up her hands in a gesture of appeasement. 'I withdraw the word "impossible". But you still haven't answered my question: if we take on this assignment and come up empty, mightn't they still put it around that psi is for the birds?'

Sarah shook her head emphatically. 'I don't believe they would. Not if we're seen to have tried our damnedest.'

'And anyway, I don't understand why Maggie's so certain we *will* come up empty,' Adams protested. 'Hell, it's not as if there aren't precedents for what they want us to do.'

'*Precedents?*' Maggie looked at him as if he were mad.

'That's right,' he replied, manhandling his left leg into a more comfortable position. 'On October 7, 1930, a seance being given by the British medium Eileen Garrett was interrupted by the first of several so-called "drop-in communicators" who'd died when the R101 crashed three days earlier on its maiden flight to India.'

Sarah braced herself. Although given to long, brooding silences, when Adams did begin arguing a case he was notoriously difficult to stop. Moreover, because he possessed not only a prodigious memory but also appeared to find everything of consuming interest, he wasn't always capable of differentiating between the relevant and the irrelevant.

'During the six seances which followed,' he continued, 'she received a mass of highly detailed technical information – much of it classified, incidentally – about what had caused it to crash, and about an attempted cover-up by the Air Ministry.'

'Fascinating,' said Sarah, anxious that the point shouldn't be lost in a long and irrelevant account of what had gone wrong with the airship.

Svenson grinned, revealing a Huckleberry Finn gap between his front teeth. 'Oh, c'mon!' he exclaimed. 'You're not seriously offering the R101 seances as proof of post-mortem survival, are you? Christ, Jack, you know as well as I do that there could be a lot of other explanations: clair-voyance, for example, or telepathic leakage, or — '

44

'Okay, then what about the cross-correspondences,' Adams interjected. 'Surely they suggest that consciousness can on occasion persist after death?'

'They might suggest it, but they don't *prove* it,' replied Svenson, rubbing the back of his bull-like neck. 'And another thing: if consciousness can survive on occasion, why doesn't it always do so? Why, for instance, has no convincing contact ever been made with Oliver Lodge or Houdini? And they were every bit as anxious to prove post-mortem survival as Sidgwick, Gurney and Myers.'

After a heated argument about whether near-death experiences were evidence of post-mortem survival or merely perinatal recall triggered by transitory cerebral anoxia, Brownrigg suddenly said: 'Okay, but what about apparitions of the dead. Most sightings certainly can't be explained in terms of transitory cerebral anoxia!'

'No, but they can be explained in terms of hallucinations triggered by heightened suggestibility!' Svenson retorted. 'Either that or observer error! Quite apart from any other considerations, the hallucination theory would explain why apparitions always appear fully clothed.

'Unless, of course,' he added with a wry smile, 'you also believe that clothes possess an etheric body capable of post-mortem survival!'

'Ah, but wait a minute,' said Sarah. 'Supposing these hallucinations were telepathically induced by a discarnate entity? If that were to be the case there'd be no logical objection to the figure being clothed. In fact clothes form such an essential part of our self-image I'd have thought it inevitable.'

'And supposing pigs could fly?' Svenson shook his head. 'I'm sorry, but all that argument does is raise more questions than it answers.

'Shit, I'd find it easier to believe in the time-slip theory of apparitions – at least we have evidence for time-slips, if only on a sub-atomic scale,' he added, and in so doing started a debate about the many-worlds interpretation of quantum theory that was ended only by the sound of Hayakawa's bleeper.

'That'll probably be Security to say Art Trumbull's arrived,' he explained, as he accepted Sarah's invitation to use her telephone.

Suddenly aware that it had become almost dark, she crossed to switch on the lights and then made the rounds with the last but one of the bottles of wine.

'Was it Art?' she asked, as Hayakawa put down the phone.

'I'm afraid so . . . '

'In that case you'd better be getting along,' she told him, not wanting that night's telepathically-induced dream experiment to get off to a bad start.

Brownrigg glanced anxiously at his watch. 'And if you don't mind, I think I had, too.'

'But of course!' said Sarah, annoyed with herself for having forgotten that he would want to visit his wife in hospital. 'Give Jean my love, and tell her I'll be along to see her just as soon as we're clear of this damned Endor thing . . . '

Looking troubled and faintly guilty, Brownrigg got to his feet. 'Umm, yes . . . Although I'm not exactly crazy about the idea of us getting involved, it's up to you,' he told her, crumpling his paper cup and dropping it into a bin. 'If you think we should take it on, fine. Just let me know if there's anything I can do.'

'And the same goes for me,' said Hayakawa, crossing to open the door. 'Anything I can do, I will.'

Sarah smiled her thanks. 'Now remember: not a word of this to anyone outside these four walls, okay?'

After waving them goodnight, she turned back to the others. 'So, where do we go from here?' she asked, raising her eyebrows enquiringly.

Again, Maggie was the first to speak. 'We've talked about whether or not we should try to raise Itzhevnikov, but what no one's mentioned so far is how we'd go about it! Do we use a ouija board, or a medium, or what?'

'No, no, *no*!' cried Svenson, thumping the back of his chair with his fist. 'The question isn't *"How* do we raise him?"', but "How do we make it *seem* as if we've raised him?"'!

'Look,' he continued, turning to Sarah, 'if you could persuade 'em to let us work here at Biotec, I could put on a show that would make the Haunted Mansion at Disneyland look like amateur night!'

'I've no doubt you could,' she said, after joining in the laughter which had greeted his suggestion. 'However, they're going to want more than that. They're going to want answers, and answers that make some kind of sense.'

Svenson look at her in astonishment. 'But as I see it, our responsibility ends with *us* having seemed to have put *them* in touch with *him*.

'So,' he added, turning to the others for support, 'is it our fault if his interrogators can't get the sonuvabitch to play ball with them?'

'No!' Sarah shook her head emphatically. 'If we get caught cheating on this one, everything we've ever done here will be called into question.'

'Okay, but let's forget all this crap about raising what's-his-name's ghost,' said Svenson, as he leapt to his feet and began pacing to and fro in front of her desk. 'What we should be doing if we *really* want to help Uncle Sam is trying to persuade that OOBEer – you know, the one who teaches Russian language studies at Harvard – to attempt an out-of-the-body intelligence-gathering mission to Moscow. Shit, if he can read target cards on the other side of town from here, I don't see why he shouldn't read top secret documents in the goddamned Kremlin!'

Sarah clutched her head. 'Andy, you must be out of your mind!' she exclaimed. 'If we start putting up suggestions like that to the Pentagon, there's no knowing where it'll all end!'

As Svenson returned crestfallen to his chair, she looked across at Adams. 'Do you have any suggestions, Jack?'

'Yes, as a matter of fact I do,' he replied, fingering the small gold ring he wore in the lobe of his right ear. 'I think we should run an EVP trial.'

Sarah's heart sank; although pleased to have found such an unexpected ally in Adams, for someone of such brilliance it was a surprisingly unoriginal idea. 'Jack, have you ever

47

listened to a typical EVP?' she asked, trying not to let her disappointment show. 'Most of them are like audio ink-blot tests. You really can make whatever you like out of them . . .

'EVPs . . . ' Maggie shrugged. 'What the hell's an EVP?'

'Electronic Voice Phenomena,' replied Sarah. 'You must have heard of Electronic Voice Phenomena!'

'Oh, *that*! Sure I've heard of it, but I've never bothered to read it up . . . '

'Well you should have,' said Adams, wagging a reproving finger at her. 'I know you think anything smacking of survival research is somehow beneath you, but – '

'Okay, okay!' Maggie interjected, wide-eyed and with an exaggerated shrug. 'So tell me about EVPs, smart-ass!'

Adams took off his jacket and hung it over the back of his chair. 'To begin at the beginning, what happened was this: In the summer of 1959, a guy named Jürgensen went into the woods near his home in Sweden to record birdsong, but when he came to play back the tape he found it also contained voices. Thinking he'd picked up a stray radio transmission, he ran more tapes as a check. This time he got voices which not only addressed him personally, but appeared to have originated from friends and relations who were dead.

'Raudive – a former professor of psychology at the Universities of Uppsala and Riga – became interested after reading a paper by someone at the University of Freiburg endorsing Jürgensen's claim that the voices had originated from discarnate entities, and between 1965 and his death in 1974 he made over 100,000 EVPs, many of them with the help of a physicist and a specialist in high frequency electronic engineering.'

'And how are these recordings made?' asked Maggie. 'I take it that there's more to it than simply putting a blank tape through a machine switched to record . . . '

'It's one way of doing it, but according to Raudive the best results are obtained by recording with a diode plugged into the microphone socket. Either that, or a radio tuned between frequencies.'

Maggie laughed aloud. 'If that was what he was doing,

I'm not surprised he got voices! He was picking up snatches of radio transmissions, for chrissakes!'

'Exactly!' Sarah glanced at her watch. It was now 9.45 and they were getting nowhere. 'Jack, I know you're keen on this EVP idea, but can we move on to discuss some other options?'

'Sure, but let me first answer Maggie's point: some of Raudive's voices might well be fragments from radio or TV transmissions, but not all of them. A lot were recorded in a screened room . . . '

'In that case, what was the point of the diode or the radio tuned between frequencies?' she asked, before Sarah had a chance to stop her.

'To provide a carrier wave, the theory being that the communicating entity in some way modulates the carrier wave to produce coherent speech.'

'What, in a screened room?' Maggie protested.

As Adams opened his mouth to reply, Sarah held up her hands. 'I'm sorry, but we really must move on. Now, does anyone else have any suggestions?'

'I know you've been hoping to find a high-tech approach to this problem,' said Svenson, stifling a yawn, 'but since there doesn't seem to be one, why don't we just hire ourselves a good medium and have done with it?'

'Is there such an animal?' she asked, taken aback that such a suggestion should have come from someone whose attitude to mediumship was even more skeptical than her own.

Svenson eyed her suspiciously. 'But you seemed very impressed with Jack's account of the R101 seances . . . '

'Sure, but how many Eileen Garretts are there around today?' she asked, rhetorically. 'And even if we were knee-deep in them, they'd still need security clearances; and that could take forever.'

'Not necessarily,' said Svenson, reaching for a yellow legal pad. 'You remember the trials we ran with faith healers a while back; well, one of them – Eleanor Mitchell – is also a medium who just *happens* to have been cleared by NASA to work on one of their classified projects.'

49

'NASA? What on earth are they doing that requires the services of a medium?'

Svenson looked up to give her one of his bland, fat-cat smiles. 'If she'd told me that, I wouldn't be recommending her for Endor!'

After giving him an equally bland, fat-cat smile in return she said: 'Okay, but what do you think about Jack's EVP idea?'

'It's all right,' he replied, without any real enthusiasm. 'There seems to be a sufficiently large body of literature to justify our getting into this neck of the woods, and providing we adopt rigorous scientific protocols — '

'Which I would insist on!' Sarah interjected.

' — it won't matter a flea's fart whether we get results or not. After all, if one is to accept the Garrett seances as prima facie evidence of survival, the fact that the data came from drop-in communicators would seem to be significant.'

Sarah frowned. 'In what way significant?'

'He means that you can lead a horse to water but you can't make it drink,' explained Adams, grinning.

'Exactly!' Svenson tore a sheet from the pad on which he had been writing and handed it to Sarah. 'That's Eleanor Mitchell's address, plus the names and addresses of several other mediums,' he told her. 'They're probably all suffering from dissociative hysteria, but at least there's no danger of them regurgitating cheesecloth ectoplasm!'

'So, just what is it that you want?' she asked Adams, as she reached for the pad and a pencil.

Adams cupped a hand to his ear. 'Come again?'

'If we're going to get into this EVP thing, I want *them* to supply the equipment,' she replied, looking surreptitiously at her watch. It was now ten o'clock, and she was beginning to feel bleary-eyed with exhaustion. 'That way, there can be no suggestion that it's anything but kosher.'

Having listed his requirements, she tore the sheet from the pad and clipped it to the one Svenson had given her. 'Okay, so who's prepared to come to Maine with me tomorrow?' she asked, looking around the room.

For a moment no one reacted. But then one after another,

50

each of the parapsychologists raised a hand.

Although she had intended going straight to bed, once back in her apartment Sarah was overwhelmed by the desire to take a shower. It was almost as if she had been raped she decided, as she dumped her blouse and underwear in the linen basket. Certainly what had been done to her had been done against her will, and she felt used and humiliated and yet at the same time curiously excited. But excited by what? Surely not the prospect of working on Endor?

Catching sight of her naked body in the bathroom mirror, it suddenly occurred to her that there might be another reason – that she would be working with Calder. Nonsense! she told herself. Banishing all thoughts of him, she tore aside the shower curtain and turned on the taps.

In order to get her colleagues to agree to work with her she'd had to sell them on the idea that it might be possible for the mind to survive the dissolution of the brain. In selling it to them, had she, she wondered, also sold it to herself? It was beginning to look as if she had. And yet since the mind clearly was the product of the brain, how could it possibly survive the dissolution of that organ and the body within which it was housed? It simply didn't make sense.

However, as she stepped under the shower she found herself trying to remember something which the philosopher C.D. Broad had once said; something which, in its own epigrammatic way, was as chastening as Shakespeare's line about there being more things in heaven and earth . . . At last it came to her: what he had said was that to think in such terms about such matters was to confuse the Author of Nature with the editor of *Nature*, and by so doing assume that there can be no productions of the former that would not be accepted for publication by the latter!

Too tired to think anymore, she finished in the bathroom, got into bed and switched off the light.

The siren grew louder and louder, then stopped. Although

tempted to get up to see what had happened, she decided against it, and instead, plumped up her pillows before once again trying to lull herself to sleep.

However, just as she was beginning to drop off, the silence was shattered by the sound of her doorbell.

Brushing the hair from her eyes, she turned to peer at the clock radio. According to the time display it was 10.45 p.m., and yet she knew it must be much later.

The bell rang again, and was followed by a sharp double rap on the door.

Throwing back the bedclothes, she pulled on a dressing-gown, and, accompanied by the now almost continuous ringing of the bell, hurried to the front door and put her eye to the spy-hole.

Standing in the dimly lit corridor, their features distorted by the spy-hole's wide-angle lens, were two heavily built men wearing white paramedic's tunics. One was carrying a black leather medical bag, while the other – who was blowing into his cupped hands – had a rolled-up canvas strait-jacket tucked beneath his arm.

With a mounting sense of trepidation, Sarah unlocked the door and opened it, but only as far as the security chain would allow.

'Dr Stuart?' asked the man with the bag.

'Yes . . . ' she replied, noticing for the first time that both men had snowflakes clinging to their hair.

'May we come in?'

'Come in? But why?'

'If you don't mind, ma'am.'

'Yes, but *why* do you want to come in?' she insisted, looking from one expressionless face to the other.

The man with the bag glanced over his shoulder, as if afraid of being overheard. 'It would be better if we were to explain inside,' he replied, dropping his voice to a discreet whisper.

Sarah lifted the chain from its latch and let the men in. 'What seems to be the problem?' she asked, closing the door behind her.

The man with the bag took a sheet of paper from his

breast pocket, unfolded it and thrust it in front of her face. 'Do you know what that is?' he demanded, as his partner began unrolling the strait-jacket.

Although the paper was blank, feeling she had to say something Sarah said the first thing which came into her head: 'It's a picture of the President! Either the President or Itzhevnikov . . . '

The men exchanged pitying glances. 'Sure, honey, but do you know what it *is*? I mean, what it *really* is?'

Without waiting for her to reply, the man with the bag plucked the paper from her hand and stuffed it back into his pocket. 'Okay, then I'll tell you,' he said, in the flat, bored voice of someone required to recite what for them had become a meaningless litany. '*That* – ' he patted the pocket containing the paper ' – that is a certificate stating that in the opinion of two physicians your condition is such that immediate restraint and detention in a hospital for the mentally ill is necessary for your comfort and safety, and the safety of others.'

Sarah woke with a start, her heart beating like a trip-hammer. Almost afraid to look, she turned to the clock radio as the blue fluorescent digits regrouped themselves to read 3.00 a.m.

Although most of her working life had been spent with people who possess paranormal abilities, the idea that her nightmare might be anything other than a product of anxiety did not cross her mind, even for a moment.

Falling back on to her sweat-soaked pillow, she set about memorising the dream in order to analyse it the following morning, not that it would require much in the way of analysis.

Obviously, what her unconscious was telling her – and telling her in an unusually direct and unequivocal manner – was that she was crazy to have taken on the task of attempting to raise Itzhevnikov's ghost for the President.

However, try as she may, the significance of one tiny detail was to elude her completely: why, particularly on a night when the temperature was in the high seventies, did the men in her dream have snowflakes on their hair?

CHAPTER 7

ACCOMPANIED BY Adams, Svenson, Maggie and Maggie's red setter, Sarah arrived back at Seacrest at 4.25 the following afternoon to be met by Calder and Piroschka. Although her colleagues had chosen to dress in a somewhat less freakishly casual manner than usual, alongside their immaculately uniformed hosts they looked as incongruous as beggars at a banquet.

'I hope you're not intending to put us up in that!' said Maggie, as they set out towards the mouldering stick-and-shingle mansion. 'You're not, are you? Hell, the last time I saw anything like that was in "The Munsters"!'

Calder's tanned face split apart in a dazzling grin. 'It had crossed our minds,' he confessed, grabbing at one of the leaves that were falling like golden snowflakes. 'That is until my executive officer pointed out that although it has fourteen bedrooms, there are only three bathrooms, and one of those is in what used to be the servants' quarters. So what in fact we've done is book you into a lodge a mile or so down the coast. You'll have your own fully-equipped cabin, and there'll be a jeep for each of you – including one we've had specially modified for Dr Adams.

'Oh, and there's one other thing I should explain,' he added, as the seagulls which had been frightened off by the arrival of the helicopter began to settle on the mansion's sagging roof ridges. 'It might sound kinda crazy, but because Seacrest is a naval establishment we use naval terms for pretty well everything. However, I guess the only one you really need to know about is "heads". Don't ask me why, but in the navy toilets are always called heads.'

By now they were halfway to the mansion, and, with

54

sweat beginning to darken the back of his sleeveless cotton jacket, Adams stopped to rest on his elbow crutches for a moment. 'Just take a look at that view!' he exclaimed, peering across the overgrown garden to where the bay lay trembling in the heat-haze. 'Y'know something?' He glanced over his shoulder at Calder. 'While I'm here I think I might try to find myself a house – somewhere I can take off to for the occasional weekend.'

Calder nodded approvingly. 'Why not? Judging by the number of For Sale notices I've seen since I've been here it's still a buyer's market. Okay, so I know it's quite a drive from Boston, but then you could always take the shuttle to Bangor if you didn't feel like the hassle.'

'Tell me, what's the fishing like on this coast?'

'If my master-at-arms is to be believed, spectacular!'

Adams chuckled. 'I'm told it's also great hunting country . . .'

'That it certainly is,' said Calder, throwing a stick for the dog. 'There's a whole mess of waterfowl and small game; deer, bear and moose – though you'll have to go inland for the big stuff.'

Maggie wrinkled her nose at Sarah. 'I don't get it,' she said, pitching her voice low but not so low that Adams would be unlikely to hear. 'I mean, this big macho trip Jack's on is bad enough, but when it comes to killing animals just for the hell of it . . .'

Sarah braced herself for what she feared might be coming next. Although Maggie admired Adams as a scientist, she had never made any secret of the fact that she regarded his refusal to denounce America's involvement in Vietnam as unforgivable.

'Still,' she added, shrugging her thin shoulders hopelessly, 'I guess it's better than — '

'Better than what?' asked Adams, his eyes fixed on the handful of gabled houses across the bay. 'Zapping gooks?'

'That wasn't what I was going to say,' she told him, but without any real conviction.

Calder took the stick which the dog had retrieved, fondled its head, and after a moment of embarrassed silence said:

55

'Getting back to the business of house-hunting, if you do find yourself talking to any of the folks hereabouts, just remember you're up for a symposium on marine ecology, okay?'

'Marine *ecology*?' Sarah frowned. 'But I've told my people – or at least the ones who weren't on your list – that we're here to discuss the possible uses of telepathy as a means of – '

'That's fine for them,' Piroschka interjected, 'but not for the locals. If you as much as hint at that to the locals it'll be all over the six o'clock news.'

With a resigned shrug, Sarah turned back to Calder. 'So, what happens now?'

'Well, that's kinda up to you,' he replied, striking a match with which to light his pipe. 'I'll have to ask each of you to sign a secrecy agreement, but when you've done that and been fixed up with IDs, I thought you might like to have a drink with the guys with whom you'll be working and – well, I guess just generally fill them in on what it is you'll be doing . . . '

In spite of the tranquillisers she had taken before leaving Boston, Sarah felt herself begin to panic. 'Is that really necessary?' she asked. 'I mean, do I actually have to stand up and *talk* to these people?'

'I think you ought to, I really do. After all, this'll be a whole new ball-game for them.'

'Them and us, too!' she retorted. 'Anyway, who *are* these people? I don't remember you saying we'd be working with anyone when I was here yesterday . . . '

'Intelligence analysts,' Calder replied, ignoring her implied rebuke. 'Mainly from the DIA.'

'The CIA?' Sarah came to an abrupt standstill. 'You certainly didn't tell me we'd be working with the CIA!'

Calder took the pipe from his mouth. 'The *D*IA!' he said, with a chuckle. 'The Defense Intelligence Agency. Of course,' he continued, urging her forward with a reassuring touch to the elbow, 'the CIA will be represented – after all, this started out as being their baby! – but I take my orders from and report back to the Assistant Secretary of Defense for Intelligence.'

As they left the lawn and began crunching their way across the gravelled forecourt, one of the gulls on the roof lifted its head and began a throbbing, high-pitched warning cry. The first gull was joined by a second and then a third, until soon they were all shrieking at the cloudless cerulean sky.

'Now, are there any other questions?' asked Calder, almost having to shout to make himself heard. 'Dr Svenson, you look as if you've got something on your mind . . . '

'No, not really. I take it there're no problems about meeting Mrs Mitchell?'

'It's all fixed,' he assured Svenson. 'Someone will be picking her up at Bangor International in an hour, and providing the weekend traffic isn't too heavy, she should be here in plenty of time to join us for dinner.'

As Adams began humping himself up the front steps, Calder looked at Maggie. 'Dr Mintz, is anything worrying you?'

'Everything about this whole *shmeer* worries me!' she replied, before turning to whistle for her dog, which was sitting just beyond the long, deep shadow cast by the *porte-cochère*.

Apart from pricking back its ears, the dog didn't move.

'Red!' she called, slapping her thigh encouragingly. 'Here, Red!'

This time the dog got up, but after taking only a few steps toward her suddenly turned as if chasing its tail and sat down again.

With a long-suffering sigh, she walked over to the dog, took hold of its collar and tried to lead it into the house, but it immediately raised a thick ruff around its neck, bared its teeth and began growling.

'What seems to be the problem?' asked Calder.

Maggie shrugged. 'I don't know,' she replied, looking around to see if she could discover what it was that had frightened it. 'I've never seen him like this before, even with other dogs . . . '

'Perhaps he's scared of the gulls,' suggested Sarah, looking up at the roof.

'What, Red?' Maggie shook her head. 'No way!'

As soon as she had succeeded in calming the dog, Maggie gathered it up into her arms, and, crooning gently, began slowly making her way back towards the house.

However, immediately it realised where it was being taken it began struggling so violently that she had to let it go. With its tail tucked between its legs, it ran from beneath the *porte-cochère*, turned, and began loping to and fro, whimpering.

'Maybe we should have the baggage detail take it to the lodge,' suggested Calder.

'I think we might have to,' Maggie replied, looking up from hugging the shivering dog. 'There doesn't seem any way of getting him into the house.' Turning shamefacedly to Sarah she added: 'I'm sorry about this. If there'd been more time I'd have left him with my sister, but her place is up in Belmont and —'

'Relax,' said Piroschka. 'Your problems are over.' Taking a walkie-talkie from his pocket, he called up the leader of the working party which was transferring the scientists' luggage from the helicopter to a Navy pick-up truck and explained what would be happening.

But Maggie's problems were not over: as soon as the dog saw that the pick-up truck was leaving without her, it broke away from the sailor who'd been holding it and leapt to the ground, barking.

'Listen,' said Calder, glancing anxiously at his watch. 'Why don't you go with him, huh? You can be back here again in half an hour, and in the meantime we can have gotten the show on the road.'

'Are you sure you don't mind?' asked Maggie, embarrassed.

'Of course I don't *mind*!' he replied, helping her up into the front passenger seat.

With the dog now settled happily between her knees, Calder slammed the door and waved the truck away.

'Well, what do you think that was all about?' he asked,

58

leading the others into the house.

'I've no idea,' Sarah replied, looking around in astonishment. During the past twenty-four hours the enormous living-hall had been transformed almost beyond recognition. The dust-sheets had been removed from the furniture and the floor had been sanded and polished until it glowed. There was a pretty red-headed girl in a white coat standing alongside a Polaroid Identification System, and behind her a score or more men, some in uniform, others in expensive-looking casual clothes. Several of the men were playing chess, while the others were reading or talking quietly over drinks.

'Maggie brings Red to work most days and he's never any trouble,' Sarah continued, hovering uncertainly near the door. 'So just why he should have freaked-out today . . . '

'You're not using an ultrasonic security system in here, are you?' asked Adams, peering up at the walls.

Calder shook his head. 'And even if we were, it would have been switched off before anyone was allowed into the room.'

'Sure, except it might have been malfunctioning.'

Piroschka eyed Adams suspiciously. 'Why do you ask?'

'Oh, it's just that they've been known to drive animals crazy.'

'Maybe it was reacting to an earth tremor,' Svenson suggested. 'One that was imperceptible to us.'

'Could be,' said Adams. 'After all, as well as being able to hear in the ultrasonic range, dogs have an extremely sensitive vibration sense, and there're – what? – something like 150,000 light tremors every year.'

'It's the house,' announced the girl in the white coat, shaking her head gloomily. 'We had to get rid of the Alsatians for the same reason . . . '

As soon as they had each signed a secrecy agreement and an ID data card, the girl in the white coat asked Sarah to sit in front of the camera, inserted her card and took aim. 'Right, here we go,' she said, before triggering the flash.

After lifting the film puller, she took the exposed sheet of

Polacolor from the automatic timer and stripped away the unwanted negative.

'Oh, no!' she cried, passing the print to Piroschka. 'Not again!'

'Are you *sure* there isn't something wrong with the goddamned camera,' he asked. 'I mean, this is just crazy!'

'Absolutely sure, sir. Away from the house it works perfectly.'

Piroschka passed the print to Calder. 'Maybe you've got a duff batch of film,' he suggested. 'It happens . . . '

'That was my first thought,' she replied, as she began reloading the camera. 'But sir, according to Polaroid the film's fine . . . '

Once again, she went through the procedure as before.

'I give up!' she said, passing the latest print to Piroschka. 'It's the house. I don't know what it is, but there's something about this *house* . . . '

Unable to contain her curiosity any longer, Sarah got up to see for herself. Although the top half of her face was evenly lit and in sharp focus, her throat, chin and part of her mouth had been all but eaten away by what appeared to be the white, felted threads of a fungus.

'Should I try again, sir?' the girl asked Piroschka.

Piroschka passed the print to Calder. 'What do you think, Admiral?'

'It'll do for now,' he replied, giving it back to the girl. 'By the end of the afternoon we'll all know one another anyway, so what the hell . . . '

With a shrug, she put the print through a laminator, trimmed it and sealed it in a plastic pouch. 'And the best of luck,' she said, as she clipped it to the lapel of Sarah's jacket.

She sounded as if she meant it.

CHAPTER 8

CALDER SHEPHERDED Sarah, Maggie, Adams and Svenson to the foot of the main staircase and held up his hands for silence.

'Gentlemen, if you'd move in a bit closer we'll begin,' he announced, his voice echoing around the huge living-hall.

As soon as everyone had settled down on or around the improvised rostrum, Calder re-stated the objective of Operation Endor in a measured, matter-of-fact tone, and then introduced each of the parapsychologists.

'Okay,' he said, rubbing his hands together briskly. 'Now I'm sure you gentlemen have a lot you want to ask our friends here, so in the interest of speed I'll leave you to introduce yourselves before you put your question.

'But first, Dr Stuart will fill you in on the general game plan. Dr Stuart . . . '

Smiling nervously, Sarah looked up from making a last-minute amendment to the notes she had begun while Adams and Svenson were being shown over the house, took a sip of her gin-and-tonic, and, after returning the glass to the half-landing on which she was sitting, clasped her hands around her knees.

'I thought it might be useful if I were to start by outlining man's attempts to contact the dead,' she began, trying to sound as relaxed as she hoped she looked. 'As we'll see, it's not a new idea. Far from it. In fact, it's something he's been trying to do at least since the beginnings of recorded history.

'However, until the comparatively recent past, what motivated him was not the wish for proof of spiritual immortality – that seems to have been pretty much taken for

61

granted – but rather the belief that the dead in some way acquire powers rarely possessed by the living. For example, when Saul asked the Witch of Endor to conjure up the spirit of Samuel, he did so for one reason only – to take advantage of Samuel's supposed clairvoyant abilities.'

After a wide-ranging historical survey of the subject ending with the rise of the Spiritualist movement, she went on to say: 'Although there are now many schools of Spiritualist philosophy, all but the reincarnationists hold that man has a soul which at death begins a journey through a hierarchy of qualitatively differing spiritual worlds, the ultimate goal being the attainment of perfection and union with God.'

Pausing to take a sip of her drink, she tried to assess how her impromptu address was being received, but the rows of professionally inscrutable faces were giving nothing away.

'So much for the philosophy, such as it is,' she continued, glancing at her notes. 'Now for a word about mediums.

'As the name suggests, mediums regard themselves as intermediaries between the physical world and the spiritual. Some simply relay messages which are whispered in their ear, while others allow themselves to be temporarily possessed either by a so-called spirit guide – one of whose functions is to pass on messages from other less experienced discarnate entities – or by the discarnate entity itself.

'Most of those with whom we'll be working – and by now it'll come as no surprise to learn that we will *be* working with mediums – are of the second type.'

After summarising the achievements of the most celebrated of the twentieth century mediums, she ended by outlining the history and theory of Electronic Voice Phenomena.

'Well, I guess that's about it,' she added. 'As we've seen, there are a number of well-attested cases of mediums imparting information which prima facie could only have originated from the dead. However, even after discounting subliminal cueing and deliberate fraud, there is one other possible explanation – telepathic leakage.

'Now, whilst I'd be happy to detail the evidence for tele-

62

pathy, would you, for the moment at least, take my word that it does exist? Would you also take my word that although we haven't as yet identified the nature of the energy used to transmit information telepathically, we know of no way of screening against such transmissions, as we'll be screening against radio transmissions when carrying out our EVP trials.

'So beware,' she said, as she began gathering together her notes. 'Although I'll be very surprised if the mediums with whom we'll be working don't produce something seemingly relevant to Endor, that something might well originate from your own conscious or unconscious minds.

'Now, if anyone has a question, either I or my colleagues will be glad to answer it as best we can . . . '

Straight away, a man wearing a blue blazer and a club tie rose to his feet. He was tall and thin and had a deeply-lined, doleful face and swept-back black hair that was greying at the temples. 'Galbraith, Defense Intelligence Agency,' he announced, staring unwaveringly at her from behind a pair of horn-rimmed bifocals. 'Dr Stuart, although your dissertation was clearly intended to be as objective as possible, you didn't, if I may say so, sound very optimistic about the outcome of what you'll be attempting here.

'What I'd like to ask, therefore, is this: just what is your position on the question of post-mortem survival? Do you believe in it, or don't you?'

'I'm afraid that's not a question I can answer in such uncompromising terms,' she replied, suddenly aware that she was beginning to get a headache. 'Indeed, were you to press me for an answer, it would have to be "I don't know".'

'Really?' Galbraith sounded almost shocked. 'And yet you were willing to participate in the project! Surely that suggests you're somewhat less than agnostic?'

Sarah slipped on a pair of sunglasses. 'With respect, I don't agree. A readiness to consider paradoxical ideas does not imply a readiness to accept them without adequate evidence. It might well be possible for the human mind to survive corporeal death rather in the way that – well, that a

63

television picture could be said to survive long after the station which originally transmitted that picture has closed down, but as of now — '

'I see,' said Galbraith, folding his arms. 'So what you're saying – and you'll correct me if I'm wrong – is that if we were thirty-three light years out in space and had a television set, we would now be watching "live" the final run-up to our 1952 Presidential election . . . '

Sarah straightened up, and, as unobtrusively as possible, began massaging the back of her neck in an attempt to dispel the headache. 'I know it isn't an awfully good analogy, but — '

'No, it isn't, is it?' said Galbraith, before she had a chance to finish. 'In fact it's singularly inappropriate, in that a television picture is not a sentient entity.'

Taken totally off her guard by the vehemence of Galbraith's attack, Sarah's mind froze.

'If you've no objection,' she heard Adams say, 'I think I may be able to help here . . . '

It was the lifeline for which she'd been hoping, and, with her headache getting worse by the minute, she conceded the floor to him willingly.

'In the end it all comes down to a question of energy,' said Adams, as a prelude to evoking the Third Law of Thermodynamics in support of the post-mortem survival hypothesis.

'So,' he concluded, after a long and exceedingly complex dissertation on energetics, 'bearing in mind that the physical concomitants of thought are at least in part electromagnetic, "soul" might well turn out to be an electromagnetic soliton.'

'Umm, yes,' said Galbraith, warily. 'You'll forgive me for saying so, but that does sound suspiciously like science fiction.'

It not only sounds like it, thought Sarah as she began rummaging in her handbag for aspirin, it probably is. Although on this occasion Adams seemed to have got away with it, she nevertheless made a mental note to speak to him later about the dangers of attempting a snow job on such men.

Adams shrugged as if to say too bad. 'Less than a hundred

years ago, the idea that matter consists mostly of space empty of anything more substantial than electric charges or electromagnetic fields would also have sounded suspiciously like science fiction,' he told him. 'Okay, so I know we're into an all-bets-are-off type of situation with this post-mortem survival deal, but y'know, if science has taught us anything, it's that not only is the world a stranger place than we imagined, it's a stranger place than we ever *could* have imagined.'

As Galbraith sat down, three of his companions each raised a hand.

'Gary,' said Calder, pointing to a four-star USAF general.

'Dr Stuart, in your opening address you seemed to be preparing us for the fact that the yield from EVPs is likely to be poor, not only qualitatively, but quantitatively. But surely, this is also likely to be true of anything we receive via a medium, isn't it? Certainly, that's the impression I've got from talking to people who've attended seances. According to them, the messages they've received have been brief, and on the whole banal. Pathetically so, in many cases . . . '

In spite of the aspirin she'd taken earlier, Sarah's head-ache had now become so bad that she could barely think. 'I can believe it,' she said, as she began massaging her throbbing temples. 'However, it isn't always the case. There're the Garrett R101 seances I mentioned earlier. And the cross-correspondences. In the case of the cross-corres-pondences, some 3,000 or so messages were received over a thirty-year period, many of them very erudite . . . '

'I hope we're going to be able to make rather better time than that!' Calder remarked, turning to point at one of the men he had passed over in favour of the general. 'Gene . . . '

As he began asking his question, a puff of breeze lifted the net curtains covering the windows in the adjoining room, bringing with it the salty tang of the sea and the chugging of a lobster boat as it beat its way up the coast.

Turning reflexively toward the window, Sarah noticed a few spots of flickering white light in the lower right-hand corner of her field of vision. Although at first they were no more than a source of minor irritation, by the time she had finished answering the man's question the phosphenes had multiplied and spread to an extent where much of her audience was all but obliterated by a shimmering, undulating aurora borealis.

And now someone from the CIA was asking a question, but one which, mercifully, was directed less towards her than Adams. Wondering how much longer she'd have to wait before she could decently bring the briefing to a close, she glanced at her wristwatch, only to discover that she was unable to tell the time. It was not that she couldn't *see* the dial; in spite of her impaired vision she could. What she seemed unable to do was make any sense of what she saw.

She would have to leave, she decided, and leave now before she really began making a bloody fool of herself. However, when she attempted to get up nothing happened. It was as if something – or someone – had seized control of those parts of her brain responsible for voluntary muscular movement, and, having done so, was now holding her prisoner within her own body.

With her heart beginning to race as if a throttle had been opened on an idling engine, she broke out into an icy sweat. Her breathing became rapid and shallow, and her mouth seemed to turn to dust.

And then – most alarming of all – she realised that she was about to be sick. To have done so in full view of her audience would have been shaming enough, but, wedged in as she was, the chances were that she'd throw up over the people sitting below her.

Without quite knowing how she had managed to regain the use of her limbs, she found herself running along the corridor towards the ground floor washroom, a hand clutched to her mouth. Arriving with barely enough time in which to snap on the light, bolt the door and lift the ancient mahogany lavatory seat, she fell to her knees, gripped the edge of the ornately decorated bowl and vomited.

After wiping her mouth she retched, and again she vomited, but this time less copiously than before. Cradling her head in her arms and moaning softly to herself, she waited until she felt it was safe to get up, then pulled the chain, but only hard enough to produce a trickle of rusty water.

With little she could do until the cistern had re-filled itself, she felt for her radial pulse, and, as the second hand of her watch touched twelve, began counting.

Apart from the fact that the muscles of her abdominal wall and diaphragm ached from having vomited, she seemed to be feeling better. Much better, in fact. Her headache had all but gone, as had the disconcerting visual and perceptual disturbances, and although her pulse was perhaps a little thready, at eighty-two beats a minute it was only slightly raised. And as for the feeling of generalised paralysis which had preceded the onset of nausea, well, the very fact that she'd been able to make it to the washroom unaided seemed to prove that that had been nothing more than a temporary aberration.

By now the cistern had stopped gurgling and, after pulling the chain – this time successfully – she crossed to the basin, sluiced her mouth out under the cold tap and began washing her face with a bar of cheap, Navy-issue soap.

'Damn!' she said, realising now that it was too late that without her handbag she would have to return to the briefing devoid of make-up.

As she rinsed the soap from her face she found herself wondering whether she would have been quite so dismayed had Calder not been there to see her. Probably not, she decided, reaching for the roller towel. Which meant what? That she fancied him? She began rubbing her face in a brisk, no-nonsense manner, as if trying to expunge all traces of such adolescent foolishness. All right, so she liked the easy way in which he wore his authority, just as she liked his frankness and his gentle if somewhat cynical, agreeably self-deprecating sense of humour. Indeed, she'd even begun to think of him as being almost handsome. It was a pity about the crew-cut, but if he were to allow it to grow out —

Christ! she thought, pausing for a moment. You really *do* fancy him! A man old enough to be your father, married, and moreover, a *sailor*! It was all too silly for words. Apart from the God-forsaken project which had brought them unwillingly together, what could she possibly have in common with a sailor?

With two sharp tugs she cleared the portion of the roller towel she'd used and returned to the basin, intending to finger-comb her hair, slick her eyebrows and pinch some colour back into her cheeks.

However, what she saw in the ancient, fly-specked mirror put all such thoughts from her mind. Although the face was hers, what were not hers were the eyes. If, as the old adage has it, the eyes are the mirror of the soul, the soul mirrored in those that were staring defiantly back at her were evil beyond redemption.

Horrified, she tried to back away, to turn and run, but the unblinking, hypnotic eyes of the creature in the wrong-way-round room behind the glass seemed to have robbed her of the power of volition.

And then in some mysterious, profoundly disturbing way everything appeared suddenly to change; change and yet remain unchanged. Everything, that is, except for one tiny, seemingly insignificant detail: the maker's name on the cistern was no longer laterally inverted.

When the truth of what had happened finally dawned, it did so with a force which left her numb with shock. The reason why the lettering was now the right way around was that she was no longer looking *into* the mirror but *out* of it.

As mute and powerless as a specimen encapsulated in a block of perspex, she watched the thing which had managed to evict her from her body turn and start towards the door, hesitate, and then turn back to the mirror again.

Manipulating her facial muscles into a sickening leer, it lifted her skirt, tore aside the leg of her white cotton panties, and, after slipping the middle finger of her right hand into her vulva, began rubbing her clitoris with a mocking, frantic brutality that was totally untypical of a woman.

Struggling desperately to prevent herself from being overwhelmed by panic and revulsion, she tried to understand what had happened, and by understanding, exorcise the thing which was vandalising her body.

It seemed as if she had been projected into another, unknown order of reality; a reality in which it was possible for her psychological self to exist independently from her physical self. Or was it rather that one *part* of her psychological self had somehow been expelled by another? Was the stranger now controlling her a stranger only because it was the unconscious component of her personality – that repository of repressed emotions and cloven-footed impulses which Freud had named the 'Id'? And yet even if this were so, how was she able to see what was happening when among the things she was seeing was not a reflection of her eyes, but the eyes themselves? What were now functioning as her retinae, optic nerves and brain? Indeed, without a brain, how was she even able to ask the question?

It was a conceptual barrier of towering monumentality, and with the thing now obviously about to take a new, perhaps even more horrendous initiative, this was not the moment to attempt to scale it.

Slipping a hand inside her blouse, it turned and began looking hungrily around the small, windowless room until it spotted what it seemed to have been searching for – an empty Coca-Cola bottle that had been left half-hidden behind the sanitary bin.

With one continuous, fluid movement, it let go of her breasts, scooped up the bottle and pulled down her panties. Gathering her skirt around her waist, it squatted down on the balls of her feet and spread her legs as wide apart as they would go.

'No!' she shrieked, aghast at what it was about to do. 'Please sweet Jesus, no!'

But her silent agony appeared only to enflame its lust; to strengthen still further its resolve to perform the ultimate act of defilement.

Having reassured itself that she would have an unimpeded view of what was about to happen, it began easing the base of the bottle up into her vagina. Once in position, it grasped the neck of the bottle with both hands, trimmed its balance slightly, and began what was clearly intended to be more an act of rape than masturbation.

Although Sarah could feel nothing of what was happening, she could see everything: the slack, salivating mouth and the glazed eyes; the erect nipples on the heaving breasts, the dark, froth-speckled ring of pubic hair surrounding the tightly-stretched, engorged labia. See and at the same time hear the panting and the moaning and the wet, rubber plunger-noises made by the bottle as it was pushed into and pulled out of her with a mounting, almost demonic savagery.

Terrified that such abuse would cause a fatal air embolism, Sarah re-doubled her efforts to will herself back into her body, but in vain.

With each thrust of the bottle forcing her closer and still closer to the edge of psychological disintegration, there was only one thing she could now do: gather together the last remnants of her strength and wait. Wait and hope that with the explosive discharge of neuromuscular tension which would accompany its orgasm, the hold it had on her body would loosen sufficiently for her to achieve what she had so far failed to achieve. It was her only chance, and she knew that if she were to fail she would be lost forever.

As the hands gripping the neck of the bottle began hammering faster and even more ferociously against the pubic bone, it lifted what had once been her head to reveal a face contorted almost beyond recognition. Sarah braced herself, like a tiger for the kill. And then as a terrible, strangled cry escaped from between its bared teeth, she pounced.

Suddenly she could see nothing: nothing, that is, except the diffuse pink glow of light percolating through closed eyelids. Her eyelids. She became aware of pain. Although it took her a moment or more to realise that the pain was in fact her pain, when she finally did so it seemed to throw open a host of other sensory channels. Suddenly she was aware of the familiar, slightly musky smell of vaginal secretions; the bitter aftertaste of bile; the sound of a bottle as it rolled to a standstill across an uncarpeted floor . . .

As if from a great distance she heard someone calling her name. 'Sarah?' It was Maggie. 'Sarah, are you all right?' she shouted, rattling the handle of the door.

Although still too stunned and disorientated to reply, she managed to raise herself on to one elbow and look around.

What in the name of God, she wondered, was she doing lying on the floor with her knickers around her ankles, when the last thing she could remember was washing after having spilled her guts? Had she been raped? She certainly felt as she imagined she would had such a thing happened, and yet clearly it hadn't. Alone in a windowless, locked room, how *could* she have been raped?

Summoning what little was left of her strength, she started to get up off the floor only to be overwhelmed by a pain so intense that she passed out.

CHAPTER 9

SUDDENLY SARAH could see light, smell antiseptic, and feel a pounding in her head. 'She's coming round,' she heard someone say above the tinkle of steel and glass. 'Dr Stuart?' It was a man's voice, louder and more insistent. 'Dr Stuart, can you hear me?'

What until then had been no more than a blur of abstract shapes slowly resolved themselves into a meaningful pattern. Screwing her eyes up against the light, she saw that she was lying in a screened-off corner of what appeared to be the casualty department of a hospital, having her forehead swabbed by a doctor holding a steel kidney bowl; a doctor whose thin face and deep-set, piercing eyes seemed somehow familiar.

'Take it easy,' he told her, as he passed the bowl to a nurse who had just moved into her field of vision. 'You fell and hurt your head, but you're going to be fine. Just fine . . . '

Lifting her wrist, he began to take her pulse. 'Incidentally, my name's Kessler,' he said, his eyes on the second hand of his watch. 'Neil Kessler.' He spoke rapidly, and in a crisp, no-nonsense manner. 'We met yesterday. I was the one doing the work-up on the guy down the corridor . . . '

Sarah frowned. 'Which guy?' she asked, still too disorientated to know what he was talking about.

'The one down the corridor. You know, the Russian. As a matter of fact,' he added, casually, 'we almost lost him half an hour ago. Cardiac arrest . . . '

At last the penny dropped. Turning to peer through a gap in the screens, she saw an expanse of bare floor, part of a

72

boarded-up fireplace and an ancient blue-and-white washbasin supported on ornate brackets. 'So I'm still at Seacrest . . . '

'Huh-huh.'

'What happened?' she asked, as she began gently exploring the swelling just below her hairline.

Kessler let go of her wrist, pulled up a chair and sat down. 'I was hoping you were going to be able to tell *me* that!' he replied, as the nurse gave her an ice-bag to hold to her forehead. 'Do you feel up to it?'

'I'll try, but it's all still a bit confused,' she warned, struggling to collect her thoughts.

With his hands clasped behind his head and his legs stretched out in front of him, he listened attentively as she described the site, quality and intensity of her headache, and how it had been followed by a scintillating scotoma, agnosia and nausea. 'The odd thing is that I felt better after I'd vomited. Much better. In fact I was about to return to the briefing when I – well, when I passed out, I guess . . .

'Except,' she added, almost as an afterthought, 'I have the feeling that something happened after I'd passed out; something pretty nasty. It's almost as if I'd been dreaming . . . '

'*Dreaming*?' Kessler frowned. 'While you were unconscious?'

'I know it sounds crazy, and yet . . . ' She shrugged, reluctant to pursue such an unlikely hypothesis any further.

'Umm . . . ' Kessler pursed his thin lips and began tapping them with his forefinger and thumb. 'You don't think you might have had an epileptic seizure, do you?'

'Good God, no!' she exclaimed, although the thought had already crossed her own mind.

'Well, y'know, all of us are potentially epileptic,' he pointed out, as if anxious to justify what might otherwise have seemed an unwarranted accusation. 'It's all a question of seizure thresholds . . . Anyway, what about migraine?' he continued, briskly. 'Have you ever had an attack of migraine?'

'No, never.'

'No history of headaches, vision disturbances, abnormally low blood-sugar — '

'Apart from the occasional cold,' she interjected, 'I can't remember when I last had anything wrong with me.'

'Huh-huh . . . Tell me, where are you in your menstrual cycle?' he asked, peering at her over the top of his tortoise-shell half-frames.

Oh God, she thought, how like a man! 'My *what*?'

'Your menstrual cycle.'

'Oh, that . . . ' she shrugged. 'As it happens it's due tomorrow, but — '

'*Tomorrow*?' Kessler raised his eyebrows. 'I see,' he said, as if not quite able to believe that he had uncovered the key to the riddle quite so quickly or so effortlessly. 'And is PMT a problem for you?'

'I suppose I do get a bit edgy and tense, but apart from that, no, not especially.'

'No oedema?'

'Not really. Okay, so I occasionally have a bit of difficulty getting my rings on and off,' she conceded, fingering the gold love-knot which Hans had given her, 'but that's all. Anyway, why do you ask?'

Kessler took off his spectacles, breathed on the lenses and began polishing them on the hem of his long white coat. 'Oh, it's just that water retention is sometimes a factor in migraine, and from what you've told me it sounds as if that's what you've had: a bad attack of migraine.'

'But I don't suffer from migraine,' she insisted. 'And anyway, what about the perceptual difficulties and the syncope? They're not typical of migraine, surely?'

Kessler checked the lenses against the light from the case-ment windows. 'Perhaps not typical, but they do often occur as a component. However, I think we'd better check you over, nevertheless . . . '

Sarah handed the ice-bag to the nurse and went to sit up, but as she did so what until then had been no more than a vague, generalised ache in the pelvis sharpened sufficiently to make her wince.

'Something the matter?'

74

'It's my abdomen,' she told him, lowering herself gently back on to the examination couch. 'The lower part of my abdomen hurts like hell.'

Kessler looked surprised. 'Why didn't you mention this before?'

'Because I've only just noticed it. Okay, so I was feeling a bit sore and achy, but I thought that was simply because I'd thrown-up . . . '

'It's probably just dysmen, isn't it?' he suggested, in an offhand manner.

'No it isn't!' she snapped, irritated that he should have thought her incapable of differentiating between period pain and any other kind of pain. 'And anyway, it's not due until tomorrow . . . '

Unruffled, he told her to relax, then placed the tips of his fingers above her appendix and began gently applying pressure. 'Does that hurt?' he asked, watching her face over the top of his spectacles.

'No, not especially.'

Moving to a point midway between her navel and her pubis, he tried again. 'How about that?'

Sarah drew in her breath sharply. 'Yes!'

'And have you ever had anything like this before?'

'No, never . . . '

'Umm.' Kessler thought for a moment. 'Well, although we're not really equipped to carry out a gynaecological examination, if you'd like me to take a look I will.

'That is if we can rustle up a vaginal speculum,' he added, turning to the nurse. 'Do you have any idea where we could get hold of such a thing around here?'

'We could try asking Dr Packman,' she suggested.

'Packman's the local physician,' he told Sarah. 'Okay, let's call him. If he can help, say you'll be right over.

'Oh, and while you're about it,' he added, as the nurse was about to leave, 'you'd better pick up a jar of obstetric cream and some sanitary towels, just in case . . . '

Turning back to Sarah he said: 'So, while we're waiting, why don't we check you over generally, okay?'

After listening to her heart and taking her temperature

and blood pressure, he helped her from the couch to a chair, palpated her carotid arteries, tested her reflexes, and then peered into her eyes with an opthalmoscope.

'Fine,' he said, laying aside the instrument. 'What I'd like you to do now is look at me with your right eye closed, and tell me when you see my finger . . . '

Suddenly it dawned on her what he was doing: he was carrying out a neurological examination for brain malfunction.

'Oh, my God!' she exclaimed, as a vision of a drill biting into her exposed skull sprang fully-formed into her mind. 'You don't think — '

'No I don't,' he said firmly. 'But we can't take any chances. So, just stop worrying,' he continued, turning her face so that her eyes were aligned with his own, 'and tell me when you see my finger.'

Kessler closed his left eye, raised a hand until it was out of sight above their heads, and, wiggling his forefinger, slowly began to lower it.

'Now!' she told him, the moment it entered her field of vision.

'Fine. Next we'll try it from below and then from either side. Right, here we go . . . '

'Now!'

'Good. And again . . . '

'Now!'

'Once more . . . '

'Yes!'

After repeating the procedure with her right eye, he took a pentorch from the lineup of ballpoints in his breast pocket, asked her to follow it with her eyes as he moved it about in front of her face, then checked to make sure that her pupils contracted when the light was shown into them.

'We're almost through,' he told her. 'In fact all I want you to do now is close your eyes and tell me what it is I'll be putting in your hand, okay?'

After correctly identifying a key, a coin and an eraser, she opened her eyes to discover that the nurse had returned with a tray equipped for a vaginal examination.

'Well, you'll be relieved to hear that there's no sign of any neurological problem,' he announced, moving his chair to the foot of the couch. 'So, if you'll just slip off your things we'll take a look at the situation down below . . . '

As he turned and put on a headlight and a pair of disposable gloves, Sarah stepped out of her skirt and panties, sat on the end of the couch, and helped by the nurse, lowered herself on to her back with her legs flexed and spread apart.

'Fine,' said Kessler, returning to his seat with the headlight on and his hands held high. 'That's absolutely fine. Now, just try to relax.'

Out of the corner of her eye she saw the nurse bend to make a small adjustment to the light, then felt him gently separate the lips of her vagina with his fingers.

'Yes, well . . . ' He paused. 'You certainly do seem to be somewhat inflamed . . . '

Using his finger and thumb, he felt the glands on either side of her labia, then passed the forefinger of his right hand up into her vagina, at the same time pressing down on the lower part of her abdomen with the palm of his other hand.

'Your uterus, oviducts – in England I believe you call them "fallopian tubes" – and your ovaries all feel to be fine,' he told her, as he withdrew his finger and turned to the nurse.

Sarah let out her breath. 'Thank God,' she said, wishing now that she hadn't been quite so sharp with him earlier.

'And you say you first noticed something was wrong, when: shortly after you arrived this afternoon?' he asked, while waiting for the nurse to finish warming and lubricating the speculum.

'Not even as long ago as that,' Sarah replied, lifting her head from the pillow. 'In fact it only seems to have come on since I threw up. I'm sure of it. Otherwise, I'd have noticed something when I visited the heads before the start of the briefing.'

With a non-committal 'Huh-huh', he took the speculum, twisted round in his chair, and, pressing down on Sarah's perineum, slipped the stainless-steel instrument into her vagina, rotated it and began opening the blades.

'Okay?' he asked, as she clenched her teeth against the pain. However, even before she could reply she heard him tighten the screw which held the blades in position and ask for a swab.

And then as quickly as her ordeal had begun, it ended. 'Fine,' he said, as he withdrew the speculum and handed it back to the nurse. 'Now, if you'd like to put your things back on again . . . '

As Sarah began dressing, Kessler stripped off his gloves and his headlight, crossed to the basin and began washing his hands. 'Okay, so to begin at the beginning, what you seem to have had was an unusually severe attack of migraine,' he told her, over his shoulder. 'Basilar artery migraine. It's a type which mostly affects women, and can be triggered either by stress or endocrinological changes associated with the onset of menstruation. In your case stress would seem to be the predominating factor – the stress of coming on to Endor.

'And as for the abdominal symptoms,' he continued, pulling a handful of paper towels from a dispenser, 'well, apart from the fact that you're a bit congested, everything seems pretty much as it should be. Of course if you want me to I'll be happy to send you back to Boston for a full gynaecological work-up, but my hunch is that you've nothing more than dysmenorrhoea.

'Okay,' he added, before Sarah had a chance to protest, 'so it's come on earlier than you expected and is more uncomfortable than you're used to, but like the migraine, it, too, has probably been induced by stress.'

Still talking, Kessler dropped the towels in a pedal-bin and turned to look into the mirror above the basin. Immediately Sarah felt a surge of alarm, much as she would had she seen him step into the path of an oncoming vehicle. '*Don't!*' she cried, as he leaned over the basin and began tightening the knot of his tie.

Kessler spun around, a look of shocked incredulity on his pale, pinched face. 'Don't *what?*' he asked, exchanging puzzled glances with the nurse. He frowned. 'Are you all right?'

Sarah nodded. By now the feeling of panic had subsided, leaving her confused and embarrassed. 'I'm sorry,' she said, pressing her fingers to her temples. 'I really am *very* sorry. I don't quite know what happened, except I suddenly had the feeling that something – that something awful was about to happen to you . . . '

'I see,' he said, after a moment of uneasy silence. 'Well, as I was about to say — '

' — before you were so rudely interrupted,' she added, in an attempt to make light of the incident.

Kessler smiled a thin, humourless smile. 'Quite so.' He cleared his throat nervously. 'As I was about to say, although there doesn't seem to be too much the matter with you, I think it would be sensible if you were to spend the night here, where we can keep an eye on you.'

'*Here?*' Sarah felt her heart sink. 'Surely not . . . ' Apart from the fact that the floor was bare, the only furniture in the great, echoing vault of a room was the two chairs they'd used earlier, a hospital-type bed and locker, and an ancient painted wardrobe.

'I know it isn't exactly the Harvard Medical Center,' Kessler conceded, 'but you'll be well looked after, and — '

'But why do I *need* looking after?' she demanded.

Kessler pulled a long face. 'Well, quite apart from anything else, you did hit your head rather badly when you fainted . . . '

'And you think I'm concussed, do you? Good God, I couldn't have hit it *that* hard!'

'No, but it isn't worth taking any chances,' Kessler insisted. 'So, can we take it that you'll stay? If nothing else, that way you'll at least be sure of getting some rest,' he added, as the nurse crossed to the bed and turned back the sheets.

CHAPTER 10

IT WAS almost dark before Sarah had been allowed to relax. First, Maggie had arrived with the overnight bag she'd packed for her. No sooner was she in bed, however, when Svenson had appeared, saying that the medium had been too exhausted by her journey to hold a seance that evening. Svenson had been followed by Adams, then Calder, Piroschka and several of the intelligence analysts. In fact by the time one of the night nurses had sent the last of her visitors packing and had cajoled her into eating a dinner she hadn't really wanted, she was feeling more tired than she would had she not been ordered to bed to rest.

But it wasn't over yet. When the nurse returned for Sarah's dinner tray, she seemed reluctant to leave.

After she had drawn the curtains, plumped up the pillows, straightened the coverlet, changed the water in the carafe for the second time since coming on duty and given Sarah her pain-killers, she picked up the tray, started towards the door and then stopped, a troubled expression on her well-scrubbed, schoolgirlish face. 'Do you mind if I ask you something?'

'Please do,' Sarah replied, curious to know what had caused the nurse to abandon her confident, almost too cheerful manner for one of such uncertainty and gloom.

'You're not a doctor, are you? I mean, not a doctor of medicine . . . '

'No, I'm a doctor of philosophy.'

'Philosophy?' The nurse seemed taken aback by Sarah's reply. 'Oh, that's odd . . . '

'Odd? In what way?'

'We heard you were a parapsychologist . . . '

'I am; but I'm also a doctor of philosophy.'

The nurse hesitated, as if still not entirely sure she was on the right track. 'Tell me to mind my own business if you want,' she said, looking down at the tray, 'but . . . '

'Go on,' urged Sarah.

The nurse began to blush. 'It's just that there've been rumours,' she continued, raising her eyes, 'well, that you're here to try to make contact with Itzhevnikov's spirit . . . '

'*Rumours*? You mean you haven't been told?'

'In the Navy you're never told more than is absolutely necessary for you to do your job,' the nurse replied, without malice. 'Of course we knew someone would be coming, but until yesterday we figured it would be still more neuro-physiologists.'

'So, how did you find out who we were?'

The nurse blushed deeper still. 'One of the other girls overheard you arguing with the Admiral,' she replied, guiltily.

Sarah shrugged. 'In that case, you know as much as I do . . . '

After hovering uncertainly for a moment more, the nurse suddenly and resolutely laid aside the tray, pulled up a chair and sat down. 'You don't mind, do you?'

'Of course not.' Sensing that their roles were about to be reversed, Sarah lifted herself higher in the bed. 'Is something the matter?'

'I think there might be,' she replied, glancing across at the door as if afraid that someone might be listening. 'In fact – well, I guess I just wanted to tell you to be careful that's all . . . '

Sarah felt a tingle of alarm. 'Be careful of what?'

'Of what's in this house. I know the other girls think I'm being silly, but . . . ' Again the nurse hesitated. 'Oh, well, what the hell,' she said, throwing the last vestiges of caution to the wind. 'You may tell me it's all a lot of hooey, but I think this place is haunted!'

'*Haunted*?' Sarah began laughing with relief, but her laughter was quickly extinguished by the hurt look in the nurse's eyes. 'I'm sorry,' she said, reaching out to squeeze

81

her hand reassuringly. 'Okay, so I know it *feels* as if it should be haunted, but what's happened to make you think it is?'

'That's what's so crazy – I don't know. I mean, it's not as if I've seen someone walking around with their head tucked underneath their arm . . . '

Sarah smiled. 'People don't necessarily have to see someone with their head under their arm to think a house haunted.'

'I suppose not,' said the nurse, making a sad little attempt to smile back at her. 'And yet surely they must see or hear or feel *something*? I just get scared!

'Actually, that's not strictly true,' she continued, after pausing to consider what she had just said. 'I *do* feel something: I feel as if someone's watching me the whole time – someone who resents my being here and who's waiting for me to make a wrong move so that they can – I don't know – get me, I guess . . . '

Chafing her bare arms as if she'd felt a sudden draught, she added: 'In fact a couple of nights ago it got so bad I had one of the guys in the path lab run a check on my blood adrenaline level, and it was *way* up. So was my free fat level . . . '

'Had you been involved in a flap of any kind?'

The nurse shook her head emphatically. 'That was the funny thing: it had been an unusually quiet shift, and yet according to my blood chemistry I'd been scared witless!'

'And you say the other girls have never complained of such feelings?'

'Not the nurses. Toni – the redhead who took your ID pictures – she's aware of them, but for some reason they don't seem to bother her nearly as much as they do me.'

'What about when you're not in the house?' asked Sarah. 'Has anything like this ever happened then?'

'No, never . . . '

'By the way, where *do* you live?'

The nurse made a small adjustment to her blue-and-gold trimmed white cap. 'My home's in Philadelphia, but I'm billeted in the stables.'

82

'In the *what*?'

'In the stables,' she replied, laughing at the look of astonishment on Sarah's face. 'But don't get me wrong – they're really very comfortable.'

'Even so, why use the stables with this place standing empty?'

'They must have figured that segregating the sexes and ranks would've been too much of a hassle. We share the stables with a couple of WAVES, and the guys have the rest of the outbuildings.'

'Incidentally, how do you manage to occupy yourselves around here when you're not working?'

'That's no problem,' replied the nurse, as if the opportunities were unlimited. 'We ride, swim, sail, go for long walks. No, the problem is occupying ourselves when we're on duty,' she added with a wry smile. 'With only one patient and all that hardware there really isn't that much for us to do . . . '

'So, what *do* you do?'

'Me? Read, mainly.'

'And what do you like reading?' asked Sarah, thinking that perhaps the girl's choice of books might have some bearing on how she felt when in the house.

Looking faintly embarrassed, she replied: 'Poetry, as a matter of fact. I know the other girls think it a bit pretentious — '

'Pretentious?' Sarah frowned. 'Why should they think it pretentious of you to like poetry?'

'I guess it must seem that way if all you ever read is *Practical Nursing* and *Cosmo* . . . '

Sarah smiled. 'And who are your favourite poets?'

'Whoever I happen to be reading at the moment,' replied the nurse, smiling back at her. 'Right now it's Yeats . . . '

'Interesting,' said Sarah, suddenly conscious of how much they had digressed. 'Anyway, to get back to the other business, have you ever considered talking to Kessler? About the way you feel, I mean.'

'What, and have him think I'm crazy?'

'Surely he wouldn't do that, would he?'

'You'd be surprised,' replied the nurse. 'I know I shouldn't be telling you this, but he's even written *you* up as being emotionally unstable.'

'Has he, now!' she exclaimed, offended and yet at the same time amused by his presumption. 'Okay, then what about asking for — '

'A transfer back to Bethesda?' The nurse shook her head. 'I'd be facing the same problem. Don't you remember the case of the Stanford psychologist who persuaded seven perfectly sane people to say they'd been hearing voices? All of them ended up in psychiatric hospitals having been diagnosed as either manic-depressive or schizophrenic! In fact if they hadn't flushed their medication down the john, some of 'em would probably still be there!'

'Umm . . . ' With her chin resting in her cupped hands, Sarah thought again. 'Tell me,' she said at last, 'have you been able to find out anything about the history of the house?'

Faint and far away, an owl began hooting.

'Sure,' replied the nurse, crossing to draw the curtains even tighter. 'But as far as I've been able to discover all of the original owners died peacefully in their beds back in Boston.'

'And do you know what it's been used for since the Navy acquired it?'

'Apart from it having once been used to give Marine medics experience of treating wounds under battlefield conditions, no I don't.'

Sarah frowned. 'But what's so sensitive about that?' she asked. 'According to Piroschka, it's always been used for what he described as "projects which were too sensitive to be contracted out" . . . '

'I guess it was the fact that they worked with live animals.'

'Oh, my God! You don't mean they actually — '

The nurse nodded. 'I know, it's horrid, isn't it,' she replied, hunching over her tightly folded arms as if suddenly feeling sick. 'And it's not laboratory-bred rats they mutilate, it's pigs, sheep, cows – sometimes even dogs and apes.'

At last Sarah thought she understood. 'If that's what's been going on here it's no wonder you've been feeling uncomfortable,' she said, indignantly. 'In fact now I think of it, I can remember feeling pretty damned uncomfortable myself when I first set foot in the house! Look,' she continued, lifting herself still higher in the bed, 'I don't know how much you know about psychometry — '

'Psychometry?' The nurse pulled a long face. 'I'm not even sure I know what it means!'

Sarah clasped her hands around her drawn-up knees. 'Then let me explain: psychometry's a form of extra-sensory perception which enables certain people to obtain information from inanimate objects, the theory being that all inanimate objects are somehow capable of retaining a record of highly-charged emotional events that've occurred in their immediate vicinity.

'Let me give you an example of what I mean,' she continued, with almost childlike enthusiasm. 'A couple of years ago we ran a series of double-blind trials with one of America's leading psychometrists. Now, even though neither the psychometrist nor the experimenters knew what they were working with, over and over again he was able to come up with results which were so much against chance it was ridiculous. For instance, when he was asked to put his hand into a box containing a fragment of dinosaur's tooth he was able to describe both the creature from which it had come and the landscape it had inhabited in so much detail it quite blew the minds of the palaeontologists who were monitoring that phase of the experiment!'

'Gee, that's fascinating!' said the nurse, but in a voice which failed to match the extravagance of her words. 'However, what I don't understand is — '

' — what any of it has to do with the way you've been feeling!' Sarah smiled. 'Okay, what I'm suggesting is this,' she continued, patiently. 'I'm suggesting that the house has somehow retained not only a memory of the animals' suffering but the emotions of the men who inflicted it on them, and that it's this you've been picking up.

'Okay, so it's pretty damned unpleasant for anyone able

85

to decode the signal, but once you understand just what it is that's happening it's no more dangerous than – well, than say watching a movie of a charging rhino!'

At last the light of comprehension dawned on the nurse's face. 'I see what you *mean*!' she exclaimed, putting a hand to her throat. But then – like a cloud passing across the sun – the radiance of her smile suddenly dimmed. 'Well, that's odd . . . ' After feeling inside her bra, she stood up, shook out her skirt, then turned to look around.

'Have you lost something?'

'My little silver crucifix . . . '

'And you're sure you were wearing it when you came on duty?' asked Sarah, leaning over the side of the bed to look with her.

'Absolutely sure. Until now I wouldn't have *dared* come into this place without it!'

'It'll turn up . . . '

The nurse shrugged indifferently. 'And if it doesn't, what the hell,' she said, turning to beam at Sarah. 'Am I glad we had this talk! Honestly, I can't *tell* you how much better you've made me feel!'

'Just between the two of us, it's made me feel better, too!' chuckled Sarah, as she plumped up her pillows before once again slipping beneath the sheets.

The nurse picked up the tray. 'Now, is there anything I can do for *you*?'

'I don't think so . . . '

'Would you like a hot drink, perhaps? Or some Seconal?'

'No, I'm fine, thanks.'

'Are you sure?'

'Quite sure,' replied Sarah, snuggling down into the bed. 'In fact I think I'll be asleep in no time . . . '

Sleep, however, was to prove elusive. No sooner had the nurse switched off the lights and left, when Sarah's mind began to fill with questions, but questions of a sort which seemed only to raise other questions, like doors opening endlessly on to other doors.

Why had she, a healthy, well-balanced and successful woman of thirty-four, suddenly fallen victim to what were obviously psychosomatic disorders? she asked herself, as she lay listening to the crooning of the night wind beneath the eaves. Had her migraine been an attempt on the part of her Unconscious to force her off the project? Although Kessler would doubtlessly have dismissed such an interpretation as mere psychobabble, it had much to commend it. After all, if, having agreed to work on Endor, she were to become too ill to do so she'd be off the hook, and with no recriminations. And yet when he had virtually invited her to have herself invalided-off the project she hadn't taken advantage of his offer. Why? Was it entirely out of loyalty to Jack, Andy and Maggie, or had it more to do with her feelings for Calder, ambivalent though they were? Indeed, might not such ambivalence be the reason for her vaginitis (and by now she'd convinced herself that she was suffering from vaginitis as well as stress-induced dysmenorrhoea)? Most puzzling of all, why had she suddenly become phobic about mirrors? Okay, so what with one thing and another she wasn't exactly looking at her best at the moment, but that neither explained why she was now finding it almost impossible to look into a mirror, or why she had reacted as she had when Kessler had looked into one.

As a psychologist she understood the mechanism of phobia-formation perfectly well: to become phobic, one would've had to have had a traumatic experience, the memory of which – for reasons of fear or guilt or a combination of both – had been repressed. However, although the incident itself would have been forgotten, the specific thing, place, person or animal most closely associated with the incident would not.

And yet there had been no such incidents in her own life. She was certain of it. Had there been, surely they would have come out during the course of her long and very thorough analysis? True, she had, as a small child, found Lewis Carroll's *Through the Looking Glass* rather scary, but there was never any question of her having repressed her memory of the book. On the contrary, she and her analyst

87

had spent many hours discussing the extent to which her choice of a career in parapsychology had been determined by having encountered such concepts as acausality – later to be the subject of her PhD thesis – at such an impressionable age.

So, had something traumatic happened to her while she had been in the ground floor washroom? Although she'd been unwilling to mention it to Kessler, she was still haunted by the feeling that she had been raped. Supposing, then, that she *had* been raped, and that her first sight of the rapist had been in the mirror above the washbasin. Assuming that the memory of the attack had been repressed, would that not explain why she had become phobic about mirrors. And yet how *could* she have been raped? The fact that they'd had to break down the door to reach her proved she had bolted it; there was nowhere in the washroom where anyone could have hidden; and anyway, who'd ever heard of a rapist using a condom?

Pausing to peer at the luminous face of her wristwatch, she was dismayed to discover that she had been tossing and turning for over an hour.

Wishing that she hadn't declined the nurse's offer of Seconal, she began untangling the sheets. It wasn't as if she was averse to taking sleeping pills; in fact she often took them for precisely the reason she should have taken them tonight – to quieten an over-active mind. Although at the time she'd told herself she simply hadn't needed them, she was now beginning to suspect that there might have been another reason – that she had been afraid to go to sleep, or at least afraid to go to sleep too deeply. But why, for God's sake? Because Maggie's dog had been unwilling to come into the house. Or was it because of what the camera operator and the nurse had told her? Either way it was just all too crazy!

Having finally managed to get the bedclothes back into some sort of order, she plumped up her pillows and turned over, determined that this time her mind would remain empty of all but the most soporific thoughts.

However, just as she was beginning to drift off the silence

which had long ago settled on the rambling warren of a house was shattered by a piercing scream.

Suddenly wide awake, she twisted around and snapped on the bedside light.

After a moment of uncertainty as to what if anything she should do, she threw aside the bedclothes, ran to the door and opened it in time to see a Naval corpsman manoeuvre a wheeled stretcher into the ICU. Although convinced that something must have happened to Itzhevnikov, when the corpsman reappeared several minutes later she was stunned to see that it was not the Russian who was lying on the stretcher, but the nurse with whom she'd been talking earlier that evening.

'Back!' he yelled, waving Sarah aside.

As the nurse was trundled past her she caught a glimpse of tousled hair, staring eyes, and, behind the transparent oxygen mask another of the nurses was holding to the girl's ashen face, lips that were drawn back in a terrified grimace.

'Oh, my God!' Sarah cried, but even as she was asking what had happened the stretcher party turned the corner at the end of the corridor and disappeared.

Still trying to make sense of what she'd seen, she closed the door and clambered back into bed. The nurse was much too young to have had a stroke, and in the equally unlikely event of her having suffered a cardiac arrest they would have been applying external heart massage. So, what on earth had happened? It was all very odd. Odd, sad and deeply disturbing.

With sleep now out of the question, Sarah picked up one of the books which Maggie had brought and began reading, but with the memory of the nurse's face still clear in her mind it was not easy to concentrate. Moreover, it seemed to be getting colder by the second. After pausing to drape a cardigan around her shoulders she began again, only to discover that she had turned over two pages instead of one without noticing her mistake until halfway through the penultimate paragraph.

'Damn!' she said, turning back to the start of the book.

However, she had not re-read more than the first hundred words when she was suddenly seized by the feeling that she was being watched. Startled, she peered into the gloom beyond the pool of yellow lamplight but could see nothing which would explain the feeling. Pulling the cardigan tighter around her shoulders, she began yet again, but still the feeling persisted.

Goddammit, she *was* being watched! she told herself, laying aside the book. She was sure of it. But by whom and from where? The door did not have an observation port, the keyhole was covered by an old-fashioned china draught-excluder and the curtains were firmly drawn. And yet no sooner had she picked up the book when the feeling returned, even stronger than before.

Was this how the nurse had felt? she wondered, as she got up to look behind the curtains as well as in the wardrobe and even under the bed. If it was, it was hardly surprising that the poor girl had hated being in the house.

Although the feeling of being watched seemed to have abated, when she went to wash her hands she found an evil-looking black spider crouching in the basin. Oh, no! she thought, aware that even if she were to succeed in coaxing it on to a sheet of paper the likelihood was that while carrying it to the window it would either drop to the floor, or, worse still, scurry back along the paper and up her arm.

However, in order to give the creature a chance of surviving she turned on the cold rather than the hot tap. As she heard the rumble of water rising in the supply pipe she looked away, but not quickly enough to avoid seeing it fail in what would be its final attempt to scale the shiny, flower-patterned porcelain. The rumble became a groan, the groan a gurgling, choking sound; the sort of sound, she imagined, that would be made by someone who had cut their throat with a straight razor. A rush of air from the ancient brass tap was followed by the sound of something splashing into the basin, and then silence.

Turning, she was confronted by a sight which, with her menstrual flow about to begin at any time now, almost caused her to faint: not only was the spider still frantically struggling to escape, but both the basin and the front of her white nightgown were splattered with what appeared to be blood. Again the tap seemed to belch, but this time it was followed by an explosive vomiting of what she could still only think of as blood.

But as the spider was sucked down into the red whirlpool which had formed above the outlet pipe, she at last recognised it for what it was – rusty water.

With the water now running clear, she raised her head to find herself staring into the mirror above the basin. Although wanting to turn away, she refused to yield to the impulse. How, she wondered, as she forced herself to study the reflection of her drawn face and bruised forehead, had she come to be reduced to such a state and in such a short space of time? She, who took such pride not only in her appearance, but in her ability to be rational at all times and under all circumstances . . .

The mirror! She felt a prickle of excitement, as if within a hair's-breadth of solving a problem which had long eluded her.

And then like a fruit-machine delivering the jackpot, the answer came to her: *the mirror was made of one-way glass*!

Of course! Why hadn't she thought of it before, especially as several of the laboratories at Biotec were equipped with such mirrors. Not only did it explain her phobia, it also explained the feeling she'd had of being watched! She *was* being watched, but by someone with whom she could come to grips.

'You mother-fucking sons of bitches!' As the full force of her anger erupted like volcanic magma, she seized a chair, and, using all her strength, drove one of its metal legs into the mirror. A web of cracks appeared in the glass, but instead of the leg disappearing into the adjoining room as she had expected, it bounced off the wall with a force which almost knocked her to the floor.

'Shit!' she muttered, staring at the now crazily distorted reflection of her shocked and ashen face.

For several minutes she just stood there, nursing her bruised palms and wondering how she was going to be able to explain away the damage. There was certainly no question of her telling them the truth; if she did, they really would think her mad.

So, what should she tell them? she asked herself, as she began clearing the basin of broken glass. That she'd knocked over a bottle of shampoo while washing her hair at half-past one in the morning? If they would believe that they'd believe anything! Supposing, then, that she were to say she'd knocked over one of the intravenous stands, or, even better, that a screen had blown over when she'd opened the window? Although still not the perfect excuse, it was the best she was going to be able to come up with feeling as exhausted as she now did.

After wrapping the broken glass in a paper towel, she placed it in the pedal-bin, washed her hands, and, with her teeth chattering with the cold, crawled back into bed.

No sooner had she switched off the light, however, when the feeling of being watched returned with an almost palpable intensity.

Pulling the covers over her head, she curled up into a tight ball and told herself that it was all in her imagination. There was no one there, and she was not being watched. For Christ's sake, hadn't she just made a complete idiot of herself *proving* that she wasn't being watched?

But still the feeling persisted. At the beginning it was as if she was being watched by something outside; now, however, that something seemed to have begun to insinuate itself into the very room, filling it with the stench of putrefaction. Something with blank protruding eyes and a swollen tongue; something with icily-cold, slimy white skin and a distended belly marbled with veins full of decomposing blood. Something which was dead and yet frighteningly alive. Something, moreover, which had come to feed on her as the hordes of squirming maggots with which it was infested were feeding on it.

And yet she knew that this was no more than a metaphor; a pathetically inadequate metaphor for something unimaginably more awful.

For the first time since she'd been a child she began to

pray, but the malevolent, suffocating sense of presence seemed only to become more palpable.

She would have to leave, and leave now before she was totally immobilised by terror. And yet how could she leave when whatever was out there in the darkness was standing between her and the door?

Somewhere in the middle of the room a floorboard creaked, then creaked again, as if the thing had suddenly acquired both mass and the ability to move. There was another creak, followed by still another. It *was* moving! She knew it was. And it was moving towards her.

Not daring to switch on the light for fear of what it might reveal, she flung back the bedclothes and made a dash for the window, neither knowing or caring about what lay beyond.

Tearing aside the heavy, dust-filled curtains, she grasped the casement fastenings and pushed. However, although she managed to force open one of the windows just far enough to hear the hollow booming of the sea as it rose and fell against the rocks far below, the other would not budge.

Sobbing hysterically, she turned and began feeling her way around the walls towards the only remaining means of escape – the door.

She had not got far when she touched something cold and slippery. With a shriek, she started back, only to find herself in the embrace of something tall and yielding. As the thing fell fluttering to the floor, she began to run. Now totally disorientated, she fought her way through a thicket of steel rods and immediately collided with something which went trundling across the bare boards, clattering and tinkling.

Soon, though, it wasn't she who was running into things, but things which seemed to be running into her; things which struck out at her, clawed her, tried to trip and smother her.

And then suddenly the room filled with a blinding light. 'Dr Stuart!' she heard someone cry, in a tone of shocked disbelief. 'What on *earth* do you think you're doing?'

CHAPTER 11

SARAH AWOKE from a dream in which she was running naked through Harvard Yard, pursued by a crowd of jeering scientists. Lawrence LeShan was there, so was Russell Targ and Hal Puthoff, Montague Ullman and Stanley Krippner. Even Carl Sagan seemed to be there somewhere, along with most members of The Committee for the Scientific Investigation of Claims of the Paranormal.

Raising herself on to an elbow, she reached out for her travelling alarm clock. Although she knew that she had overslept, it couldn't really be *that* late! Throwing back the covers, she ran to the window and drew the curtains. As the cabin filled with the mellow light of an autumn afternoon, suddenly it all came tumbling back.

'Oh, no!' she groaned, turning to bury her face in the curtains. With a clarity which left her numb with shame, she remembered how she had fought with the nurses when they'd tried to get her back into bed, and how she'd had to be brought to the lodge before allowing Kessler near her with the hypodermic.

She'd made a fool of herself: such a complete and utter bloody fool that if a word of what had happened were ever to leak out – and this clearly was the message of her dream – she would become the laughing-stock of her profession. It wasn't surprising that no one had bothered to wake her: anyone capable of behaving as she had behaved was more than just an embarrassment, they were a positive liability.

And yet by the time she had finished in the bathroom, found a classical music station on the radio and set the coffee perking, the events of the past twenty-four hours seemed as remote from her as they would had they happened to some-one else. In a sense they had happened to someone else, for now that her menstrual flow had finally begun she felt relaxed, clear-headed and totally in command of her emotions.

After filling a mug with coffee, she moved out on to a patio overlooking the beach. Although the weatherman had forecast storms for later that night, so far the only thing to flaw an otherwise flawlessly blue sky were the bands of fluffy white altocumulus which were just beginning to edge in from the northwest. With the mug cradled between her hands, she leaned over the rail, delighting in the feel of sun-warmed timber beneath her bare feet and elbows. It was, she decided, one of those still, pearly afternoons which Renoir might have enjoyed painting; the sort of afternoon which blended perfectly with the music from the radio: Victoria de los Angeles' haunting recording of Chausson's *Poème de l'amour et de la mer.*

Even though she would have liked nothing more than to have spent the remainder of the day mindlessly watching the terns as they ferried silver fish snatched from a silver sea to their now almost fully-fledged chicks waiting at the water's edge, it was a luxury she could not afford. She was in trouble – deep, deep trouble – and the sooner she came to grips with it the better.

So, what should she do? she wondered, grabbing at a thistledown as it went floating by. Offer to resign from the project? After last night's débâcle, the chances were that they'd be only too happy to accept. However, although the idea of a ticket out was immensely appealing, it wasn't really on. Tagged as yet another victim of burnout, she would quite likely lose her job at Biotec. Worse still, once the story of *why* she had lost it became known she might well find it impossible to get another.

There was, therefore, only one thing for it: she would somehow have to re-establish her credibility with the people at Seacrest, and fast. But in order to do that, she would first have to come up with a plausible reason for why she'd behaved as she had.

Explaining what had happened to her during the briefing

would be easy enough; after all, there was nothing particularly unusual or shaming about having had a migraine. No, the real problem lay in explaining away her behaviour during the early hours of the morning. Clearly, there was no question of her telling them the truth – they would never have believed it. In fact the more she thought about it the less inclined she herself was to believe it. A more plausible explanation, surely, was that after falling into a deep sleep (and, as she was to remind herself, by the time she had cleared away the remains of the broken mirror she'd been feeling pretty exhausted) she'd had another Type 2 false awakening – a dream in which the dreamer appears to awaken in their own bed. Okay, so last night's false awakening had been even more terrifying than the one she'd had before leaving Boston, but that wasn't too difficult to understand bearing in mind all that had happened before she had finally fallen asleep. In fact had it not been for the nurse's story, the idea that she was being watched might never have entered her head.

But what about her attempt to escape through the window? Had that been part of the same dream? It must have been, she decided. A dream followed by a sleepwalking episode. Indeed, the very fact that she had been sleep-walking would explain why it had been necessary to tranquillise her: to awaken a sleepwalker abruptly – as she had been awoken – invariably does induce overwhelming feelings of panic and confusion.

Feeling much happier now that she had found an explanation she was sure would not only satisfy the people at Seacrest, but which also went a long way towards satisfying her, she returned to the kitchen and made herself an omelette.

So that was that! she told herself, smugly sliding the omelette on to a warmed plate. Now all she had to do was change into something flattering but not too obvious, get her ass over to Seacrest and the show on the road.

Sarah cleared the checkpoint behind the imposing, wrought-

iron gates of Seacrest at 4.45, driven by the Marine corporal
she'd found standing guard at the door of her cabin. Ahead
of her she could see Svenson supervising the unloading of
what looked like sections of a screened room from a rig
parked alongside the *porte-cochère*. As they came to the end of
the long, tree-lined driveway and began rounding the
fountain, Svenson looked up from his clipboard and did a
double take. 'Hey Maggie!' he yelled, pushing back the
headphones of his Sony Walkman, 'come and see who's just
turned up!'

Rushing forward, he lifted Sarah down from the jeep and
hugged her. 'Well, how are you?' he asked, looking her over
at arm's length.

'Great!' she replied, turning to embrace Maggie.
'Absolutely great!'

After handing his clipboard to a naval quartermaster,
Svenson and the two women began to crunch their way
towards the house.

Turning from one to the other, Sarah recited her carefully rehearsed account of what had happened during the
early hours of the morning. 'And that's about it, except for
one thing,' she concluded, although the driver had already
answered the question she was about to ask. 'How come
everyone just pissed off leaving me behind at the lodge this
morning, huh?' She snorted indignantly. 'A fine bunch of
friends you turned out to be!'

'But we were told that on no account were you to be
disturbed,' Maggie explained, as they began climbing the
front steps. 'According to Kessler, you'd had an hysterical
seizure — '

'A *what*?' Sarah demanded, stopping abruptly.

'He said — ' Maggie cleared her throat nervously and
began again. 'Well, according to Kessler, you'd had some
kind of a — '

' — panic attack,' Svenson interjected. 'I think the term he
actually used was "panic attack".'

Sarah laughed. 'Bullshit!' she said, in a manner intended
to leave them in no doubt that from now on hers was to be
the authorised version of what had happened. 'Okay, so

maybe I did blow my stack, but I knew that if I didn't get out of this dump I'd be fit for nothing today.'

After taking the remainder of the steps two at a time, she strode across the veranda and entered the living-hall. As if anticipating the arrival of bad weather, a fire had been lit in the inglenook. Here and there, open books and unfinished board games awaited the return of their owners, giving the hall a comfortable, lived-in look – an effect which was heightened still further by the faint but curiously reassuring aroma of smoldering pine cones, pipe tobacco and well-polished leather.

'So, where is everybody?' Sarah asked, as the long-case clock began softly chiming the hour.

'They're in the library, listening to Jack's tapes,' replied Svenson, as if he expected her to know what he was talking about.

'They're doing *what?*' asked Sarah, thinking for a moment that he must be referring to Adams's collection of Jimi Hendrix recordings.

Svenson frowned. 'Haven't you heard? Last night, Jack managed to make some tapes of It. Or rather tapes of a guy speaking Russian,' he added, only just in time to avoid having her rebuke him for making an unwarranted assumption. 'I'm sorry, but it never crossed my mind that you hadn't been told.'

Sarah took a deep breath. 'Okay, so how were these tapes of his made?' she asked, thrusting her hands deep into the pockets of her tan doeskin skirt.

'On his portable radio-cassette recorder . . . '

'Oh, shit!' exclaimed Sarah, as angry with herself for not having been there to stop such an act of foolishness as with Adams for having committed it. 'But it was agreed that all experiments were to be carried out on equipment supplied by them!

'And, anyway, what about the screened room?' she added, as one of the eight feet by four feet steel-and-plywood panels from which the room would be constructed was carried past her by two sailors. 'Surely he realises that any EVP not produced in a screened room is highly suspect?'

98

'Sure,' said Svenson, rubbing his blond beard unhappily. 'But honestly, all we were doing was — '

'All *we* were doing?' echoed Sarah, looking from one to the other. 'You mean you were in on this too?'

'Not guilty!' said Maggie, backing away with her hands in the air. 'As soon as I'd left you, I high-tailed it back to the lodge for an early night. As it happens, I really should split now,' she added, glancing at her man-sized wristwatch. 'Mrs Mitchell - the medium - is due here at seven-thirty, and I still haven't finished fixing a room for her . . . '

After waving her away, Sarah turned back to Svenson. 'So, it was just you and Jack, then?' She tut-tutted. 'Really, you ought to have had more sense . . . '

'Okay, but let me try to explain,' said Svenson, moving her out of the way as another of the steel-and-plywood panels was manoeuvred through the front door. 'What happened was this: after dinner last night Jack and I got to talking about this EVP idea of his, and to cut a long story short he thought it might be interesting if we went back to the house with his radio-cassette recorder to see what we could get using one of the traditional methods.'

Sarah began impatiently tapping the toe of one of her high-heeled Italian leather boots. 'Since when has using a radio-cassette recorder been considered a traditional method for making EVPs?' she demanded.

'The principle's just the same,' Svenson assured her, digging into the breast pocket of his plaid shirt for a packet of chewing gum. 'When Raudive wasn't using a diode, he would plug a radio tuned between frequencies into the microphone socket of a standard radio, which was basically what we were doing, except in our case the whole thing was fully integrated.'

After Sarah had declined his offer of gum, Svenson slipped a stick into his mouth and began chewing furiously. 'Anyway, by the time we'd fooled around with the recorder for maybe an hour or so and come up empty, I decided to call it a day. Jack, however, wanted to go on trying for a bit longer, so, when I got a chance of a lift back to the lodge - and we'd come in his jeep, right? - I left him to it.

'But then,' he continued, glancing over his shoulder to reassure himself that there was no one else within earshot, 'just as Jack was beginning to think that maybe the whole thing was a waste of time, a guy speaking what he assumed was Russian suddenly started coming through loud and clear.'

'What time was this?' asked Sarah.

'Between one and one-thirty.'

'That's odd,' she said, remembering that it had been about then that she'd first had the feeling of being watched.

'Odd?' Svenson gaze her a puzzled look. 'In what way odd?'

'Forget it,' she told him, anxious to avoid having anything undermine her painstakingly constructed rationale. 'So, what happened then?'

'That's about it. Although as far as Jack knew the guy could've been reading the fat stock prices in Pushtu, he was sufficiently intrigued to keep the machine rolling until he ran out of tape at three-thirty or thereabouts. Okay, so I know his tapes are about as much like typical EVPs as a mountain is like a molehill, but I just felt it would be a mistake to wipe 'em before he'd checked them out with someone able to speak Russian.'

'Let me get this straight,' said Sarah, narrowing her eyes. 'You mean Jack wanted to wipe them but *you* persuaded him not to, is that what you're saying?'

'Right,' he replied, sheepishly.

Sarah groaned, knowing what the end of the story would be.

'Anyway, Calder had Galbraith listen to them, and – well, Galbraith lit up like a Christmas tree. He rounded up the rest of the guys, herded them into the library along with Jack, where they've been since . . . ' Svenson paused to consult his wristwatch, ' . . . I guess since about eleven-thirty this morning.'

'You're out of your mind!' exclaimed Sarah. 'I still don't know what you thought you were doing fooling around with this thing in the first place, but having done so you might at least have had the sense to check with me before involving

Calder. Shit, Andy,' she added, despairingly, 'when it's discovered that these tapes of yours are nothing more than a freak pick-up from Moscow Radio or whatever the hell, we're going to look as if we're just off the bus from Poughkeepsie!'

'Oh, c'mon!' Svenson protested. 'If that's all they are, why would the brass have spent the last five hours listening to them?'

'That's exactly what I'm about to find out!' Sarah announced, as she stormed across to the library.

CHAPTER 12

AS SARAH threw open the richly panelled mahogany doors, the babble of voices from the men seated around the table in the middle of the otherwise empty library dwindled away as one by one they became aware of her presence.

After a moment of embarrassed silence, Calder pushed back his chair and crossed to greet her. 'Well, how are you?' he asked, making an all too obvious effort to shake off the air of troubled preoccupation which hung like a pall in the room.

'Fine,' she replied, as they shook hands. 'I really am most terribly sorry about all the trouble I caused you — '

Calder stopped her short. 'As long as you're all right,' he said, in a manner which suggested that apologies were unnecessary. 'You *are* all right, aren't you?' He frowned as if having second thoughts about her competence to judge such matters.

'I'm fine!' she insisted. 'After nearly twelve hours sleep I'm ready for pretty well anything!'

'Umm . . . ' he said, doubtfully; and for a moment she thought that in spite of her assurances he was about to insist on her leaving. However, with a resigned shrug he motioned her towards a vacant chair across from Galbraith and returned to his own place at the head of the leather-topped library table.

'But tell me, how is the nurse today?' she asked, hooking the strap of her Fiorucci shoulder-bag over the back of her chair. 'You know, the one who was — '

'The nurse?' Calder seemed taken aback. 'How do you know about the nurse?'

'Because I saw her being wheeled away on a gurney,' she replied, puzzled as to why her enquiry should have had such an unsettling effect. 'She is all right, isn't she?'

'I'm afraid not,' he replied, gravely. 'I'm afraid – well, the fact of the matter is that she died on her way to Bethesda . . . '

'Died?' Sarah felt herself grow cold with shock. 'But what on earth happened?'

Calder struck a match and began lighting his pipe. 'It's still a bit of a mystery,' he told her, between puffs. 'Right now they're talking about something called "autonomic dystonia", which as I understand it is a fancy way of saying she died of fright . . . '

'Oh, come *on*!' Sarah protested, aware that if what he had said was true she would have to bear a large measure of responsibility for the girl's death. 'People don't die of *fright*, or at least not in sophisticated Western societies . . . '

'I'm only telling you what I've been told,' said Calder, shaking out the match. 'It seems that Itzhevnikov's heart suddenly went on the blink while she was alone in the ICU checking his blood gases, and the shock of it — '

'I see,' Sarah interjected, thankfully. 'Well, I suppose that does make it a little easier to understand. After all, the poor wee thing was very young . . . '

A telephone standing on one of the window seats began ringing.

'She wasn't all *that* young,' Calder pointed out, as Piroschka got up to answer the phone. 'And anyway, as a fully trained, experienced nurse she should've been able to handle a cardiac arrest without turning a hair.'

'It's for you,' said Piroschka, with a nod towards Sarah.

'For *me*? But it can't be,' she protested. 'No one knows I'm here . . . '

'The guy on the line does,' he told her, a trace of impatience in his voice.

'Did he say who he was?'

'Only that it was a personal call.'

Mumbling her apologies, Sarah crossed to the window and took the phone from Piroschka. 'Hello?'

103

'Sarah?' The voice at the other end of the line was deep and heavily accented. 'Is that you, Sarah?'

'Yes it is,' she replied, as she tried desperately to work out who it could possibly be.

The caller began to snicker.

'Who is this?' she demanded.

However, instead of identifying himself he stopped snickering, and, in a voice which had become shrill and accusatory in tone, launched into a stream of blasphemous obscenities.

Clapping a hand over the mouthpiece, Sarah took the phone from her ear and turned to face the table. 'Would someone please come and take a listen to this?' she asked, as the tiny, insectile-like voice continued to pour out its still audible torrent of filth.

With a weary sigh, Piroschka rose from his chair. 'What's the problem?'

'Just take a listen,' she replied, thrusting the phone at him as if it had become infected.

'All I can hear now is the dialling tone,' he grumbled.

'Are you sure?'

'Sure I'm sure!' he replied, holding out the phone so that she could hear for herself. 'So, just what was all the hassle about?'

Feeling suddenly very foolish, she said: 'You're not going to believe this, but I've just had my first obscene telephone call!'

'Do you have any idea who it was?' asked Calder, as Piroschka rang through to the switchboard and began questioning the operator.

'Not the foggiest . . . '

Piroschka banged down the phone. 'Well, it wasn't an outside call,' he announced, as he ushered Sarah back to her place at the table. 'Which means it must have come from someone either in the house or in one of the outbuildings.'

'In that case, surely you'd have recognised him?' said Sarah, aware that she had begun to shake. 'I mean, how many people do you have stationed here with an accent like that?'

'None that I can think of,' replied Piroschka. 'But then he wouldn't have used his real voice, would he?' he added, as if it were self-evident. 'Not unless he was crazy . . . '

'He'd have to be crazy to make a call like that!' she retorted. 'My God, I've never heard anything *like* it!'

'If it happens again keep him talking and have someone else call the switchboard on another line,' Calder told her, before turning to the papers that lay scattered across the table in front of him. 'Now, if you don't mind I'd like to get back to the business in hand. I don't know if you know this or not,' he continued, 'but Dr Adams thinks he might have already made contact with Itzhevnikov.'

'I see,' she said, non-committally. For the first time since entering the library she looked directly at Adams. Although used to seeing him in the laid-back, aggressively non-conformist style of dress affected by many of the younger members of her staff, on this occasion his appearance took even her by surprise. Unshaven and wearing a forward-tilted flat leather cap, a zippered silver bomber jacket, T-shirt and jeans, he looked more like a drug pusher than one of America's top scientists.

Sarah listened attentively as Adams described how the tapes had been made. Although substantially the same as Svenson's, he ended his account by giving his colleague the full credit for having recognised their significance. 'I know it's crazy to admit this,' he added, shaking his head in a self-deprecating manner, 'but if it hadn't been for Andy I'd just have wiped 'em!'

'Yes, well . . . ' Wishing to God that he had, Sarah turned back to Calder. 'I take it you've no objection to my hearing these tapes of Jack's?'

'On the contrary, we'd be grateful for your opinion.' He looked enquiringly at Galbraith. 'Which do you suggest we begin with?'

Galbraith pulled a cigarette from a packet of Carlton and lit it. 'What about Tape Three, side B,' he suggested. 'It's more audible than most of the others, as well as being some-what easier to follow . . . '

Adams shuffled through the cassettes which were

scattered across the table in front of him, took one out of its box and slipped it into his matt black radio-cassette recorder. 'The batteries might be getting a bit low by now,' he warned, as he pressed the play button. 'Anyway, let's see how we get on . . .'

The first voice to emerge from the speakers was his own. Against the distant chiming of the long-case clock, he gave his name, the date and time, and how and where the recording had been made.

'What you're hearing now is white noise obtained by tuning between frequencies,' he explained, as a sound like softly falling rain began oozing from the speakers.

'By the way, after I'd made the opening announcement I unplugged the external microphone,' he added, turning the volume up a fraction. 'Which means that everything you'll be hearing from now on must either have originated from a transmitter or have been created within the machine itself . . . '

'Created by what and how?' Sarah asked, rather more sharply than she had intended.

Adams shrugged. 'A discarnate entity which has somehow managed to modulate the white noise to produce an analogue of the human voice?' he suggested. 'Quite frankly, until we've had a chance to come to grips with this thing it really is anyone's guess . . . '

Sarah leaned forward, listening intently. Amid the half hum, half hiss, she fancied she could hear a low-pitched, conspiratorial murmur, but, just as she was about to ask if this was what she was supposed to be listening to, a man's voice suddenly broke through, loud enough to make her jump.

The voice was coarse and rasping, and, as if the man were talking in his sleep or was delirious, ranged from barely audible, often near-to-tears whispers to angry outbursts which boomed around the room like thunder.

'God Almighty!' she cried, looking wide-eyed at Piroschka. 'It's – well, don't you recognise it?'

'Recognise what?'

'The voice, of course! It's the same voice that was speaking on the phone!'

106

'Well?' Calder asked Piroschka.

'I don't agree,' he replied, talking as softly as he would had he been in church. 'Okay, so it's not *unlike* it, but so what?'

Calder turned to look enquiringly at Sarah.

However, by now her initial feeling of certainty that the voice she was hearing was the same as she had heard a few minutes earlier was beginning to ebb rapidly away. 'It still sounds very like it to me, but I just can't be sure, not with him speaking Russian . . . '

Looking none too pleased to have had his meeting interrupted by yet another irrelevancy, Calder turned to Galbraith. 'Since your Russian is better than mine, perhaps you'd translate for Dr Stuart . . . '

Galbraith nodded. 'Okay, well right now he's cursing what he calls his "feelings of disorientation and helplessness",' he explained, as the voice rose to a crescendo. 'And before that – well, it was just a lot of garbled, stream-of-consciousness stuff about his childhood, the war, people he'd loved and people he'd hated . . . '

Sarah felt her heart sink. Although still reluctant to believe that what they were listening to was an EVP, of one thing she was sure: it quite clearly wasn't Moscow Radio. And yet if it wasn't an EVP – and, as she reminded herself, every EVP she'd ever heard had consisted of no more than a few indistinct often polyglot words spoken at great speed – what on earth was it?

But then she found herself remembering something which Svenson had said when she'd first had them into her office to tell them about Endor. Something about putting on a show that would make the Haunted Mansion at Disneyland look like amateur night . . . Oh, no! she thought. They couldn't have been *that* stupid! And yet the more she thought about it the more convinced she became that she now knew how the voice had been produced. At the instigation of Svenson and with the help of a Russian-speaking accomplice, all but the introductory announcements had been pre-recorded by Adams before he had left Boston! It was so simple that it was amazing they had fallen for it. And yet judging by the rapt expressions on the faces of the men around the table, they'd fallen for it hook, line and sinker.

In the circumstances there was only one thing she could do: without denouncing Svenson or Adams, she would somehow have to disabuse the others of the idea that contact had been made with the dead Russian. However, in order to do that, she would first have to discover why they seemed so certain that the voice they were listening to was his.

As it dwindled away to a whimper, Galbraith cocked his head to one side, frowning. 'Ah, now this is where it gets interesting,' he told her, as the voice suddenly became both more audible and much more controlled. 'He's begun talking about the difficulties of communicating across what he describes as ''different states of existence'',' he explained, fumbling for a cigarette. 'Although when in the physical body he spoke English tolerably well, he never mastered it sufficiently to actually *think* in English, and on what he calls the ''astral plane'' communication is by thought alone. This, he goes on to say, is a problem for many would-be communicators – communication by thought alone, that is – because as in life, in the afterlife much of our thinking is austistic.

'Incidentally,' he added, peering at Sarah through the top half of his horn-rimmed bifocals, 'what do you think he means by that?'

'Autistic thinking?'

Galbraith nodded.

'Put at its most simple, it's the random flitting from one half-formed idea to another.'

With his hands thrust deep into his trouser pockets and the cigarette dangling from the corner of his mouth, Galbraith got up and ambled across to one of the huge sash windows overlooking the bay. 'As well as having to marshal his thoughts in a way which avoids what he calls a ''heterogeny of ideas'',' he continued, staring out at the gathering storm clouds and at a sea which had taken on the ominous sheen of molten metal, 'he also has to make them audible, all of which – and here again I'm translating literally – requires an even greater degree of determin-

ation and effort than communicating by means of oesophageal speech.

'Or in other words,' he added, after pausing to scratch his
backside, 'talking without the benefit of a larnyx.'

Sarah nodded at Adams, indicating that she had heard
enough. 'Tell me, what makes you so certain that this *is*
Itzhevnikov?' she asked, addressing the question to
Galbraith's back.

While awaiting his reply, she suddenly realised that everything had gone quiet outside the room as well as within it, as
if the whole world were holding its breath anxiously. Gone
was the distant rush of breakers up the beach, the rustling of
leaves and the chirping of crickets; even the gulls seemed
finally to have ceased their incessant clamouring.

After remaining at the window for a moment more,
Galbraith returned to the table and flopped heavily into his
chair. 'No one has said they are certain,' he replied, in his
characteristically schoolmasterish manner. Taking the
cigarette from between his lips, he lifted his spectacles and
began massaging the bridge of his nose between forefinger
and thumb. 'Right now, all I'm certain about is that whoever
it is that's talking on those tapes wants us to believe they're
Itzhevnikov . . . '

'Then I'll re-phrase my question: why are you so certain
that he does want you to believe he's Itzhevnikov? Has he
said that's who he is?'

Galbraith took a long, deep pull at his cigarette. 'No,
but – '

'Well, there you go!' said Sarah, with a wry smile. 'Okay,
so he's Russian, but all I've heard so far is *so* generalised
that it could apply to almost anyone!'

Galbraith began to cough. 'Actually, it isn't all that
generalised,' he said, his face reddening from the effort of
speaking at the same time as he was coughing. 'For
example, take his mention of oesophageal speech. I'd have
thought that a most unlikely choice of metaphor.' He paused
to light another cigarette from the end of the one he had just
finished. 'Unless, of course, one has known someone who'd
had to learn oesophageal speech, and, as it happens,

109

Itzhevnikov did know such a person – his own father. In 1964 his father was diagnosed as having cancer of the throat and underwent a laryngotomy at the October Hospital in Kiev.'

Sarah looked unimpressed. 'That could be nothing more than a coincidence,' she told him. 'Now, if he'd said something which could *only* have come from someone who'd held a top job within the Kremlin – well, that would be far more evidential. Has he said anything of that sort?'

'Well, let's just put it like this,' Galbraith replied, after considering the question for several seconds. 'Although so far he hasn't told us anything we didn't already know, he has told us a lot that only a very few people know.'

'Such as?' she demanded, irritated by what she considered to be his unncessarily cryptic reply.

'Well, such as where the Russians are at with — '

Piroschka cleared his throat noisily. 'Jim, just let me remind you that although our guests have been cleared for temporary access to classified material, we're still operating on a strict need-to-know basis.'

Galbraith began again, but in a manner which suggested that he hadn't taken kindly to the younger man's attempt to teach him his job. 'In an admittedly rather roundabout way, the guy on the tapes has told us where the Russians are at in the field of particle beam weapons; what their thinking is — '

'Oh, come on!' said Sarah, laughing. 'These days you can't open a newspaper or turn on the TV or radio without coming across *something* about particle beam weapons!'

Galbraith shook his head. 'Not the sort of stuff that's on those,' he said, pointing a nicotine-stained forefinger at the tapes.

'And if you'd done me the courtesy of allowing me to finish,' he added sourly, 'I'd have told you that they also shed new light on Soviet intentions in Latin America, Africa and the Middle East.'

Sarah's eyes blazed. 'And if you had done *me* the courtesy of taking me fully into your confidence of — '

'Now just hold it!' said Calder, spreading his open hands as if separating boxers in a clinch. 'Just hold it, okay?' He turned to Sarah. 'Although Jim's choosing his words carefully, my hunch is that deep down he's pretty much convinced that these tapes could only have originated from Itzhevnikov, and that they must therefore be EVPs.'

'However, what I'm not clear about is why you, Dr Stuart, seem so convinced that they're not EVPs?'

'For a start, the signal-to-noise ratio is too good. Also, they go on for too long. Far too long. Even at their best, EVPs rarely consist of more than a few words.'

'But if they're not EVPs, what are they?' Calder asked.

'A freak radio pick-up,' she replied, with as much conviction as she could muster. 'Look, these tapes were made at night, and at night the ionosphere reflects radio signals better than it does during the day, which means that Jack could have picked up any one of a number of distant stations.'

Ignoring the fact that Galbraith had begun shaking his head, Sarah pressed home her point. 'And that's not all: radio signals can be strengthened still further by unusual meteorological or even astronomical conditions.'

'No, no, no!' said Galbraith, unable to contain himself any longer. 'With respect, that was *so* obvious an idea that we had it checked out before doing anything else,' he told her. 'However, the CIA's broadcast monitoring service have assured us that no Russian-speaking radio or TV station anywhere in the world has put out anything even remotely like what is on those tapes.

'Oh, and incidentally, we didn't just have them check out last night's transmissions,' he added, with a chilling smile. 'Because there was always a possibility that they might have been pre-recorded, we also had the Company check on everything that went out over the air since you were first told about the project!'

'Well, thanks a million!' she said scathingly. 'All right, so if it wasn't a scheduled broadcast maybe it was a pick-up from a diplomatic transmitter. Hell, the Russian Embassy in Washington must be sending out and receiving stuff right around the clock, especially with the situation which is developing in Nicaragua.'

'Not the kind of stuff that's on those tapes,' Calder pointed out. 'And anyway, honey, diplomatic radio traffic is always coded . . . '

There was a tap on the door and a steward carrying a tray laden with glasses of iced tea entered the room. Without anyone speaking, he distributed the tea, sugar and lemon, emptied the ashtrays and gathered up the curling remains of a sandwich lunch which was stacked on one of the empty bookshelves.

As he closed the doors behind him, Piroschka looked across at Sarah. 'Of course, there is always one other possibility,' he said, as he began spooning sugar into his tea. 'And that is that your colleagues may have pre-recorded the tapes with the help of a Russian-speaking accomplice.'

'That, if I may say so, is an absolutely monstrous suggestion!' she exclaimed, looking to the others for support. However, all of them – including Calder, who seemed suddenly to have become preoccupied with reaming his pipe – carefully avoided catching her eye.

Piroschka took a sip of tea. 'Well, there's one very easy way to settle the matter,' he told her, 'and that's to have them take a lie-detector test.'

Sarah shook her head vehemently. 'No way!' she snapped, as furious with Adams and Svenson for having placed her in such an invidious position as with Piroschka for having made such a suggestion. They were bound to fail such a test, and when they did it wouldn't just be their reputations which would suffer, but those of everyone working at Biotec. Worse still, they could even end up being charged under the Espionage Act.

But then to her amazement she heard Adams say: 'Listen, if it'll help clear up this matter I've no objection to taking a lie-detector test . . . '

Sarah slapped the table with the palms of her hands, hard enough to set the ice tinkling in her still untouched glass of tea. 'Over my dead body!' she cried, before Piroschka had a chance to reply. 'If you don't trust us, get someone you do trust!'

'Cool it,' Calder told her, as she pushed back her chair to

leave. 'Just cool it, huh?

'Look,' he continued, in a more relaxed, almost avuncular manner, 'we all know that when under pressure to produce results even a scientific superstar may sometimes yield to the temptation to fake his experiments. Okay, so I'll admit that the thought that Dr Adams *might* just have gotten into this neck of the woods has been bugging us ever since he first played us his tapes. However, I'm sure my colleagues will agree with me that we can now dismiss that as a possibility.'

Piroschka took a break from nibbling his fingernails. 'But since Dr Adams is prepared to take a lie-detector test, why not have him take one?'

'Because that'll mean him having to go to Washington,' Calder replied. 'And for what? Shucks, Hank, have you ever heard of anyone offering to take a lie-detector test knowing they were going to have to lie?'

'At Langley, lie-detector tests are mandatory for all personnel having access to classified material,' said the man from the CIA, shaking his head unhappily.

Calder brushed aside the implied criticism with an airy wave of his hand. 'The British security services don't use – or at least they didn't until very recently – and their record's no worse than our own,' he pointed out. 'Anyway, there just wasn't time, and there's even less time now.'

As Sarah slumped back into her chair and breathed a sigh of relief, another of the telephones on the window seat started to ring. 'If that's for me,' she began, as Piroschka snatched up the handset, 'you can tell him to go — '

After shaking his head at her, Piroschka listened for a moment and then turned to Calder. 'Are we expecting a Mrs Eleanor Mitchell?' he asked, pressing the mouthpiece to his chest. 'Checkpoint have a dame — '

'It's all right,' Sarah told him, in a flat exhausted voice. 'Mrs Mitchell's the medium who should've been here last night . . . '

CHAPTER 13

SARAH PUT her head around the library door. 'Andy,' she called. 'Andy, will you come in here for a moment, please. You, too, Maggie . . . '

After gathering up his winnings, Svenson left the inglenook where he had been playing cards with the men who had delivered the screened room, and, followed by Maggie, sauntered across the hall, a glass of tea in one hand and a lumber-jacket in the other.

'How much longer do you expect to be?' he asked Sarah.

'We're almost through. Why?'

Svenson entered the library. 'Oh, it's just that I'd like to make a start on assembling the screened room . . . '

'You mean it isn't up yet?' she exclaimed.

'Well, no,' he replied, with a sideways glance at Adams. 'I mean, we couldn't very well start building it with all of you in here, could we?'

'But why did it have to be in here?' she demanded. 'Good God, there are at least a half a dozen other rooms into which it could have gone!'

Taking a firm grip on his steel crutches, Adams heaved himself to his feet. 'Sure it could, but that would have been a pretty dumb thing to have done,' he told her, peevishly. 'Look, I know you think the tapes are just a lot of horse manure, but this was the room in which I made them, right? Now, doesn't that suggest that it might – just *might* – be the epicentre for the phenomena?'

Ungrateful bastard, thought Sarah. I've just finished busting my ass trying to save his, now he's giving me a hard time. 'All right,' she said flatly, 'but I'm going to need Andy with me for the next couple of hours, which means

114

you'll have to oversee its installation,' she told him, as he went stumping past her on his way to the door.

'And another thing,' she added firmly, but not so firmly as to risk raising the suspicions of the others, 'I want to talk to the two of you as soon as we're through with Mrs Mitchell, okay?'

'Sure,' he said indifferently, as he disappeared through the doorway.

'Now,' Sarah continued, turning back to Svenson, 'what I want *you* to do is to give us a quick run-down on Mrs Mitchell.'

'A *quick* run-down! How quick, for chrissakes?'

'You've got as long as it takes her to get from the gates to the front door!'

'Shee-it!' Swallowing the remainder of his tea, Svenson deposited the glass on one of the empty bookshelves and turned to address the men at the table. 'Well,' he began, wiping his mouth with the back of his hand, 'I guess the first thing to get a handle on is that she's *different*. Although she's here as a medium, she's also a psychic, and a damned good one at that . . . '

Calder finished gathering together his papers, got up, and followed by the others, began making his way towards the door. 'Surely, they're one and the same thing, aren't they?'

Svenson grimaced. 'We're into a very iffy area here,' he explained, falling into step between Calder and Sarah. 'Generally speaking, a psychic is someone whose super-normal powers are inherent, whereas a medium is an instrument through whom discarnate entities manifest themselves.

'For example, although we can't actually see it, we know that all living organisms are surrounded by an electro-magnetic field which appears to fluctuate according to the psychophysical state of the organism. Mrs Mitchell, however, claims not only to be able to ''see'' it as a corona of pulsating, coloured lights – what she calls an ''aura'' – she's also able to make statistically significant diagnostic assessments on the basis of what she sees. Okay, so I know it sounds crazy, but then it wasn't all that long ago that hypnotism was thought to be crazy — '

115

'Andy,' Sarah interjected. 'Andy, I know this is all very interesting, but Mrs Mitchell's here as a medium, not a psychic. So, what *kind* of a medium is she?'

'She's a trance medium. Very briefly what'll happen is this: first, she'll pick half a dozen of us to sit with her. Once we've settled down – and in order to boost what she likes to call her "psychic energy" we'll be asked to link hands – she'll "go under Control". Going under control means being possessed by what she describes as a "highly evolved spirit", one of whose functions is to relay messages from other, I guess less highly evolved, spirits. Incidentally,' he added, 'Mrs Mitchell's Control is called Tsung Dao Chung, which I very much fear will mean us having to put up with messages being delivered in an "Ah, so" accent, and with the definite article omitted!'

As they moved out on to the veranda, Galbraith took a final pull at the cigarette he'd been smoking and ground it out under his heel. 'Are you telling us that this way we don't get to talk to Itzhevnikov directly?' he asked, in a manner which made it sound less like a question than a complaint.

'Probably not,' Svenson replied, watching the limousine which had brought Mrs Mitchell from her hotel in Bar Harbor as it made its slow, majestic way down the long, tree-lined driveway. 'However, occasionally a Control will allow a communicator direct access to a medium, but only, it would seem, when the communicator is able to organise his or her thoughts well enough to make sense.'

'Huh-huh . . . ' Piroschka made a small adjustment to the angle of his cap. 'So what you're saying is that the function of a Control is to edit out precisely the kind of stream-of-consciousness stuff that took up so much time on the tapes, right?'

'Right,' said Sarah, afraid that if she didn't get in ahead of Svenson he would make the mistake of revealing that he knew more about what was on the tapes than would have been possible had he not had a hand in their production. 'That, and to act as a sort of chairperson.'

With the coming of twilight the temperature had dropped appreciably, and there was now an unmistakable smell of rain in the air. Drawing her cardigan more tightly around her shoulders she added: 'According to mediums I've talked to, would-be communicators are attracted to a seance like bees to a honey-pot, and it's the Control who has to decide who gets priority.'

'Okay, but just tell me this,' said Piroschka, as the limousine rounded the fountain and came purring to a standstill alongside the *porte-cochère*. 'Just how much does this Mrs Mitchell know about what's going on here?'

'Nothing.' Slipping on his jacket, Svenson started down the steps to greet her. 'No reputable medium ever does expect to be briefed before a seance.'

To Sarah's surprise, Mrs Mitchell turned out to be a short, plump, rather motherly figure who had dressed as if going to a wedding. She had white hair, a round, unlined face and rosy cheeks, and her hat, coat, gloves and shoes were a perfect match of her twinkling, cornflower-blue eyes.

After she and Svenson had embraced one another warmly, he introduced her to Sarah.

'Ah, I see you're a sensitive, too,' said the medium, as they shook hands. Although her voice was thin and wavering, it had a certain edge to it, as if she were used to getting her own way.

Sarah smiled. 'Alas, no. Not at all . . . '

'Really?' The medium looked her over from head to toes. 'Well, you *do* surprise me!' she said, as if suspecting her of not telling the truth. 'In fact the impression I have is that you're highly gifted psychically.

'Tell me,' she continued, apparently oblivious of the fact that there were others waiting to be introduced, 'how much do you know about the etheric body?'

Sarah shrugged. 'A little, I suppose . . . '

'Mrs Mitchell,' said Svenson, deferentially. 'Mrs Mitchell, I think perhaps we should be — '

The medium silenced him with an imperious wave of her hand. 'Then you'll know it's the counterpart of and inter-penetrates the physical body, and that of its seven specialised centres, or ''chakras'', as they're sometimes known, the most important is the etheric centre.'

117

'So I believe . . . ' With a gentle touch to the elbow, Sarah tried to get her moving, but still she stood her ground.

'Well – and I do hope you won't mind me saying this – your etheric centre doesn't look to be at all strong.' Inclining her head to one side, the medium stared at Sarah's midriff through half-closed eyes for a moment. 'Dear me, no! In fact we must do something about strengthening it, we really must. I don't know if you're aware of this, but a weak etheric centre can render one vulnerable to a possessing entity.'

Looking suitably shocked, Sarah managed to move the medium forward, but after taking only a few steps she stopped and for some unaccountable reason began lecturing her on the dangers of ouija boards.

Aware of the problem she was having, Calder hurried down the steps, and, interrupting the medium in full flow, introduced himself forcefully.

'I was just telling this young lady how dangerous ouija boards can be,' she said, after Calder had finished thanking her for having made the journey to Seacrest.

Taking her firmly by the arm, he led her beneath the *porte-cochère*. 'And why should that be, ma'am?' he asked, with a polite show of interest.

'Oh, it's just that the inexperienced seem to imagine the spirit world to be all sweetness and light,' she told him, as they began slowly climbing the steps. 'But it isn't. Dear me, no.' At last on the veranda, she stopped to catch her breath. 'In fact there are as many evil spirits as there are evil people, and on the whole it is they who seem to manifest themselves through ouija boards, often with disastrous consequences for the sitters. And yet you know, until very recently ouija boards were outselling Monopoly as America's most popular indoor game.'

As soon as the introductions were over, Calder ushered her into the hall, and, after he'd helped her out of her coat, passed it to a steward along with her hat and gloves. 'Now, what about a drink?' he asked, rubbing his hands together briskly.

However, since entering the house the medium seemed to

have become preoccupied with her own thoughts. Thinking she might not have heard, Sarah repeated his invitation.

'Oh, no,' she replied, making an effort to smile. 'Thank you all the same, but not just yet . . . '

Shuffling to the centre of the hall, she cocked her head to one side as if straining to catch a barely audible voice. 'Yes, yes!' she muttered, addressing the unseen presence somewhat querulously.

After a minute or more of uneasy silence, she turned frowning to Calder. 'I have a young woman here,' she told him. 'A very persistent but disturbed young woman who passed over recently and in very tragic circumstances.'

But, before Calder had had a chance to reply the medium put a hand to her eyes and turned away. 'There, there, there,' she said, as if trying to comfort a child who had just awoken from a nightmare. 'Now, my dear, if you could only tell me your name . . . ' After listening intently for a moment, she turned to Sarah. 'Have you lost anyone recently. A sister, perhaps . . . '

'I'm afraid I don't have a sister.'

'A close friend, then? Someone – ' Again the medium hesitated. 'Someone who – yes, someone whose passing was a result of an illness of the mind rather than the body . . . '

'As far as I know, all of my friends are alive and well.'

'This really is *most* odd,' said the medium, looking deeply troubled. 'One sometimes gets this feeling of – how can I best describe it? – this feeling of – well, of *disintegration* when someone has taken their own life, and yet I don't believe that this girl did. However,' she added, regretfully, 'I'm afraid no useful purpose will be served by pursuing it any further at the moment . . . '

Shaking off her air of gloomy preoccupation, she turned back to Calder. 'Tell me, have you been troubled by RSPK of any sort?'

Calder looked at Sarah, a puzzled expression on his face.

'Recurrent Spontaneous Psychokinesis,' she said, smiling. 'In other words, have there been any unexplained happenings here at the house?'

119

'Unexplained *happenings*?' Looking even more puzzled than before, he turned from Sarah to Piroschka.

'Well, there was the business with the ID camera,' he offered, before beginning to bite his nails.

'Ah, yes . . . ' At last Calder seemed to have understood what had been asked of him. 'And what about the way the electronic security system kept false alarming? Now that really was weird!' he continued, turning back to Sarah. 'In fact we were getting so many false alarms – all of 'em totally inexplicable! – that in the end we had no option but to rip out the whole goddamned system, double the guards and put up barbed-wire on the perimeter walls!'

'And there was another thing,' Piroschka began, but by now the medium had heard enough.

'I'm not surprised,' she said, fingering her pearl necklace unhappily. 'Indeed, the only surprising thing is that nothing more serious has happened.'

Now looking even more deeply troubled than before, she turned to Sarah. 'You know, my dear, until we've had a chance to do something about your etheric centre, you really shouldn't be here at all. Not with what's in this house.'

'How do you mean, "What's in this house"?' asked Piroschka, with a sideways glance at Calder.

Ignoring his question, the medium took something from her bag and pressed it into Sarah's hand. 'Here, I think you should have this . . . '

'What is it?' she asked, staring down at a glass phial containing a clear liquid.

'Holy water.'

Sarah felt herself begin to blush with embarrassment.

'I hope you won't have need of it, but if an occasion should arise just sprinkle a little around you . . . ' The medium turned to Piroschka. 'Now, Major, what was your question?' she asked, as Sarah – mumbling her thanks – slipped the phial into the pocket of her cardigan.

'I was wondering what you meant when you talked of there being – I think the expression you used was "something in the house"?'

'All I can tell you at the moment is that whatever it is –

120

and it could be an earthbound spirit, an elemental, or even a thought-form – it's very malevolent,' the medium replied, looking around the now almost dark hall. She turned again to Sarah, frowning. 'Surely *you* can sense it, can't you?'

However, before she'd had a chance to decide whether any useful purpose would be served by describing what had happened to her during her first few hours in the house, the medium had begun padding towards the staircase.

'Ah, yes!' she said, plucking a lace handkerchief from the cuff of her long-sleeved jersey dress. 'Now it's getting clearer . . . ' She blew her nose loudly. 'But, the odd thing is that although I can sense it, I can't *see* it – and usually I can when it's as strong as this,' she continued, peering into the gloom at the top of the staircase. 'Now wait a minute . . . '

Resting one hand on the ornately carved newel-post, she pressed the bridge of her nose between her forefinger and thumb and closed her eyes. 'Tell me, is the spirit you're hoping to contact that of an elderly but very powerful man who passed over quickly and with his life's work still unfinished?'

No one replied.

The medium bristled. 'Well?' she demanded, turning to glare at Calder.

'I guess so . . . '

'What do you mean, you "guess so"?'

'I guess you could say his passing was quick,' Calder told her, obviously ill-at-ease with the medium's choice of euphemism. 'And he certainly had a very great deal left to do.'

'Ah!' She wagged a reproving finger at him. But was this something *he* wanted to do, or were others driving him to do it?'

'Well, let's just say this: although he wouldn't have chosen to do it, there was an alternative open to him had he *really* not wanted to do it.'

The medium eyed him warily. 'I see,' she said, but in a manner which suggested that she didn't much like what she saw. 'All right, then let me ask you another question: just

121

how important *is* it that you make contact with him?'

'Very!' Calder replied, firmly. 'What he has to tell us could be of immense practical value not only to the United States, but to the whole of the free world.'

'Umm . . . ' Fingering one of her pearl earrings, the medium considered the implications of what she had been told. 'Very well, in that case I suppose we'd better try,' she said, after an interval of several seconds. 'However, I must tell you that had you not told me what you just have, I'd have advised against opening a channel of communication with this man. Indeed, I'd have gone further than that, I would have advised you to have him exorcised . . . '

'Have him exorcised!' Calder looked totally non-plussed. In what was clearly an attempt to give himself time in which to both recover from the shock and to think how he should handle this new and unexpected turn of events, he dug into his breast pocket for his tobacco pouch and began clumsily filling his pipe. 'Look,' he said at last, 'I know that as a human being he left a lot to be desired, but to suggest that he should be *exorcised*! Good God, surely that's something one only resorts to in order to rid oneself of a devil?'

The medium shook her head gravely. 'Well, I can only tell you that the impression I have – and I pray to God I'm wrong – is of someone so spiritually degraded and so full of hatred that even if you couldn't properly call him a devil, "devilish" would be entirely appropriate.

'Oh, and incidentally,' she added, 'you might be interested to know that he's the one who has been causing you all your difficulties . . . '

Calder looked up from lighting his pipe. 'You mean — '

The medium nodded. 'However,' she continued, 'there is another less drastic alternative to exorcism, and that's to hold a rescue circle.'

Calder blew out the match, but only just in time to prevent his fingers from being burned. 'A rescue service?' he said, squinting at her through the smoke from his pipe. 'What the hell's a — '

' — a rescue circle?' After asking for the lights to be switched on, the medium rejoined the others. 'A rescue circle is an attempt by the living to help the dead come to terms with the fact that they *are* dead; redress real or imagined wrongs that have either been done by the dead or to them – that sort of thing . . . ' The medium gave him a bleak, sad smile. 'Now, shall we begin?'

CHAPTER 14

THE ROOM which was to be used for the seance had originally been the butler's pantry, and had been chosen by Svenson because of all the rooms in the house it seemed the most cosy.

Standing in the middle of the floor was a large, stoutly built circular table surrounded by six high-backed chairs, and, hanging above it, an ancient rise-and-fall pendant lamp lit by a single red bulb. Alongside the table was a two-tier folding trolley on which was a voice-activated reel-to-reel tape recorder and microphone, a carafe of water covered with a beaded linen napkin and six glasses. A fire had been lit, rugs had been scattered across the floor, and there were bowls of flowers everywhere.

After lowering a roller blind in front of the now rain-streaked casement windows, Svenson looked expectantly at the medium.

'Whenever possible I like the sexes to alternate, so if you were to sit here, dear,' she said, indicating that he was to take the chair to her left, 'and Admiral Calder were to sit to my right, Maggie – it is Maggie, isn't it? – could sit between the admiral and Mr Galbraith, and Sarah between Mr Galbraith and Andy.'

As soon as everyone was in their appointed place, the medium asked them to put their palms downward on the table with the little finger of each hand touching the little finger of the sitter on either side.

After reassuring herself that everyone was comfortable and relaxed, she bowed her head and recited a short prayer asking for guidance and protection.

Without opening her eyes, she lifted her head and began

breathing deeply and sonorously. For several minutes the only other sounds to be heard in the warm, dimly lit room was the sighing of the wind and the soft, sporadic drumming of rain on the windows.

And then she began moaning. As the moaning grew louder, her fingers started to twitch, and her face began to change. First her neck appeared to lengthen, then her face. Her eyes narrowed and developed what in the poor light seemed to be epicanthic folds, her cheekbones became more pronounced and her mouth turned down at the corners.

Although Sarah was in no doubt as to how she'd achieved the apparent transmogrification – she had, she was sure, done no more than simply straighten her spine, drop her lower jaw, and, at the same time as she'd sucked in her cheeks, changed the angle of her head sufficiently to increase the depth of the shadows beneath her cheekbones and brow – she had nevertheless succeeded in creating a passable likeness of an archetypal Mongolian face.

Assuming an expression of aloof inscrutability, she began to speak in the clipped, high-pitched voice a child might use when attempting to mimic a Chinaman.

'Faith for Spiritualist involves belief in God, and in man's survival after death of physical body. At moment of death, divine element in man departs physical body to live in spirit . . .'

Sarah's attention immediately began to wander. After what seemed to have been an impressive display of generalised extra-sensory perception, the platitudes being mouthed by what she was convinced was no more than a dramatisation of the medium's secondary personality had come as something of a disappointment. Indeed, as she continued to drone on Sarah found herself wondering if what she had witnessed earlier had been quite as impressive as it had seemed at the time. If Svenson had been prepared to help Adams fabricate the tapes, why should he have stopped short of entering into a conspiracy with the medium? In fact the more she mulled over what the medium had said, the more she came to realise that little had been added to what Svenson would have been able to tell her about Itzhevnikov.

125

True, there'd been the stuff about the Russian's innate wickedness, but that had almost certainly been arrived at by nothing more than inferential deduction. After all, anyone who had risen to the top of a repressive military hegemony was more likely to have been a son-of-a-bitch than not.

But how had she known about the malfunctioning ID camera and the electronic security system which had given them so much trouble. The answer to that was simple: she hadn't! All she had done was to *ask* if there had been any instances of unexplained happenings in the house, and, having been answered in the affirmative, had used the information as one more element in her cleverly constructed and artfully presented scenario!

And as for all the nonsense about her being a sensitive with a vulnerable etheric centre, well, that clearly had been nothing more than an attempt to create a feeling of kinship and dependancy.

However, although so far it had all gone better than they could have ever dared to hope, the difficult part lay ahead. Or *did* it? Given that Svenson had briefed her properly, all she would in fact have to do once she had come to the end of her long and unbelievably boring preamble was to drop a few references to particle beam weapons and the Marxist-Leninist conspiracy for world revolution and she'd have them eating out of her hand.

If they were still awake to hear her, that is. Already everyone except Svenson seemed to have succumbed to the warm, womb-like atmosphere of the room, and Sarah could feel her own eyelids growing heavier by the minute. Knowing that if she allowed them to close, she, too, would soon be nodding off, she blinked, straightened her back and concentrated her mind on the question of how she could best deal with this latest act of betrayal.

However, with the medium now chuntering on about spiritual enlightenment and how it could be acquired through the practice of deep relaxation, it was not long before the temptation to close her eyes proved irresistible.

As she began to drift off, she was seized by the feeling that someone had entered the room. Suddenly wide awake, she twisted around in her chair intending to send the intruder packing, only to discover that no one was there.

How on earth, she wondered, could she have been so misled by her senses? But even before she could attempt an answer a dank and curiously melancholy chill seemed to descend on the room, as if she had passed from sunshine into the shadow cast by an iceberg. Although her immediate reaction was to assume that the feeling was entirely subjective, when she turned back to the table she was startled to see that her breath – like that of everyone else – had begun to condense.

'What in God's name is happening?' she whispered, but the words were barely out of her mouth when the medium suddenly went rigid. Her eyes popped open, and, as the look of oriental inscrutability was replaced by one of naked terror, she attempted to get up from the table. Halfway out of her chair she crumpled. As the blood drained from her face, her eyes rolled back behind their lids and her head plopped on to her chest with sufficient force to dislodge one of her white Kirbigrips.

The bulb flickered, went out and came on again, and the table began to vibrate.

At first the vibration was no more than would have been caused by a heavily laden truck passing close to the house. However, instead of fading away, the vibration grew in intensity until finally the table began to creak and groan as if something was attempting to wrench it apart.

And then as if the house had been hit by an earthquake, everything began to rattle: the fire-irons, the glasses and the bowls of flowers, and finally the countless pieces of china inside the cabinets with which the room was lined. With the bulb now pulsing eerily, water began gushing from the taps, the roller blind shot up, the windows flew open, and the lamp began swinging wildly, throwing grotesque shadows on to the trembling walls. As the recorder began spewing out yard after yard of tape, the trolley on which it was standing spun around on its axis and went careening across the floor to hit the door with a crash which sent the carafe and the glasses cannoning into one another.

With the tumult at last beginning to subside, Sarah saw Svenson dart across to the sink, turn off the taps and close the windows.

'Andy — ' She swallowed hard and began again. 'Andy, just what the hell is — '

'I only wish I knew!' After pulling down the blind, he returned to his seat, blowing into his cupped hands. 'It's crazy,' he continued, as he began chafing his arms. 'Absolutely crazy! I mean, physical phenomena just isn't her bag . . . '

Although it was still bitterly cold, she noticed that his breath was no longer condensing. 'All right, but if — '

'Sarah!' It was Maggie. 'Sarah, *look*!' she hissed, nodding at the medium.

For a moment she could see nothing which would explain the horror in Maggie's voice. But then, as the still swinging lamp illuminated the medium's ashen face she saw that what appeared to be mucus had begun oozing from her nostrils.

Hugging the contours of her face, the pearly, viscid liquid crept past the corners of her mouth to the point of her chin, hung for a moment and then dropped to the table like a spider on a thread.

Fed by the continuing flow from her nostrils, the swaying, semi-translucent thread thickened and began to coil around on itself to form what was not so much a pool as a mound. A mound which increasingly took on the colour, texture and consistency of dough.

With a mixture of disgust and indignation, Sarah watched as a bubble trapped within what was clearly intended to be ectoplasm was squeezed into an ellipse as it began its journey from the medium's chin to the table.

It was a trick. A brilliantly engineered trick, but a trick nevertheless.

And yet as she continued to watch, she began to have her doubts.

With the mound growing more voluminous by the minute, it began to take on an asymmetrical shape, as if it was sliding down an inclined surface. Except it wasn't sliding, it was creeping. She was sure of it; creeping by means of what appeared to be wave-like muscular contractions of its underside, like a gigantic slime-mould at the plasmodium stage of its life-cycle.

Praying that the bulb would soon stop pulsing, she watched the leading edge draw itself up to form a warty protuberance. As one peristaltic wave followed another, the protuberance not only lengthened and acquired a more structured appearance, but it, too, began to put out protuberances of its own – grey, wrinkled, finger-like protuberances.

And then suddenly it dawned on Sarah that they weren't just finger-like, they were fingers; four fully-articulated fingers and an opposable thumb.

'Jesus Christ Almighty!' It was a man's voice, but because fear had so tightened the speaker's throat she couldn't be sure if it belonged to Calder or Galbraith.

As a faint, flickering light threw a shadow of the glazing bars on to the blind, the hand flexed, and, just before the bulb finally died, began feeling around as if familiarising itself with the surface on which it was lying.

Above the distant rumble of thunder, she heard Svenson ask Maggie where she'd put the spare bulbs.

'The *what*?'

Svenson's voice became thin and frantic. 'The bulbs! What did you do with the fucken bulbs?'

Without waiting for an answer, Svenson pushed back his chair and went blundering off into the darkness. 'For chrissakes don't anyone switch on a torch or strike a match! With her producing ectoplasm, a bright light could be disastrous! In fact we'd better put something else up in front of the window. A jacket, maybe, or a rug; anything to make sure that the room stays dark . . . '

But the warning had come too late. As she was getting up from her chair, there was an ear-splitting crack and the room was flooded with the dazzling whiteness of forked lightning.

Although the flash could only have lasted a few milliseconds, for what seemed an eternity she could see every detail of the scene confronting her with appalling clarity.

The medium lay sprawled across the table. Attached to

129

her by what had now come to resemble an umbilical cord was the organism she had somehow brought into being. During the few minutes since the bulb had burned out, not only had it quadrupled in size, it had begun to organise itself into a crumpled, partially-formed humanoid. Indeed, the image which came immediately to Sarah's mind was of a car which, having been impacted into a cube, no longer looked like a car, and yet was still clearly recognisable as such.

Although the face – if it had a face – was hidden behind its drawn-up knees, she could see what appeared to be a head and a neck, an arched back and buttocks, elbows and ankles, hands and feet, and what looked like the beginnings of male genitalia.

However, no sooner had she seen it than it was gone. Almost as if air had been let out of a balloon, the creature suddenly shrivelled and went zigzagging back into the medium with a force which lifted her out of her chair. As the room was once again plunged into darkness, Sarah heard her land with a thud against one of the china cabinets.

With the cups still tinkling from the impact, Svenson lunged across the room. 'Someone get a doctor!' he yelled.

No one moved.

From somewhere near where the medium had landed, his voice rose in a lurid scream. 'For Christ's sake will someone get a *doctor*!'

CHAPTER 15

'WELL, HOW is she?' asked Svenson, even before Kessler was through the door of the candle-lit kitchen in which they had been waiting for news of the medium. Although Sarah had said little, Svenson, Maggie and then Adams had spent most of the past hour arguing either among themselves or with Calder and Galbraith about the significance of what had happened during the seance.

'Physically, not too bad,' Kessler replied, taking a seat at the head of the long, well-scrubbed pine table at which the others were sitting. 'The scalp laceration required a couple of stitches and her back's badly bruised, but at least no bones were broken.'

Sarah poured him a mug of coffee from the enamel pot that was being kept warm on one of the original wood-burning stoves. 'So, what happens now?' she asked.

After declining her offer of cream and sugar, Kessler took a packet of Sweet'n'Low from his trouser pocket and tapped two of the tablets into his coffee. 'That depends on how she is in the morning,' he replied, wiping the spoon he had borrowed from Galbraith on the hem of his white coat. 'She'll probably wake up feeling as if she'd gone the distance with the world heavyweight champion, but apart from that she should be fit enough to return home.'

By now the storm had moved out to sea, and above the distant rumble of thunder he added: 'Incidentally, where does she live?'

'Providence, Rhode Island,' Svenson replied, taking his mug across to the stove for more coffee. 'She shares a house with her sister in Providence, but since coming on to the project she's been staying at a hotel in Bar Harbor.'

131

'Why Bar Harbor?'

'We thought that if we had her with us at the lodge, she'd be bound to absorb a lot in the way of background information, which would have made it a bad experiment.'

Kessler nodded. 'If we were to get her back to Bar Harbor, could her sister pick her up from there?'

'Now just hold your horses for a moment!' said Galbraith, lighting a fresh cigarette from the end of the one he had just finished. 'If all she has are a few bruises, why are you in such a hurry to send her home?'

Flapping a hand in front of his face, Kessler extinguished the butt which Galbraith had left smouldering in his overflowing ashtray. 'After what's just happened, why are you so keen on having her stay?'

'Because these people seem to think that she might have been about to materialise Itzhevnikov for us,' he replied, with a nod towards Svenson and Maggie.

Kessler tut-tutted. 'Oh, boy!' he said, shaking his head disbelievingly. 'This whole goddamned operation's getting crazier by the hour. In fact if I didn't know different, I'd have sworn you were all bucking for a Section Eight discharge!'

'Okay, so how *do* you explain what happened?' demanded Galbraith.

Pulling a long face, Kessler spread his hands.

'Well, I'll tell you this much,' said Calder, as soon as he realised that the doctor wasn't to be drawn further, 'if I hadn't been scared rigid I'd have been outta there faster than a greased hog!'

'Anyway, to get back to the question of Mrs Mitchell,' Kessler continued, with a resigned shrug. 'What that lady needs is psychiatric help, not a repeat performance of this evening's fiasco.'

'Psychiatric help!' Svenson started back. 'Oh, c'mon,' he chuckled, 'I've known her for years and she's as sane as I am!'

Kessler looked unimpressed. 'Then God help you, son, because in my book she's showing all the signs of paranoid schizophrenia!'

'She's *what*?' Outraged by the suggestion, Svenson turned to Sarah for support.

'Although I'm no more a psychiatrist than you,' she told Kessler, relishing the opportunity to get back at him for having written her up in his case notes as being emotionally unstable, 'she certainly didn't strike me as being schizoid. An hysteric, maybe, but certainly not — '

'That's because you weren't there to hear her!' he retorted, as Galbraith began coughing. 'Look, before I sedated her she was banging on about how *we're* in danger; how *she's* in danger; in fact according to your Mrs Mitchell even the goddamned *President* is supposed to be in some sort of imminent danger!'

'The President?' Red-faced and with his eyes watering, Galbraith looked up from examining the contents of his handkerchief. 'What the hell's the President got to do with it?' he wheezed.

'She seems to have gotten it into her head that he's due here – here at the house, that is – any day now.'

Thumping his chest, Galbraith turned to look enquiringly at Calder.

'It's the first I've heard of it,' he replied, as the fluorescent lights suddenly pinged on.

'At last!' Sarah got up and began pinching out the candles. 'Anyway, what's that to do with him being in danger?'

'Exactly,' added Calder, as if his professional reputation had in some way been impugned by the suggestion. 'He'd be as safe here as in the White House.'

Kessler shrugged. 'At the time I had more important things on my mind, but according to Mrs Mitchell – ' He paused, mouthing the words silently to himself. 'Yes, what she actually said was that although he'll come here as President and *leave* as President, he'll no longer be the President . . . '

'Are you sure she used the word ''President''?' asked Svenson. 'I mean as distinct from – well, say, emperor or king . . . '

'Sure I'm sure.' Kessler peered at him over the top of his

133

half-frames. 'How else would I have known who she was talking about?' he grumbled, before taking a sip of his coffee. 'But why do you ask?'

'Oh, it's just that it sounds as if it might be a line from a quatrain by Nostradamus . . . ' Svenson looked across at Maggie, but by now she was sprawled across the table with her head cradled in her arms, apparently fast asleep.

'It might sound like it,' she mumbled, 'but it isn't . . . '

Svenson smiled. 'Maggie fancies herself as something of an expert on Nostradamus,' he explained to Kessler. 'What was the line again? Although he will come as President and leave as President — '

' — he will no longer be the President.' Kessler drank some more of his coffee. 'It seemed to me the only way that could happen in mid-term is for him to die while he's here. Although dead, strictly speaking I suppose he'd still be President until such time as the Vice-President was able to take the oath of office.'

'So, what are you suggesting?' asked Calder. 'That we report this to the Secret Service?'

Kessler sighed. 'All I'm suggesting,' he replied, as if regretting that he'd ever introduced the subject, 'is that Mrs Mitchell's in need of psychiatric advice.'

'Just — ' Svenson held up his hands. 'Let's just hold it a minute, huh? Obviously I'll talk to her about all of this first thing in the morning, but let me say here and now that her record at precognition is pretty damned impressive. In fact if he were to decide to pay us a visit, my advice would be to — '

'There's no way that's going to happen,' Calder insisted. 'Quite apart from the fact that the last thing he'll want is to be directly implicated in what's going on up here, right now he has his hands full trying to persuade Congress that his Central America package isn't just money down the tubes.' He yawned. 'Now, I don't know about the rest of you, but I'm about ready to hit the sack.'

Kessler finished his coffee and got up. 'Incidentally, I'm sorry it took us so long to get to Mrs Mitchell,' he said, as Sarah signalled to Svenson and Adams that they were to remain where they were. 'But while you were having your problems down here, we were having our own problems up aloft.'

'What problems were those?' asked Calder, picking up his cap.

'For the third time in twenty-four hours we nearly lost Itzhevnikov.'

Calder groaned. 'Not *again*? What happened this time?'

'The same thing as happened on the previous occasions: his heart suddenly stopped beating,' replied Kessler, crossing to open the door for the Admiral.

'Apart from the problems with his heart, how's he holding up?'

Kessler took a deep breath. 'Right now we're treating him for septicaemia, pneumonia, hepatic failure, fat embolism, gastrointestinal tract haemorrhage – '

'In other words you're saying that all you're *really* doing is holding off the onset of decomposition, right?'

'Right! What I don't understand is *why* we're doing it.'

'We're doing it because no one's prepared to take the decision to stop doing it,' Calder replied, turning to see what had become of Sarah. 'You won't; I won't; the Chairman of the Joint Chiefs won't; and the President's religious scruples won't allow him to. What'll happen if he ever has to authorise a retaliatory nuclear strike, God alone knows!' he added, before asking Sarah if she was ready to leave.

'You go ahead,' she told him. 'I want to talk to Andy and Jack.'

Maggie raised her head. 'Does that mean I can go too?' she asked, bleary-eyed.

'Sure,' she replied, waving goodnight to the others. 'See you in the morning . . . '

'Now,' Sarah began, as soon as they were alone, 'would you mind telling me just what the hell you think you're playing at?'

The two men exchanged looks of total bewilderment.

'Come again?' asked Adams, reaching into a pocket for his wrist-exerciser.

'For a start, I want to know how those tapes of yours were made.'

Adams shrugged. 'Like I told you,' he began, wearily. 'First, I tuned the radio between frequencies — '

'Jack, *please!*' she said, in a manner which suggested that by persisting with his original story he was wasting everyone's time. 'What I want to know is how you *actually* made them, not how you were supposed to have made them.'

'Are you suggesting — ' Apparently lost for words, Adams ran his fingers through his mop of curly red hair. 'Let me get this straight: are you saying that the tapes are phoney?' he asked in a pained, disbelieving voice. 'That I somehow – well, that I *fabricated* them?'

Sarah laughed. 'Of course you fabricated them!' she replied, amused by his display of outraged innocence. 'They're as phoney as a three-dollar bill!'

Adams, however, did not join in her laughter. Tight-lipped and white with anger, he slipped his arms into his crutches, heaved himself up from behind the table and turned to leave.

'Jack,' said Svenson, putting a hand on his shoulder. 'Jack, just cool it . . . ' He turned back to Sarah. 'Look, maybe they aren't EVPs. I haven't heard more than a snatch, so I don't have an opinion one way or the other. But tell me this: what would've been the point of Jack fabricating them?'

'Coming from you that's very funny!' she replied, although she was no longer laughing. Indeed, Adams's indignation had seemed so real that she was beginning to wonder whether her assessment of what had happened was correct. 'Hell, Andy, you were the one who first suggested we should cheat!'

Svenson looked askance. 'I see,' he said, fingering his beard unhappily. 'I was wondering why you'd had so little to say about what happened at the seance. You think that was a put-up job, too, don't you?'

'I'm less certain about the seance than I am about the tapes,' she replied, as Adams lowered himself slowly back into his chair. 'However, this much I do know: of all the

136

areas of mediumistic phenomena, materialisations have unquestionably been the most discredited.

'Look, you've seen Schrenck-Notzing's photographs of figures said to have been materialised by Marte Béraud,' she continued, as she crossed to get the coffee pot. 'I mean, Christ, Andy, they've so obviously been made from cheese-cloth and paper that I don't understand how anyone could ever have been taken in by them.'

'Sure, but as we know from our work with paranormal metal-benders, the occasional appearance of a counterfeit dollar bill doesn't mean that all dollar bills are counterfeit,' Svenson pointed out. 'Now, are you going to answer my question?'

'What question was that?'

'Do you or do you not think that this evening's seance was a put-up job?'

Having refilled their mugs with coffee, Sarah returned to her chair and sat down. 'I think it probably was,' she replied, unwillingly. 'All right, so I've no idea how the trick was worked — '

'But nevertheless you think it was a trick?' Clasping his hands behind his head, Svenson leaned back in his chair and swung his feet up onto the table. 'Okay, well let's see if we can't break it down,' he continued, with the easy confidence of someone who knew they'd only to allow an opponent enough rope and they would eventually hang themselves. 'What about the drop in temperature? How do you think that was worked? And remember, we're talking about a drop of something like forty degrees in as many seconds.'

'Andy, I don't *know*!' she replied, feeling the first stirrings of panic. 'I'm not even sure if any of it actually happened, or whether we just imagined it!'

'Oh, c'mon!' Svenson chuckled. 'I know it happened, Maggie knows it happened, and so does Calder and Galbraith! We couldn't *all* have been imagining things!'

'If we'd been hypnotised we could!' she protested. Although intended as no more than a debating point, it suddenly dawned on her that she might have stumbled upon the truth of what had happened.

137

'But what about the screwed-up tape recorder?' Svenson asked, as she hurriedly assembled the evidence with which to support her contention. 'Are you suggesting that that's a figment of our imaginations?'

'Of course not. However, that proves nothing. Arranging for the recorder to self-destruct would've been as easy as falling off a log.'

Svenson frowned. 'I'm sorry, but now you've lost me completely . . . '

'Me, too,' said Adams, as he began rolling himself a joint. 'Why would anyone want to zap the recorder?'

'To conceal the fact that we were hypnotised!' Sarah replied. 'She'd have had to use some form of induction procedure, and since the recorder was voice-activated it would have been essential to erase the tape.

'Look, it was the perfect set-up for hypnosis,' she continued with renewed confidence. 'For a start, she was allowed — '

'I'm sorry, but when you say "she", are you referring to Maggie or to Mrs Mitchell?' asked Svenson.

'Mrs Mitchell, of course. She was allowed to pick her own sitters; the room was warm, quiet and dimly-lit; and from the outset she talked of little else except how important it was for everyone to relax. With all that going for her, hypnotising us would have been no problem. And once hypnotised, having us all experience the identical positive hallucination would have been a push-over.

'Goddammit,' she added as Adams put a match to the joint and inhaled deeply, 'how else do you explain why not a single piece of china or glass was broken; why there was no sign of rain on the window-sill even though it was pouring at the time; that the — '

'Hold it right there,' said Svenson. 'Okay, so I agree that the whole thing could have been a positive hallucination induced under hypnosis.' He shrugged. 'I don't believe it was, but it could've been. However, let me ask you this: without testing for hypnotic susceptibility, how would she have known who to pick?'

'No problem!' Sarah began counting off points on the

fingers of her left hand. 'One: you knew from the experiments we did a couple of years ago on psi-favourable states that both Maggie and I are susceptible. Two: she *did* test, or at least she tested for suggestibility. If you remember, by the time she'd finished with Calder he'd have been prepared to swear that black was white!'

'Oh, really, Sarah!' exclaimed Svenson, as if he had just caught her cheating at solitaire. 'To have known whether or not Calder was susceptible she'd have had to have him take the sway test, or the hand-clasp test. And anyway, what about Galbraith? How would she have known to pick him? As I recall, he didn't say or do a thing while we were in the hall . . . '

'He didn't have to!' she protested. 'Jack knew he'd become hooked on the whole survival deal from listening to the tapes. He could have told you, and you could have told Mrs Mitchell!'

Adams looked at his wristwatch. 'Listen you guys, we're just going round in circles,' he said, passing the joint to Svenson. 'So, why don't we agree to do this? Why don't we give this Mitchell dame a couple of days to get over what happened and then try again, only next time we'll video the whole show? Hell, we could even monitor her body weight to see if any loss occurs should she succeed in materialising another figure. And if she does, we could try getting it to plunge its hands into a bowl of paraffin wax so we can compare the shells with Itzhevnikov's hands. We could use a thermography camera to try to understand what happens when the temperature drops, and a gaussmeter to — '

'Jack!' Shaking her head, Sarah crossed to the window to reassure herself that it had finally stopped raining. 'Jack, it all sounds great except for one small detail,' she told him. 'There's no way Mrs Mitchell would ever agree to play ball!' Returning to the table, she began gathering up the empty coffee mugs. 'Have you ever heard of a medium who would? According to Andy, she wasn't exactly wild about the idea of there being a tape recorder in the room!'

Svenson stifled a yawn. 'We can but try,' he said, as the wall-mounted telephone began ringing. 'Now, as for the question of Jack's EVPs, why don't we just wait and see how he makes out in the screened room using factory-fresh tapes and equipment?' he suggested, before finally getting up to answer the phone. 'If he continues to get results under those conditions we'll know we're on to something pretty damned interesting . . . '

Svenson lifted the handset, listened for a moment, and after saying 'We'll be right with you!', hung up.

'It's Mrs Mitchell,' he said, turning back to the others. 'Something's happened to Mrs Mitchell!'

Sarah followed Svenson up the service staircase two steps at a time, and through a labyrinth of dark, draughty passage-ways.

'What do you think that is?' she asked, as she suddenly became aware of a faint, somewhat sweet but sickly smell.

'It's – I dunno, it's as if someone's been barbecuing spare-ribs,' he replied, as they turned into the brightly lit corridor leading to the ICU.

Ahead of her she could see two nurses and a steel-helmeted member of the Shore Patrol standing outside the open door of the room in which she had spent part of the previous night. Although the SP made no attempt to prevent Svenson from entering, when Sarah tried to follow him he blocked her way. 'I wouldn't go in there, ma'am,' he told her. 'Not right now, I wouldn't.'

Ignoring his warning and the warning from one of the ashen-faced nurses, she pushed past him, only to be brought to an abrupt halt by a scene from a nightmare. 'Oh, my God,' she cried, clapping a hand to her mouth.

Even though the windows were wide open, the room was stiflingly hot and the ceiling was hidden behind a pall of blue-grey smoke.

The medium was lying with her head on the pillow and her left leg hanging over the side of the bed as if she had been about to get up. However, apart from the leg, her head, shoulders, and the hand she'd used to throw aside the blankets, her body had been reduced to ashes.

140

'I don't get it,' said Kessler, turning away from Sarah and Svenson to stare disbelievingly at the empty, crumbling pelvis and the heat-eroded prosthetic hip joint that were lying on top of the mattress's exposed coil springs. 'I just do not get it. I mean, how the hell could this have happened to a hundred and seventy pound woman in just half an hour?'

The chief of the naval fire-fighting crew – a big-bellied, red-faced man who was perspiring heavily – looked up from examining the underside of the bed. 'And it's not just the speed at which she burned-up that's weird about this one,' he told them, as a sudden breeze stirred the hair on the medium's head. 'Okay, so I know subcutaneous fat catches fire easily, but when you remember it takes anything up to four hours at two thousand degrees Fahrenheit to incinerate a body in a crematorium, the heat required to do this in just half an hour must have been like outta this *world*!

'And yet look,' he continued, clambering to his feet to shine his flashlight on the bedhead. 'The fucken paint hasn't even blistered! You know something?' he added, shaking his head as if unable to believe the evidence of his own eyes. 'I've been fighting fires for more years than I care to remember, and this has to be the goddamndest thing I've *ever* seen! I kid you not . . . '

'Have you ever come across the term ''Spontaneous Human Combustion''?' asked Svenson, glancing over his shoulder to reassure himself that Sarah was still all right.

The fireman lifted his helmet and wiped his brow with the back of his hand. 'Sure, but I never really believed it was possible. And anyway, how was she supposed to have got the fire started in the first place?' he asked, looking around the room. 'There's no sign of any matches; the fireplace is boarded-over; and the candles were removed as soon as the lights came back on again.'

'Ah, but the thing about SHC is that the heat appears to originate from *inside* the victim's body,' Svenson explained, as Piroschka and another naval officer entered the room carrying a green zippered body-bag. 'One theory is that the bones in some way act as dielectric resonators.'

'They *what*?' exclaimed Kessler. 'How can bones possibly

141

act as dielectric resonators?'

'You'll probably think it bullshit,' Svenson warned, as he brushed away a speck of soot which had settled on his nose, 'but the work we've done on psychic healers suggests they're able to release an as-yet-unidentified source of energy.

'Now, supposing it were possible for this energy to suddenly go critical – and the likelihood seems to be that it originates within the skeleton – it might well cause the bones to act as dielectric resonators, turning the victim into what is in effect a microwave oven.'

'Umm . . . ' Kessler took out a handkerchief and began polishing his spectacles. 'Tell me, do you think that this has anything to do with what happened downstairs?'

'How do you mean?'

'*By the blast of God they perish, and by the breath of his nostrils are they consumed.*' Kessler put his spectacles back on again and pocketed his handkerchief. '*The Book of Job,*' he explained, with an embarrassed smile. 'Anyway, disregarding the divine retribution angle, could there be a connection? I mean, perhaps I shouldn't have been so dismissive when you talked earlier of – what was it again? – ''psychic reper- cussion''?'

However, before Svenson had a chance to reply, Piroschka cut in to ask the fireman if there was any more he and his men had to do.

'Apart from clearing up, no, I don't think so,' he replied, as he began gathering together the fire extinguishers that were scattered about the room.

With his arms spread wide, Piroschka moved Sarah, Svenson and Kessler towards the door.

'What're you going to do with her now?' she asked, watching his companion as he laid the body-bag alongside the bed and unzipped it.

'Don't you worry about any of that,' replied Piroschka, as he continued to back them towards the door. 'It's all being taken care of.'

Through the open windows, Sarah heard a jeep screech to a halt on the forecourt. 'But I *am* worried,' she insisted. 'Quite apart from anything else, what're we to tell her sister?'

'You're to tell no one a damned thing,' Piroschka replied. 'As far as you're concerned, Mrs Mitchell was never here, okay?

'Look,' he continued, less aggressively, 'if we were to play it by the book we'd find ourselves up to our asses in cops, Feds, medical examiners and the goddamned media, and believe me, that would be as much a disaster for you as it would be for us. So just try to forget all about it.' He moved her aside to allow two men carrying decorator's equipment into the room. 'By sunrise, it'll be as if nothing's happened.'

Out of the corner of her eye, Sarah saw Calder striding down the corridor, his hands thrust deep into the pockets of a blue raincoat. 'Admiral, we've got to talk to you.'

'In the morning . . . ' he replied, as he attempted to push past.

Sarah stood her ground. 'No, now!'

Muttering under his breath, Calder opened the door of a room across the corridor from the one in which the medium had died and switched on the lights. Followed by Svenson and Piroschka, Sarah entered and looked around. Apart from a few boxes of medical supplies and some intravenous stands, the room was bare.

'Well, what is it?' he demanded, closing the door behind them. He was looking tired and dishevelled, and by now was in need of a shave.

'I want to know what's to happen to Mrs Mitchell.'

'Hasn't the major explained?'

'He hasn't told us what's to happen to her,' replied Sarah. 'Only why it has to happen. Or rather, why he *thinks* it has to happen.'

Calder rubbed a hand over his stubbled chin. 'Is there any real reason why we shouldn't tell 'em?' he asked Piroschka. 'I mean, they're going to find out eventually, so why not now?'

'It's up to you,' he replied, in a manner which suggested that while he was prepared to accede to the admiral's wishes, he would be doing so against his better judgement.

143

Calder turned back to the others. 'Right, what'll happen is this: we're going to fix it to look as if Mrs Mitchell crashed her car – '

'But she came up here by plane!' Sarah protested. 'Christ, I'm not even sure she could *drive*!'

'The first thing she did after checking in at her hotel was hire herself a Lincoln Continental.'

'She did *what*?'

Calder shrugged. 'I guess she thought that since Uncle Sam would be picking up the tab, she might as well. We didn't worry too much because – well, I guess that's what folks do when they're on vacation.'

'But she wasn't *on* vacation!'

'She told her sister she was.' Piroschka nodded towards Svenson. 'At your colleague's suggestion, as a matter of fact.'

Sarah clapped a hand to her forehead. 'She might have *said* she'd tell her sister that, but how do you know she did?'

'Because we've just had someone call her, and they were told she was vacationing at Bar Harbor,' replied Piroschka. 'And before you ask, the reason we had one of our own people drive her here this evening is that if we'd left it to her she'd probably not have made it. Judging by the number of citations she's had over the years,' he added, with a wry smile, 'driving wasn't one of her strong points!'

'Which is why Hank's scenario is a good one,' Calder pointed out.

Svenson began shaking his head. 'You'll never get away with it,' he told them. 'Even the hottest gasolene fire doesn't approach the kind of temperatures required to produce such massive destruction. And if you don't believe me, check with your fire officer.'

'We already have,' said Piroschka. 'And according to him it isn't the extent of the destruction which is significant, but the speed at which it occurred.' He paused to look anxiously at his wristwatch. 'We're planning to have her come off the road at a spot where she won't be found 'til morning, so providing we don't waste any more time here the fire will

144

have been burning long enough for it all to seem perfectly kosher.'

'Look, I can understand perfectly well how you feel,' Calder told them, in a softer, more sympathetic tone of voice. 'And if playing it by the book would bring her back that's what we'd do. Obviously. But since it won't, why not do it this way? Mrs Mitchell will still get a decent burial; any insurance she has won't be prejudiced — '

'All right!' said Sarah, pressing her fingertips to her forehead. 'I'll go along with it, but on one condition: *I* must be the one who breaks it to her sister. Goddammit,' she added, suddenly near to tears, 'if we hadn't asked her up here she'd still be alive . . . '

'Do you know her sister?' asked Piroschka.

Sarah took a handkerchief from her pocket. 'No, I don't,' she replied, before blowing her nose. 'But I do know she's very old and frail.'

'Do you?' he asked Svenson.

'No, I'm afraid I don't either . . . '

'That's great!' Piroschka turned away, exasperated. 'That's just *great*!'

'I see what Hank's getting at,' said Calder, scratching the side of his face unhappily. 'Having you suddenly turn up is going to seem mighty odd, isn't it?'

'I don't see why,' she replied. 'Although I myself hadn't met Mrs Mitchell until this evening, she's had a long association with Biotec.'

'What d'you think?' asked Calder.

Piroschka sighed wearily. 'I suppose if it'll make her feel any less guilty she'd better go ahead,' he replied, crossing to the door. 'But *after* the news has broken, not before.'

'It's not a question of making me feel less guilty,' she called after him. 'I just want to be sure that everything possible is done for the sister.'

Slipping a hand beneath her shoulder-length hair, she began massaging her aching neck. 'So, when can I reasonably have heard the news?' she asked Calder.

'Hank?'

'I guess they'll have identified the remains in time to

145

make the morning papers.'

'*Tomorrow's* papers?'

'No, Tuesday's,' he replied, opening the door. 'I'm sorry, but I really am going to have to go . . .'

'All right, then I'll take the first available flight to Rhode Island on Wednesday morning,' she told Calder.

CHAPTER 16

WITH HER mind numbed by what she had witnessed, Sarah collected her things from the kitchen, said goodnight to Adams and Svenson and left the house.

As she picked her way between the puddles on the sodden forecourt the crescent moon was swallowed up by scudding cloud and once again it began raining.

Although too dark to see inside her jeep, as she reached for the door handle she was seized by the feeling that there was someone waiting for her.

Wishing that she'd taken the trouble to have the interior light repaired, she opened the door and peered inside. 'Hello?' she said, pushing back her wind-tousled hair. 'Hello, who's that?'

There was no reply.

However, so powerful was the sense of presence that in spite of the rain she considered returning to the house, saying she'd been unable to start the jeep.

'Oh, shit!' she exclaimed, aware that to have done so would have meant ruining her already badly-spotted doeskin skirt.

With one swift, decisive movement she slipped into the driver's seat, slammed the door, and, after buckling on her seat belt, turned the key in the ignition and snapped on the headlights, wipers and heater.

In an attempt to exorcise the now faint but still lingering sense of presence, she found an all-night pop music station on the radio, revved the engine several times and went roaring down the avenue of wind-lashed beeches.

After the Marines manning the checkpoint had waved her past the raised red-and-white pole, she eased the nose of the

147

jeep out on to the narrow coast road, looked right, left and right again, then pulled away. Buffeted by the wind and with her view of the road ahead reduced by the torrential rain that was swirling in her main beams, she eased the speed up to thirty m.p.h. and held it there; anxious as she was to get back to the lodge and into a hot bath, to have driven any faster on a night such as this would have been suicidal.

With the music becoming increasingly inaudible because of static, she switched off the radio, and, for the first time since leaving Seacrest, glanced at her rear-view mirror to reassure herself that the road behind was clear.

What she saw there almost caused her to lose control of the jeep: although the face was hers, the unblinking, hypnotic eyes that were staring mockingly back at her were definitely not hers.

Although by now a mile or more from the house, such was her terror that she immediately pulled over to the side of the road with the intention of abandoning the jeep. However, when she attempted to transfer her right foot from the gas to the brake pedal she found she was unable to move it.

'Jesus, no!' she cried, as all of her repressed fears erupted with an almost explosive force.

Fighting to keep control both of herself and the vehicle, she slammed her left foot hard down on to the brake pedal. As the jeep went aquaplaning across the flooded road, she somehow managed to steer it out of the skid, pumped the brakes for a moment, then changed from third to second. But with her immobilised right foot still pressing down on the gas pedal, instead of reducing speed the move to a lower gear only increased it still further.

Not daring to look into the mirror again, she glanced over her shoulder to make sure that the road behind was still clear, switched off the ignition and began pumping the brakes until the car had rolled silently to a standstill. Without stopping to move the gearshift into neutral or apply the handbrake, she unfastened her seat belt, threw open the door and went to get out, only to discover that she was still unable to lift her foot from the gas pedal.

Grabbing hold of her ankle, she tried to pull the foot free but still she could not move it. Pausing before making another attempt, she heard the key turn in the ignition. The engine caught immediately and the jeep shot forward. Horrified, she seized the wheel with one hand and slammed the door with the other. After steering back on to her side of the road, she re-buckled her seat belt and once again went to switch off the engine. However, although she could feel the ignition key between her finger and thumb, she seemed to have lost either the will or the ability to turn it.

Switching her left foot from the brake to the clutch pedal, she tried to move the gearshift into neutral, but again the muscles of her right arm were unable to execute the command.

Through eyes now blurred with tears, she suddenly became aware of taillights in the road ahead of her. With the speedometer needle touching forty-five and climbing, it was not long before she saw that they belonged to an ancient Ford pickup truck.

Aware that they were approaching a blind hillbrow followed by a narrow, winding descent into a valley, she felt herself break into a cold sweat. Although the road was still wide enough to overtake, no one in their right mind would ever have attempted to do so. And yet if the pickup trundling along in front of her didn't increase its speed to match hers she'd have no option but to overtake. Either that or run smack into the back of it.

As the distance between the two vehicles shortened, she flashed her headlights and began hammering on the horn. But it was to no avail: instead of accelerating, the driver of the pickup began to brake.

There was now only one course open to her: she would have to overtake and hope to God that nothing was coming up the hill.

Taking a deep breath, she braced herself, flicked down the turn indicator and pulled out.

As they crested the hill side by side she was suddenly blinded by the headlights of an oncoming vehicle. Swinging the steering wheel violently to the right, she cut in ahead of

149

the pickup only just in time to avoid a head-on collision with a Mercedes Tourer.

With the blare of its horn still ringing in her ears and the driver of the pickup furiously flashing his headlights at her, she prepared herself for what lay ahead: a right turn so tight that even on a dry, bright day she'd always taken it at a snail's pace. For a moment she considered running the car into one of the steep, grassy banks flanking the road, but quickly put the thought from her mind. At the speed she was travelling she would almost certainly have been flipped over. However, providing she didn't lose control while trying to take the corner and wasn't rammed as she crossed the intersection at the foot of the hill, the chances were that the car would stall while climbing out of the valley, if, that is, she was able to get it into top gear.

Keeping tight to her side of the road she drove straight at the turn, waited until the front wheels were clear of the bank to her right, then stood on the brakes. Throwing up a great sheet of grit and water, the jeep immediately went squealing into a clockwise skid. With a bone-jarring thud it slammed against the left-hand bank and stopped, its rear wheels spinning impotently in the torrent of muddy water that was cascading down the ditch alongside the road.

However, as she was about to make another attempt to get out the wheels suddenly caught, hurling the car across the road to bury its nose in the grassy bank opposite.

As she was flung violently forward, something seemed to break deep inside her. 'Oh God, no!' she cried. After snapping open her seat belt, she reached into the glove compartment for a flashlight, pulled the blouse from the waistband of her skirt and peered down. Relieved to discover that whatever it was she could feel seeping into her lap wasn't blood, she began cautiously checking herself for other injuries.

By now the driver of the pickup – a lantern-jawed old man in blue farmer's coveralls – had caught up with her. 'Whaddaya think you're playing at, lady?' he bellowed, as he clambered down from the cabin and came hobbling across to her. 'Goddammit, anyone with a lick of sense

150

would've known that what you did back there could've gotten us all killed!'

Sarah began to apologise, but, suddenly relenting a little, the farmer interrupted her to ask if she was all right.

'I think so,' she replied, as he bent to help her out of her seat. 'Just a little shaken up, I guess . . . '

'You and me, too,' he grumbled. 'So, for Pete's sake what happened?'

'It was the gas pedal,' she told him, hunching her shoulders against the rain. 'I don't know how, but the gas pedal seems to have got stuck . . . '

The farmer kicked one of the front tyres. 'And you didn't think to switch off the engine?' he asked, as if unable to believe that even a woman driver could have overlooked so obvious a move.

'I did, but something seems to have gone wrong with that, too,' she replied, miserably.

Muttering to himself, he climbed into the car, started it with one turn of the ignition key, reversed it off the bank, straightened-up and stopped. Although the front fender was bent and the fog lamp shattered, it was now running perfectly.

As the farmer began sermonising about her lucky escape, Sarah suddenly remembered the phial of holy water which Mrs Mitchell had given her earlier that evening. Slipping her fingers into her cardigan pocket she felt shards of broken glass and a sodden handkerchief. 'Good God!' she exclaimed, as the truth of what had happened seemed to dawn on her: not only was she now free of whatever it was which had held her in its power since first getting into the car, but it had left her at the very instant that the phial of holy water had been crushed between her body and the seat belt.

However, by the time the farmer had escorted her to the lodge she had formulated another, seemingly more rational theory to account for her terrifying experience. What had happened was that one part of herself – the part which disapproved of her participation in what was happening at Seacrest – had tried to destroy the part which, for the sake of

151

expediency, was prepared to go along with what was happening.

Not that she derived any comfort from such an interpretation. Quite the contrary; she would have been far less worried had she been able to lay the blame on a jinxed car or a possessing entity which had been exorcised with a sprinkling of holy water. However, viewed in the context of all that had happened to her since coming on to the project it could mean only one thing: as Kessler had suspected, she was badly in need of psychiatric help – help she promised herself she would seek the moment she was free to return to Boston.

Although she'd been dreading her coming visit to Rhode Island, as she got ready for bed she suddenly found herself almost looking forward to it. Not only would it help assuage her guilt about what had happened to Mrs Mitchell it would also give her a much needed break from what she was by now convinced was the cause of all her troubles: the claustrophobic, anxiety-laden atmosphere of Seacrest and her absurd but none the less obscene attempt to commit what must surely be the ultimate act of desecration.

CHAPTER 17

'SO, WHERE do we go from here?' asked Calder, as soon as everyone was seated at the leather-topped table which had been moved from the library to the living-hall while a replacement for the first screened room was being erected.

'I guess we begin our EVP trials,' replied Svenson.

Calder looked questioningly at Sarah.

'When do you expect them to be through with everything?' she asked, turning to peer down the table at Adams.

'Within the next hour or so,' he replied, between sips of his coffee. 'However, we're unlikely to be fully operational until this evening.'

'This evening?' Calder exclaimed. 'But Dr Stuart will've left for Rhode Island by then . . . '

Adams shrugged. 'Is it my fault that they goofed-up with the equipment?' he asked, wiping his Zapata moustache with the back of his hand. 'If they'd sent us what we asked for we wouldn't have had to sit around kicking our heels for the past two days.'

'Yes, well . . . ' said Calder, before turning back to Sarah. 'What is it they say about the best laid schemes of mice and men?'

'Gang aft a-gley,' she replied, exaggerating her soft Scots accent. 'Anyway, I'll be back in forty-eight hours, so there's no real problem.'

'Fine, then perhaps Dr Adams would like to fill us in on what will be happening when everything is in a Go condition . . . '

As soon as he had finished his coffee, Adams crossed to a blackboard which had been set up in front of the inglenook, picked up a piece of chalk and drew a plan of the library as it

153

would appear with the equipment installed. 'This,' he began, pointing to a square near the right-hand edge of the blackboard, 'represents the screened room, right? Now, the idea is that I'll be inside it relaying your questions to the tape recorder. Each of us will be equipped with — '

'Just hold it a minute,' said Piroschka, narrowing his eyes. 'Why does it have to be you who's in the screened room? Quite apart from anything else, you don't - or so you'd have us believe - speak a single word of Russian.'

'No, but Itzhevnikov understands English even if he chooses to answer in Russian,' he replied, ignoring Piroschka's jibe.

'Even so, why scratch your ear with your foot when you have a hand?'

'And just what is that supposed to mean?' asked Adams, laying aside the chalk.

'It means that I think it would make more sense if we had one of our own people in the screened room.'

'Huh-huh.' After brushing the chalk dust from his fingers, Adams picked up his crutches and began making his way back to the table. 'Well, if you still don't trust me,' he began, in a hurt voice, 'I guess there's nothing for it but to — '

'It's not my job to trust you,' Piroschka told him. 'Now, if you'd been prepared to take a polygraph test — '

Adams stopped dead in his tracks. 'But I *was* prepared to take one!' he cried, indignantly. 'For chrissakes, it was the Admiral who said it would be a waste of time!'

Oh no, not again! thought Sarah. However, having confronted Adams and Svenson with her suspicions she was now far less certain that a polygraph test would expose them as cheats. So much less certain that she found herself thinking that it would be no bad thing if they *were* to take the tests, if only to remove the last lingering traces of doubt from her own mind.

Calder grimaced. 'The fact that our parapsychology friends haven't taken lie-detector tests really is bugging you, isn't it?' he asked, in a voice which betrayed his concern.

'I just think it's bad security.'

Looking suddenly very discomforted, Calder ran a finger around the inside of his shirt collar. 'Well, I guess if you feel *that* strongly about it . . . '

'I'll be goddamned!' exclaimed Adams, lifting his baseball cap to scratch his head. 'Have you guys taken a look at my army record? I did two tours of duty in Nam, where I was awarded the Legion of Merit, the Bronze Star and the — '

Calder nodded. 'He's right, y'know,' he told Piroschka. 'His service record is as good as any man stationed here.'

'So was Lieutenant Colonel What's-his-name's – the one who was working in the Pentagon – but that didn't stop him from betraying his country!'

After Calder had insisted on Piroschka apologising to Adams, he turned to Sarah and said: 'If we *were* to ask you to take a lie-detector test, would you still feel that your integrity was somehow being impugned?'

'I guess not,' she replied, with a resigned shrug. 'However, let's not forget one thing: because no one is more anxious than us that this experiment should be beyond reproach, it's been designed to rule out any possibility of experimenter fraud. Whoever's finally chosen for the screened room will have video cameras trained on them the whole time; they'll be working with sealed, two-track tape — '

Calder nodded. 'So what you're saying is that even if anyone was predisposed to cheat, there's no way they'd be able to?'

'Exactly,' she replied, as the man from the CIA picked up a telephone which had begun ringing. 'Still, if taking lie-detector tests will make you feel easier, let's take 'em and have done with it.'

'It's the checkpoint to say they have a Major Lawford from the Army Medical Corps to see you.'

'Me?' Calder shook his head. 'It must be Kessler he wants . . . '

'Not according to the checkpoint.'

'Here, let me have it,' said Piroschka, reaching around the back of Maggie for the handset.

After questioning the guard for a moment, he interrupted Calder to say: 'Apparently he's here on some sort of inspection. I've no idea what it's all about, other than that he's come armed with a letter from the Chairman of the Joint Chiefs . . . '

'Hell's teeth! This is supposed to be a top secret operation and they're sending guys in off the street!'

'Do you want me to call General Brogan's office?' enquired Piroschka.

Calder considered the proposal for a moment. 'If this guy Lawford is listed and the letter looks kosher, let's not get into that kind of hassle.'

After telling the guard to hold the major at the gate until he rang back, Piroschka left the room.

When he returned several minutes later he was carrying a sheet of hard copy. 'Well, he's here all right,' he told Calder. 'Lawford, Melvin F., Born Hartford, Connecticut, 1938, the second son of General and Mrs — '

'In that case you'd better have 'em send him down,' said Calder, rubbing his red-rimmed eyes. 'Oh, and while you're on the horn see if you can raise Kessler . . . '

Major Melvin F. Lawford turned out to be a thin, freckle-faced, prematurely bald man wearing rimless spectacles and carrying a brown leather document case. 'I'm sorry to have arrived unannounced,' he told Calder, transferring his trench coat from his right to his left arm in order to shake hands, 'but I was assured that would be taken care of by someone in the Joint Chiefs' office.'

Calder finished reading the letter the major had produced from the tunic of his immaculate dress uniform and passed it to Piroschka. 'Ah, well, these things happen,' he replied, with a resigned smile. 'Anyway, what can we do for you?'

'With respect, Admiral,' he replied, fingering the lobe of his right ear as if embarrassed by the question, 'it's not so much what you can do for me, but what I can do for you.'

'How do you mean?' asked Piroschka, handing the letter back to him.

156

'I take it you're still having problems with — ' The major paused to glance uncertainly at the parapsychologists.

'With Itzhevnikov, do you mean?' asked Calder.

'Exactly!' he replied, as if relieved to find himself able to speak freely.

'We are, but frankly I don't quite see how — '

The major shrugged. 'General Brogan thought I might be able to help in some way,' he explained in a manner which suggested that he did not necessarily share his superior's optimism. 'Anyway, now I'm here I guess I may as well take a look. Providing, of course, that you and Commander Kessler have no objections.'

'No, none at all,' replied Calder. 'However, I'm afraid the commander isn't expected back much before noon.'

'Noon!' The major glanced anxiously at his wristwatch. 'To be honest with you, I was hoping to be back in Bangor by then . . . '

Calder turned to Piroschka. 'Who's minding the store this morning?'

'Only the nursing staff,' he replied. 'Still, I guess we could always wake O'Hanlon . . . '

'Dr O'Hanlon is second-in-command of the medical team,' Calder explained.

'And he has just come off duty?'

'He has, but I'm sure he — '

The major shook his head. 'In that case I wouldn't hear of it,' he said. 'Look, all I need to do is reassure the general that everything that can be done for the patient is being done – and knowing the commander's reputation I've no doubt it is – and that'll be the end of the matter.

'So,' he added, with an understanding smile, 'why don't you have one of your nurses give me an update on the situation and I'll leave you to get on with more important matters?'

'Well, how did you find him?' asked Calder, when, escorted by a nurse, Major Lawford returned from visiting the ICU ten minutes later.

157

'Although admittedly he's in pretty bad shape, there's no way anyone could do more for him than is already being done right here, which is what I'll tell the general on my return to Washington.'

Looking relieved and somewhat surprised that the major's visit should have ended as quickly and satisfactorily as it had, Calder asked him if he and his driver would like coffee.

'It's a nice idea,' he replied, almost wistfully, 'but I think we'd better be cutting along.'

After shaking hands with the nurse, Calder and Piroschka, the major nodded his goodbyes to the others and left.

However, no sooner had he closed the door behind him when Adams grabbed hold of his crutches, hoisted himself to his feet and went hobbling after him. 'Major, hold it a minute!' he yelled, as he yanked open the door.

'What's gotten into him?' asked Calder, twisting around in his chair.

'I've no idea,' replied Sarah, as the major's jeep pulled away from the front of the house.

Through the open door she saw Adams turn to speak to one of the guards.

'Hank, will you find out just what the hell is going on?' However, the words were barely out of Calder's mouth when Adams suddenly threw aside his crutches and snatched the automatic rifle from the guard. As he went to retrieve it Adams drove the stock into the guard's solar plexus, and, as he doubled up, brought the barrel hard down on to the back of his exposed neck.

With the speed of a striking cobra the second guard hurled himself at Adams, only to be sent crashing through the veranda railings by a great scything blow to the side of his head.

Bracing himself against one of the pillars, Adams raised the rifle to his shoulder, took aim at the now rapidly retreating jeep and fired.

'Oh my God, *no*!' screamed Sarah, rising to her feet. With the sound of the shot still reverberating around the

158

hall, she saw the driver throw up his arms. It's tyres squealing, the jeep veered off the driveway, mounted the grass verge and crashed into one of the purple beeches, sending the major hurtling through the blood-spattered windshield.

'Freeze!' yelled Adams, as the major reappeared from out of the smoke rising from the crumpled hood and began pulling himself painfully up into the passenger seat.

After turning the visor of his baseball cap to the back of his head, Adams tightened his grip on the rifle, squinted along the sights and once again squeezed the trigger. There was a sharp *rat-a-tat-tat*, a flicker of flame from the muzzle, and, as the last of the brass cartridge cases flashed briefly in the morning sun, the major's bald head blew apart like an egg.

Laying aside the still smoking rifle, Adams turned to confront the stunned and silent onlookers in the hall. 'Are there any bomb disposal people on the base?' he asked, as unruffled as if he had just come in from shooting skeet.

'Bomb disposal people?' echoed Calder, in a faint, disbelieving voice.

Adams nodded towards the men who were now racing towards the stalled jeep. 'And someone had better tell those dudes to back off – there's a radio-controlled detonator somewhere aboard that thing.'

After a moment of hesitation, Piroschka snatched the handset from one of the telephones and ordered that a warning be relayed over the public address system.

'I knew something wasn't quite right when Lawford turned up wearing a Korean campaign ribbon,' Adams explained, above the hubbub from the driveway. 'If he wasn't born until 1938 there was no way he could have served in Korea. And then when he returned from upstairs without his attaché case — '

'His *attaché* case!' exclaimed Calder. 'But he had it when he left!'

'He had his raincoat but not his case,' said Adams, glancing over his shoulder. 'That was the other thing that struck me as odd: why carry a raincoat on a day like this except as a cover for leaving the case behind?

159

'Anyway, go take a look for yourselves,' he added, before turning to help one of the still dazed guards to his feet. 'Five'll get you ten it'll be behind Itzhevnikov's bed.'

'I just hope you're right, son,' said Calder, ominously. 'By God I hope you're right . . .'

By the time everyone had been allowed back into the house the bomb had been defused, and, along with its radio-controlled detonator, removed by a Navy bomb disposal team.

'It seems as if the real Major Lawford is alive and well and stationed in Indiana,' announced Piroschka, as he rejoined the others. 'Although we still haven't come up with a positive ID on his stand-in, the driver has been identified as one Daniel Nathan Goldberg, a small-time hood from Miami who was mixed up with the pro-Castro movement back in the late sixties.'

'You're not suggesting that this was carried out on the orders of Castro, are you?' asked Adams.

Piroschka shook his head. 'This is definitely KGB,' he replied. 'I guess their only reason for picking him was that as a known communist sympathiser he could be relied upon not to go running to the Feds.'

'So, what do we do now?' asked Kessler, who had arrived back at the house only minutes earlier. 'If we have to move Itzhevnikov again the chances are we'll lose him.'

'I don't think there's any reason to move him,' replied Piroschka. 'Let's face it, they'd have to be out of their minds to try anything like this again.'

'I agree,' said Calder, as he set out to make the rounds with a bottle of brandy. 'However, what does worry me is that since they obviously believe him to be alive, anything we do get from him will be worthless.'

'Why?' asked Sarah, waving away his offer to re-fill her glass.

'Because if Moscow thinks he's still alive they'll be busy unscrambling as many of the plans he was privy to as is humanly possible,' Calder explained.

'Except wait a minute,' he continued, coming to an abrupt standstill behind Adams's chair. 'Of course! Whoever tipped them off as to his whereabouts must only know half the story! If they knew he was brain-dead, what would've been the point of trying to assassinate him?'

'Good thinking,' said the man from the CIA.

Calder placed a fatherly hand on Adams's shoulder. 'Now, if we were to let it be known that Goldberg and his buddy had *succeeded* with their mission . . . '

'But how do we do that with them both on their way to The Farm in body-bags?' asked Adams.

'No sweat,' said the man from the CIA. 'Whoever tipped off the Russians has to be working in one of our intelligence agencies, in which case all we have to do is route a memo through all the departments which knew we had Itzhevnikov saying he's been zapped!'

'But what about Jack's point?' asked Piroschka.

The man from the CIA shrugged. 'Again, no sweat,' he told him. 'In the memo we say that they triggered the bomb prematurely and were gunned down while attempting to make their getaway!'

'I know I was pretty zonked out at the time,' said Maggie, pressing her fingertips to her temples, 'but didn't someone say something about the *firing* mechanism having short-circuited?'

'They did, and it had,' replied Calder. 'But the perpetrators wouldn't have known that.'

'Okay, but according to the bomb disposal officer there was enough explosive in that thing to have blown away the corner of the house,' Piroschka pointed out. 'So, what happens if they send someone up to take a look?'

'They find we've covered the corner of the house with a tarpaulin!' said Calder, with the easy grace of a conjurer producing a rabbit from a hat. 'And to make it look even more as if we've something to hide, we leak a story to the local press saying the house was damaged during the storm! Now,' he added, turning to look back at Sarah, 'shouldn't you be leaving for Rhode Island?'

'You mean I can go in *spite* of what's happened?'

'I don't see why not, do you?' he asked Piroschka.

'Not if it's something she still has a hankering to do . . . '

Feeling as if she had just been woken from a nightmare, she bundled her things together and left before anyone had a chance to change their mind.

CHAPTER 18

WHEN SARAH returned to Seacrest on the following Saturday, she found the gates guarded by civilians as well as Marines.

'May I see your ID, ma'am?' asked a young man wearing a three-piece suit and what looked like a hearing aid. Although it was dusk, his eyes were hidden behind a pair of steel-rimmed sunglasses.

'What's this all about?' she asked, passing him the card.

Without replying, he checked it against the clipboard he was carrying, compared her with the photograph and handed it back. 'And how was your trip? Cape Cod, wasn't it?'

'As a matter of fact it was Rhode Island . . . '

'Ah, yes!' he said, eyeing the suitcases that were lying on the back seat of the jeep. 'I'm sorry, but we're going to have to take a look inside those.'

'You *what*?' she exclaimed, as he handed one of the cases to the colleague who'd been inspecting the rear of the vehicle, and the other to a Marine. 'Just what *is* going on here?'

'If you'd bring your purse with you and step this way, please,' he said, opening the door of the jeep.

Still protesting, she followed the men into the brightly lit sentry booth and unlocked her luggage.

The man in the sunglasses held out his hand. 'If you've no objection, I'll take a look in your purse,' he told her, as another of his colleagues began checking her over with a metal-detector.

'Won't someone *please* tell me what this is all about?' she demanded, trying to make out the insignia on the tiny

163

metallic lapel badges the men were wearing.

'They'll explain everything at the house,' he told her, as he finished examining the contents of her bag.

Turning, he picked up a telephone. 'This is Checkpoint One,' he announced, as her cases were being returned to the jeep. 'Applejack has just been cleared and'll be with you in two minutes. Please advise Keystone.'

After hanging up, he escorted her from the booth, helped her into the jeep and slammed the door. 'Thank you for your co-operation, and have a nice evening,' he said, waving her away.

Sarah switched on the engine, engaged gear and drove off. At the end of the colonnade of purple beeches the house stood silhouetted against a blueberry-coloured sky in which a harvest moon was rising, fat and golden as a pumpkin. Not that she was able to enjoy the spectacle; on the contrary, she felt as if she were driving to her doom. If, as she now suspected, the men at the checkpoint were FBI agents, it could mean only one thing: the attempt to dispose of Mrs Mitchell's body had failed.

And yet as she got closer to the house she noticed that other less ominous changes had taken place during her absence. The lawns had been mowed, the planting beds restocked, and the gravelled forecourt weeded and raked. Although the fountain was still not working, the pendants of dripping green algae which had once hung from the rims of its three stone basins had been removed, and the pool had been cleaned and filled with water.

Waiting for her in front of the line of large, impressive-looking cars which were parked in front of the house were Calder and Svenson.

'Where have you been?' Calder grumbled, as he stepped forward to open the door of the jeep. 'We've been trying to reach you for the past twenty-four hours.'

'But I told Jack my plans when I rang yesterday morning,' she protested, at the same time looking more closely at the cars. As well as having Washington licence plates, all of them were equipped with both roof-top and boot radio antennas. 'Anyway, what's happening?'

'What's happening?' echoed Calder, as if the answer were self-evident. 'The goddamned President's decided to pay us a visit, that's what's happening! In fact,' he added, pausing to glance at his wristwatch, 'he should be leaving Hyannis Port about now.'

Sarah began laughing. 'So the guys at the gate aren't — '

'Aren't what?' Calder demanded, with a puzzled frown. 'They're Secret Servicemen. Who did you think they were?'

Sarah sniffed. 'It doesn't matter,' she replied, fumbling in her bag for a handkerchief. 'So Mrs Mitchell *was* right . . . '

'We'll talk about all of that later,' Calder told her, glancing over his shoulder to reassure himself that they hadn't been overheard. 'Now, I suppose you'll want to freshen-up?'

Sarah looked down at her creased jumpsuit. 'And change . . . '

'All right, but don't take all night about it,' he told her, before ordering a passing ensign to carry her suitcases into the house. 'He'll be here in half an hour, and anyway it's all supposed to be very informal.'

'So, what changed his mind?' she asked, as they hurried across to the house. 'According to you, wild horses wouldn't have dragged him here . . . '

'Yes, well that's as maybe,' said Calder, saluting two Marines in full dress uniform who were standing guard at the front door. 'What happened was this: during the past seventy-two hours we've been getting some pretty hot stuff from Itzhevnikov.'

Inside the screened room?' Sarah exclaimed, as she attempted to come to terms with yet another totally unexpected turn of events. 'But Jack didn't mention any of that!'

Calder snorted. 'I should hope *not*! Not over an open line!'

'But he could've let me know what was happening without breaking security,' she insisted. 'Anyway, what's he been saying, for God's sake?'

'There's been a lot about how we and the Soviets should be working towards a peaceful settlement of our differences;

165

the dangers of a nuclear arms race, that kind of thing. Not that it's been all do-gooder waffle, by any means. He's had some interesting things to say about the power struggle within the Kremlin; the deployment of chemical-warfare weapons in Western Europe and so on. However, the item which seems to have caught the President's interest has to do with matters much closer to home. Obviously we're taking nothing on trust, but if Itzhevnikov is to be believed certain very highly placed persons with the Administration have been taking kick-backs from some of the biggest arms manufacturers in this country to do all they can to scuttle the more important of the President's peace initiatives.'

Suddenly Sarah's mouth felt as dry as dust, and she had to make a determined effort to conceal that she had begun to tremble. 'And is this the same voice as Jack taped on his radio-cassette recorder?' she asked, turning to Svenson.

'It is,' he replied, almost apologetically. 'We've compared them on a spectrograph, and there's absolutely no doubt about it.'

'Oh, *shit*!' she heard herself say.

Calder looked surprised. 'I'd have thought you'd been delighted . . .'

'I am,' she lied. 'It's just that – I don't know, I guess it's just that I wish I knew why we're getting better results than anyone else working in this field.'

Calder shrugged, as if to say why worry about *how* you're getting them, as long as you're getting them. 'If you're going to do anything about changing, you'd better hurry,' he told her, as the long-case clock chimed the quarter-hour. 'But before you go, let me quickly fill you in on the game plan. The President's been briefed on the basic set-up, so as soon as he arrives we'll take him straight to the library. Since he's said he doesn't want to disrupt anything, everyone's been told to carry on as normal.

'He's pretty squeamish, so it's unlikely he'll want to visit the ICU, but if he does – well, Kessler can handle it from that point on.

'All I hope is that he doesn't use the opportunity to give him a repeat of the lecture on medical ethics he's been giving me

166

for the past couple of days,' he added, gloomily. 'The President's an easy going guy, but when Kessler gets a bee in his bonnet he could try the patience of a saint.'

Taking her suitcases with her, Sarah went to the first floor bathroom, washed, changed into a skirt, blouse and jacket, left the cases with one of the nurses and returned to find Calder waiting anxiously on the veranda. 'They're just coming in to land now,' he told her, above the thumping of a distant helicopter engine.

'Jack's obviously in the library doing his number, but where's Maggie?' she asked Svenson, as they hurried towards the group of Secret Servicemen who had assembled alongside the ambulance which was parked on the periphery of the floodlit north lawn.

'She had something for dinner last night which didn't agree with her, so she's spent today in her cabin,' he explained, watching the huge blue-and-white Marine helicopter as it dropped slowly from the darkening sky, it's tailplane and nose lights flashing red. 'However, she seems to think she'll be fine by tomorrow.'

Guided by a landing signal officer wielding a pair of luminous batons, the helicopter settled gently in the middle of the pool of light. Its engines were shut down and its wheels chocked, the passenger door was thrown open and a set of steps lowered to the ground. As the rotor blades spun to a standstill the President appeared.

Closely followed by an Army officer carrying the black leather briefcase which contained the coded release messages that would be required in the event of a nuclear war, he ran down the steps, strode across to Calder and shook him warmly by the hand. 'Chuck, it's good to see you again,' he said, in a voice which was uncannily like that of the late John F. Kennedy. 'How are you?'

He was tall and athletic-looking, with a strong, handsome face, good teeth and an attractive smile, and he was wearing the same blue, oak-leaf encrusted utility cap and zippered windcheater he'd worn during his recent and widely-publicised visit to the nuclear-powered attack carrier *Nimitz*.

'I'm fine, Mr President. Just fine.'

167

'And Dorothy and the kids? Are they well?'

'Dorothy's fine, too. Johnny started high school this semester, and Tom's flying choppers with the Seventh Fleet.'

The President shook his head, disbelievingly. 'It seems only yesterday that they were both in short pants. I was about to say give 'em my love,' he added, with a sad smile, 'but in the circumstances I guess that wouldn't be a good idea . . .'

Calder smiled back at him. 'I guess it wouldn't at that,' he replied, before introducing Sarah and Svenson.

'First let me say how grateful I am to you and your colleagues for coming up here at such short notice,' the President told them, as they began to make their way back across the dew-laden lawn. 'And for getting such quick and impressive results with this technique of yours.'

'That's kind of you, Mr President, but we can't claim the technique as ours,' Sarah confessed. 'The credit for that belongs to a Swede named Friedrich Jürgenson.'

'Even so, I'm told that the results you've been getting are light years ahead of Jürgenson's,' said the President, thrusting his hands deep into the diagonal pockets of his windcheater. 'Anyway, without getting too technical, perhaps you'd fill me in on just what it is you've been doing?'

After waiting a moment to see if Sarah would reply, Svenson said: 'Basically it's very simple: what we're been doing is feeding white noise into a tape recorder — '

'White noise being, what?' asked the President.

'A mix of sound waves covering a wide frequency range,' replied Svenson. 'However, although it leaves the electronic noise generator as a hiss, somewhere between the input socket and the recording head it's converted into human speech. But how it happens and what causes it to happen – well, as of now, Mr President, that's still anyone's guess . . .'

'Does that mean you don't buy the ghost in the machine theory?'

As they began climbing the steps to the veranda, the

Marines posted on either side of the door snapped to attention and presented arms.

'I think I probably do buy it, bearing in mind the reaction we've had from people who knew Itzhevnikov.'

The President removed his cap and tucked it into the back pocket of his slacks. 'And what about you, Dr Stuart?' he asked, running his fingers through his shock of auburn hair. 'Where do you stand on all this?'

'I think it's too early to take a stand one way or the other,' she replied. 'What was it that Sherlock Holmes said? That when you've eliminated the impossible, whatever remains, however improbable, must be the truth.

'Although we're working on it, frankly we've a long way to go before we can claim to have eliminated the impossible.'

'I know someone who'd say "Hear hear!" to that,' said the President. 'Dick Copeland.'

Sarah looked puzzled.

'Richard Cardinal Copeland,' Calder explained. 'His Eminence and the President are friends from way back.

'As a matter of interest,' he added, turning back to the President, 'have you discussed Endor with him?'

'I have, and as you'd expect he's against it. Don't get me wrong: it's not that he refuses to countenance any attempt to communicate with the dead, he doesn't.' The President's widely-spaced blue eyes twinkled mischievously. 'How could he, when Christ himself raised the spirits of Moses and Elias?

'No,' he continued, serious once again. 'Dick's objection is pragmatic rather than theological. According to him – and interestingly enough he spent quite a while investigating Spiritualism back in the early thirties – the big problem is being certain that the communicating entity actually *is* who he or she claims to be.

'As a matter of fact,' he added, 'his last words to me were from John 1, Chapter 4: *Beloved, believe not every spirit, but try the spirits whether they are of God; because many false prophets are gone into the world.*'

Looking suitably impressed, Calder led the President

across to a table laden with bottles and glasses and offered him a drink.

'Chuck, I won't,' he replied, as all but two of his retinue of Secret Servicemen dispersed to take up positions at various points through the hall. 'Tricia's organised a cook-out, and I promised I wouldn't be too late getting back.'

'Mr President, say no more!'

After telling the steward to see if the others wanted anything, Calder led the President across the hall and opened the library door.

'I'll be goddamned!' he exclaimed, as he surveyed the scene before him. To their right was the screened room – a huge, free-standing box of polished steel in which was reflected a constellation of varicoloured lights – and facing it, three rows of trestle tables at which the intelligence analysts were seated. Most of them were in their shirt-sleeves, and, like students in a language laboratory, all were wearing light-weight headsets. Each man's place was illuminated by a pool of yellow lamplight, and each had his own computer terminal, telephone and television monitor. Although most were silently listening to what was being relayed over their headsets, others were keying information into or calling it up on their terminals, studying maps or consulting with one another in barely audible whispers. Hanging from the ceiling was an enormous screen showing a closed-circuit television picture of Adams sitting in front of a Revox reel-to-reel tape recorder and microphone, an electronic noise generator and an oscilloscope. Like the men outside, he, too, was wearing a headset.

With the self-conscious, reverential air of late-comers to a church service, the presidential party tiptoed to a table at the back of the room and sat down.

'Although in theory it's impossible for Dr Adams to receive radio signals on any of the equipment he's using, it could just happen,' Svenson told the President, as soon as he'd explained the basic set-up. 'Hence the screened room, the function of which is to block out all electromagnetic radiation.'

'Another precaution they've taken is to work with two-track tape,' Calder pointed out. 'One track is used to record Dr Adams's questions, the other Itzhevnikov's answers.'

Svenson nodded. 'If we'd recorded question and answer on the same track, we could never have been absolutely certain that Dr Adams wasn't responsible for both.

'Fraud apart,' he added, as Calder began passing out headphones, 'there's often so much activity in the larynx even when people are just thinking that there's always a possibility of something being picked up by a sufficiently sensitive mike.'

Along with the others, Sarah slipped on the headphones she'd been given. 'Say that the stuff about Russia's relationship with South Africa was fascinating, and that we'd like him to expand on it,' she heard Galbraith tell Adams. 'Okay?'

'Will do,' he replied.

Looking up at the television screen, she saw him lean forward and switch on the table microphone. 'Andrei Ilich, what you've just been telling us about the Soviet's relationship with South Africa was immensely interesting,' he said, as if speaking to an old friend. 'In fact what we'd like you to do is tell us anything else you know about the situation. Do you think that would be possible?'

After a pause during which all she could hear was the hiss of the white noise, the same eerie, disembodied voice she'd first heard on Adams's original tapes began speaking.

'One small step for man,' muttered the President, 'one giant step for mankind . . . '

Sarah pushed back her headphones. 'I beg your pardon?'

'I don't know if it's occurred to you,' he replied, in a voice which sounded as if it were being kept under tight control, 'but what we're witnessing right here in this very room could well turn out to be the most important single event since the Resurrection!'

Still not understanding, Sarah nodded cautiously.

'Anyway, we can talk more about that in a minute,' he told her, before turning to Svenson. 'Why's he answering in Russian, when the question was put to him in English?'

Svenson explained that on the astral plane communi-

171

cation is by thought alone, so that unless one was able to think in a language as well as speak it, communicating across differing states of existence was an almost insuperable problem. 'Or at least that's what Itzhevnikov tells us,' he added, with a shrug.

'In that case, why doesn't Mr Galbraith put the questions to him directly, rather than through Dr Adams?' asked the President. 'Wouldn't that make things a lot easier for everyone?'

'It would, except we've tried it and it doesn't work. In fact we've tried it with several people, but for some reason it's only Adams who he'll talk to.'

The President turned to Calder. 'What's he saying, Chuck?'

'He's been talking about Russia's gold reserves, but he seems to have moved on to — ' Calder paused. 'Now this is interesting, because he's obviously aware that you're present,' he continued, putting his fingers to the headphones. 'He says to tell you that the reason why the Kremlin isn't reacting to your programme of economic initiatives in Central America . . . is that it believes . . . that if left alone . . . they will in the long run work against us . . . in so far as they will serve to stiffen the determination of the freedom fighters . . . to rid themselves of the yoke of fascist repression.'

Chuckling, the President removed his headphones, took a coin from his pocket and began rolling it from one finger to another. 'Tell me, do you think having Itzhevnikov in the building in any way explains why you're doing so much better than the people who pioneered EVPs?' he asked Sarah. 'In fact, since I'm here, I suppose I should really take a look at him,' he added, before she had a chance to reply. 'Would that be a problem for you?'

Sarah looked across at Calder. 'It wouldn't, would it?'

'Not at all.'

The President pocketed his coin and stood up. 'In that case, why don't we discuss it on our way up?' he suggested.

With a wave to the intelligence analysts, he followed Calder out of the library. 'One thing I absolutely must do before I leave is to personally thank Dr Adams for his action on Wednesday,' added the President. 'If ever anyone deserved the Congressional Medal of Honor it's that boy.'

Calder looked surprised. 'You're not — '

'Alas no, not on an operation like this,' replied the President, before turning to Sarah. 'Now, where were we?' he asked, as they began climbing the stairs.

'You were wondering whether having Itzhevnikov on the premises in any way explains why we seem to be doing better than the people who pioneered EVPs.'

The President nodded. 'And what do you think?'

'It's possible,' she replied. 'After all, the fact that there are no reliable accounts of EVPs appearing on unmanned tape recorders suggests that psychokinesis is a vital factor in their production. However, since psychokinesis is essentially a function of a living organism, the question we have to ask ourselves is this: although Itzhevnikov's brainstem is undoubtedly dead, is the rest of his brain as dead as an electroencephalograph would have us believe, bearing in mind how pitifully little we know about the workings of the brain? If it is, I don't see how his presence here can be a factor. If it isn't, it might well be.'

'Could I add one extra thought?' asked Svenson. 'These days we recognise two kinds of death: clinical and absolute; clinical death being the cessation of vital functions, absolute death the dissolution of the cells responsible for those functions.

'Now, supposing that there is such a thing as a supra-physical body, could it not be that until the advent of absolute death this supraphysical body remains attached to the physical body, and it is *this* which is giving us our results?'

'It could,' she conceded. 'The trouble is that as a theory it raises as many questions as it answers.'

As they arrived at the half-landing, the President hesitated. 'Tell me something,' he said, looking at Sarah. 'We all have a dream about what we'd ultimately like to achieve during our lifetime. In a sentence, mine is to make the world a safer place in which to live. But what's yours?'

173

'In a sentence?' She frowned. 'I suppose I'd like to think I could create the environment in which it was possible for someone, someday, to re-write the laws of physics in such a way as to remove the para from paranormal.'

'And you?' he asked, turning to Svenson.

'I'd like to be that someone!' he replied, without a moment's hesitation.

After joining in their laughter, the President said: 'The reason I ask is this: I have a hunch that what you're doing here could have consequences far beyond simply stealing a march on the Soviets.

'Let me try to explain,' he continued, as they started up the second flight of stairs. 'I know that even if we were able to ban nuclear weapons it wouldn't be the end of the problem, because the real problem isn't *how* we fight wars, but *why* we fight them.

'So, what has this to do with communicating with Itzhevnikov? It's this, I guess: if as a result of this exercise you were able to perfect a technique whereby it could be proved beyond any shadow of a doubt that man was more than an electro-chemical organism with built-in obsolescence, it seems to me that it must change the whole way in which we view ourselves, and change it for the better. Indeed, as an evolutionary step it might well rate as equivalent to man's primordial emergence from the sea.

'Anyway, think about it. I know that to date you've avoided getting into survival research, and I certainly wouldn't want to divert you from what you see as being your principal goal. However, if you do get interested, call me.

'Shucks,' he added, 'for the cost of a new missile system, we might actually be able to do something worthwhile for once!'

By now they were at the top of the stairs, and after the President had been introduced to Kessler and two of the nurses, they began walking slowly down the corridor towards the ICU.

'And how's the patient making out?' he asked, solicitously.

Kessler clasped his hands behind his back. 'With respect,

Mr President, "patient" is hardly the word, in so far as it implies the possibility of cure, or, in the case of the terminally ill, an easy and painless death.

'Itzhevnikov, however, has been clinically dead since he was first brought here, which means all we've been able to do is hold off the onset of absolute death.'

After listening impassively, the President said: 'I can quite see that this has been a demanding and demoralising job for both you and your staff. Nevertheless, I'd be grateful if you'd continue for a little while longer, simply to give our parapsychologist friends an opportunity to establish whether or not there's a connection between what's happening up here and what's happening downstairs. Always providing, of course,' he added hastily, 'that by so doing we're in no way prolonging the patient's suffering.'

'The only ones suffering in this situation are his medical staff,' grumbled Kessler, as he opened the door of the softly lit ICU. Although the room had recently been sprayed with air freshner, it had done little to mask the unmistakable smell of necrosis. 'The "patient", as you insist on calling him, ceased to feel anything as from the moment they allowed his brain to die in Frankfurt!'

With the exception of his head and shoulders, Itzhevnikov was covered with a white sheet and he was now receiving blood as well as saline. Although only the second time she had seen him, Sarah immediately experienced a powerful feeling that somewhere in her past they had known one another intimately. And yet it wasn't a pleasant feeling; quite the contrary, it was one which made her flesh crawl.

As Kessler began explaining the meaning of brain death to the President, she tried to remember what she knew about *déjà vu*.

Had they, perhaps, known one another in a previous incarnation? Although a psychiatrist friend of hers at the University of Virginia had written a paper in which he'd made what was prima facie a strong case for reincarnation, she immediately dismissed the idea as preposterous. There had to be a more prosaic explanation, but what was it? Still

175

more evidence that there was something seriously the matter with her? As she was quick to remind herself, even though *déjà vu* is sometimes experienced by perfectly healthy people, it is also symptomatic of several diseases of the central nervous system.

Again she found herself wondering why she was still having so much trouble looking into mirrors. While changing to meet the President, it had required a considerable effort of will to look into one even for a moment. And it wasn't just here at Seacrest that the problem manifested itself; she'd been plagued by it throughout her trip to Rhode Island.

Could there be a connection between the phobia and the *déjà vu*? she wondered. However, no sooner had the thought occurred when it was wiped from her mind by a high-pitched, insistent bleeping from the cardiogram monitoring Itzhevnikov's heart.

Although in mid-sentence, Kessler turned on his heel, and, followed by the nurses, raced to Itzhevnikov's side.

As one of the nurses threw back the sheet Sarah suddenly understood the reason for it: not only had the scar on his now hugely distended and discoloured belly begun to fester, but both legs had become gangrenous.

After making sure that none of the ECG leads had become detached, Kessler pulled the pillows from beneath Itzhevnikov's head, felt his carotid artery for a moment, then thumped his chest with his clenched fist.

With the Russian's yellow, waxen face now beginning to turn blue, he clambered on to the bed, placed one hand over the other above the lifeless heart and began bearing down on it in short, sharp, rhythmic thrusts.

However, he had only been applying EHC for a moment or so when the overhead lights flickered and died. Immediately, the ICU became a bedlam of warning lights, bells and klaxons.

'Everyone stay where they are!' he yelled above the uproar. 'Everybody stay right where they — '

But even as the Secret Servicemen were drawing their revolvers, the room was once again flooded with light.

'Jesus H. Christ!' he exclaimed, looking around him in amazement.

And then as suddenly and as mysteriously as they had started, the flashings and the ringings and the raspings dwindled away into an eerie silence.

Anxious to make up for the lost seconds, one of the nurses began hurriedly charging an array of hypodermic syringes, while the other disconnected the endotracheal tube, clamped a face-mask over the Russian's mouth and began inflating his lungs with oxygen.

'What happened?' asked the President, as the Secret Servicemen re-holstered their weapons.

With his eyes on the cardiogram, Kessler called for ten millilitres of adrenaline. 'He's had a cardiac arrest,' he replied, after pausing to draw breath. 'But as to why the hardware went berserk, your guess is as good as mine.'

Pale and visibly shaken, the President asked if there was anything he could do.

Taking the syringe from the nurse, Kessler felt for the fourth left interspace and thrust the needle through the chest and into Itzhevnikov's heart. 'Just keep well back,' he told him, as he withdrew the needle and turned again to the cardiogram.

Although the light spot had begun to leap fitfully, within a few seconds it was once more travelling in a straight line.

'Defibrillators!' he yelled, but the nurse who had charged the syringes had anticipated him and was already coating the defibrillator paddles with electrode jelly.

Kessler jumped down from the bed, took a paddle in each hand, and, as the nurse crossed to the power unit, placed one paddle above the apex of Itzhevnikov's heart and the other at the base. 'Let's begin with a hundred joules at point one of a second,' he told her, before ordering the nurse who was administering the oxygen to stand clear of the bed. 'Right, here we go: three, two, one!'

As he pressed the power buttons on the defibrillator paddles, the Russian's back arched and a waveform appeared on the cardiogram, hung uncertainly for a moment and then disappeared.

After several more equally unsuccessful attempts had been made to shock the heart back to life, Kessler flung aside the paddles and ordered the nurses to prepare for a thoracotomy.

'I'll have to try internal heart massage,' he told the President, as he hurried to the washbasin and began to scrub. 'So if you take my advice, you'll leave now.'

The President, however, appeared to be transfixed by the drama being enacted before him.

'The commander's right,' Calder told him, as one of the nurses, having sterilised Itzhevnikov's chest, broke open a large thoracotomy towel. 'Since there's no way any of us can help, wouldn't it be better if we were to leave?'

Still the President didn't react.

Now gowned and masked, Kessler snapped on a pair of rubber gloves and returned to the bed. 'Mr President, do you really want to stay for this?' he asked, picking up a scalpel.

But still the President made no move to leave.

With a resigned shrug, Kessler cut through the flesh immediately below Itzhevnikov's left nipple, forced apart his ribs with a retractor, and, thrusting his hand inside the chest, began massaging the exposed heart.

'Nothing's happening,' he told the girl who was acting as his scrub nurse. 'We'd better try another ten millilitres of adrenaline and five of calcium chloride.'

With his gown, gloves and paper shoe coverings now splattered with blood, Kessler injected one drug and then the other directly into the left ventricle and once again began massaging the heart. But still he could not get it to re-start.

Shaking his head sadly, he withdrew his hand from inside Itzhevnikov's chest, removed the retractor, and, leaving the nurses to close the incision with metal wound clips, stripped off his mask and gloves. 'I'm sorry, Mr President, but frankly we'd been expecting this for some time now,' he told him. 'I just wish it hadn't happened while you were here . . . '

The President blinked and began rubbing his eyes with

178

his forefinger and thumb, as if he had just awoken from a deep sleep. 'What was that?' he mumbled.

'I said I just wish that — ' Kessler stopped, only now aware that something was seriously wrong with the President. 'Are you all right, sir?' he asked, peering at him over the top of his half-frames.

Still rubbing his eyes, he nodded uncertainly.

'Here, come and sit down,' said Kessler, guiding him on to the chair which one of the nurses had brought across. After taking his pulse, he persuaded him to put his head between his knees for long enough to restore some of the colour to his ashen face.

'How're you feeling now?'

'Okay, I guess,' he replied, unconvincingly. Placing a hand on the back of his neck, he rotated his head several times with his eyes closed, opened them, blinked, and looked around as if he were no longer sure where he was. 'What happened?'

'I'm afraid we lost Itzhevnikov. We did everything we could — '

'Lost him?' The President scowled. 'What the fuck are you talking about?' he asked, in an off-key, petulant voice. 'How could you have *lost* him?'

Now looking very perplexed, Kessler turned to the Secret Servicemen and asked if the President's personal physician was in the house.

'He's downstairs,' one of them replied, reaching for his walkie-talkie. 'Do you want us to have him come up?'

'I think you'd better . . . '

'I don't want that asshole up here,' growled the President, as he began massaging his temples. 'Now for chrissakes will you just leave me alone for a minute!'

'All right, but then I think we ought to have him take a look at you,' said Kessler, in a placatory tone of voice. 'It's probably no more than a faint, but let's not take any chances.'

Dismissing the suggestion with an airy wave of his hand, the President stood up, tried walking to and fro several times, and then, turning to look at Sarah with undisguised

179

sexual interest, said: 'I have to be going now, but we'll get together again soon, okay?'

Kessler quickly placed himself between the President and the door. 'I'm sorry, sir, but I really don't think you should go anywhere until your own doctor has examined you.'

'Bullshit!' Sweeping Kessler aside, the President strode angrily from the room, followed by his puzzled-looking Secret Servicemen.

'What the hell was that all about?' asked Kessler, turning from one stunned face to another. 'Jesus, it wasn't my fault the guy died!'

'Forget it,' Calder told him, as he, too, left the room. Followed by Sarah and Svenson, he hurried along the corridor and down the stairs, arriving in the hall only just in time to see the President and his entourage leave by the front door.

'What the — ' Calder began, but the President's abrupt and discourteous departure had left him speechless. He cleared his throat and began again. 'I mean, he didn't even wait to say goodbye, for chrissakes!'

'Perhaps he's embarrassed about having nearly passed out,' Sarah suggested.

Calder shrugged, disconsolately. 'I just don't get it,' he said, as the helicopter's engine roared into life. 'I've known him since he was a freshman Senator, and for him to behave like that – well, it just isn't him. It isn't him at *all*!'

CHAPTER 19

'AH, WELL, what the hell!' said Calder, ushering Sarah into his austere ground floor office. Used originally as a billiard room, it contained an imposing desk flanked by a pair of flags, half a dozen chairs, a locker and some filing cabinets. 'Why don't we have ourselves a drink and forget all about it?'

'That's the best suggestion I've heard all evening,' she replied, turning from studying the assortment of framed photographs of naval vessels that were hanging above the mantelpiece.

Calder looked surprised. 'You don't sound as if you were very impressed with his offer . . . ' Switching on a green-shaded desk lamp, he crossed to the locker, produced a bottle of White Label and held it up for her approval. 'Or did you think it was just happy talk?' he asked, as he returned to the desk and half-filled two glasses with whisky and branch water.

'No, I think he probably meant it.'

As they clinked their glasses and sat down either side of the desk, Calder said: 'So, how come you're not more excited?'

'After the number he's just pulled!' she exclaimed, picking up a framed photograph of two small boys and an attractive, middle-aged woman cradling a dachshund in her arms. 'You don't mind, do you?'

Calder waved a hand, as if to say feel free. 'That was taken at our place on Long Island,' he explained. 'Of course, the kids have grown up a lot since then . . . '

'You're very lucky. Having a family, I mean . . . '

'Except in this job I don't get to see them as often as I should,' he said, with a resigned shrug.

Wondering what lay behind his choice of the phrase 'as I should' rather than the more conventional 'as I would like', she replaced the first photograph and picked up another of General MacArthur wading ashore at Corregidor. Scrawled across the bottom of the picture were the words: *To Chuck, for helping me keep my feet dry at Pusan. Douglas.*

Sarah frowned. 'Pusan?' she said, fearing that he might be much older than he looked. 'Now, just let me think . . . '

'It's in North Korea,' he replied, as if anxious to change the subject. 'Anyway, tell me some more about your reaction to the President's offer.'

'I don't know that there's much more to tell,' she said, putting down the photograph. 'Except I'm not really sure if I'd ever be able to trust anyone capable of quite such a sudden and spectacular about-face.'

Calder swung his feet up onto the corner of the desk and loosened his tie. 'Well, I've never known him behave that way before. Usually he's the one guy who can be relied upon to keep his head when all about him are losing theirs.'

'I wonder,' she said, before pausing to take a sip of her drink. 'Let's face it, he must have become a little unglued to have ordered an operation like this.'

'You mean Endor?' Calder looked doubtful. 'I know that was my initial reaction, except – goddammit! – it seems to be paying off.'

'You really believe that, do you?'

'Don't you?'

Sarah shrugged. 'How would I know? Remember, I'm the one who's not being told what it is you're getting.'

'Yes, I'm sorry about that,' he said, rubbing his chin unhappily.

'There's no need to be; I doubt if I'd be able to appreciate the significance of it anyway.'

'It's this damned need-to-know rule,' he explained, as if trying to think of a way around an insoluble but unnecessary problem.

'I realise that,' she said, touched by his obvious concern.

'Honestly, I wasn't complaining – simply making the point that I personally have no way of knowing whether it's paying off or not. However, even if it is I'm still not sure we should ever have embarked on it . . . '

Calder started back, a bemused expression on his face. 'Really?'

'The trouble with scientific knowledge is that once it's learned, it can never be unlearned,' Sarah explained. 'Which is what makes a mockery of his nuclear disarmament initiatives.

'Don't get me wrong,' she added hastily. 'I'm all for nuclear disarmament, just as I'm all for what he's doing in the Third World. God knows we've waited long enough for a President with the sense to realise that it isn't communism which is the enemy but the repression and poverty which gives rise to communism, and that if you help rather than hinder the revolution of rising expectations — '

'Fine, but let's stay with the question of nuclear disarmament for a moment longer,' he said, holding up a hand. 'If I understand you correctly, what you're saying is that even if he does get rid of nuclear weapons, because there's no way he can get rid of nuclear know-how, all he'll have done is put Doomsday on hold.'

'Unless and until we correct the imbalance between our technological and our psychological development,' she told him. 'Hell, as people we've hardly changed at all since the days we were hitting one another over the head with stone axes, and yet we now possess the means of destroying the entire ecosphere.'

'But surely, that was exactly the President's point,' he said, glancing at his wristwatch. 'Anyway, why don't we continue this in – well, in rather more convivial surroundings? It's not all that late, and I know of a very nice little spot overlooking Frenchman's Bay . . . '

'Fantastic!' Sarah felt her mood lighten still further. 'I don't know why, but I really feel like doing something this evening!'

'Then we're in business,' he said, as they finished their drinks and got up from the desk.

183

'Aren't you going to change?'

Calder looked down at his uniform. 'I guess I better had,' he replied, before switching off the desk lamp and escorting her across the room.

'In which case I don't have to feel guilty about taking the time to change, too.'

'That depends on *how* long you take!'

As he opened the door, Sarah suddenly became aware of a buzz coming from somewhere upstairs, and behind it a rhythmic thumping. 'Do you hear what I hear?' she asked.

Calder closed the door behind him and cocked his head to one side. 'It sounds just as if someone's having a party . . . '

'Someone *is* having a party!' she cried, delightedly. Taking his hand, she hurried him up the stairs and along the corridor leading to the ICU. By now the buzz had become the rumble of animated voices; the rhythmic thumping, music. Commingled in the warm air were the unmistakable party smells of alcohol and pot, perfume and perspiration. As she opened the door the rumble became a roar, but one which drained quickly away to a guilty silence.

'I'll be goddamned!' exclaimed Calder, above Frank Sinatra's bittersweet rendition of *September Song*.

Itzhevnikov had been disconnected from the monitoring equipment, put into a sealed, watertight body-bag, and, along with his bed, moved to a corner of the crowded, candle-lit room. Where the bed had been was a table on which was standing a record-player and a pile of LPs, as well as a great many bottles, bowls of ice and plates laden with sandwiches and cookies. Above the table hung a huge cluster of blown-up surgical gloves.

'Chuck!' cried Kessler, breaking free from the embrace of the nurse with whom he'd been dancing. 'Chuck, we thought you'd left for the night . . . '

'So I see! Now, if someone wouldn't mind telling me what the hell this is all about . . . '

'We thought it might be a nice idea if we were to hold a wake for our friend here,' explained another of the doctors, nodding towards the dead Russian. The name on the ID card pinned to his white shirt was O'Hanlon. 'You've no objections, have you?' he added, anxiously.

'I guess not . . . '

'In that case, why don't you come on in?' he asked, as if a great weight had suddenly been lifted from his shoulders.

Calder turned to Sarah. 'What d'you think?'

'I think it sounds great! Except wait a minute,' she added, with a frown. 'Isn't it a rule that you have to say something good about the deceased before you're allowed a drink?'

'Strictly speaking, yes,' replied O'Hanlon. 'But since the best any of these dudes could come up with was that he'd never once complained about anything, we decided to give it a miss!'

'In that case there's no problem,' laughed Sarah.

With a roar of approval from the others, Calder led her into the middle of the room, slipped an arm around her waist and began dancing. For such a tall, heavily-built man he turned out to be not only an accomplished dancer, but also surprisingly light on his feet.

However, they had not been dancing for long when they were approached by a worried-looking naval corpsman. 'I hate to interrupt you, sir — '

'Sorry, sailor,' said Calder, tightening his hold on Sarah, 'but this isn't an excuse me.'

The corpsman smiled uncertainly back at him. 'I realise that, sir. It's just that some of the nurses are holding a seance in — '

'Did you say a *seance*?'

'Aye, aye, sir,' he said, raising his voice in order to make himself more easily heard above the din. 'You know, one where you use an upturned glass . . . '

'But I thought this was supposed to be a party?'

'It is, sir.'

Calder rolled his eyes. 'Then why fool around with an empty glass when you could be fooling around with a full one?' he asked, in the manner of Groucho Marx.

'That's a good question, sir!' replied the corpsman ruefully. 'Although I guess it just kinda started out as a joke, the fact of the matter is, sir, that we've gotten through to someone who keeps asking for Dr Stuart.'

'*Me*!' she exclaimed, suddenly taking more than just a casual interest in what was being said.

The corpsman shrugged unhappily. 'We haven't been able to think of anyone else on the base called Sarah . . . '

'And who is it who's supposed to be asking for me?' she enquired, as they were jostled by other dancers.

'Someone calling themselves Joan . . . '

'Joan?' After thinking for a moment, Sarah shook her head. 'I've never known anyone called Joan.'

'In that case it must be Joan Lansdale,' the corpsman told her, as he began scratching one of his tattooed forearms. 'You know, the nurse who looked after you the night you were taken ill . . . '

'You mean the one who *died*?' she asked, withdrawing her arms from around Calder's neck.

'Yes, ma'am. We thought all along that it might be Joan, but we just couldn't be sure.'

Sarah tut-tutted. 'You know, you really should have more sense than to mess around with a thing like this.'

'I guess so, ma'am, but like I said, it started out as a — '

'And you'd like us to come and take a look, is that it?' interjected Calder.

'Aye, aye, sir. That's if you and the lady wouldn't mind, sir . . . '

Reluctantly, Sarah allowed herself to be led out of the ICU and back along the corridor to what had obviously once been the nurses' station. Sitting at a table in the centre of the large, dimly lit room were three middle-aged women, each of whom had a forefinger resting on the base of an upturned wine glass that was slowly rotating in the middle of a circle of sheets torn from a small scratch pad. A felt-tipped pen had been used to write the letters A to Z on twenty-six of the twenty-eight sheets, and the words YES and NO on the remaining two.

With a screech which set Sarah's teeth on edge, the glass suddenly shot across the polished surface of the table to nudge the sheet on which the letter S had been written.

'It's starting again!' announced the stockily built, bespectacled nurse, who, Sarah suddenly remembered, had helped try to restrain her on the night she had gone berserk.

After criss-crossing the table to touch the letters A, R and A again, the glass veered off at a tangent and struck the H sheet hard enough to send it fluttering to the floor.

As the corpsman bent to retrieve the fallen sheet, the nurse began calling out the letters being touched by the rapidly moving glass. 'C...A...N...N...O...T - "Sarah cannot" — ' The nurse frowned. 'Cannot *what*?' she demanded of her unseen communicator.

Again the glass started moving, but with what appeared to be less certainty than before. 'E...A...S...I...L...Y - "easily" - S...A...Y - "Sarah, cannot easily say" - W...H... ' On arriving at the A sheet the glass stopped, as if it had suddenly run out of energy. 'I know it isn't *easy*, dear,' said the nurse, in a polite but unforgiving voice. 'Now, do please try a little harder — '

No sooner were the words out of her mouth when the table began to vibrate with sufficient force to set the glass trembling beneath the sitters' fingers. 'Who's doing that?' she asked, peering accusingly at the others over the top of her steel-rimmed spectacles.

However, before any of them had a chance to protest, the table stopped vibrating as abruptly as it had started and the glass once again began racing to and fro between the letters.

'Was that S or R?' she asked, stretching across the table in an attempt to keep her finger on the glass.

'It looked like the S to me,' replied one of the other women.

Turning to glare up at the corpsman, the nurse said: 'Well don't just stand there, get it down!'

Taking a pen and a pad from the pocket of his white tunic, he wrote frantically until the glass came shuddering to a standstill several minutes later.

'Well?' she demanded, removing her finger from the glass in order to light a cigarette.

With a puzzled shrug, the corpsman handed her the pad.

After she had borrowed his pen and spent a moment or so organising the rows of letters into words, she took the

187

cigarette from her mouth, flicked the ash on to the floor and began reading aloud: *'Its hour come round at last slouches towards Bethlehem to be born . . . '* She looked up at Sarah. 'Does that mean anything to you?'

'Slouches towards *where* to be born?'

'Bethlehem.'

Sarah shook her head. 'I'm sorry, it doesn't mean a thing.'

'Are you sure?' asked the nurse, as if she suspected her of being deliberately obtuse.

'Absolutely sure!'

After the sitters had spent the best part of ten minutes trying unsuccessfuly to cajole the glass into producing something other than meaningless gibberish, Calder made his excuses and left. 'Well, what did you think of all that?' he asked Sarah, as they began making their way back towards the ICU.

'It's just a lot of nonsense, isn't it?'

'I guess so, except it really did look to me as if they were being pulled by the glass rather than pushing it.'

'I'm not saying they *were* pushing it, or at least not consciously,' she told him. 'Have you ever seen the pendulum trick? The one where you tie a ring on to a piece of string and hold it over a table?'

Calder shook his head.

'Okay, well what you do is rest your elbow on the table, and without moving your hand you'll find that you can will the ring to swing in any direction you choose as often as you choose – clockwise, anti-clockwise, north to south or east to west.'

'Which proves what?' he asked, opening the door of the ICU for her.

'That the mind can cause physical reactions of which we're simply not aware.'

'I see,' he said, as they once again began dancing, this time cheek to cheek. 'So, what you're suggesting is that any messages which do come through originate in the sitters' unconscious, unless, of course, one or more of them is deliberately cheating.'

188

'Exactly. Which is why fooling around with upturned glasses and ouija boards isn't to be recommended.'

Moving to the slow, sensuous beat of a bossa nova, they approached the table at which Adams, Galbraith and several of the other intelligence analysts were sitting.

'What you seem to be proposing is that we should start World War Three now and get it over with,' she heard Galbraith say.

Adams dismissed the suggestion with an unco-ordinated wave of his arm, knocking over the glass which one of the nurses had just refilled for him. 'No, no, no!' he cried, either unaware of or unconcerned by what he had done. 'Not *start* it, stop it!

'Look,' he continued, as the nurse returned with a box of medical wipes and began mopping up the rapidly spreading pool of wine, 'right now the Russkies are spending something like fifteen per cent of their GNP on armaments, okay? How are they able to do it? By imposing a low standard of living! And what is the long-term effect of a low standard of living? Widespread discontent with the system which imposes it!'

Galbraith began hiccuping. 'So?'

'So, instead of halving our defence budget we double it and watch the sons-of-bitches screw themselves trying to catch up with us!'

Calder chuckled. 'Beneath that radical exterior beats a heart of John Wayne!' he whispered into Sarah's ear. 'Incidentally, just why *did* he go to Vietnam?' he asked, serious once again. 'With his qualifications, dodging the draft would've been as easy as falling off a log.'

'Maybe it had something to do with him being the son of an immigrant,' Sarah suggested, as she tried to remember where she'd first seen the pretty red-head with whom Svenson was dancing. 'Maybe it was his way of repaying the debt he felt he owed to the country of his adoption. After all,' she added, 'it's always struck me as significant that the most decorated American unit in the Second World War consisted entirely of Japanese immigrants.'

Like a bolt from the blue, it suddenly occurred to her that

she might have at last discovered the reason for Adams's apparent success in conjuring up Itzhevnikov's ghost: because of his continuing anxiety to help the country of his adoption, he had produced the Russian from his own unconscious and projected it on to the tape psychokinetically.

However, no sooner had the idea formed than it collapsed like a house of cards. She was, she reminded herself, making the classic mistake of attributing mysterious causes to mysterious effects. The explanation – both in terms of motivation and mechanism – had to be much simpler, and, before surrendering herself to the beat of the music and the feel of Calder's body next to hers, she resolved that before another day passed she would crack the riddle once and for all.

CHAPTER 20

SARAH SHOOK him gently. 'Darling, it's six o'clock.'

With his eyes still closed and murmuring sleepy endearments, Calder rolled over and took her in his arms.

'Charles, no!' she giggled, as she felt him beginning to harden. 'There isn't time, not if you want to be out of here before reveille . . . '

Suddenly wide awake, he leapt from the bed and began pulling on his clothes. 'All right, but what are you doing tonight?'

'Tonight?' Wrapping a sheet around herself, she hurried into the kitchen to make him a cup of instant coffee. 'It depends on when you think you'll be through at the house . . . '

'If it's anything like the past couple of days it could be late,' he warned.

'The later the better,' she replied, gently teasing him. 'That way I'll at least be sure of getting *some* sleep!'

After he'd gulped down his coffee and kissed her goodbye, he slipped quietly away into the incandescent mist of what promised to be yet another perfect Indian Summer's day.

For several minutes Sarah remained leaning against the door jamb, trying to come to terms with what had happened. However, with the memory of his powerful body still reverberating in her mind it wasn't easy to think, let alone think rationally. And yet that was what she'd have to do, she told herself as she began gathering up the cast-off clothing that lay between the settee and the bed. Although even before their first kiss he had made it clear that he could never leave his wife, what had subsequently emerged about the state of their twenty-year old marriage had given her cause to hope.

But was that what she really wanted? she wondered, turning on the bath taps. So far each had been as careful as the other not to use the word love, albeit for what she suspected were very different reasons. For him it would almost certainly have been tantamount to making a commitment he felt himself unable or unwilling to honour, while for her it would simply have been meaningless to do so. After all, how could one love someone about whom one knew so little?

However, of one thing she was certain: she wanted to be allowed the opportunity to find out if she could love him, and since that would take time she was more determined than ever to root out and remove what had now become a threat to her private as well as her professional future.

Sarah climbed the steps leading to Maggie's cabin and rapped on the door. Immediately, the dog began barking. 'Red!' she heard her call. 'Red, be quiet!' There was a patter of approaching feet, followed by the sound of locks being unbolted. The door was opened as far as the security chain would allow, and Maggie appeared. 'Sarah! Well, hi there!' she cried, looking like an overgrown schoolgirl in her dark blue shorty dressing gown and pigtails. 'What're you doing up at this hour on a Sunday?'

'It's not *too* early, is it?' she asked, wishing now that she had left it until later. 'It's – well, it's just that I need to talk to you . . . '

'Of course it isn't too early!' she replied, lifting the security chain from its slot. 'Come on in . . . ' After waving her through into the cabin, Maggie closed the door and then hurried across to draw the curtains. Although she'd been there for little more than a week, she had already managed to make it look as chaotic as her apartment in South End. As well as a great many books, newspapers and magazines, there were items of clothing scattered everywhere, some of it clean and some of it not so clean. There were things she had picked up from the beach – oddly-shaped pieces of driftwood, shells and pebbles – and other things which looked as if they might have been bought at barn sales – a Stolpe-Walton oil lamp without a shade, a painted wood candle box and a chipped fox-head creamer.

'So, how did you make out in Rhode Island?' she asked, as Red came bounding from the kitchen to leap up at Sarah, its tongue lolling and its tail wagging excitedly.

'Fine,' she replied, fondling the dog's head. 'In fact having met the old lady, I was very glad that they did what they did. Losing her sister was bad enough, God knows, but if she'd known just what *had* happened . . . ' Sarah covered her eyes for a moment, as if the prospect were too terrible to contemplate. 'Anyway, what about you? How're you feeling now?'

Maggie began making a desultory attempt to clear the worst of the mess. 'I'm fine. I told the guys I'd picked up a tummy bug, but I think it was probably just a delayed reaction to everything that's happened during the past week.'

After Sarah had finished discussing the events of the previous evening, omitting nothing other than that she and Calder had slept together, Maggie suddenly said: 'By the way, have you had breakfast?'

'No, not really. But honestly, don't make — '

'I was about to make some for myself, so why don't you join me,' said Maggie, leading her into a kitchen stacked with health foods. There were packets of ginseng and herbal tea; tins of brewer's yeast and wheat germ; bottles of cider vinegar and sunflower oil; and jars of honey and black strap molasses.

'As well as all this,' said Sarah, looking around in amazement, 'you didn't also happen to bring along a dictionary of quotations?'

'Damn!' Maggie clapped a hand to her forehead. 'I knew I'd forgotten *something*!' she replied, gently mocking her. 'Anyway, what d'you want with a dictionary of quotations, for chrissakes?'

'Oh, it's just that I've a hunch I've come across the ''slouches towards Bethlehem'' line somewhere before . . . '

'It's not from a Christmas carol, is it?'

193

'What, with the word "slouches" in it?' exclaimed Sarah. 'And then there's the use of the impersonal pronoun – "Its hour come round at last" – no one would ever refer to Christ as It. The Antichrist, maybe . . . '

'Perhaps it has something to do with Itzhevnikov? Don't forget, most of us ended up calling him It . . . '

'Except that doesn't make sense either, not on the night he died . . . '

'Breakfast!' said Maggie, suddenly bored with trying to guess the meaning of the message. 'Now, have you ever tried my Dragon's Milk?'

'I'm not sure I've even heard of it.'

'Then you've a treat in store,' she promised, crossing to the refrigerator. 'So, tell me some more about the President's offer to fund us.'

'I don't know that there's a lot left to tell,' Sarah replied, watching her as she half-filled a blender with milk and began spooning in brewer's yeast, wheat germ and ground almonds. 'In fact I'll be very surprised if we hear any more about it, particularly after what happened.'

Having by now added yoghurt, sunflower oil, orange juice, honey and a banana, Maggie broke an egg into the mixture, screwed on the cap and pressed the start button. 'That's weird, isn't it?' she said, above the roar from the blender. 'I mean, him suddenly doing a Jekyll and Hyde like that . . . '

'Very weird, because up until then he really couldn't have been nicer,' Sarah explained. 'But I suppose one shouldn't be too surprised. After all, he couldn't have been *that* nice to have got where he is.'

Maggie switched off the blender and began pouring the Dragon's Milk. 'I wonder . . . ' she said, passing a glass to Sarah. 'The trouble is that since Watergate it's automatically assumed that anyone who gets to be President has to be a son-of-a-bitch. Anyway, what do you think of it?' she asked, after Sarah had taken a sip of the thick, creamy liquid. 'It's great, isn't it?'

'It really is!' she replied, nodding her approval.

'One more question about last night, and then we'll talk

194

about whatever it is that you want to talk about,' said Maggie, as she returned the ingredients to the refrigerator. 'What effect did It's death have on the taping?'

Sarah smiled sadly. 'As it happens, that's exactly what I wanted to talk to you about. It was as if *nothing* had happened! Absolutely nothing!'

'That's odd, isn't it?' said Maggie, frowning. 'I mean, I'd have thought that – I dunno, but I'd have expected *some* kind of reaction . . .'

'Exactly. But then don't forget, no one in the library knew what had happened until they'd shut up shop for the night.'

Maggie eyed her suspiciously. 'What're you suggesting?'

'I'm suggesting that — ' Sarah hesitated. 'Look, why don't we take a walk along the beach?'

'What now?' Suddenly realising what lay behind the suggestion, Maggie's eyes popped open in alarm. 'Christ!' she said, in a hushed voice, 'you don't think — '

Sarah put a finger to her lips. 'I just think it would be nice to take a walk along the beach . . .'

Looking very perplexed, Maggie hurried off to change into a track suit, and, after they'd spent several minutes searching for her sneakers, she called the dog and they left.

By now the sun had all but burned away the early morning mist, revealing a great crescent of untrodden sand that was deserted but for the gulls which were scavenging along the tide-line.

'So, what's on your mind?' she asked, as her dog went tearing off across the beach.

'Maggie, do you know what it is that Jack and Andy are up to?'

'Are you talking about the tapes or the seance?'

Sarah stopped abruptly. 'Ah! So you *do* know!' she said, looking at her over the top of her sunglasses.

'I only know what they told me, which is that you'd accused them of cheating.'

'Well they are, aren't they?'

'No, of course they aren't!' she replied, with a derisory laugh. 'Don't you think I'd have spotted it if they were?'

'Not necessarily, honey,' said Sarah, as they began

195

walking again. 'After all, you're a biologist, not an electrical engineer.'

'Sure, but I do happen to come from a long line of electrical engineers,' Maggie told her. 'Anyway, why in God's name would they want to cheat?'

'Oh, because they think that unless we come up with results Biotec will find itself in trouble. Who knows? All I do know is that if they're not stopped they'll eventually get caught and then we really *will* be in trouble!'

Stepping out of her sneakers, Maggie said: 'Tell me, why are you so certain they *are* cheating?'

'Because there's no way that voice could be anything but phoney. My God, have you heard it? It goes on for *hour*, after *hour*, after *hour*!'

'Of course I've heard it! In fact for most of the time you were away I did little else except work with them on it.'

'And you don't think it's phoney?'

'No, I don't!' Maggie replied, indignantly. 'Okay, so I hated the way Jack just shot the shit outta those two guys as if they'd been vermin; but that apart, like Andy he's a responsible, highly respected scientist. And you should know that better than anyone; it was you who hired him, for chrissakes!

'Okay, so I'll admit I've had my doubts,' she continued, in a more placatory tone of voice. 'In fact I'll go even further than that: I think Jack probably *is* responsible for it, but without knowing he is.'

Sarah frowned. 'Come again?'

'Well, he could be producing it psychokinetically, couldn't he?' said Maggie, kicking unhappily at the sand. 'I mean, if the mind can deflect a laser beam, affect the fall of dice, or — '

'Maggie, will you please get to the point!'

'All I was going to say was that if the mind can do that – and we know it can – I don't see why it shouldn't be able to modulate white noise or vary the strength of a magnetic field on a strip of tape.'

Sarah nodded. 'That's fine but for one thing: Jack doesn't speak a word of Russian! Not a single word!'

196

'Well, now just hold it a second,' Maggie cautioned. 'Jack's grandparents emigrated from Russia when his mother was ten, right? Okay, so we know he was never *taught* Russian, but with a Russian mother and Russian grandparents around the house during his formative years, it would've been very surprising if he hadn't absorbed a helluva lot of Russian without necessarily realising he'd done so. It's called cryptomnesia . . . '

'I know what it's *called*,' said Sarah, a trace of irritation in her voice. 'And although it's entirely plausible, I don't happen to think it's the explanation.'

Once past the tide-line they sat down, Sarah on an out-crop of rock and Maggie beside her on the sand.

'Okay, then let's try to decide what it *isn't*, rather than what it is,' Maggie suggested. Clasping her hands behind her head, she lay back on the sand and closed her eyes. 'One: we know it isn't a freak radio pick-up, right?'

'Right.'

'Two: we know Jack doesn't have one of his buddies beaming the stuff to him, because quite apart from the fact that none of the equipment he's working with is able to receive radio transmissions, everything's being done inside a screened room. Three: he's not — '

'Wait a minute,' said Sarah, pressing her fingertips to her temples. 'Supposing he's tampered with the equipment so that it *is* able to receive radio signals . . . '

Maggie shook her head. 'There's no way he could've done that. Not only is it CIA equipment that he's using, they lock it away when he's *not* using it. And even if he'd somehow managed to find a way around that, he'd still have the screened room to contend with . . . '

Sarah picked up a handful of pebbles and began throwing them listlessly into a sea that was as flat as a millpond. 'Is there any way in which he could have got at the tapes?'

'How do you mean?' asked Maggie, as her dog came lolloping back to deposit a deflated, oil-stained beach ball at her feet.

'Could he, for instance, be substituting pre-recorded tapes for blanks?'

197

'No way,' replied Maggie, hugging the dog as if it had unearthed a priceless treasure. 'Even if the guy who deals him the tapes was in on the act, you'd still have to explain the fact that a lot of what Itzhevnikov says arises directly from questions asked by the analysts while the tape's running.

'Look, it's still too early for there to be anyone at the house,' she added, squinting up at her wristwatch. 'So, why don't we drive over there so you can see for yourself?'

Sarah shook her head. 'I'll take your word for it . . . '

'I'd be happier if you didn't.' Maggie sat up, brushed the sand from the soles of her feet and began pulling on her sneakers. 'Quite apart from anything else, this way you'll at least be certain that *I* haven't been conning you.'

Sarah and Maggie arrived at Seacrest just before eight o'clock. After parking in the deserted forecourt, they entered the house, followed by the dog.

'I've just realised something,' said Maggie, as she opened the library door. 'Red's with us!'

'So?'

'Don't you remember? When we first came here we couldn't get him near the house, let alone inside it,' she replied, watching in astonishment as it began exploring the empty library, its nose to the floor and its tail wagging happily. 'And it wasn't just the once: because I felt guilty about leaving him with the people at the lodge I tried bringing him with me on another occasion, and still he wouldn't set foot in the place . . . '

With a bemused shrug, she crossed to the screened room, opened the door and switched on the light and the air conditioner.

Dumping the bag she had brought with her from the cabin on to the now empty table, she took out a transistor radio and a circuit tester.

'Okay, so the first thing we do is make sure this is working,' she told Sarah, as she took the transistor outside the screened room and switched it on. Immediately, the

198

library was filled with the hand-clapping, foot-stomping beat of a Baptist congregation singing *This Little Light of Mine*. 'It's working!' she cried, as she sashayed her way back into the room and shut the door.

After first checking the earth with the circuit tester, she picked up the now silent transistor and used it to sweep the door and the door threshold, the floor, ceiling and walls, as well as every inch of the supporting framework.

'Well, that rules out radio transmissions,' she announced, as she began massaging her aching shoulder and arm muscles. 'There's obviously nothing wrong with the earth, and if Jack had tampered with the shielding we'd have been bound to pick up something on the tranny.'

Sarah crossed to the table, pulled out the chair and sat down. 'I don't get it. *I just do not get it*! Even supposing Jack is producing the voice psychokinetically, where's he getting his information from? Okay, so I know we're not being allowed to see transcripts of what's been said, but even from the little we've been told we know it's all pretty high-powered stuff.'

'I wonder if it *is* all that high-powered?' asked Maggie, as she began gathering together her things. 'Perhaps it just seems that way because it appears to be coming straight from the horse's mouth.'

'The horse's *what*?'

Maggie smiled. 'Listen, if I were to telephone you to say that I thought America was about to declare war on Russia, it would go in one ear and out the other, right?

'However, if the call came from someone who said he was Calder, sounded like Calder and could offer evidence which appeared to support his contention that he *was* Calder, you'd probably head straight for the nearest fall-out shelter even though you couldn't be absolutely certain that it was Calder.

'And that's what I think has been happening on this gig: material which in our so-called "open society" could have been picked up from scores of different sources has acquired a totally spurious worth because by now everyone's convinced themselves that it's originating from a former

199

member of the Politburo.'

'Well, I guess that's that.' Feeling oddly dejected, Sarah got up to leave. However, as she was about to open the door her eye was caught by a small grey metal box set low into the wall alongside the door jamb. 'What's that?' she asked.

Maggie looked up from packing her bag. 'That? Oh, that's just the filter box . . . '

'Uh-huh.' Sarah bent to take a closer look. 'And what does it do?'

'It's really just to – well, I guess it just irons out mains-borne interference . . . '

'And you don't think we should check it?'

'We can if you like,' Maggie replied, unenthusiastically. 'Not that I can see any point in him fooling around with the filter box. After all, the power leads into here are all shielded, so there's no way they could have been acting as aerials. However,' she added, digging into her bag for a wallet of assorted screwdrivers, 'while we're here I suppose we might just as well take a look inside.'

As Sarah returned to the chair, Maggie crossed to the filter box, and, squatting down on her heels, began removing the first of eight cross-head screws from the cover. 'Incidentally, have they taken away Itzhevnikov's body yet?' she asked.

'I think I heard someone say that it would be flown back to Camp Peary later today.' Taking an emery-board from her bag, Sarah began filing her nails. 'Why do you ask?'

'Oh, I was just wondering if that might have explained why Red was prepared to come into the house . . . '

'By now it's probably in a casket, but I'm sure I heard them say that they wouldn't be shipping it out until later . . . ' Sarah frowned. 'But let me ask you a question: assuming you're right about Jack having produced the voice psychokinetically, what would his motivation have been?'

'I wasn't suggesting that he'd done it consciously!' Maggie protested.

'Obviously not. No, I'm talking about his *un*conscious motivation.'

200

'Okay, well that's easy enough to explain,' Maggie replied. 'As you yourself suggested earlier, he was terrified that if we didn't come up with something, Biotec's credibility would have been shot, along with his own. After all, it was Jack who sold you on the EVP idea in the first place.

'I guess the other thing one has to remember is that being disabled, he's bound to be subjected to an above average amount of frustration of one sort or another,' she added, as she began undoing the final screw. 'And as was well demonstrated in the Rosenheim poltergeist case, frustration appears to be an essential ingredient in all PK phenomena.'

Laying aside the screwdriver, Maggie lifted the cover and the RF gasket and peered inside. 'Terrific!' she said, in a flat, exasperated voice. 'Well, I *really* goofed up on this one!'

Sarah raised her head. 'Something the matter?'

'You'd better come and see for yourself . . . '

After dropping the emery-board into her bag, Sarah crossed to the filter box and squatted down alongside Maggie. 'What am I supposed to be looking at?'

'Those!' she replied, pointing to a pair of leads fitted with tiny crocodile clips which had been used to bypass a bundle of vari coloured wires. 'What Jack's done is to short-circuit the fucking thing!'

'But why would he have done that?' asked Sarah, having resisted the temptation to remind her that only a few minutes earlier she had said that there would have been no point in Jack tampering with the filter box.

Maggie began chewing unhappily at the end of one of her pigtails. 'I'm damned if I know . . . Except wait a *minute*!' she added, looking as if she was trying to think in ten different directions at once.

After a brief pause, her face suddenly lit up. 'I've got it!' she exclaimed. 'I think I know what the crafty son-of-a-bitch has been doing! He's had someone feed Itzhevnikov's voice to the recorder via the mains!'

'Oh, shit!' groaned Sarah, burying her face in her hands.

'What they must have done — ' Maggie snapped her fingers. 'Yes, of course!' she continued, in a voice that was a mixture of excitement and disbelief. 'They must have hidden a transmitter beneath the overhead power-lines somewhere between here and the transformer! Obviously the guy who's been impersonating Itzhevnikov wouldn't have wanted to spend his nights crouched over the transmitter – quite apart from any other considerations he'd have been spotted sooner or later – so what he would've done is use a second transmitter to broadcast his voice to the one they'd hidden. Having bypassed the filter box, all Jack would then have had to do was make sure that the mains cable to the tape recorder was always lying across the input lead from the white noise generator, and the signal radiating from the mains cable would've been induced into the input lead! Once in the input lead, the signal would pass via the record amplifier to the recording head, and from the recording head on to the tape!

'It couldn't have been more simple,' she added, as she clambered to her feet and began rummaging in her bag. 'Simple, elegant and typically Jack!'

Sarah lifted her head from her hands. 'What're you going to do?' she asked, as Maggie returned to the filter box carrying a pair of insulated pliers.

'Remove the bypass, of course . . . '

'But if we do that he'll simply deny it was ever bypassed! No, what I want to do before confronting Jack is find out who else is in on this caper with him.'

'So, you want me to leave everything just the way we found it, right?'

'Right . . . '

With a resigned shrug, Maggie replaced the RF gasket and the cover, dropped the first of the screws into its hole and began tightening it.

'Tell me something,' said Sarah. 'If they were feeding the signal in via the mains, why wasn't it ever picked up on any of the other recorders in the house?'

'Again, that's where Jack's been very clever: the Revox B77 – his choice, remember – produces a bias frequency which is way above what your average recorder's bias oscillator produces, so the signal simply wouldn't have been decoded.'

'Okay, but what about broadcasting the voice to the hidden transmitter? I know we're in a very thinly populated area, but even so I'd have thought that sooner or later someone would've been bound to pick it up on their radio . . . '

'They've probably been using either an unallocated or underemployed segment of the electromagnetic spectrum,' Maggie suggested, as she finished tightening the last of the screws and began wiping her finger-prints from the cover. 'However, what I'm still trying to figure out is how the guy impersonating Itzhevnikov knew what question he was supposed to answer. They couldn't have bugged the room, because it's swept for bugs before the start of every session. So, just how the hell *did* they do it?'

'Unless . . . ' Suddenly her face brightened. 'Holy Christ, I think I've got it!' she cried, scrambling to her feet. 'Here, come with me . . . '

After picking up her bag she switched off the air-conditioning and the light and led Sarah across to the three huge windows overlooking the bay. 'Anyone talking in a room sets the windowpanes vibrating, right? So, if the guys working with Jack were to have bounced a laser off the glass – and before you ask, a laser beam doesn't *have* to be visible – it would've come back modulated by the sound waves in the room!'

'But of course!' exclaimed Sarah. 'That was another reason why Jack had to make it appear as if he were the only one who could raise Itzhevnikov – he had to be sure that the others remained outside the screened room where they could be heard!'

Maggie nodded. 'It also explains why Thursday's session ended up a fiasco. Shortly before midnight a gale force wind started blowing in off the sea, and with wind rattling the windowpanes a laser microphone would've been useless.

'Okay,' she continued, 'so if we're right about them having used a laser, they'd have needed a clear line-of-sight to the windows . . . Which means — ' Maggie clapped her hands to her head. 'Shit, this is all falling together quicker than I ever dared hope! What it means is that they've *got* to be operating out of one of the houses across the bay from here!

'So, what're we waiting for?' she asked, her eyes gleaming. 'Why don't we high-tail it over there and give 'em the shock of their lives?'

Sarah shook her head. 'We'll wait until the start of this evening's session and then hit them. That way we not only catch all of them in the one net, it'll be impossible for them to flim-flam their way out of it.

'The bloody fools,' she added, bitterly. 'If it had been Piroschka and not us who found them out – well, I dread to think what the consequences would have been.'

After leaving the library, they wandered through into the kitchen, poured themselves some milk and took it out into the overgrown and weed-choked garden on the seaward side of the house.

'Where do you think they've been getting their equipment?' asked Sarah, as soon as they'd found somewhere to sit. 'As far as I know we don't have anything like that at Biotec.'

Maggie kicked off her sneakers and crossed her legs under her. 'They'd have borrowed a bit here and a bit there,' she explained. 'Jack, I know, has buddies in half the universities and R&D plants in and around Boston, and so has Andy. So, getting hold of the hardware wouldn't have been any big deal.'

'Okay, but what about the house? I know Jack started looking for what he called a "weekend retreat" the moment he arrived, but the odds against him finding it on that exact spot must've been billions to one against.'

'Having a house wasn't essential,' Maggie replied, between sips of her milk. 'In fact something very like this could've been done by a couple of guys working out of trucks.

'Anyway,' she added, with a sideways glance at Sarah, 'what are you going to do about it all? Fire 'em?'

'Ask for their resignations.'

'And you really do think that's necessary, even though they were doing it for – well, I guess all our sakes?'

'I don't see that I have any alternative. Once a scientist has allowed himself to cheat, how can one be sure that he won't cheat again the moment the going gets rough?'

Shielding her eyes against the sun, Maggie turned to watch the last of the terns as they began their migration south. 'Incidentally, how'll you explain away the fact that as from this evening there's to be no more cosy, fireside chats with It?'

'I suppose we'll have to cobble together some bullshit story about — ' Sarah began tapping the rim of her glass against her teeth. 'Actually, you know, this couldn't have happened at a better time. I imagine even those assholes at Camp Peary will lay on some sort of committal service for him, so all we have to do is tell the people here that with his immortal soul now laid to rest — '

'I like it!' chuckled Maggie. 'In fact I like it a lot!'

'Well,' said Sarah, suddenly brightening, 'the one good thing about all this is that within twenty-four hours we should be on our way back to Boston.'

CHAPTER 21

AS SOON as that evening's taping session had begun, Sarah and Maggie slipped out of Seacrest and drove to the headland across the bay.

The house outside of which they stopped was built in the style known as Salt Box Colonial. It was a two-storeyed, shingle-covered structure with double-hung windows and storm shutters, a central chimney and a steep gable roof which at the rear extended to the first floor. Staring out to sea from a plinth mounted above the blue front door was a nineteenth-century ship's figurehead carved in the shape of a woman with vine leaves entwined in her hair and a fully-blown rose clutched to her bosom.

Identifying it as the house in which Adams's accomplices were working had been easy enough: even through binoculars, it had been obvious that it was the only one on the headland which had not already been shuttered in preparation for the winter.

However, what had been far less easy was coming to terms with the consequences of their discovery. Although Maggie still seemed caught up in the excitement of having solved the mystery of the phantom voice, for Sarah the ten-minute drive along the bumpy coast road had been an occasion of mounting sadness. Not only was she soon to lose several of the best and the brightest members of her team, she would also be losing people she had come to regard as true and trusted friends.

Taking a deep breath, she stepped down from the jeep, strode across to the door and twice in rapid succession brought the dolphin-shaped brass knocker crashing down on to the striking plate, sending the gulls which had settled on the roof ridges and chimney wheeling away into the blood-red sky.

Impatient to have it over and done with, she was about to knock again when she heard the sound of approaching feet. There was the rattle of a key being turned in the lock and the door was opened by a tall, thin man with an intelligent, aquiline face and prematurely grey, close-cut hair. He was wearing horn-rimmed spectacles, an open-neck silk shirt and a cashmere sweater, slacks and leather carpet slippers, and he was carrying a copy of the Boston *Globe*. From somewhere within the house, Mozart's Violin Concerto No 3 in G Major was being played on what sounded like very good stereo equipment.

'Oh . . . ' said Sarah, taken aback to find herself not only confronted by a stranger, but one as unlike either Adams or Svenson as it was possible to imagine. 'I'm sorry, but I was – that is, we were — '

'We've a message from Dr Adams,' Maggie interjected.

The man took off his spectacles and frowned. 'Dr Adams?' He shook his head regretfully. 'I'm sorry, but I think you must have the wrong address. There's no Dr Adams staying here . . . '

Determined to make up for her fumbling, ineffectual start, Sarah said firmly: 'But there *are* people from Biotec staying here, aren't there?'

'Biotec?' Again the man shook his head. 'I'm not being very helpful, am I . . . '

After excusing himself, he walked to the corner of the house, turned, and, shielding his eyes against the glare of the setting sun, peered back at the other houses on the headland. 'You don't think they could be at one of the — '

'No, this is the house,' replied Sarah, with a great deal more conviction that she felt.

Suddenly the man's face brightened. 'I think I know what's happened,' he said, retracing his steps. 'Look, the owners rent out this place when they're not using it, so it was probably your friends who were here before us. Let's just think. What would be the best way of finding out where they are now?'

Faced with such urbane and amiable implacability, Sarah began to have second thoughts not only about whether they had got the right house, but about the whole basis upon which the deduction had been made. Could Maggie have totally misunderstood the significance of what she had seen in the filter box? After all, although they had spent much of the afternoon searching for the hidden transmitter, they had found nothing.

However, just as she was about to apologise to the man for having troubled him, she heard Maggie say: 'It's a good try, but let's cut the crap, huh? Look, we've found the bypass and the transmitter you used to get the signal into the mains.

'Now,' she added, with a nod in the direction of Seacrest, 'are you going to talk to us or the brass?'

'I see . . . ' The man began tapping his pursed lips with his forefinger and thumb. 'You wouldn't be Sarah Stuart by any chance, would you?' he asked, raising an eyebrow.

Maggie shook her head. 'This is Dr Stuart. My name's Mintz.'

The man smiled to himself, as if at a secret joke. 'In that case you'd better come in,' he said, ushering them through the hall and into a comfortably furnished sitting-room hung with whaling prints. Facing a brick chimneybreast on which was displayed a collection of harpoons was a brown leather chesterfield flanked by a pair of rush-bottomed captain's chairs, and behind the chesterfield a sofa table laden with drinks.

'You'll forgive me if I don't introduce myself,' he said, turning down the volume on the stereo amplifier, 'but in the circumstances I think it would be – well, shall we say *inappropriate*.' Rubbing his hands together briskly, he bent to examine the array of bottles on the sofa table. 'Now, what can I offer you? Let me see, we have gin, vodka — '

'I don't want anything,' replied Sarah, icily.

'Really?' The man looked up at her with a pained expression. 'Are you quite sure?'

'*Quite* sure!'

'And what about you, Dr Mintz? You'll have something, won't you? A brandy, perhaps . . . ' He turned back to the bottles. 'I know we have a rather splendid cognac here somewhere . . . '

208

Maggie shook her head. 'Thank you, no.'

'Oh, dear . . . ' The man straightened up and for a moment seemed at a loss as to know what to do next. 'Well, shall we sit down?' he suggested, motioning them towards the chesterfield. 'I take it you've no objection to *sitting* with me?'

After several seconds of embarrassed silence, both Sarah and the man suddenly began speaking at once. 'Please,' he said, conceding the floor to her with a gracious wave of his hand.

Sarah cleared her throat and began again. 'Apart from Adams, is anyone else from Biotec involved in this ill-judged venture of yours?'

'No one.'

'Are you sure?' she asked, studying his face closely for any sign of duplicity.

'Absolutely sure,' he replied, raising his right hand as if swearing an oath. 'The only people involved in what you quite understandably but in my view wrongly describe as this ill-judged venture of ours have been Jack, myself and the gentleman who's been impersonating Itzhevnikov.

'Which reminds me,' he added, leaping to his feet. 'If you'll forgive me for a moment, I'd better do something about alerting Jack as to what's happened!'

'Well, what do you think?' asked Maggie, as soon as they were alone.

Sarah looked uneasily around the twilit room. 'I think there's something wrong with the whole set-up,' she replied, as she began drumming her fingers on the arm of the chesterfield. 'For a start, why has a guy like that allowed himself to become involved in a thing like this? Christ, he looks as if he should be teaching composition at Juilliard, not trying to sabotage a top secret defence project! And why an outsider anyway? I mean, it isn't as if he has anything to gain from helping Biotec, if that's what he thought he was doing.'

As Maggie began totting up the probable cost of such a venture, the man came bounding back bearing a box of Astleys Romeo and Julietta Petit Corona. 'Well, that's all taken care of,' he announced. Perching on the edge of the chair, he broke the seal on the cedar box, offered the women a cigar, and, having had his invitation declined, took one for himself. 'You don't mind if I do, do you?' he asked, rolling it beside his ear.

Sarah shook her head. 'So, what happens now?'

'My colleague – who'll be joining us shortly – has just transmitted a prearranged phrase which will let Jack know he's wanted back here at the house,' he replied, as he peeled the band from the cigar, pierced the end and moistened it with his lips. 'He'll spend a few minutes coming on like the mad scene from *Lucia di Lammermoor* and then close down. After Jack has failed in his attempt to coax him back on to the line, so to speak, it'll just be a question of how quickly he can leave Seacrest without arousing suspicion. My guess is that he'll be with us within – ' he paused to look at his wafer-thin gold wristwatch ' – oh, certainly within the next twenty minutes.'

The man struck a match and began rotating the end of the cigar in the flame. 'Interestingly enough, the only really difficult part of the whole operation has been to avoid trans-mitting extraneous and readily identifiable noises,' he continued, as if at the end of an excellent dinner with old friends. 'Seagulls, for instance, or those damned helicopters they seem constantly to be flying into and out of Seacrest. Although we finally solved the problem by having our man use a throat microphone, we were still left with the worry of what would happen if he were suddenly to sneeze.' After pausing to draw on his cigar, he shook out the match and tossed it into the grate. 'Explaining away a disembodied spirit with a head cold might have over-taxed even Jack's undoubted ingenuity,' he added, jovially.

From somewhere at the top of the house a door banged, and was followed by the sound of feet pounding down the stairs.

The man who entered the room a moment later was enormous. Although somewhat shorter than his companion, he was at least three times as heavy. He had a bald head with small, closely-set, almost babyish features, and his grotesquely over-developed weight-lifter's body was clothed in a skin-tight black T-shirt and slacks. 'Why isn't anyone drinking?' he grumbled, in a deep, heavily accented voice.

The thin man made a vague motion with his hand, as if he'd been asked an unanswerable question. 'Perhaps later . . . By the way,' he added, almost as an afterthought, 'this is Dr Stuart, and the young lady next to her is Dr Mintz . . . '

After acknowledging their presence with no more than a nod, the fat man lowered himself carefully into the chair on the opposite side of the fireplace to his companion and crossed one muscular thigh over the other. As well as having no hair on his head, Sarah could now see that he had neither eyebrows nor eyelashes. 'So, what's happening?' he asked of nobody in particular.

The thin man shrugged his narrow shoulders. 'We're waiting for Jack . . . '

'Tell me something,' said Sarah, when the ensuing silence finally became unbearable, 'just why *did* the two of you agree to become involved in this thing?'

By now the light had almost gone, and, after getting up to switch on a pair of electrified oil lamps, the thin man turned over the record. 'We've known Jack for a long time now, so when he asked us to help – well, I guess we just didn't think twice about it,' he replied, as the room filled with the sensuous sonority of the Concerto in D Major.

'And anyway, we found the prospect of pitting our wits against the might of the Pentagon really rather exhilarating,' he added, returning to his seat. 'Much as other men seem to find it exhilarating to pit their wits against sailfish or moose . . . '

'But didn't you realise the risk you were running?' Sarah demanded.

The thin man blew a smoke-ring at the ceiling. 'Were we running all that much of a risk?' he asked, rhetorically. 'At no time did we enter a prohibited place, damage government property or pass on information useful to an enemy. In fact as far as I can see the only offence we've committed was to illegally obtain the few kilowatts of electricity needed to power the buried transmitter, and I really can't believe they'd be so foolish as to allow us to be charged with that bearing in mind the circumstances of the case.'

Suddenly the fat man cocked his head to one side. 'That'll be Jack,' he said, seconds before the sound became discernible to Sarah.

As the jeep screeched to a standstill outside the house, the thin man left the room, closing the door behind him.

After what seemed to Sarah like an inordinately long time, the door was thrown open and Adams came stumping into the room. 'You know why I did what I did, and I know you'll never forgive me for having done it,' he began, in a crisp, unrepentant manner. 'Which at least means we can skip the agonising and get straight down to the business of what's to be done about it.

'Now, what I think we should do,' he continued, lowering himself into the chair which had previously been occupied by the thin man, 'is carry on with the deception for maybe a couple of days more — '

'No!' exclaimed Sarah, so angry that she could barely bring herself to look at him. 'Absolutely not!'

Adams ran his fingers through his mop of red hair. 'But won't that look mighty suspicious?' he asked, as the thin man slipped back into the room and removed the record from the turntable. 'And anyway, there's another reason why we should carry on for a while longer,' he continued. 'On several occasions voices other than that of our friend here have appeared on the tape.'

'I don't understand,' said Sarah.

Adams turned from the fat to the thin man. 'We don't have all that stuff about the kick-backs on *our* tape, do we?' he asked, wrinkling his brow.

'Not on ours. That's how we knew it was an extraneous pickup.'

Nodding, Adams turned again to Sarah. 'If you remember, it was because of this that the President decided to come and take a look for himself, or at least that's what everyone seemed to think.

'According to Itzhevnikov,' he continued, after waiting a moment to see if she would react, 'both the Secretary of State and the President's National Security Adviser have

212

been taking kick-backs from some of the biggest defence contractors in the United States to — '

'What do you mean, ''according to Itzhevnikov''?' Maggie interjected. 'You've just admitted that your buddy's been playing the part of Itzhevnikov!'

'That's exactly my point!' Adams told her. 'Although ninety-five per cent of what's on the tape is him, the remaining five per cent cannot be accounted for except in terms of genuine electronic voice phenomena!

'Now, I know it's still too early to be sure,' he added with renewed, almost boyish enthusiasm, 'but my hunch is that we're on the verge of something very exciting!'

Sarah chuckled. 'Jack, it's a clever move – damned clever – but the answer's still no.'

'I'm sorry,' said Maggie, rubbing her eyes, 'but all of this is way over my head . . .'

'What he's trying to suggest is that from time to time Itzhevnikov broke into the tape with genuine messages,' Sarah told her. 'They've obviously been keeping a tape of everything they've been putting out, and what they were about to suggest was that if we were to compare *their* tape with the tape made in the screened room we'd be persuaded to allow them to carry on with the experiment.'

Maggie shrugged. 'Well, maybe we *should* take a listen. After all, if they're telling the truth — '

'*If* they're telling the truth!' said Sarah, scornfully. 'For a start, it's highly unlikely that we could get our tape back from the CIA, and certainly not without us having to answer some very awkward questions. And even if we could, what would it prove? Oh, sure, I've no doubt that the stuff about the kick-backs won't be on *their* tape, but how would we know they hadn't simply erased it?' She shook her head vehemently. 'No, I'm sorry, but it's all over. Finished.'

Adams turned to look into the empty grate, as if trying to conceal that he was near to tears. 'You're making a mistake,' he told her. 'A helluva mistake. Listen, all I'm asking for is a few more days. Just a few more days in which to fade the whole thing out nice'n'easy and in a way which – you know, which'll seem to make some kind of sense . . .'

'Jack, I'm not kidding,' said Sarah, narrowing her eyes. 'I'll be in the library tomorrow evening, and if there's as much as a croak out of fatso here I'll blow the whistle and damn the consequences. Now, is that understood?'

'Okay, well I guess that's that,' said Adams, looking across at the thin man. 'The first thing we'd better do is get the main transmitter back here and then start packing the rest of the equipment.'

Turning to the fat man, Adams asked if he felt up to driving to Boston that night.

'Sure, why not? If we really are wrapping the operation, I guess the quicker we get everything back to where it came from the better.'

Adams shrugged. 'And that's about it,' he told Sarah. 'Except to say that the Massachusetts Institute of Technology has been making overtures to me for some time now, so I'll be happy to let you have my resignation whenever you think it's appropriate. Now, I don't know about you, but I'm about ready for a drink! So, what'll it be?'

Sarah hesitated for a moment. Although the deception had ended with far fewer casualties than she'd feared, she was in no mood to celebrate. And yet to have refused his invitation would have seemed unmagnanimous. 'Oh well, go on then,' she said, wearily. 'I'll have a brandy.'

'Maggie?'

'I'll have the same.'

Adams looked across at the thin man. 'In that case, why don't we all have brandy . . . '

'Hey, listen,' said Maggie, turning to Sarah. 'Maybe Jack knows where that line comes from; you remember, the one about slouching towards Bethlehem . . . '

Thankful for something with which to fill the awkward silence which had followed Adams's farewell toast, Sarah repeated the story of the nurses' seance.

'It's from W.B. Yeats's *The Second Coming*,' he told her, the moment she had finished. 'Let me see now, how does it go? *And what rough beast its hour come round at last, slouches toward*

214

Bethlehem to be born.'

'Is that the sort of thing you'd have expected her to know?' asked Maggie.

Sarah took another sip of her drink. 'That's the odd thing: not only was she fond of poetry, she'd just begun reading Yeats before she died . . . '

'Oh, God,' said Maggie, in a troubled voice. 'But if it was the nurse, what do you think she was trying to tell you?'

'*If* it was the nurse, my hunch is that all she was trying to do was let me know she'd survived by instancing something only I could have known.'

Adams looked unconvinced. 'I wonder . . . '

'About what?' asked Sarah.

'About whether you were the only one to know she was reading Yeats,' he replied. 'After all, since she told you the chances are she'd also have told the other nurses.'

'Except I remember her telling me that they weren't interested in poetry.'

'Okay, so maybe she read them *The Second Coming* in the hope of getting 'em interested,' he suggested. 'If she did, it's hardly surprising that the line turned up when and where it did.'

Sarah shrugged indifferently. 'Anyway,' she said, stifling a yawn, 'tell me about this job you've been offered at MIT.'

Adams had not been talking for long when Sarah suddenly realised that not only were her eyelids beginning to grow heavy, but that her speech was becoming slurred and her movements uncertain. 'Have you put something in my drink?' she asked, staring down into her now empty brandy balloon.

'Just a little chloral hydrate,' replied the thin man, as he reached over the back of the chesterfield to take her glass and then Maggie's.

As Sarah tried to force herself to her feet, Adams lifted one of his crutches, placed the rubber-tipped end between her breasts, and, smiling benignly, pushed her gently back on to the couch and held her there until she passed out a few seconds later.

215

CHAPTER 22

ARTHUR TRUMBULL arrived at Biotec at 9.25 p.m. and rang the night bell. He was a short, plump, dandified man in his late forties with alert, watchful eyes, a petulant mouth and the reputation for being difficult.

Having chided the security guard for keeping him waiting a moment longer than he considered reasonable, he took the elevator to the basement, and, leaving a trail of *Paco Rabanne pour Homme* in his wake, bustled along a length of locker-lined concrete corridor and put his head around a door marked DREAM LABORATORY.

Sitting drinking coffee from china cups were two men and a stiff-backed, matronly woman with a white streak in her upswept auburn hair. The men he knew, but not the woman: Minoru Hayakawa was project director for the series of telepathically-induced dream experiments Trumbull had been participating in for the past ten days; Lewis McGilly, his partner in the experiments.

'Art!' cried Hayakawa. 'Art, come on in and have some coffee.'

Trumbull plopped his overnight bag on to a laboratory bench. 'What me with my bladder!' he exclaimed, flicking a handkerchief at the only available chair before entrusting his white suit to it. 'Sweetie, you must be *joking!*' He had a high-pitched, almost eunuchoid voice, and he spoke rapidly and with a lateral lisp.

After introducing him to the woman, Hayakawa explained that she was from the National Institute of Mental Health and would be spending the night with them observing the experiment.

'The National Institute of Mental Health!' Trumbull's blue eyes twinkled mischievously. 'I was wondering why we were using the best china,' he said, before launching into an obscene and totally untrue account of what they got up to during their nights in the dream laboratory.

Hayakawa leapt from his stool. 'I think it's about time we made a start, don't you?' he announced, hurrying Trumbull and his partner from the room.

Shaking his shock of straight, glossy black hair, Hayakawa closed the door behind them and returned to his stool. 'I'm sorry about all that,' he said, shamefacedly. 'Now, where were we?'

'Talking about Jung's theory that we receive a great deal of telepathic information while we're dreaming,' the woman replied, in a prim, schoolmarmish voice.

'Ah, yes . . . ' Hayakawa took a tissue from the pocket of his white lab coat and began wiping the condensation from his tinted aviator spectacles. 'I was saying that the reason why we here have become interested in telepathically-induced dreams is that it seems to us that the technique could be used with considerable effect in the field of mental health. Supposing, for example, a specific target element were to be — '

'Just a minute,' said the woman, firmly. 'Before we get down to details, I'm going to need a great deal more background information.'

Hayakawa replaced his spectacles. 'But of course,' he said, with an understanding smile. 'Okay, well although there's still a lot we don't know about the phenomena of dreaming, this much we do know: it's an altered state of consciousness unlike either waking or sleeping. For example, stimuli which would awaken a sleeper who *isn't* dreaming will not awaken him if he *is* dreaming. Now, while this would seem to suggest that the dreamer is in a very deep sleep, in fact the opposite is true. Not only is his neuronal activity increased, so, too, is his heart and respiration rate, his blood pressure and his body temperature. What we have, then, is a situation in which the dreamer's brain is no longer swamped by the sensory impressions, thoughts and fantasies

217

which characterise the waking state, and yet is electro-chemically primed for action.

'Indeed,' he added, 'it's been our experience that REM sleep – Rapid Eye Movement sleep, that is — '

'I am familiar with the term,' the woman was quick to point out.

Hayakawa ducked his head deferentially. 'It's been our experience that REM sleep favours telepathic reception even better than the ganzfeld technique, largely because of an improved signal-to-noise ratio.'

'Tell me, Dr Hayakawa, what would you say to those people who believe that the mind rejects thoughts coming from another mind much as the body rejects grafts from another body?'

'I'd say they might well be right, but that the technique we're using here is the psychological equivalent of employing immunosuppressive drugs in transplantation surgery,' he replied, as his intercom began buzzing. 'That'll be Trumbull to tell us he's in bed and ready to be wired-up to the electroencephalogram.'

Still talking, Hayakawa ushered the woman through into the adjoining room. It was small, windowless, and accoustically shielded, and contained a wardrobe, a bed and a bedside table on which was standing an intercom, a bundle of EEG leads, a carafe of water and a glass.

'During a typical night we have anything up to eight REM cycles,' Hayakawa continued, as he began applying adhesive to the silver EEG electrodes. 'Although the first cycle rarely lasts more than a few minutes, they become longer as the night progresses until by morning they can last for up to an hour.

'However, the younger we are the more we seem to dream,' he added, as he stuck the first of the electrodes close to Trumbull's eyes. 'For example, a middle-aged adult will on average spend fifteen per cent of the night dreaming; a teenager twenty per cent; and a newborn baby fifty per cent.'

After sticking the remaining electrodes to the front and back of Trumbull's skull, Hayakawa wished him goodnight, doused the lights, and, accompanied by the woman, returned to his laboratory and switched on the electroencephalogram.

'Okay, so what'll happen now is this,' he told her, as he refilled their cups with coffee. 'As soon as the EEG tells us he's asleep, I'll buzz through to McGilly and ask him to select one of the twenty-four envelopes he was given earlier, open it and take out the postcard that's inside. Let's say it's a reproduction of Dali's *Temptation of St Anthony* – and incidentally, neither he nor I have any idea what *is* in any of the envelopes – he'll start projecting an image of a man in a desert confronted by a caravan of elephants with insectile legs. Once we see that Trumbull has been dreaming, I'll awaken him and ask him to describe his dream. When he's gone back to sleep, McGilly will open a second envelope and the whole cycle will begin again.'

After asking Hayakawa if he minded if she were to smoke, the woman took a cigarette from her crocodile-skin handbag, inserted it into a holder and lit it. 'But what about your own thoughts, or the thoughts of other people in the building? Security guards, for example. Or cleaners. Aren't they ever picked up by the percipient?'

'Oh, certainly,' replied Hayakawa, passing her an ashtray. 'However, signal strength, selectivity and directionality appear to be vital factors in telepathic transmission. In fact I suppose the only essential difference between electromagnetic and telepathic transmission is that with telepathy there appears to be no attenuation with distance.

'Anyway, come and have a look at this,' he added, as his attention was suddenly taken by what was happening on the electroencephalogram.

Laying aside her coffee, the woman crossed to look over his shoulder.

'What's beginning to come through now are theta waves measuring from four to seven cycles per second as distinct from the thirteen or so cycles one would expect in alert, waking consciousness,' he explained, pointing to the tightly-bunched patterns of zig-zag lines which were being drawn by the chart pens on the slowly turning roll of calibrated paper. 'Which means that it won't be long now before he's fast asleep . . . '

After buzzing through to McGilly to tell him to open the first of his envelopes, Hayakawa returned to the task of trying to convince the woman that since the National Institute of Mental Health had funded much of the pioneering work in the field of telepathically-induced dreams, it should fund the follow-up work being done by Biotec. 'Although what we're doing at present is little more than replication experiments, our ultimate aim is to see if the technique can be adapted for use as a diagnostic tool in the field of mental health,' he explained, after a lengthy preamble. 'Although free-association is a useful tool with which to explain the workings of the unconscious mind, just think how much more revealing it would be if one were able to telepathically implant a specific target element into a patient's mind as he or she began dreaming! Surely, it would make such things as Rorschach tests seem positively Stone Age!'

However, before he could develop his theme further his eye was caught by a change in the EEG trace. Instead of the large, slow waves indicative of dreamless sleep, they had suddenly become compact and irregular.

'He's just beginning his first REM cycle,' Hayakawa announced, before pressing a switch on the intercom. 'Art, it's Minoru,' he said into the microphone. 'Art, are you awake?'

There was the sound of bedsprings creaking, and then Trumbull's voice boomed from the loudspeaker. 'Holy Christ!' he exclaimed. 'McGilly's certainly coming through loud and clear tonight!'

Again there was the sound of bedsprings creaking, followed by the clink of glass on glass and the gurgle of water being poured.

'Art, don't leave it too long or you'll forget what it was you were dreaming,' warned Hayakawa, as he switched on a tape recorder.

'Not this one, I won't!' Trumbull retorted. 'Right, here

we go: I'm in a house . . . It's a shingled house with storm shutters and some sort of carved figure above the door . . . In fact since the house is close by the sea it's probably a ship's figurehead . . . There are several people in the house, but one of them – a woman – is telling me she's in terrible danger . . . The odd thing is that although I feel sure I know her – in fact I *know* I know her! – I can't for the life of me remember who she is . . . '

Hayakawa waited a moment and then said: 'Is that it, Art?'

'I think so . . . No, hold it, I've just remembered something else: one of the men in the house was walking with sticks, as if he were crippled . . . '

'Anything else?'

'No, that seems to be about it, except to say that the overwhelming feeling of the dream was one of impending death.'

'Fine,' said Hayakawa. 'We'll talk again later. In the meantime sleep well.'

After releasing the first switch, he pressed a second. 'Lew, he's just reported a dream, so if you'd like to take a break I'll come back to you as soon as he's asleep. Now, what was the target number?'

'The target number on that one was – let me see – yes, zero three.'

'Zero three.' Hayakawa released the switch, taped a footnote to Trumbull's description and then turned back to the woman. 'By the way, I don't think I've explained how we score the tests, have I? Okay, well in order to avoid experimenter bias, that's left to an independent panel of assessors. I'll give them the tape and the target pictures in the morning, and with a bit of luck their report will be waiting for me when I come on duty tomorrow evening.'

'And you will send me a copy, won't you?'

'But of course,' he replied, before returning to the subject of telepathically-induced dreams as a possible diagnostic tool in psychiatric practice.

However, twenty minutes later the reappearance of a trace indicating that Trumbull had begun dreaming again brought the discussion to an abrupt end.

'Art,' said Hayakawa, his lips close to the intercom micro-phone. 'Art, it's time to — '

'I'm awake!' he snapped. 'Listen, you did tell McGilly to change the target card, didn't you?'

'Of course. Why do you ask?'

'Because I've just had exactly the same dream as before!'

Hayakawa switched on the tape recorder. 'Fine, so describe it.'

'But I've just told you; it's the same goddamned dream as before!'

'It doesn't matter; tell it to me again.'

Trumbull sighed. 'I'm in a wooden house beside the sea,' he began, in a long-suffering, sing-song voice. 'There's a ship's figurehead above the door, and one of the women in the house is about to be killed by a man who walks with a limp.

'Minoru, I want you to do something for me,' he added, in a less peevish manner. 'I want you to check with McGilly just to make absolutely sure he isn't still working with the first target card.'

'Art, you know that any exchange between percipient and agent is against the rules . . . '

'Screw the rules! Look, I'm not asking to be told *what* the target card is, only whether it's the same one as before.'

Shit! thought Hayakawa. If he did what he'd been asked he risked having the woman accuse him of influencing the outcome of the experiment; and yet if he didn't, he risked having Trumbull walk out on him in a huff. 'Art, you've never asked me to do anything like this before,' he said, mainly for her benefit. 'So why tonight?'

'Because I have a feeling that this might be an extraneous pickup.'

'I'll be right back to you.' Hayakawa released the switch and ran his fingers through his hair. 'What he's saying is he thinks that the dream is a message from someone in trouble,' he told the woman, as he tried to decide how best to handle the situation.

'Then why don't you do as he suggests?'

Hayakawa shrugged. 'Why not . . . We'll just have to

weight the scoring accordingly.' Turning back to the intercom, he pressed the switch which would connect him with McGilly. 'Lew, I'm sorry about this, but would you confirm that you're not still working with the first target card?'

'No, of course I'm not,' he replied, in a puzzled voice.

'That's all I wanted to know,' said Hayakawa, before switching back to Trumbull. 'Art, I've just spoken to McGilly and he *did* change the target.'

'In that case it's an extraneous pickup and I'm coming out!' he announced, above the creaking of the bedsprings.

'Art, stay where you are!' said Hayakawa, sharply. 'What's probably happened is that you picked up an echo from the first target.'

'Echo, my ass! Look, I've just checked my pulse and it's a hundred and twenty; and I've only ever had that happen with crisis premonitions!'

Hayakawa sighed. 'Okay, well I'll tell you what I'll do,' he said, unhappily. 'If you promise to stay right where you are, I'll check to see how the dreams match up with the target card.'

When Hayakawa returned to the laboratory a couple of minutes later he handed the woman a postcard of Manet's *Le Dejeuner sur l'Herbe*, strode across to the intercom and said: 'Art, you're doing fine. Just fine . . . '

'What's that supposed to mean?' he squawked. 'Has McGilly changed target cards or hasn't he?'

'He has, but for reasons I'll explain in the morning, what you seem to have been getting is an unusually powerful echo from the first target. So please go back to sleep. I can promise you'll not be troubled by it again.'

After signing off, Hayakawa turned beaming to the woman. 'Don't you think he did rather well?'

'I'm not sure,' she replied, peering at the card at arm's length. 'I must say I don't see *all* that much similarity between it and the dreams.'

'Ah, but just think about it for a moment,' said

Hayakawa, politely but firmly. 'Trumbull talked about people in a wooden house near water and a woman whose life was being threatened, right? Now, take another look at the picture,' he continued, crossing to look at it with her. 'You have two fully-clothed men sitting with a naked woman in a wood beside a lake. One of the men is pointing the forefinger of his right hand at the woman's head much as one might if one were miming the action of firing a pistol, and, moreover, he has a cane in his left hand.

'In fact you can even see where he got the ship's figure-head from,' he added, pointing to the half-naked girl who was standing knee-deep in the lake.

'Yes, I suppose so,' said the woman, grudgingly. 'However, why should he have dreamed the same dream twice?'

'That's easy to explain,' replied Hayakawa, with a chuckle. 'McGilly found the whole setup so sexually exciting that try as he may he couldn't get it out of his mind, even when he was supposed to be concentrating on the second target card!'

After relieving her of the postcard, he crossed to the tape recorder and began dictating a detailed report of the incident. However, he'd not got far before he was interrupted by a muffled cry from the adjoining room.

'What was that?' asked the woman, looking up from a copy of the *Journal of the Society for Psychical Research* as Hayakawa crossed to the electroencephalogram.

'Good God!' he exclaimed, staring disbelievingly at the line of now stationary chart pens. 'The EEG trace – it's suddenly gone flat on all channels!'

Turning on his heel, he raced to the door and wrenched it open, only to collide with a dishevelled-looking Trumbull.

'What the hell do you think you're doing?' he demanded, as Trumbull strode over to the percolator. 'I thought you'd had a heart attack!'

'Sweetie, I almost did,' he replied, as he slopped coffee into a cup. 'I'm sorry, but we're going to have to do something about it.'

'Do something about what?'

'The dream. I've had it again, except this time I know who the woman is: it's your boss, Sarah what's-her-name . . . '

'Sarah *Stuart*?'

Trumbull nodded. 'I'm certain it's her.' Turning to face Hayakawa, he suddenly caught sight of the postcard. 'Is this the target card?' he asked, snatching it up before Hayakawa had a chance to hide it. 'It is, isn't it? And it's not what I've been dreaming about. No way!'

Hayakawa began to protest, but Trumbull stopped him. 'I'm sorry, but I know she's in some sort of danger. Now, are you going to ring her or aren't you? Because if you don't, I will . . . '

CHAPTER 23

'SHIT!' CRIED Svenson. Ever since arriving at Seacrest, he'd been trying to get the pretty, red-headed ID camera operator into bed with him, and now that he'd finally succeeded his telephone had begun ringing.

'Leave it,' she said, between kisses.

'Honey, it may be important . . . '

The girl tightened her embrace. 'If it's that important they'll call back.'

Svenson began again, but his potency was quickly undermined by the high-pitched, insistent shrilling. 'It's no good,' he told her, as he disentangled himself from her limbs and dragged the handset from the cradle.

'Yes, who is it?' he growled.

'*Minoru,*' the voice replied.

Exasperated, he rolled over on to his back. 'Minoru, what in the name of God do *you* want?'

As Hayakawa began telling him about what had happened in the dream laboratory, the girl reawoke him with her mouth, straddled him, and, after slipping him back inside her, began rocking backwards and forwards with an increasing urgency.

'All I know is that Sarah and Maggie were supposed to be driving to Bar Harbor for dinner,' said Svenson, raising his voice in the hope of drowning out the girl's orgasmic moaning. 'Anyway, there's nothing more you can do, so leave it with me, okay?

'Oh, and by the way,' he added, 'you can tell that fag Trumbull that if this turns out to be a false alarm I'll ream his ass for him.'

226

Svenson paused. 'I guess you're right at that,' he chuckled. 'Okay, then tell him I *won't* be reaming his ass for him!'

After hanging up, he wrestled the girl on to her back and quickly ejaculated. 'Hey, what about me?' she complained, as he got out of bed, put on a robe and slippers and padded across to the door.

'What's good for the goose is good for the gander,' he told her, closing the door behind him only just in time to avoid being hit by a pillow.

Hugging himself against the cold night air, he hurried over to Sarah's cabin and knocked on the door. After getting no reply, he climbed the steps to Maggie's cabin and tried again. This time he did get a response: the whimpering of her dog. 'Maggie,' he called, as he tried the handle. 'Maggie, it's Andy.'

Leaving the dog scratching frantically at the door, he ran to the seaward-side of the cabin, climbed over the railings and let himself in through the French windows. As the dog slipped past him to lift his leg against a tub of mugho pine, he switched on the lights and looked around.

By Maggie's standards the room was comparatively tidy, which suggested she'd not been there since the maid had turned back the coverlets at 7.00. But what did that mean? Nothing, he decided. Except . . . Looking instinctively at his left wrist, he discovered he'd come without his watch. However, Minoru had rung around 11.15, so by now it must be at least 11.30. Although he knew Maggie had been bribing the maid to take the dog out for a few minutes during her evening rounds, would she, he wondered, have left it locked in the cabin for a further four and a half hours? Knowing her as well as he did, it seemed unlikely. In which case there was only one thing for it: he'd have to ring Calder. Crossing to the telephone, he picked up the handset, hesitated, put it down again and cracked his knuckles. The trouble was that although he had been sufficiently impressed by Minoru's story to have checked it out this far, what would Calder make of it?

Svenson grimaced. The short answer was that he'd

227

probably think them all mad, especially if he happened to know that sleep research had revealed that two dreams out of three are unpleasant, and almost all involve someone known to the dreamer.

After the dog had come loping back into the room with its tail wagging happily, Svenson closed the French windows, switched off the lights, and, after letting himself out through the front door, returned to his own cabin.

'So, what was that all about?' demanded the girl, laying aside the copy of *Playboy* she'd been reading.

Svenson took off his robe, climbed back into bed and hugged her tightly.

'My God!' she cried, as he buried his face between her breasts. 'You're freezing!'

'Well, you know what to do about that . . .'

'Not until you've told me where you've been,' she said, fighting him off.

'If you must know, I went to see if Sarah Stuart was in . . .'

The girl drew back her head. 'You did *what*?' she asked, her voice heavy with suspicion. 'You weren't thinking of —'

'With Sarah?' Svenson grinned. 'I mean, there's nothing wrong with it as an *idea,* it's just that I can't imagine — '

'Andy, I'm serious,' she said, lifting his hand from her thigh. 'What was the call about just now?'

'It was from a friend to say that he'd dreamed that Sarah was in some kind of trouble, that's all.'

The girl frowned. 'And?'

'And, what?'

'Well, is she in trouble?'

'No, of course not! She isn't even in her cabin . . .'

'In that case, how can you be sure?' Slipping from under him, she propped herself up on to an elbow. 'A couple of years ago I dreamed that my sister had been in an automobile accident,' she told him. 'And she had, just the way I dreamed it.'

'Okay, but how many times have you dreamed of things that *didn't* come true?' asked Svenson. 'Listen, on average we have five dreams a night. That's one thousand, eight hundred and twenty-five dreams a year. What age are you? Twenty-four?'

The girl punched him playfully on the chest. 'Twenty-three, if you *don't* mind!'

'Okay, twenty-three. So, to date you've had – what? – I guess somewhere between forty and fifty thousand dreams.' Svenson shrugged. 'A few of those dreams are bound to have coincided with events that were unknown to you at the time, but that doesn't prove they were clairvoyant or prophetic. In fact the only thing it proves is the soundness of probability theory.'

'Bullshit!' she said. 'Anyway, what're you going to do about Dr Stuart?'

'What can I do, for chrissakes?'

'Well, for openers you could try calling Piroschka . . . '

'No way! If you feel that strongly about it, *you* call him,' he told her, reaching for the phone.

'If I call he's going to want to know *how* I know, and it's all going to get – well, kinda flaky.'

Svenson laughed. 'Then will you just forget about it,' he said, as he went to kiss her.

'Andy, no!' Covering his mouth with her hand, she turned her head aside. 'Not until you've done something about Dr Stuart . . . '

With a long-suffering sigh, Svenson picked up the phone and asked to be put through to Calder's quarters. After a wait of almost a minute the operator came back on the line to say that there was no reply. 'In that case put me through to Seacrest,' he told her.

'It's Svenson for you,' said Galbraith.

With a puzzled frown, Calder got up from the table at which he'd been listening to that evening's tapes and took the phone.

As Svenson began re-telling the story he'd been told by Hayakawa, Calder signalled to Piroschka to pick up the extension. 'Andy, would you begin again,' he said, as soon

as Piroschka had the phone to his ear. 'This isn't a very good
line . . . '

'Well, what do you think?' asked Calder, as soon as he'd
finished talking to Svenson.

'The same as I've thought all along: that we're dealing
with a rack of eight balls.'

'And you don't think we should check it out?'

'What's there to check out? There could be any number
of places between here and Bar Harbor with a ship's figurehead over the door: seafood restaurants, waterfront coffee
houses, yacht chandlers, you name it . . . '

'Except Svenson was quite definite about it being a
house,' Calder reminded him. 'A house overlooking the
sea.'

'But overlooking the sea *where*? For God's sake, Maine
has something like two and a half thousand miles of
coastline!'

Calder turned to the others. 'Has anyone ever noticed a
house near here with a ship's figurehead over the door?' he
asked.

After a moment's puzzled silence, the man from the CIA
replied: 'I'm not sure if it's a *ship's* figurehead, but there's a
house across the bay which has a wooden figure of some sort
over the door. In fact,' he twisted around in his chair
to point at the prickle of yellow lights that lay beyond
the expanse of moonlit sea, 'if there's such a thing as a pair
of night glasses on the premises you'd be able to see it from
here.'

'It belongs to a couple from Augusta,' said the steward, as
he handed the night glasses back to Piroschka. 'When
they're not using it they rent it out as a vacation home.
Right now two fags from Lewiston have it – teachers,
according to the guy who runs the general store . . . '

'Teachers?' echoed Calder. 'October's a funny time of the
year for teachers to be taking a vacation . . . '

230

'Maybe they're on a sabbatical,' Piroschka suggested. 'Anyway, the Secret Service would've checked them out before the President's visit.'

Calder looked unimpressed. 'You mean like the way they checked out John Hinckley, Sara Jane Moore and Squeaky Fromme?' he said, glancing at his wristwatch. 'Look, it's a little after twenty-three forty, so why don't we make sure the girls haven't returned during the past ten minutes, then drive over to the house?'

'You're really taking this thing seriously, aren't you,' said Piroschka, as he lifted the phone and began dialling the number of the lodge.

'I just think we should check it out, that's all . . . '

After talking to the lodge operator for a moment, Piroschka thanked her and hung up. 'They've still not returned.'

'Then let's roll,' said Calder, slipping on his jacket.

'Now just hold it a minute,' Piroschka told him. 'We're going because you're afraid they're being held against their will, right?'

'I'd just sleep easier if I knew they weren't . . . '

'Okay, but in that case there's only one way to handle it: we go prepared for a hostage situation.'

Calder sat down again. 'But Hank, that means — '

'We do it as it should be done or not at all. Admiral, I'm sorry, but if we go bursting in there unprepared and find that they really are being held against their will, we could screw things up for them, for ourselves — '

'If you're *that* worried, why don't you just call the cops?' asked Galbraith.

Piroschka shook his head. 'Because if it is a hostage situation we'd have too much explaining to do afterwards.' He returned to the phone. 'And anyway, God knows where the nearest SWAT unit is to here . . . '

Svenson woke with a start. 'What the fuck is that?'

'It's only my bleeper,' the girl replied. After slipping a hand beneath her pillow to switch it off, she reached across him for the phone.

'Your *what*?' he asked, rubbing the sleep from his eyes.

'Seacrest, please,' she told the operator. 'And as quick as you can, it's an emergency.' Covering the mouthpiece with her hand, she looked back over her shoulder. 'My bleeper. You did know I was attached to the Security Detail, didn't you?'

'The *Security* Detail? I thought you — '

The girl held up a hand. 'Hi, it's Toni Truda. You wanted me . . . ' After listening for a moment she said, 'I'll be with you in ten minutes,' slammed down the phone, and, scooping her clothes up from the floor, ran into the bathroom.

'Sorry about this, honey, but I'm wanted back at the house,' Svenson heard her yell above the sound of running water.

'But why, for chrissakes?' he yelled back at her, as he turned to peer bleary-eyed at his alarm clock. 'It's well past midnight!'

Truda popped her head around the bathroom door. 'Because they think they might know where Sarah is! Sarah and Maggie . . . '

CHAPTER 24

AT EXACTLY 12.30 a.m. Truda got back into her white VW Scirocco having put up her hair and changed her T-shirt and jeans for a full-length silver lamé evening dress and a white fox fur jacket. Followed by two blacked-out troop carriers and a tow-truck, she set out for the house across the bay.

The first of the carriers had been equipped as a mobile command centre. Sitting at a bench laden with radio transmitters were half a dozen men, some with earphones, others headsets. At the end of the bench were Calder and Piroschka. With the exception of the major – who had changed into white overalls – everyone was wearing blue fatigues.

The second carrier contained twenty-four Marines. Each man was dressed in full combat uniform and their hands and faces were smeared with Night Fighter cosmetic. Some carried M16 assault rifles fitted with starlight sniperscopes, others Colt Commando submachine-guns or 12-gauge Remington pump-action shotguns. All had been issued with walkie-talkies and night-vision goggles.

Half a mile from the house the carriers and the tow-truck pulled into a field and stopped, leaving Truda to continue on for another 400 yards.

By the time the Marines had been filing swiftly and silently past her, she had stopped the Scirocco by the side of the road, switched on the hazard warning lights and lifted its hood.

At 12.55 the walkie-talkie she had placed on top of the cylinder block crackled into life. 'Night Rider to Moonflower.' It was Piroschka. To avoid arousing the suspicion of any outsider who happened to intercept the radio traffic between members of the task force, each had been assigned a CB handle and told to use CBer's lingo and codes as far as possible. 'Ready when you are, Good Buddy,' she replied, her breath smoking in the cold night air.

'A big ten-four, Night Rider.' After checking to make sure that her wristwatch transmitter was working, she dirtied her hands, lowered the hood and began walking towards the only house on the headland with lighted windows.

Five minutes later she arrived and knocked on the door, waited a moment and then knocked again. From inside she heard muffled voices followed by the sound of approaching footsteps. After the porch light had been switched on and a key turned in the lock, the door was opened by the fat man.

'I'm awfully sorry to bother you,' she began, in a suitably flustered voice, 'but when I saw your lights I – well, you see my car's broken down and I was wondering whether you'd mind very much if I used your phone to call a garage?'

The fat man shook his head. 'Sorry, lady, but don't have a phone,' he replied, as he went to shut the door.

'Really?' She peered up at the telephone line, a puzzled expression on her face.

'Have phone, but – how you say? – phone out of order.'

'Ah!' Suddenly she seemed to understand. 'In that case, as soon as I find one which is working, I'll have them come and fix yours. I'll tell them there's someone sick in the house,' she added, turning to leave. 'That should speed things up.'

As the fat man started to protest, the thin man appeared at the door. 'What seems to be the problem?' he asked, amiably.

Truda began a long and deliberately complicated story about where she'd come from and where she was going and how her ex-husband had always said that no one should be allowed on the roads who didn't understand the basic principles of the internal combustion engine.

'Just hold it right there!' said the thin man, stopping her in full flood. 'I take it what you want to do is call a garage, right?'

234

'Well, yes . . . ' She hesitated for a moment, as if not quite sure what he was getting at. 'But your friend has just told me that your phone's out of action . . . '

'It was earlier, but now it seems to be fine,' he said, waving her inside.

Still chattering twenty-to-the-dozen, she was led to a telephone that was standing on a bamboo hall table to the right of the staircase. 'God, what a mess!' she exclaimed, looking at her dirty hands. 'Would you mind very much if I were to use your bathroom?'

'Don't worry about it,' he told her, as he tried to get her to take the area telephone directory.

Truda made a pitiful face. 'Actually, that isn't the only reason I'd like to go to the bathroom . . . '

'Oh, I see.' Looking somewhat perplexed, the man thought about it for a moment. 'All right, but wait here until I've made sure it isn't being used.'

As he went sprinting up the stairs Truda took a small self-adhesive transmitter microphone from her sequinned purse and attached it to the underside of the table.

'It's all clear,' she heard him call, as she was reaching up to drop a second bug on top of a stuffed fish in a glass case that was hanging on the hall wall.

Lifting the hem of her dress, she hurried up the stairs, entered the bathroom and locked the door. After examining the contents of the mirrored cabinet that was mounted above the basin, she washed her hands, flushed the toilet and returned to make her call.

'They say they'll send someone around within half an hour,' she beamed, after she'd hung up. 'I really am most grateful to you.'

The thin man beamed back at her. 'Not at all,' he said, moving her gently but firmly towards the front door. 'I'm just glad we were able to be of help . . . '

By the time Truda had arrived back at the command vehicle it was buzzing with activity.

'Well?' asked Piroschka, above the babble of voices.

235

Squeezing her way to the end of the bench, she pulled up a stool and sat down. After describing the men in minute detail, she went on to say: 'There were only two tooth-brushes and razors in the bathroom, so I think it's safe to assume there's only the two of them.

'Apart from the fact that the fat guy was a little jumpy – he was the one you heard telling me that they didn't have a phone – everything seemed to be on the level.'

Piroschka shook his head. 'Not according to the row they had about whether you should've been allowed in,' he said. 'No, they're definitely up to *something*; what we don't yet know is whether that something has anything to do with us or not.'

'I take it there was no sign of the girls?' asked Calder.

Truda shook her head. 'Nothing I was able to spot,' she replied, as she reached for a pad of graph paper and a felt-tipped pen and began sketching a plan of the house. 'If they're there at all, they've gotta be in one of the bed-rooms . . .'

Piroschka raised an eyebrow. 'You don't think — '

'No.' Truda shook her head emphatically. 'Although the guys didn't strike me as being gay, they certainly weren't their type, and anyway they were both fully dressed.

'Incidentally,' she added, 'there was no sign of Maggie's jeep anywhere. No track marks, nothing.'

'A couple of our technical people are trying to figure out a way of getting a look inside the garage,' he told her. 'But the problem seems to be that it has a radio-controlled up-and-over door and they're afraid that even if they find the right frequency to activate it they'll be — '

Piroschka broke off as one of the men wearing a headset began snapping his fingers at him. After signing off, he lifted the microphone arm from in front of his mouth and turned to the major. 'Sergeant Harris has just reported that one of the suspects has arrived on the beach carrying a rubber dinghy which he's now inflating. It sure is getting to seem more and more as if it's drugs they're hustling.'

'Drug smuggling in Maine!' exclaimed Truda. 'Surely not?'

'Since Operation Florida, New England's become one of the main points of entry for drug smugglers,' replied the radio operator. 'Only last week the Coast Guard intercepted a fishing boat with half a million dollar's worth of coke aboard.'

Laying aside his headphones, Calder lifted his blue crew-chief's cap and scratched his head. 'But if it is drugs, where the hell's the supply vessel?'

'Maybe they've been stood up,' Piroschka suggested, before turning back to the radio operator. 'I take it there's still no sign of any activity out at sea?'

After relaying the question to the sergeant, he said: 'No, none at all. Incidentally, the dinghy's now fully inflated and the guy's on his way back to the house . . . Hold it!' Pressing the headphones tight against his ears, he listened for a moment, acknowledged the call and turned back to Piroschka. 'The second suspect's just appeared carrying what looks like a bundle of clothes . . . '

'Clothes?' Piroschka frowned. 'I don't get it!'

'Are they women's clothes?' asked Calder.

'He doesn't — ' The radio operator broke off to listen to what was coming over his headphones. 'Ten-four, Firefly,' he said into the microphone. 'As soon as you can, take a look at them, huh? Ten-ten.'

'Oh, boy! Things really *are* beginning to happen now!' announced another of the radio operators, almost having to shout to make himself heard. 'The fat guy's just taken Mintz's jeep from the garage and parked it in front of the house!'

'Are they sure it's hers?' asked Piroschka, motioning to the other men to lower their voices.

The radio operator nodded. 'The first thing they did was to check on the licence plates.

'By the way,' he added, 'they caught sight of a second jeep while the first was being backed out . . . '

'A second jeep?' Piroschka exchanged puzzled glances with Calder.

'It can't be Sarah's because we know she left it back at the lodge,' Calder told him. 'Anyway, I think the time has come to find out just what the hell is going on, don't you?'

'Definitely!' Piroschka unzipped his white overalls to the waist, and began pulling on a bullet-proof vest. 'Okay, fill me in on the house,' he said, looking over Truda's shoulder at the plans she'd drawn.

Starting with the type of lock used on the front door, she described everything she had seen or had been able to surmise about the layout of the house.

'Great,' he said, as he zipped up his coverall and slipped a walkie-talkie into one pocket and a packet of Marlboro and what looked like a silver Dunhill cigarette lighter in the other. 'So, let's get the show on the road and hope it doesn't turn out to be a turkey.'

By the time Piroschka and the driver of the tow-truck had arrived at the house, two of the Marines had taken up positions behind the bushes on either side of the front door.

Piroschka got out of the truck, walked up the path and tapped out a dum-diddy-dum-dum rhythm on the brass knocker.

Out of the corner of his eye he saw someone peek at him from behind the sitting-room curtains. The porch light came on and a moment later the door was opened by the thin man.

'Are you the party that called about a stalled Scirocco half an hour ago?'

With a weary sigh, the thin man lifted his spectacles and squeezed the bridge of his nose between his finger and thumb. 'No, I did *not* call about a stalled Scirocco half an hour ago,' he began, in a voice that was patient but unforgiving. 'The party who — '

Piroschka read aloud the address and telephone number that was on the clipboard he was carrying. 'That is you, isn't it?'

'It is, but the young woman who made the call is waiting in the car a couple of hundred yards down the road.'

'Down the road?' Piroschka shook his head. 'We ain't seen no Scirocco.'

238

'Which direction did you come from?' snapped the thin man.

'From the north, I guess . . . '

'In that case it's not surprising you didn't see it.' Taking Piroschka by the elbow, he moved him off the porch and pointed south. Immediately, a Marine sergeant stepped from behind the bushes and brought the calloused outer edge of his right hand crashing down on the back of the thin man's neck. For a moment he seemed not to react. But then with the slow, silent splendour of a falling chimney stack, he toppled forward to land face down in a planting bed.

Piroschka caught the pump-action shotgun which the driver of the tow-truck tossed to him, chambered a round, and, followed by the two Marines, slipped into the hall.

Ahead of him was a dog-leg continuous tread staircase, and to either side a door, one closed and the other open. As soon as the Marines were in position – the sergeant to the right of the open door and the private covering them – Piroschka darted forward. As he did so, he saw the fat man dive for cover behind the chesterfield.

'Up!' yelled Piroschka. 'Up with your hands on top of your head!'

However, when the fat man reappeared a millisecond later it was to fire a burst from a Uzi submachine-gun.

Amid a shower of wood splinters, Piroschka fired back, chambered a second round and fired again. Although the first round did no more than plough a furrow across the back of the chesterfield, the second blew away the fat man's ear and much of the left-hand side of his scalp.

As he reached for his fallen Uzi, Piroschka chambered a third round and squeezed the trigger.

This time the tightly bunched cluster of black, ball-bearing sized shot caught him full in the chest. Leaving a cloud of blood droplets in his wake, he hit the wall to the left of the fireplace with a force that brought several of the whaling prints and an ancient harpoon crashing to the floor.

Followed by the Marines, Piroschka made his way cautiously up the stairs. After looking in the bathroom, the

239

closet and two of the bedrooms, he and his sergeant took up positions on either side of the remaining bedroom door – Piroschka to the left and nearest the handle, the sergeant to the right. With his back flat against the wall, Piroschka reached down, turned the handle and pushed the door ajar. Reaching around the jamb, the sergeant swung it fully open and the two men dived into the dimly lit bedroom.

'Hold it right there!' someone yelled from the far side of the room.

Raising his head cautiously, Piroschka looked over the top of the bed behind which he had taken cover. 'Holy Shit!' he gasped.

Lying face down and naked on the first of two single beds was Maggie. Her wrists and ankles had been bound and her mouth sealed with a length of adhesive strapping.

Crouched behind the second bed and using Sarah's bound-and-gagged but fully clothed body as cover was Adams. In his right hand was a Smith & Wesson .44 Magnum, and in his left an M.2 fragmentation grenade from which the safety pin had been pulled.

'Okay, now get on the horn and tell the others not to try to take me from the rear,' he said, nodding towards the curtained-off window behind him. 'And make sure they understand that if I loosen my grip we all end up as hamburger.'

Laying aside his shotgun, Piroschka put the walkie-talkie to his lips and pressed the transmit button. 'Night Rider to all units. We have a ten forty-seven at Castle. All units are therefore ordered to withdraw and await further instruction.'

After the message had been acknowledge, Piroschka looked across at Adams and said: 'So how do you want to play this thing?'

'I take it you wasted the other guys?'

'It was either them or us . . . '

Adams shrugged indifferently. 'Okay, then what I want is a helicopter. But one *only* big enough to take a pilot and two passengers.'

'A chopper's no problem, except where are you planning to board it?'

'Here, of course.'

'What, on the headland? There's nowhere for a chopper to land — '

'Not on the headland, on the beach,' Adams told him. 'The tide'll be almost out by now. And I'm going to need money,' he added, as Piroschka put the walkie-talkie to his lips. 'A hundred thousand dollars in used, non-sequential bills.'

Piroschka lowered the walkie-talkie. 'Ah, now that *could* be a problem. As far as I know we don't hold that kind of dough at Seacrest, and to get it from a bank at this time of night will mean us having to make the whole thing official.'

'How do you mean, official?'

Piroschka grimaced. 'Strictly speaking we shouldn't be here at all,' he explained, as if he and Adams were in an identical predicament. 'In fact if the cops get wind of what's going on I don't know which of us will be in the worst trouble!

'Now, let me think,' he continued, as he began fingering his earlobe. 'What you're obviously intending to do is take one of the girls with you as a hostage, have the pilot put you down somewhere remote but not so remote that you won't be able to pick up a car, then high-tail it to the nearest international airport, right? For chrissakes, you're not going to need a hundred thousand bucks to do that!'

'Fifty grand, then.'

Piroschka beamed. 'Fifty grand it is!' he said, raising the walkie-talkie to his lips.

After Adams had allowed him to cover Maggie with a blanket, Piroschka pulled up a chair and sat down. 'Now we've got everything fixed, how about telling me what this is all about?' he asked, as he shook out a cigarette and lit it with his silver Dunhill. 'You know, like they do in the movies.' With the cigarette dangling from the corner of his mouth and the lighter in his right fist, he folded his arms, felt for the dummy flame control wheel, and while waiting to see

241

if Adams would reply, began tapping out a detailed description of the situation.

As Piroschka came to the end of his transmission, the radio operator who had been translating the morse into clear text ripped the sheet from his typewriter and passed it to Calder. 'It doesn't look good,' he told him, as he removed his headphones.

'It doesn't, does it.' Calder handed the sheet to Truda. 'Stun grenades and CS gas are out, and even if a pretext could be found for opening the drapes, there's no way a sniper could be sure of hitting the motherfucker where it matters without having the bullet pass straight through him and into her.'

'Maybe if we were to use hollow-nose with a quarter load?' suggested the radio operator.

Calder's master-at-arms pulled a long face. 'Not with the safety pin out. Christ, that thing'll blow three seconds after he releases the lever!'

'Tell me something,' said Truda. 'Can we get a message back to Major Piroschka without having to use a walkie-talkie?'

The radio operator nodded. 'Providing he's still holding the dummy lighter, sure we can. The transmitter button doubles as a receiver, tapping out dots and dashes which can be felt but not heard.'

'Okay, then let me ask another question. I take it I am right in thinking that grenades are detonated by means of a percussion cap?'

'Right,' replied the master-at-arms, with a puzzled frown.

'So, even if quite a heavy electrical charge were to be put through one it wouldn't explode?'

'In principle, no . . . '

'Fine,' said Truda, turning the plan of the house so that the others could follow. 'In that case what I suggest is — ' She hesitated. 'Shit, it's going to make a helluva mess of the bedroom!'

242

'I don't know what it is you have in mind, but forget about any mess,' said Calder. 'As soon as we're through we're going to have to burn the house down anyway. In fact they're working on it now.'

'Do we really have to do that?' she asked, in a pained voice. 'I mean, couldn't we just clean up after us?'

'We could, but suppose we were caught doing it?' Calder pointed out. 'And if we leave the place the way it is – well, that's just as risky. No, burning is the neatest way of handling the situation. After all, the owners are bound to be insured . . . '

Truda shrugged. 'In that case, what I think we should do is this . . . '

Clasping his hands behind his head, Piroschka leaned back in his chair and swung his feet up on to the corner of the bed on which Maggie was lying. 'Okay, so if you won't tell me what this is all about let me see if I can guess,' he said, as amiably as if he were about to play Twenty Questions. 'The tapes were phoney, right? These two found out about it and came to warn you off, not realising that you were working for the Russians. You are working for the Russians, aren't you? Of course you are! It's the only thing which makes sense. I mean, all that stuff about the Soviets putting laser battle stations into space: that was only to get us to make the same mistake we made with the Mig 25 Foxbat. If we hadn't believed those stories about the Foxbat having a top speed of three mach, super-sophisticated avionics and Christ knows what else, we wouldn't have been panicked into trying to match it with the MacDonald Douglas F15 – a machine which is so goddamned over-developed that it's out of commission forty-five per cent of the time.

'Still, it was a clever idea,' he conceded. 'Bloody clever. And as for gunning down those poor dumb bastards you had sent in like lambs to the slaughter – well, that was pure genius. From then on any misgivings we had about you – and believe me, we had plenty! – just disappeared in a puff of smoke.'

243

Piroschka frowned. 'But what did the girls think you were up to?' he asked, looking from one to the other. 'I guess they must have figured you were doing it to – I dunno – boost your reputation as a parapsychologist. Anyway, they'd have given you an ultimatum: cut it out pronto, or they'd blow the whistle on you. The trouble was you needed more time if the disinformation you were feeding us was to do any significant damage, which meant having to get rid of them. So, the impulsive Dr Mintz was supposed to have gone for a moonlight swim not realising just how cold the water is on this coast at this time of year. She gets into trouble. Sarah rushes fully clothed into the sea to try to save her and they both drown.' Piroschka nodded approvingly. 'It's a pity you had to wait for the tide to go out, or you'd probably have gotten away with it if you'd made sure their blood alcohol levels were high enough for the whole thing to have made sense to a coroner.'

'You're a regular little Sherlock Holmes aren't you?' said Adams, raising the hand holding the grenade just high enough to see the time. 'Anyway, where the hell's this chopper?'

'Give 'em a chance,' replied Piroschka, glancing at his own watch. 'The ETA is zero two-thirty, and it's only just turned two.

'So, where were we?' he continued. 'Ah, yes: Sherlock Holmes. Flattered as I am by the compliment, there are a couple of things I don't understand. One: what was a Russian agent doing working in a place like Biotec? MacDonald Douglas I could understand; but *Biotec*? Were you put there as a sleeper, or — ' He snapped his fingers. 'Of course!' he exclaimed, grinning broadly. 'Why didn't I think of it before? The Soviets are heavily into psi, aren't they? How many millions of roubles a year are they spending on trying to train psychics to jam radar screens, read minds and go on out-of-the-body intelligence-gathering missions? Twenty-five million? Fifty million? Or have the boys in Science City already passed the billion mark?' Piroschka shook his head sadly. 'And to think they mightn't ever have gotten into it but for that bullshit story about the telepathy experiments we were supposed to have conducted on board the *Nautilus* back in 1959!'

'You said you wanted to ask two questions, not six. So either shit or get off the pot.'

'They were only supplementaries,' explained Piroschka. 'My main question is this: what decided you to switch sides? Did you really believe that there was a military potential in psi that needed to be shared in order to maintain parity, or were you just so pissed off with the way Vietvets like yourself were treated that you decided not to get mad but even?'

As Adams began his reply, Truda – who by now had . changed back into a T-shirt and jeans and had put on a hard hat, safety goggles and rubber-soled shoes – was cutting away a section of the wooden ceiling directly beneath his abdomen with a thermic lance, having located his position with a thermal radiation detector.

The moment the saucer-sized disc of wood had fallen into the waiting hands of one of the Marines, she turned off the lance and the extractor fans, examined the exposed joists and cross bridging, then climbed down the platform ladder on which she'd been working and crossed to the dining table. On top of the table was a large step-up transformer, one end of which was attached to a mains outlet, the other to a coil of electrical cable which had been welded just below the barb of a vicious-looking steel harpoon

Truda picked up the harpoon-gun that was lying beside it, loaded it with a carbon dioxide cartridge, and, after sliding the two-foot long harpoon down the barrel, carried it to the top of the ladder.

Adams's bitter denunciation of the way Vietnam veterans had been treated was suddenly interrupted by the tinkle of breaking glass from behind the curtains.

'For chrissakes get back!' yelled Piroschka, waving away the imaginary intruder.

Still clutching the grenade, Adams spun round and began firing at the billowing curtains. As the room filled with the acrid smell of burnt cordite, Truda tightened her grip on the harpoon-gun, released the safety catch and squeezed the trigger.

Trailing its coil of electrical cable behind it, the razor-sharp harpoon zipped up out of the floorboards like a missile from a silo, and, entering Adams by way of his groin, passed through his bladder, intestines, stomach and lung to impale itself in his left shoulder blade.

Even before Adams's agonised scream had left his throat, the Marine standing beside the step-up generator threw a switch, sending a 500-volt surge of alternating current up the cable and into his body. Immediately, each of his muscles contracted with a violence which not only made it impossible for him to release the grenade, but dislocated joints, fractured bones and caused him to bite off the tip of his tongue.

With blood spurting from between his tightly-clenched teeth, Adams crashed to the floor, and, as Piroschka swung Sarah off her bed and into the arms of a Marine, he began thrashing around as if he'd been dropped on to a red-hot skillet.

As another Marine rushed Maggie from the room, Piroschka stamped the floor twice with the heel of his combat boot and Adams suddenly went limp. Snatching the grenade from his twitching fingers, he bound it tightly with a length of adhesive tape, paused a moment to take a deep breath, and then called downstairs for a body bag.

CHAPTER 25

BY MID-NOVEMBER the temperature in Boston had dropped dramatically. However, it wasn't only the bitterly cold east wind which was making Sarah shiver, but what she had just discovered during a visit to a hypnotherapist.

Until now things had worked out better than she had dared hope. It had been almost ten days before Adams's decomposed and sand-filled body had been washed ashore twenty miles down the coast from Seacrest, and although the coroner had been unable to understand why anyone – much less someone physically handicapped – would have been crazy enough to have gone spearfishing in October, he had nevertheless returned a verdict of accidental death.

Even the burning of the house in which they'd been held hostage and the disappearance of Adams's accomplices seemed to have been treated as routine matters by the police. (Since both men had given the renting agency false names and addresses the police had been unable to question them as to why they'd made no attempt to summon help when a live coal had rolled from the sitting-room fireplace, setting the carpet ablaze.)

Sarah's application to become an American citizen had been accepted; she had learned that along with several of her colleagues she'd been nominated for the first ever Nobel Prize in the field of parapsychology; and the dozen or so sessions she'd had with her analyst had helped her avoid what might otherwise have developed into a serious post-traumatic stress disorder. However, no amount of free association had shed any light on what lay behind her fear of mirrors. Indeed, it had become such an intractable and distressing problem that her analyst had finally conceded

247

defeat and referred her to a hypnotherapist.

Sarah was a good subject and it had not taken the therapist long to talk her into a deep trance. After testing the level
of her trance he had taken her back to the afternoon on
which she'd arrived at Seacrest to begin work. With startling
clarity she had relived the experience of stepping down from
the helicopter to be greeted by Calder and Piroschka.
Svenson, Maggie and Maggie's dog were there, and, as if
brought back from the dead specially for the re-enactment,
so was Adams. As on that dazzlingly hot, never-to-be-
forgotten Indian Summer afternoon, they had entered the
gloomy warren of a house. Leaving Maggie to take the dog
to the lodge, she'd once again had her ID photograph taken
by the girl with whom Svenson was now living, and had
retired to the library to prepare her introductory talk.

Although the therapist had sought to explain what had
happened next in terms of a dissociative reaction to feelings
of intense anxiety, Sarah had left his consulting room
knowing not only that she had been possessed, but by whom
she had been possessed.

Once inside her apartment she went straight into the
living-room, and, without stopping to take off her raccoon
coat, switched on the television set just in time to catch the
start of the early evening news shows.

' — in the most intense information campaign since John
F. Kennedy went public on the Cuban missile crisis,' the
newscaster was saying, 'the President today sought to justify
his decision to bomb Nicaraguan military airfields by — '

With trembling fingers Sarah switched channels. As she
did so the face of NBC's star anchorman appeared on the
screen. 'Behind the President's new, hard-line approach to
what he today described as "the menace of worldwide Soviet
interventionism" is the belief that Russia could not afford to
fight a nuclear war with the United States,' he explained.
'Were she to do so – or so the argument goes – her losses
would be such as to make her easy prey to the Chinese, the
Afghans, the Poles, the — '

Again she switched channels.

'Replying to what UN Secretary-General Carl Ericsson

248

today described as his "reckless and indefensible overreaction to events in Central America", the President – speaking at a White House press conference – said — '

As the picture of the newscaster was replaced by one of the President, Sarah turned down the sound, picked up the telephone and dialled Calder's Washington number.

'It's me,' she began, after waiting several minutes for the switchboard to answer her call.

'Honey, what a wonderful surprise! Where're you calling from?'

'Boston . . .'

Calder lowered his voice. 'God, I've missed you.'

'I've missed you, too,' she told him. And she had. Apart from the weekend they'd spent together at Cape Cod, she'd only seen him twice since leaving Seacrest. 'Look, I hate to ask this with all that's going on right now, but do you think there's any chance of us meeting tonight?'

'*Tonight?*' She heard him draw in his breath sharply. 'That might be difficult; you've seen the story in the *Washington Post* about us calling up the Reserves, haven't you?'

'But I thought that had been denied?'

'Yes, well . . . ' he replied, in a tone which implied that the denial wasn't to be taken seriously. 'Anyway, to get back to tonight: is anything the matter?'

'I think there might be. Which is why I have to talk to you, but not over the phone.'

'And it's not something which can wait until the weekend?'

Sarah bit her lip. 'I don't think it can,' she replied, glancing across at the TV screen as a story about the attempts that were being made to ward off the imminent collapse of the world banking system was followed by another about the riots which had recently laid waste to half a dozen major American cities. 'I honestly don't . . . '

After what seemed a long silence, he suddenly said: 'You're not — '

'No, of *course* I'm not!' she told him, with a gentle laugh. 'That I could've handled . . . '

'Okay, then I'll tell you what I'll do,' he said, in a more relaxed tone of voice. 'One of our guys'll be flying to the Naval War College later tonight, so I'll hitch a ride with him. However, it means my having to drive up from Newport, so it could be late . . . '

Sarah was awoken from a nightmare by the sound of her doorbell – a nightmare in which a naked sun blazed down through an ozone-depleted stratosphere on to an irradiated world in which the only surviving organisms were insects and grass.

Leaping up from the couch on which she'd been lying, she smoothed the wrinkles from her house-coat, shook out her hair and ran to the door. 'Darling!' she cried, throwing herself into Calder's arms. 'Oh, darling, I'm sorry about all this.'

'I'm just sorry I couldn't get here earlier,' he told her, between kisses. 'With half of Washington cordoned off because of the riots, getting to Andrews turned out to be more of a hassle than we'd anticipated.'

Calder took off his sheepskin coat and hung it in the hall closet. In response to Sarah's coaxings, he'd not only abandoned his crew-cut for a longer, more flattering style, he was also dressing younger and he'd given up smoking a pipe.

'However, if nothing else,' he added, as she led him into her handsomely appointed kitchen, 'bringing back the draft should take most of the trouble-makers off the streets.'

'Great!' said Sarah, with more than a trace of mockery in her voice. 'Instead of burning our cities we'll send 'em abroad to burn someone else's! Anyway, what can I get you?' she asked, opening the refrigerator door. 'Ham and eggs? Or there's — '

Calder pulled a chair from beneath the kitchen table and sat down. 'Just some coffee,' he replied. 'Now, what's the problem?'

'How long have you been in analysis?' he asked, after

250

listening with granite-faced impassivity to her account of what had led her to seek help from a hypnotherapist, and what she'd discovered as a result of having been regressed.

'It must be – what? – six or seven years now.'

Calder began fingering his car keys as if they'd been worry beads. 'I'd no idea . . .'

'Darling, I'm not *crazy*!' she assured him, reaching across the table to take his hand. 'All analysts and a lot of psychologists undergo analysis as a matter of routine. If one doesn't understand oneself,' she added, with a small shrug, 'how can one possibly hope to understand others?'

Withdrawing his hand from hers, he crossed to the window. Outside the wind was busily scavenging the trees lining the sidewalk of their few remaining leaves and the clouds were low and heavy with the threat of snow.

'Is something the matter?' she asked, puzzled by his apparent lack of concern about what had happened to her while she'd been at Seacrest.

Still jiggling his car keys, he returned to the table and sat down. 'I guess it's just that I don't like the idea of you talking to outsiders about Endor.'

'But darling, one's analyst is hardly an outsider!' she protested.

'Even so, if you felt you needed help you should have let me send you to one of our own people,' he told her, as he began peeling the cellophane wrapper from a panatella. 'Anyway, what does your guy make of all this — ' He hesitated, as if not quite able to bring himself to use the term. 'Well, this possession business?'

Sarah waved her hand in a dismissive manner. 'He waffled on about it being a dissociative reaction to anxiety . . .'

'I'm not sure I understand what that means,' he said, turning to drop the wrapper into a pedal-bin.

'Oh, just that one part of me did what another part disapproved of and therefore tried to forget, except it never quite managed it.'

'And you don't buy that?' he asked, putting a match to the panatella.

251

Sarah shook her head. 'If it had happened in isolation I might have; but not along with everything else.'

'You're going to have to explain that, too.'

'All right, but before I do let me ask you something: do you think the President's changed since his visit to Seacrest?'

Calder frowned. 'Do I think he's *changed*?' he echoed, as if seeking a hidden meaning in the question. 'I think circumstances have changed, and that in meeting those changes he's had to change with them.'

'Oh, come on!' she protested. 'I mean, take his decision to send troops to El Salvador – not to mention the stroke he's pulled in Nicaragua! Would he have done that before he visited Seacrest? I'm damned sure he wouldn't! Quite apart from the fact that it runs counter to all of his previous policies, surely he must know that to commit forces to a conflict over which he has no political control is a recipe for disaster?'

Calder took off his grey herringbone jacket and hung it over the back of his chair. 'I wonder,' he said, doubtfully. 'As his popularity ratings show, there're a helluva lot of guys out there who think it's high time we stopped letting the Russians jerk us off whenever and wherever they have a mind to.

'However, you didn't ask me up here to discuss the international situation,' he pointed out. 'So, just what is the problem?'

Sarah braced herself. 'Do you want it with novocain or without?'

'It's as bad as that, is it?'

'If I'm right it's a disaster, not just for us here in America, but for the whole world,' she told him, as she began fiddling nervously with the sugar spoon. 'Okay, well here goes: I think the President's been possessed by Itzhevnikov!'

Calder looked at her in astonishment. 'You *what*?'

'I think the President's been possessed by Itzhevnikov,' she said, more firmly than before. 'How do I know? One, because it happened to me. Two, because of the way Maggie's dog reacted — '

252

'Maggie's *dog*?'

'You remember how we couldn't get him into the house on that first afternoon? Well, on the day following Itzhevnikov's death – the day we discovered what Jack had been getting up to – the dog followed us inside without as much as a whimper. And it wasn't just the dog which noticed it; again without us quite realising, we all noticed it.'

'Noticed *what*?'

'That the whole atmosphere at Seacrest suddenly changed with the President's departure.'

Calder frowned. 'I don't remember there being any change in the atmosphere . . .'

'You don't remember the party? Or what happened afterwards?'

'Of course,' he replied, shifting uncomfortably in his chair. 'But that was just – well, I guess just a reaction to the sudden release of tension.'

'Really?' Sarah pulled a long face. 'So *that* was all it was, was it?' she said, nodding gravely. 'A reaction to the sudden release of tension . . .'

Calder began to protest that he hadn't meant what she'd thought he had meant, but she waved away his protestations as unnecessary. 'Anyway, what about the mediums we brought in during the final couple of days?' she continued. 'Unlike Mrs Mitchell, they sensed nothing! Why? Because by then Itzhevnikov's spirit had left the house having taken possession of the President!'

'Hold it!' With his eyes closed, Calder clasped his head in his hands as if his brain was about to go into overload. 'Just hold it a minute, huh? Listen, do you realise what we're doing? We're talking about possession as if it were as much a fact of life as – I dunno – depression, say.

'So, c'mon,' he continued, opening his eyes to give her a long, hard look, 'just what *do* you mean by "possession"?'

'I can define it, but not explain it.'

'I can *define* it,' he grumbled. 'What I can't do is explain it. Nor, I suspect, can anyone else.'

'Can you explain how the brain works?'

Calder considered the question for a moment. 'No, *I* can't,' he replied, in a manner which suggested that he was beginning to regret ever having opened this particular can of worms. 'However – and this is the real point – there *are* people who can.'

'Are there?' Sarah raised an eyebrow in feigned surprise. 'As a matter of fact the people who know most about the brain are the first to admit that next to the universe itself, the brain is probably one of the least understood things in the universe.

'Oh, and incidentally,' she added, almost as an after-thought, 'the man who did perhaps more than anyone else to make the idea of psychosomatic illness respectable – an English psychiatrist named Kenneth MacAll – not only believes in possession as a reality, he's also effected a number of remarkable cures based on the possession hypo-thesis.'

With the sky now beginning to lighten, Calder rubbed his bloodshot eyes. 'All right, but just answer me this: why did Itzhevnikov choose to possess the President rather than Piroschka or Galbraith, or even me if it comes to that?'

'Because possessing the President was the only way he could continue with what he was doing when he left Russia.'

Calder frowned. 'Which was what?'

'Avenging himself *on* Russia, of course!' she replied. 'Christ, no one as highly placed as Itzhevnikov chooses to betray their country unless they feel they've been betrayed by it.'

'But honey, he didn't *choose* to betray his country,' said Calder, forcing a smile. 'He was blackmailed into it! Black-mailed by the CIA . . . '

Sarah looked dumbfounded. 'You didn't tell me *that*!' she cried, suddenly feeling herself to have been betrayed by the man she'd come to trust more than any other.

'I didn't think it necessary . . . '

'You *what*?'

'I didn't think it necessary,' Calder replied, staring defiantly back at her. 'We were operating on a strict need-

254

to-know basis, and in my judgement there simply wasn't any need for you to know. Anyhow,' he added, in a less belligerent manner, 'you were always warning us not to tell you or your people more about Itzhevnikov than was absolutely necessary in case it – what was your phrase? – "prejudiced the outcome of the experiment".'

Although still shocked and angry, Sarah made a determined effort to defuse what was threatening to become an explosive situation. 'Okay, fine,' she said, in a forgiving voice. 'But you're going to have to tell me now. You do see, that, don't you?'

'Actually, there isn't a lot more to tell,' he replied, a little belatedly. 'Or at least nothing which has much bearing on what we've been discussing . . . '

'Let me be the judge of that,' said Sarah. 'For a start, you can tell me what it was he'd done that enabled them to blackmail him. Whatever it was, it must have been pretty nasty,' she added. 'At Itzhevnikov's level one can get away with murder in Russia . . . '

Calder blew a plume of smoke at the ceiling. 'Not quite murder,' he said, taking care to avoid her eyes.

'*What* was that?'

'I said that even someone as highly placed as Itzhevnikov couldn't get away with murder, or at least not one which hadn't been officially sanctioned.'

'Oh, no!' Sarah felt the palms of her hands begin to sweat. 'You're not suggesting that . . . '

A pained expression passed across Calder's face. 'What the hell, you might as well know,' he said, in a flat, apathetic voice. 'The reason why the CIA were able to get him to turn traitor was very simple: they had evidence proving that he'd been responsible for the sadistic murder of at least one Moscow prostitute.

'What happened was this,' he continued, his eyes fixed on the glowing tip of the panatella. 'One of the girls who'd been lucky enough to survive his attentions spotted him in the line-up on top of the Lenin mausoleum during last year's May Day parade. However, instead of taking her story to the KGB she decided it would be more profitable and a helluva lot safer if she were to take it to the CIA. The CIA put him under around-the-clock surveillance, so that when he next struck they were able to video the whole thing from start to finish on infra-red cameras.'

'Oh my God!' cried Sarah, as her look of shocked incredulity changed to one of horror. 'You mean they just stood there and let him do what he tried to do to me?'

'Honey, spying's a tough game,' Calder continued, ignoring her interjection. 'Okay, so I don't condone what the CIA did, but I understand. Given the size of the game they were stalking, they doubtlessly felt that on this occasion the end more than justified — '

Without waiting for him to finish, she leapt up from the table, ran into her book-lined study and returned a moment later carrying a copy of *The Collected Poems of W.B. Yeats*. 'Do you remember Joan Lansdale's message?' she asked, as she began leafing frantically through the index.

'Joan who?'

'The nurse who died,' she replied, turning to the page on which *The Second Coming* was printed. 'You know, the one who came through during the session with the upturned glass . . . I've just realised what it was she was trying to tell us!'

Calder frowned. 'According to you, that was all a lot of— '

'I know I know!' she snapped, brushing aside his objection with a wave of her hand. 'But I was wrong. Terribly wrong! Now just shut up for a minute and listen:

'Turning and turning in the widening gyre – '

'The widening *what*?' he asked.

'Gyre: a circle or spiral,' she explained. 'But for Yeats it also had a mystical meaning. In his *A Vision* – which, incidentally, was based largely on spirit communications received by his wife – he writes about Primary and Antithetical gyres. By a Primary gyre he means — '

'That's fine,' said Calder, helping himself to more coffee. 'Anyway, go on . . . '

> *'Turning and turning in the widening gyre*
> *The falcon cannot hear the falconer;*
> *Things fall apart; the centre cannot hold;*
> *Mere anarchy is loosed upon the world,*
> *The blood-dimmed tide is loosed, and everywhere*
> *The ceremony of innocence is drowned;*
> *The best lack all conviction, while the worst*
> *Are full of passionate intensity.'*

Sensing that his interest was beginning to wane, she passed over the following nine lines and began anew.

> *'The darkness drops again; but now I know*
> *That twenty centuries of stony sleep*
> *Were vexed to nightmare by a rocking candle,*
> *And what rough beast, its hour come round at last,*
> *Slouches towards Bethlehem to be born?'*

Sarah put the book aside. After a moment during which each waited expectantly for the other to respond, Calder – looking warily at her over the rim of his raised cup – suddenly said: 'Well?'

'But don't you *see*?' she demanded, as he took a sip of his coffee. 'What she was telling us was that as a result of his having been possessed by Itzhevnikov, the President has become the Antichrist!'

'The *Antichrist*!' he spluttered. Banging the cup down into its saucer, he said: 'For crying out loud, how did the Antichrist get into this?'

'Because Yeats was heavily into cabalism, neo-Platonism, hermetics, theosophy and God knows what else, he had a very specific time in mind when the Antichrist of *The Second Coming* would "slouch towards Bethlehem to be born",' Sarah told him, ignoring his question. 'And like the poem says, it's *now*! – twenty centuries after the birth of Christ!

'Oh, I know what you're going to say,' she added, even before he'd had a chance to open his mouth. 'You're going to say that we've not yet arrived at the two-thousandth anniversary of his birth.'

257

'No I wasn't!' he snapped back at her. 'I was going to ask why – if that *was* what she wanted to tell you – she didn't just come right out with it, for fuck's sake?'

'Because – ' Sarah paused, then abruptly changed tack. 'You'll remember me mentioning the cross-correspondences during the talk I gave at Seacrest, right? So you'll also remember Frederick Myers's line about how difficult it was to communicate through a medium.'

'I can't say I do, or at least not specifically . . . '

'Okay, well what he said was that communicating through a medium was – and I quote – "like being behind a sheet of frosted glass which blurs sight and deadens sound, dictating to a reluctant and obtuse secretary".'

Somewhere to the east, the driver of a police car switched on his siren.

'I'm sorry,' said Calder, as the first siren was joined by a second and then a third, 'but I still don't understand what it is you're suggesting.'

Sarah got up, and, with her hands thrust deep into the pockets of her house-coat, began restlessly pacing between the window and the door. 'I'm suggesting that given the difficulties which Myers had described, the nurse seized on the one line that told the whole story better than a thousand of her own, even if she'd been able to find a way of getting them across!'

'All right, so I know that most chronologists agree that Christ was born at least ten years earlier than the Gregorian calendar would have us believe,' said Calder, stubbing out the remains of his panatella with more force than was necessary. 'But as for the two-thousandth anniversary heralding the arrival of the Antichrist – well, I'm sorry, but anyone who believes that is ready for the funny farm!'

Sarah stopped abruptly. 'Okay, so you won't buy the Antichrist proposition,' she said. 'But tell me this: was Itzhevnikov turned on by blood?'

'Blood?' Calder considered the question for a moment. 'Yes, I suppose he must have been,' he replied. 'Why do you ask?'

258

'Just wait a minute,' she told him, before once again leaving the kitchen.

When she returned several minutes later she was carrying an open copy of Trevor-Roper's *The Last Days of Hitler*. 'Listen to this,' she said, as a prelude to reading from the book. '*Though he was physically afraid of the sight of blood, the thought of it excited and intoxicated him, just as destruction in all its forms seemed to have appealed to the inherent nihilism of his spirit.*

'*Nor did it matter to him whose blood he shed: for it was the spectacle, the imaginary contemplation of rivers of human blood that inspired him . . .*

'*Throughout the war Hitler continually gave evidence of this lust for blood, this physical delight in the intellectual contemplation of slaughter for its own sake . . .*' Sarah passed the book to Calder. 'But go ahead, see for yourself.'

After reading to the end of the chapter he said: 'So, what is it you're suggesting now?'

'I'm suggesting that Itzhevnikov has taken possession of the President not just to stir up trouble between the super-powers, but to destroy them,' she replied, in a deliberately flat, matter-of-fact voice.

'*Destroy* them? His people as well as ours?'

'Exactly!' Snatching the book from him, she once again began reading aloud. '*Satisfaction never abated this terrible appetite for blood, which, like his appetite for material destruction, seemed rather to grow when the price was to be paid not in inferior currency but in good Aryan coin. In his last days . . . Hitler seems like some cannibal god, rejoicing in the ruin of his own temples.*'

'Okay, so both Hitler and Itzhevnikov were political and military leaders who happened to have been turned-on by blood,' Calder conceded. 'But honey, apart from that their situations were totally different. Hitler felt he'd been betrayed by his generals, his — '

'So had Itzhevnikov,' she insisted. 'Good God, if he'd trusted his own people he'd have told them that the CIA was trying to put the squeeze on him and that would've been the end of the matter. Don't you remember the case of Khrushchev's second-in-command? The one who'd made a fortune out of the black market. Well, when he was caught

259

off base he wasn't even demoted! So why didn't Itzhevnikov come clean about the mess he'd got himself into?'

'Quite apart from the fact that sadistic murder is in an altogether different league to black marketeering, there were a lot of guys on the Politburo who were just waiting for the chance to pull the rug from under Itzhevnikov's feet. *And* he knew it . . . '

'Well, there you go!' Sarah spread her arms wide. 'You've just proved my point!'

'Okay, so let's assume you're right about Itzhevnikov,' said Calder. 'Let's assume that he's obsessed by an insane wish to take his revenge on both America and Russia, and that in order to do so he's somehow managed to possess the President.

'Now,' he added, hooking an arm over the back of his chair, 'where does he go from there?'

'He launches a nuclear attack on Russia, of course,' she replied, tossing the book aside. 'Russia responds with a nuclear attack on — '

'What, just like that?' Calder chuckled. 'Honey, it's not that simple. The President can't just press a *button*! In fact if he were to order a nuclear attack without having a damned good reason for doing so, it wouldn't get further than the National Command Authority!'

'Which is why he's doing what he's doing now,' she told him. 'Don't you see? He's creating the very conditions in which it *will* be possible for him to order such an attack, and have the order carried out.'

'Okay, but if we launch a nuclear attack on Russia, they're going to retaliate . . . And if that happens the chances are that the President will die along with every other poor son-of-a-bitch. And if the *President* dies — '

'Yes, go on,' she urged.

Looking decidedly embarrassed, Calder began rubbing his nose. 'I was going to say that if the President dies, Itzhevnikov would die with him,' he explained. 'But then I remembered that – well, that . . . '

'He's already dead.' Sarah nodded grimly. 'Exactly!'

After several minutes of icy silence, Calder suddenly

looked up from his coffee cup and said: 'All right, but just what is it you're expecting me to do about all this?'

'Well, for a start you could talk to Cardinal Copeland,' she suggested. 'You do know him, don't you?'

'Sure, but talk to him about what?'

'About the President being possessed, of course.'

Calder looked at her as if she was mad.

'But why not? After all, much of Christ's ministry was concerned with casting out evil spirits — '

'No way!' he interjected. 'Okay, so maybe he's no longer entirely responsible for his actions. As you yourself said on the night he freaked out, anyone capable of dreaming up a stunt like Endor has to have a screw loose. But as for him having been *possessed* — '

Sarah started to say something but Calder stopped her. 'Do you know what they'd do if I did what you're suggesting?' he demanded, suddenly very angry. 'They'd bust my ass, that's what they'd do!'

After glancing at his wristwatch, he got up and put on his jacket. 'Honey, I'm due back in D.C. at ten and if I don't leave now I'll never make the shuttle.'

Slipping her arm through his, Sarah walked with him into the hall. 'All right, but we're going to have to talk some more about all this at the weekend,' she warned, as she helped him into his sheepskin.

'The weekend . . . Listen, I'm going to have to call you about that . . . '

'But it was all arranged!' she told him, trying not to let her disappointment show. 'Don't you remember? We'd planned to — '

He kissed her on the cheek. 'Honey, I must go,' he said, opening the door. 'Take care, and we'll be in touch, okay?'

It was after her tenth unsuccessful attempt to get Calder on the telephone that Sarah decided to take matters into her own hands. As soon as his secretary had finished explaining that he was in conference and could not be disturbed, Sarah hung up, turned to watch the end of NBC's coverage of the

American take-over of the Iranian oil-fields, then dialled her attorney's number. 'Hold on to your hat,' she began, 'but what I want to know is how one goes about removing from office a president of the United States who's been possessed by an evil spirit!'

Sarah began telling him about what had happened at Seacrest, but after a moment of stunned silence he stopped her in mid-sentence. 'Dr Stuart, this isn't something we should be talking about over the phone,' he told her. 'I'm tied up in court for the rest of the day, but could you get over here first thing tomorrow morning?'

The siren grew louder and louder, then stopped. Although tempted to get up to see what had happened, she decided against it, and instead plumped up her pillows before once again trying to lull herself to sleep.

However, just as she was beginning to drop off, the silence was shattered by the sound of her doorbell.

Brushing the hair from her eyes, she turned to peer at the clock radio just as the blue fluorescent digits regrouped themselves to read 10.45 p.m.

The bell rang again, and was followed by a sharp double rap on the door.

Throwing back the bedclothes, she pulled on a dressing-gown, and, accompanied by the now almost continuous ringing of the bell, hurried to the front door and put her eye to the spy-hole.

Standing in the dimly lit corridor, their features distorted by the spy-hole's wide-angle lens, were two heavily built men. One was carrying a black leather medical bag, while the other – who was blowing into his cupped hands – had a rolled-up straitjacket tucked beneath his arm.

Both men had snowflakes clinging to their hair.